OTTO PENZLER PRESENTS
AMERICAN MYSTERY CLASSICS

GOLDEN AGE DETECTIVE STORIES

OTTO PENZLER, the creator of American Mystery Classics, is also the founder of the Mysterious Press (1975); Mysterious-Press.com (2011), an electronic-book publishing company; and New York City's Mysterious Bookshop (1979). He has won a Raven, the Ellery Queen Award, two Edgars (for the *Encyclopedia of Mystery and Detection*, 1977, and *The Lineup*, 2010), and lifetime achievement awards from NoirCon and *The Strand Magazine*. He has edited more than 70 anthologies and written extensively about mystery fiction.

GOLDEN AGE DETECTIVE STORIES

OTTO PENZLER, EDITOR

AMERICAN MYSTERY CLASSICS

Penzler Publishers
New York

Published in 2021 by Penzler Publishers
58 Warren Street, New York, NY 10007
penzlerpublishers.com

Distributed by W. W. Norton

Cover image: Andy Ross
Cover design: Mauricio Diaz

Paperback ISBN 978-1-61316-216-3
Hardcover ISBN 978-1-61316-215-6
eBook ISBN 978-1-61316-217-0

Library of Congress Control Number: 2021908058

Printed in the United States of America

9 8 7 6 5 4 3 2 1

CONTENTS

GOLDEN AGE
DETECTIVE STORIES

INTRODUCTION

ONE OF the favorite sports of mystery critics, historians, and scholars is trying to determine when the mystery genre began, who invented it, and what is the first story or novel in the genre. The other favorite occupation is defining what a mystery is in the first place.

I am not eager to get sucked into the first controversy, in which some have claimed the Bible, specifically Cain slaying Abel, as the first murder story, though there's not much mystery involved. Others point to Shakespeare, notably *Macbeth*, but murder and puzzlement turn up in other of his plays as well.

The first memorable act of pure detection is often credited to Voltaire, when his character Zadig makes observations of ordinary facts and then infers events that he could not have seen. Although not specifically involved with crimes, his deductions made him the first systematic detective in literature in 1748.

Embracing the notion of observation and deduction in the solution to criminal mysteries, Edgar Allan Poe can claim with great justification the honor of inventing the detective short story in 1841 when he produced "The Murders in the Rue Morgue." William Leggett's "The Rifle" preceded Poe's tale by fourteen years and is largely a textbook of observation and deduction, but the author was not as gifted a storyteller as the master and his story quickly faded into obscurity. Most writers of introductions to mystery books are quite content to leave the honor of invention to Mr. Poe.

While more and more bits of what is now regarded as the mystery novel were added to gothic fiction, they finally coalesced in Charles Dickens's *Bleak House* (1852-1853) to produce a detective, Inspector Bucket, within the confines of a larger novel with greater ambition than producing a detective novel. Wilkie Collins, a close friend to Dickens, soon followed with *The Woman in White* (1860) and *The Moonstone* (1868), described by T.S. Eliot as the first, the longest, and the best detective novel ever written.

With the creation of Sherlock Holmes in *A Study in Scarlet* (1887) and, more significantly, the short stories that followed in 1891 and after, the detective story was in full bloom and has never again lost its position as a successful and much-loved literary form.

The history of mystery fiction does not have definitive moments, chiseled in granite, that define the exact time when it can be inarguably stated that—aha!—*that* is the moment, or the author, or the story, that changed literature forever.

Defining what is a mystery is just as elusive as pinpointing its invention. I have customarily described "mystery" as any work of fiction in which a crime, or the threat of a crime, is central to the plot or theme of the work. I would not argue against anyone who suggests that this is an extremely expansive view of the genre, as it includes the detective story, crime fiction, psychological suspense, espionage, thriller, noir, police procedural, private eye, and variations and sub-genres of seemingly infinite variety.

It is an imperfect definition, to be sure, as it would necessarily have to include western fiction, which almost invariably includes a crime or crimes but, since it is its own genre (which has its own challenges, both in claiming the date of its creation and in being defined) it can be left aside.

An area where we may come to a little more accuracy and general agreement about its parameters is the Golden Age of detective fiction.

Most people glibly define it as books and stories written between the two world wars, and point to the first Agatha Christie novel, *The Mysterious Affair at Styles* (1920) as the benchmark novel. Of course, nothing is quite so simple, as it was published two years after the Great War ended and the time frame ignores E. C. Bentley's masterpiece, *Trent's Last Case* (1913). At the other end of the time continuum, many of the Golden Age writers who got their start in the 1920s were still going strong after World War II ended in 1945. Two of the genre's giants, in fact, Christie and Ellery Queen, were still releasing novels in the 1970s, as was John Dickson Carr, whose first book was published in 1930.

The Golden Age may be considered in the same fashion as we refer to art, which is that we know it when we see it. The time frame, and even the specific sub-genre of the detective story as one of the buckets of water in the deep well of mystery fiction, may be elastic enough that they do not fit little pigeon holes of dates and genre, nor should we care.

Which brings us to *American Golden Age Detective Stories*, which features virtually all the giants of mystery fiction produced between the world wars. Alas, no Charlie Chan, no Philo Vance, no Mr. Moto, as their authors never wrote short stories featuring those detectives.

This delightful cornucopia of crime does feature Ellery Queen, of whom Anthony Boucher once gushed, "*is* the American detective story" in a *New York Times* book review, and Boucher, for whom the World Mystery Convention was unofficially named the Bouchercon, is in these pages, too. So is Mary Roberts Rinehart, who, for about a quarter of a century, was one of the two bestselling authors in America. For aficionados of impossible crimes, you will find Clayton Rawson and his magician detective, the Great Merlini. For charming couples rivalled only by Nick and Nora Charles (who appeared only in a single novel, *The Thin Man*), we offer Peter and Iris Duluth and Mr. and Mrs. North, who got their name from a bridge hand. Masters of suspense are here, too, with Cornell Woolrich, the Poe of the twentieth century, and Charlotte Armstrong, whose work has inspired outstanding films of suspense. If your like humor, there's a story by Craig Rice, the first mystery writer to grace the cover of *Time* magazine, and Stuart Palmer's Hildegarde Withers, she of the weird and wild hats. Baynard Kendrick, who holds card number one from the Mystery Writers of America, which he co-founded, is here with his blind detective, and so is Mignon G. Eberhart, the Mary Higgins Clark of her era. Iconic detectives? How about Mr. Mycroft, who some seem to think is a pseudonym for Sherlock Holmes who only wants privacy as he keeps bees in Sussex, and Perry Mason, Erle Stanley Gardner's lawyer detective who is the bestselling American mystery writer of all time.

Here, then, for our pleasure and edification, our scrutiny and curiosity, our solace and joy, are some examples of the most illustrious writers of the traditional and classic detective story.

OTTO PENZLER
New York, July 2020

THE ENEMY
Charlotte Armstrong
Detective: Mike Russell

ALTHOUGH NOT a household name, in spite of the acclaim given to her by fellow mystery writers and critics, Charlotte Armstrong (1905-1969) enjoyed a long and successful career. She found a highly specialized niche when she wrote frequently about peril to the young and to the elderly, creating stories and novels of suspense that focused on that theme.

In no work is this characterized more graphically than in *Mischief* (1950), in which a psychopathic hotel babysitter gradually becomes unglued as she contemplates killing her young charge. Filmed as *Don't Bother to Knock* (1952), it starred the young and beautiful Marilyn Monroe in a rare villainous role. Directed by Roy Baker, it also starred Richard Widmark, Anne Bancroft, and Elisha Cook, Jr.

Another of Armstrong's powerful suspense novels to be filmed was *The Unsuspected* (1946), a controversial novel that was both praised by critics for its writing skill but lambasted for disclosing the identity of the killer almost at the outset. A famous radio narrator steals money from his ward's inheritance and, when his secretary discovers his thievery, he kills her. More deaths follow before he confesses—on air. It was filmed under the same title and released in 1947 to excellent reviews.

Directed by Michael Curtiz, it starred Claude Rains, Joan Caulfield, and Audrey Totter.

During the filming of *The Unsuspected*, Armstrong and her family permanently moved from New York to California, where she continued to write stores and more than twenty novels, one of which, *A Dram of Poison* (1956), won the Edgar as the best novel of the year. She also wrote television scripts, including several that were produced by Alfred Hitchcock.

"The Enemy" was originally published in the May 1951 issue of *Ellery Queen's Mystery Magazine*; it was first collected in *The Albatross* by Charlotte Armstrong (New York, Coward-McCann, 1957).

The Enemy
By Charlotte Armstrong

THEY SAT late at the lunch table and afterward moved through the dim, cool, high-ceilinged rooms to the Judge's library where, in their quiet talk, the old man's past and the young man's future seemed to telescope and touch. But at twenty minutes after three, on that hot, bright, June Saturday afternoon, the present tense erupted. Out in the quiet street arose the sound of trouble.

Judge Kittinger adjusted his *pince-nez*, rose, and led the way to his old-fashioned veranda from which they could overlook the tree-roofed intersection of Greenwood Lane and Hannibal Street. Near the steps to the corner house, opposite, there was a surging knot of children and one man. Now, from the house on the Judge's left, a woman in a blue house dress ran diagonally toward the excitement. And a police car slipped up Hannibal Street, gliding to the curb. One tall officer plunged into the group and threw restraining arms around a screaming boy.

Mike Russell, saying to his host, "Excuse me, sir," went rapidly across the street. Trouble's center was the boy, ten or eleven years old, a towheaded boy, with tawny-lashed blue eyes, a straight nose, a fine brow. He was beside himself, writhing in the policeman's grasp. The woman in the blue dress was yammering at him. "Freddy! Freddy! Freddy!" Her voice simply did not reach his ears.

"You ole stinker! You rotten ole stinker! You ole nut!" All the boy's heart was in the epithets.

"Now, listen . . ." The cop shook the boy who, helpless in those powerful hands, yet blazed. His fury had stung to crimson the face of the grown man at whom it was directed.

This man, who stood with his back to the house as one besieged, was plump, half-bald, with eyes much magnified by glasses. "Attacked me!" he cried in a high whine. "Rang my bell and absolutely leaped on me!"

Out of the seven or eight small boys clustered around them came overlapping fragments of shrill sentences. It was clear only that they opposed the man. A small woman in a print dress, a man in shorts, whose bare chest was winter-white, stood a little apart, hesitant and distressed. Up on the veranda of the house the screen door was half-open, and a woman seated in a wheelchair peered forth anxiously.

On the green grass, in the shade, perhaps thirty feet away, there lay in death a small brown-and-white dog.

The Judge's luncheon guest observed all this. When the Judge drew near, there was a lessening of the noise. Judge Kittinger said, "This is Freddy Titus, isn't it? Mr. Matlin? What's happened?"

The man's head jerked. "I," he said, "did nothing to the dog. Why would I trouble to hurt the boy's dog? I try—you know this, Judge—I try to live in peace here. But these kids are terrors! They've made this block a perfect hell for me and my family." The man's voice shook. "My wife, who is not strong . . . My stepdaughter, who is a cripple . . . These kids are no better than a slum gang. They are vicious! That boy rang my bell and *attacked* . . . ! I'll have him up for assault! I . . ."

The Judge's face was old ivory and he was aloof behind it.

On the porch a girl pushed past the woman in the chair, a girl who walked with a lurching gait.

Mike Russell asked, quietly, "Why do the boys say it was you, Mr. Matlin, who hurt the dog?"

The kids chorused. "He's an ole mean . . ." "He's a nut . . ." "Just because . . ." ". . . took Clive's bat and . . ." ". . . chases us . . ." ". . . tries to put everything on us . . ." ". . . told my mother lies . . ." ". . . just because . . ."

He is our enemy, they were saying; *he is our enemy.*

"They . . ." began Matlin, his threat thick with anger.

"Hold it a minute." The second cop, the thin one, walked toward where the dog was lying.

"Somebody," said Mike Russell in a low voice, "must do something for the boy."

The Judge looked down at the frantic child. He said, gently, "I am as sorry as I can be, Freddy . . ." But in his old heart there was too much known, and too many little dogs he remembered that had already died, and even if he were as sorry as he could be, he couldn't be sorry enough. The boy's eyes turned, rejected, returned. To the enemy.

Russell moved near the woman in blue, who pertained to this boy somehow. "His mother?"

"His folks are away. I'm there to take care of him," she snapped, as if she felt herself put upon by a crisis she had not contracted to face.

"Can they be reached?"

"No," she said decisively.

The young man put his stranger's hand on the boy's rigid little shoulder. But he too was rejected. Freddy's eyes, brilliant with hatred, clung to the enemy. Hatred doesn't cry.

"Listen," said the tall cop, "if you could hang onto him for a minute . . ."

"Not I . . ." said Russell.

The thin cop came back. "Looks like the dog got poison. When was he found?"

"Just now," the kids said.

"Where? There?"

"Up Hannibal Street. Right on the edge of ole Matlin's back lot."

"Edge of *my* lot!" Matlin's color freshened again. "On the sidewalk, why don't you say? Why don't you tell the truth?"

"We are! *We* don't tell lies!"

"Quiet, you guys," the cop said. "Pipe down, now."

"Heaven's my witness, I wasn't even here!" cried Matlin. "I played nine holes of golf today. I didn't get home until . . . May?" he called over his shoulder. "What time did I come in?"

The girl on the porch came slowly down, moving awkwardly on her uneven legs. She was in her twenties, no child. Nor was she a woman. She said in a blurting manner, "About three o'clock, Daddy Earl. But the dog was dead."

"What's that, Miss?"

"This is my step-daughter . . ."

"The dog was dead," the girl said, "before he came home. I saw it from upstairs, before three o'clock. Lying by the sidewalk."

"You drove in from Hannibal Street, Mr. Matlin? Looks like you'd have seen the dog."

Matlin said with nervous thoughtfulness, "I don't know. My mind . . . Yes, I . . ."

"He's telling a lie!"

"Freddy!"

"Listen to that," said May Matlin, "will you?"

"She's a liar, too!"

The cop shook Freddy. Mr. Matlin made a sound of helpless exasperation. He said to the girl, "Go keep your mother inside, May." He raised his arm as if to wave. "It's all right, honey," he called to the woman in the chair, with a false cheeriness that grated on the ear. "There's nothing to worry about, now."

Freddy's jaw shifted and young Russell's watching eyes winced. The girl began to lurch back to the house.

"It was my wife who put in the call," Matlin said. "After all, they were on me like a pack of wolves. Now, I . . . I *understand* that the boy's upset. But all the same, he cannot . . . He must learn . . . I will not have . . . I have enough to contend with, without this malice, this unwarranted antagonism, this persecution . . ."

Freddy's eyes were unwinking.

"It has got to stop!" said Matlin almost hysterically.

"Yes," murmured Mike Russell, "I should think so." Judge Kittinger's white head, nodding, agreed.

"We've heard about quite a few dog-poisoning cases over the line in Redfern," said the thin cop with professional calm. "None here."

The man in the shorts hitched them up, looking shocked. "Who'd do a thing like that?"

A boy said, boldly, "Ole Matlin would." He had an underslung jaw and wore spectacles on his snub nose. "I'm Phil Bourchard," he said to the cop. He had courage.

"We jist know," said another. "I'm Ernie Allen." Partisanship radiated from his whole thin body. "Ole Matlin doesn't want anybody on his ole property."

"Sure." "He doesn't want anybody on his ole property." "It was ole Matlin."

"It was. It was," said Freddy Titus.

"Freddy," said the housekeeper in blue, "now, you better be still. I'll tell your Dad." It was a meaningless fumble for control. The boy didn't even hear it.

Judge Kittinger tried, patiently. "You can't accuse without cause, Freddy."

"Bones didn't hurt his ole property. Bones wouldn't hurt anything. Ole Matlin did it."

"You lying little devil!"

"*He's* a liar!"

The cop gave Freddy another shake. "You kids found him, eh?"

"We were up at Bourchard's and were going down to the Titus house."

"And he was dead," said Freddy.

"*I* know nothing about it," said Matlin icily. "Nothing at all."

The cop, standing between, said wearily, "Any of you people see what coulda happened?"

"I was sitting in my backyard," said the man in shorts. "I'm Daugherty, next door, up Hannibal Street. Didn't see a thing."

The small woman in a print dress spoke up. "I am Mrs. Page. I live across the corner, Officer. I believe I did see a strange man go into Mr. Matlin's driveway this morning."

"When was this, Ma'am?"

"About eleven o'clock. He was poorly dressed. He walked up the drive and around the garage."

"Didn't go to the house?"

"No. He was only there a minute. I believe he was carrying something. He was rather furtive. And very poorly dressed, almost like a tramp."

There was a certain relaxing, among the elders. "Ah, the tramp," said Mike Russell. "The good old reliable tramp. Are you sure, Mrs. Page? It's very unlikely . . . ."

But she bristled. "Do you think I am lying?"

Russell's lips parted, but he felt the Judge's hand on his arm. "This is my guest, Mr. Russell . . . Freddy." The Judge's voice was gentle. "Let him go, Officer. I'm sure he understands, now. Mr. Matlin was not even at home, Freddy. It's possible that this . . . er . . . stranger . . . Or it may have been an accident . . ."

"Wasn't a tramp. Wasn't an accident."

"You can't know that, boy," said the Judge, somewhat sharply. Freddy said nothing. As the officer slowly released his grasp, the boy took a free step, backwards, and the other boys surged to surround him. There stood the enemy, the monster who killed and lied, and the grown-ups with their reasonable doubts were on the monster's side. But the boys knew what Freddy knew. They stood together.

"Somebody," murmured the Judge's guest, "somebody's got to help the boy." And the Judge sighed.

The cops went up Hannibal Street, toward Matlin's back lot, with Mr. Daugherty. Matlin lingered at the corner talking to Mrs. Page. In the front window of Matlin's house the curtain fell across the glass.

Mike Russell sidled up to the housekeeper. "Any uncles or aunts here in town? A grandmother?"

"No," she said, shortly.

"Brothers or sisters, Mrs. . . . ?"

"Miz Somers. No, he's the only one. Only reason they didn't take him along was it's the last week of school and he didn't want to miss."

Mike Russell's brown eyes suggested the soft texture of velvet, and they were deeply distressed. She slid away from their appeal. "He'll just have to take it, I guess, like everybody else," Mrs. Somers said. "These things happen."

He was listening intently. "Don't you care for dogs?"

"I don't mind a dog," she said. She arched her neck. She was going to call to the boy.

"Wait. Tell me, does the family go to church? Is there a pastor or a priest who knows the boy?"

"They don't go, far as I ever saw." She looked at him as if he were an eccentric.

"Then school. He has a teacher. What grade?"

"Sixth grade," she said. "Miss Dana. Oh, he'll be okay." Her voice grew loud, to reach the boy and hint to him. "He's a big boy."

Russell said, desperately, "Is there no way to telephone his parents?"

"They're on the road. They'll be in some time tomorrow. That's all I know." She was annoyed. "I'll take care of him. That's why I'm here." She raised her voice and this time it was arch and seductive.

"Freddy, better come wash your face. I know where there's some chocolate cookies."

The velvet left the young man's eyes. Hard as buttons, they gazed for a moment at the woman. Then he whipped around and left her. He walked over to where the kids had drifted, near the little dead creature on the grass. He said softly, "Bones had his own doctor, Freddy? Tell me his name?" The boy's eyes flickered. "We must know what it was that he took. A doctor can tell. I think his own doctor would be best, don't you?"

The boy nodded, mumbled a name, an address. That Russell mastered the name and the numbers, asking for no repetition, was a sign of his concern. Besides, it was this young man's quality—that he listened. "May I take him, Freddy? I have a car. We ought to have a blanket," he added softly, "a soft, clean blanket."

"I got one, Freddy . . ." "My mother'd let me . . ."

"I can get one," Freddy said brusquely. They wheeled, almost in formation.

Mrs. Somers frowned. "You must let them take a blanket," Russell warned her, and his eyes were cold.

"I will explain to Mrs. Titus," said the Judge quickly.

"Quite a fuss," she said, and tossed her head and crossed the road.

Russell gave the Judge a quick nervous grin. He walked to the returning cops. "You'll want to run tests, I suppose? Can the dog's own vet do it?"

"Certainly. Humane officer will have to be in charge. But that's what the vet'll want."

"I'll take the dog, then. Any traces up there?"

"Not a thing."

"Will you explain to the boy that you are investigating?"

"Well, you know how these things go." The cop's feet shuffled. "Humane officer does what he can. Probably, Monday, after we identify the poison, he'll check the drug stores. Usually, if it *is* a cranky neighbor, he has already put in a complaint about the dog.

This Matlin says he never did. The humane officer will get on it, Monday. He's out of town today. The devil of these cases, we can't prove a thing, usually. You get an idea who it was, maybe you can scare him. It's a misdemeanor, all right. Never heard of a conviction, myself."

"But will you explain to the boy . . . ?" Russell stopped, chewed his lip, and the Judge sighed.

"Yeah, it's tough on a kid," the cop said.

When the Judge's guest came back, it was nearly five o'clock. He said, "I came to say goodbye, sir, and to thank you for the . . ." But his mind wasn't on the sentence and he lost it and looked up.

The Judge's eyes were affectionate. "Worried?"

"Judge, sir," the young man said, "*must* they feed him? Where, sir, in this classy neighborhood is there an understanding woman's heart? I herded them to that Mrs. Allen. But she winced, sir, and she diverted them. She didn't want to deal with tragedy, didn't want to think about it. She offered cakes and cokes and games."

"But my dear boy . . ."

"What do they teach the kids these days, Judge? To turn away? Put something in your stomach. Take a drink. Play a game. Don't weep for your dead. Just skip it, think about something else."

"I'm afraid the boy's alone," the Judge said gently, "but it's only for the night." His voice was melodious. "Can't be sheltered from grief when it comes. None of us can."

"Excuse me, sir, but I wish he *would* grieve. I wish he would bawl his heart out. Wash out that black hate. I ought to go home. None of my concern. It's a woman's job." He moved and his hand went toward the phone. "He has a teacher. I can't help feeling concerned, sir. May I try?"

The Judge said, "Of course, Mike," and he put his brittle old bones into a chair.

Mike Russell pried the number out of the Board of Education.

"Miss Lillian Dana? My name is Russell. You know a boy named Freddy Titus?"

"Oh, yes. He's in my class." The voice was pleasing.

"Miss Dana, there is trouble. You know Judge Kittinger's house? Could you come there?"

"What is the trouble?"

"Freddy's little dog is dead of poison. I'm afraid Freddy is in a bad state. There is no one to help him. His folks are away. The woman taking care of him," Mike's careful explanatory sentences burst into indignation, "has no more sympathetic imagination than a broken clothespole." He heard a little gasp. "I'd like to help him, Miss Dana, but I'm a man and a stranger, and the Judge . . ." He paused.

". . . is old," said the Judge in his chair.

"I'm terribly sorry," the voice on the phone said slowly. "Freddy's a wonderful boy."

"You are his friend?"

"Yes, we are friends."

"Then, could you come? You see, we've got to get a terrible idea out of his head. He thinks a man across the street poisoned his dog on purpose. Miss Dana, *he has no doubt!* And he doesn't cry." She gasped again. "Greenwood Lane," he said, "and Hannibal Street—the southeast corner."

She said, "I'll come. I have a car. I'll come as soon as I can."

Russell turned and caught the Judge biting his lips. "Am I making too much of this, sir?" he inquired humbly.

"I don't like the boy's stubborn conviction." The Judge's voice was dry and clear. "Any more than you do. I agree that he must be brought to understand. But . . ." the old man shifted in the chair. "Of course, the man, Matlin, is a fool, Mike. There is something solemn and silly about him that makes him fair game. He's unfortunate. He married a widow with a crippled child, and no sooner were they married than *she* collapsed. And he's not well off. He's encumbered with that enormous house."

"What does he do, sir?"

"He's a photographer. Oh, he struggles, tries his best, and all that. But with such tension, Mike. That poor misshapen girl over there ties to keep the house, devoted to her mother. Matlin works hard, is devoted, too. And yet the sum comes out in petty strife, nerves, quarrels, uproar. And certainly it cannot be necessary to feud with children."

"The kids have done their share of that, I'll bet," mused Mike. "The kids are delighted—a neighborhood ogre, to add the fine flavor of menace. A focus for mischief. An enemy."

"True enough." The Judge sighed.

"So the myth is made. No rumor about ole Matlin loses anything in the telling. I can see it's been built up. You don't knock it down in a day."

"No," said the Judge uneasily. He got up from the chair.

The young man rubbed his dark head. "I don't like it, sir. We don't know what's in the kids' minds, or who their heroes are. There is only the gang. What do you suppose it advises?"

"What could it advise, after all?" said the Judge crisply. "This isn't the slums, whatever Matlin says." He went nervously to the window. He fiddled with the shade pull. He said, suddenly, "From my little summer house in the backyard you can overhear the gang. They congregate under that oak. Go and eavesdrop, Mike."

The young man snapped to attention. "Yes, sir."

"I . . . think we had better know," said the Judge, a trifle sheepishly.

The kids sat under the oak, in a grassy hollow. Freddy was the core. His face was tight. His eyes never left off watching the house of the enemy. The others watched him, or hung their heads, or watched their own brown hands play with the grass.

They were not chattering. There hung about them a heavy, sullen silence, heavy with a sense of tragedy, sullen with a sense of wrong, and from time to time one voice or another would fling out a pronounce-ment, which would sink into the silence, thickening its ugliness . . .

The Judge looked up from his paper. "Could you . . . ?"

"I could hear," said Mike in a quiet voice. "They are condemning the law, sir. They call it corrupt. They are quite certain that Matlin killed the dog. They see themselves as Robin Hoods, vigilantes, defend-ing the weak, the wronged, the dog. They think they are discussing jus-tice. They are waiting for dark. They speak of weapons, sir—the only ones they have. B.B. guns, after dark."

"Great heavens!"

"Don't worry. Nothing's going to happen."

"What are you going to do?"

"I'm going to stop it."

Mrs. Somers was cooking supper when he tapped on the screen. "Oh, it's you. What do you want?"

"I want your help, Mrs. Somers. For Freddy."

"Freddy," she interrupted loudly, with her nose high, "is going to have his supper and go to bed his regular time, and that's about all Freddy. Now, what did you want?"

He said, "I want you to let me take the boy to my apartment for the night."

"I couldn't do that!" She was scandalized.

"The Judge will vouch . . ."

"Now, see here, Mr. what'syourname—Russell. This isn't my house and Freddy's not my boy. I'm responsible to Mr. and Mrs. Titus. You're a stranger to me. As far as I can see, Freddy is no business of yours whatsoever."

"Which is his room?" asked Mike sharply.

"Why do you want to know?" She was hostile and suspicious.

"Where does he keep his B.B. gun?"

She was startled to an answer. "In the shed out back. Why?"

He told her.

"Kid's talk," she scoffed. "You don't know much about kids, do you, young man? Freddy will go to sleep. First thing he'll know, it's morning. That's about the size of it."

"You may be right. I hope so."

Mrs. Somers slapped potatoes into the pan. Her lips quivered indignantly. She felt annoyed because she was a little shaken. The strange young man really had hoped so.

Russell scanned the street, went across to Matlin's house. The man himself answered the bell. The air in this house was stale, and bore the faint smell of old grease. There was over everything an atmosphere of struggle and despair. Many things ought to have been repaired and had not been repaired. The place was too big. There wasn't enough money, or strength. It was too much.

Mrs. Matlin could not walk. Otherwise, one saw, she struggled and did the best she could. She had a lost look, as if some anxiety, ever present, took about nine-tenths of her attention. May Matlin limped in and sat down, lumpishly.

Russell began earnestly, "Mr. Matlin, I don't know how this situation between you and the boys began. I can guess that the kids are much to blame. I imagine they enjoy it." He smiled. He wanted to be sympathetic toward this man.

"Of course they enjoy it." Matlin looked triumphant.

"They call me The Witch," the girl said. "Pretend they're scared of me. The devils. I'm scared of them."

Matlin flicked a nervous eye at the woman in the wheelchair. "The truth is, Mr. Russell," he said in his high whine, "they're vicious."

"It's too bad," said his wife in a low voice. "I think it's dangerous."

"Mama, you mustn't worry," said the girl in an entirely new tone. "I won't let them hurt you. Nobody will hurt you."

"Be quiet, May," said Matlin. "You'll upset her. Of course nobody will hurt her."

"Yes, it is dangerous, Mrs. Matlin," said Russell quietly. "That's why I came over."

Matlin goggled. "What? What's this?"

"Could I possibly persuade you, sir, to spend the night away from this neighborhood . . . and depart noisily?"

"No," said Matlin, raring up, his ego bristling, "no, you cannot! I will under no circumstances be driven away from my own home." His voice rose. "Furthermore, I certainly will not leave my wife and step-daughter."

"We could manage, dear," said Mrs. Matlin anxiously.

Russell told them about the talk under the oak, the B.B. gun.

"Devils," said May Matlin, "absolutely . . ."

"Oh, Earl," trembled Mrs. Matlin, "maybe we had all better go away."

Matlin, red-necked, furious, said, "We own this property. We pay our taxes. We have our rights. Let them! Let them try something like that! Then, I think the law would have something to say. This is outrageous! I did not harm that animal. Therefore, I defy . . ." He looked solemn and silly, as the Judge had said, with his face crimson, his weak eyes rolling.

Russell rose. "I thought I ought to make the suggestion," he said mildly, "because it would be the safest thing to do. But don't worry, Mrs. Matlin, because I . . ."

"A B.B. gun can blind . . ." she said tensely.

"Or even worse," Mike agreed. "But I am thinking of the . . ."

"Just a minute," Matlin roared. "You can't come in here and terrify my wife! She is not strong. You have no right." He drew himself up with his feet at a right angle, his pudgy arm extended, his plump jowls quivering. "Get out," he cried. He looked ridiculous.

Whether the young man and the bewildered woman in the chair

might have understood each other was not to be known. Russell, of course, got out. May Matlin hobbled to the door and as Russell went through it, she said, "Well, you warned us, anyhow." And her lips came together, sharply.

Russell plodded across the pavement again. Long enchanting shadows from the lowering sun struck aslant through the golden air and all the old houses were gilded and softened in their green setting. He moved toward the big oak. He hunkered down. The sun struck its golden shafts deep under the boughs. "How's it going?" he asked.

Freddy Titus looked frozen and still. "Okay," said Phil Bourchard with elaborate ease. Light on his owlish glasses hid the eyes.

Mike opened his lips, hesitated. Supper time struck on the neighborhood clock. Calls, like chimes, were sounding.

". . . 's my Mom," said Ernie Allen. "See you after."

"See you after, Freddy."

"Okay"

"Okay"

Mrs. Somers's hoot had chimed with the rest and now Freddy got up, stiffly.

"Okay?" said Mike Russell. The useful syllables that take any meaning at all in American mouths asked, "Are you feeling less bitter, boy? Are you any easier?"

"Okay," said Freddy. The same syllables shut the man out.

Mike opened his lips. Closed them. Freddy went across the lawn to his kitchen door. There was a brown crockery bowl on the back stoop. His sneaker, rigid on the ankle, stepped over it. Mike Russell watched, and then, with a movement of his arms, almost as if he would wring his hands, he went up the Judge's steps.

"Well?" The Judge opened his door. "Did you talk to the boy?"

Russell didn't answer. He sat down.

The Judge stood over him. "The boy . . . The enormity of this whole idea *must* be explained to him."

"I can't explain," Mike said. "I open my mouth. Nothing comes out."

"Perhaps *I* had better . . ."

"What are you going to say, sir?"

"Why, give him the facts," the Judge cried.

"The facts are . . . the dog is dead."

"There are no facts that point to Matlin."

"There are no facts that point to a tramp, either. That's too sloppy, sir."

"What are you driving at?"

"Judge, the boy is more rightfully suspicious than we are."

"Nonsense," said the Judge. "The girl saw the dog's body before Matlin came . . ."

"There is no alibi for poison," Mike said sadly.

"Are you saying the man is a liar?"

"Liars," sighed Mike. "Truth and lies. How are those kids going to understand, sir? To that Mrs. Page, to the lot of them, Truth is only a subjective intention. 'I am no liar,' sez she, sez he, 'I *intend* to be truthful. So do not insult me.' Lord, when will we begin? It's what we were talking about at lunch, sir. What you and I believe. What the race has been told and told in such agony, in a million years of bitter lesson. *Error*, we were saying. Error is the enemy."

He flung out of the chair. "We know that to tell the truth is not merely a good intention. It's a damned difficult thing to do. It's a skill, to be practiced. It's a technique. It's an effort. It takes brains. It takes watching. It takes humility and self-examination. It's a science and an art . . .

"Why don't we tell the *kids* these things? Why is everyone locked up in anger, shouting liar at the other side? Why don't they automatically know how easy it is to be, not wicked, but mistaken? Why is there this notion of violence? Because Freddy doesn't think to himself, 'Wait a minute. I might be wrong.' The habit isn't there. Instead, there are the heroes—the big-muscled, noble-hearted, gun-toting heroes, blind in a righteousness totally arranged by the author. Excuse me, sir."

"All that may be," said the Judge grimly, "and I agree. But the police know the lesson. They . . ."

"They don't care."

"What?"

"Don't care enough, sir. None of us cares enough—about the dog."

"I see," said the Judge. "Yes, I see. We haven't the least idea what happened to the dog." He touched his *pince-nez*.

Mike rubbed his head wearily. "Don't know what to do except sit under his window the night through. Hardly seems good enough."

The Judge said, simply, "Why don't you find out what happened to the dog?"

The young man's face changed. "What we need, sir," said Mike slowly, "is to teach Freddy how to ask for it. Just to ask for it. Just to want it." The old man and the young man looked at each other. Past and future telescoped. "*Now,*" Mike said. "Before dark."

Supper time, for the kids, was only twenty minutes long. When the girl in the brown dress with the bare blonde head got out of the shabby coupé, the gang was gathered again in its hollow under the oak. She went to them and sank down on the ground. "Ah, Freddy, was it Bones? Your dear little dog you wrote about in the essay?"

"Yes, Miss Dana." Freddy's voice was shrill and hostile. *I won't be touched!* it cried to her. So she said no more, but sat there on the ground, and presently she began to cry. There was contagion. The simplest thing in the world. First, one of the smaller ones, whimpering. Finally, Freddy Titus, bending over. Her arm guided his head, and then he lay weeping in her lap.

Russell, up in the summer house, closed his eyes and praised the Lord. In a little while he swung his legs over the railing and slid down the bank. "How do? I'm Mike Russell."

"I'm Lillian Dana." She was quick and intelligent, and her tears were real.

"Fellows," said Mike briskly, "you know what's got to be done, don't you? We've got to solve this case."

They turned their woeful faces.

He said, deliberately, "It's just the same as murder. It is a murder."

"Yeah," said Freddy and sat up, tears drying. "And it was ole Matlin."

"Then we have to prove it."

Miss Lillian Dana saw the boy's face lock. He didn't need to prove anything, the look proclaimed. He knew. She leaned over a little and said, "But we can't make an ugly mistake and put it on Bones's account. Bones was a fine dog. Oh, that would be a terrible monument." Freddy's eyes turned, startled.

"It's up to us," said Mike gratefully, "to go after the real facts, with real detective work. For Bones's sake."

"It's the least we can do for him," said Miss Dana, calmly and decisively.

Freddy's face lifted.

"Trouble is," Russell went on quickly, "people get things wrong. Sometimes they don't remember straight. They make mistakes."

"Ole Matlin tells lies," said Freddy.

"If he does," said Russell cheerfully, "then we've got to *prove* that he does. Now, I've figured out a plan, if Miss Dana will help us. You pick a couple of the fellows, Fred. Have to go to all the houses around and ask some questions. Better pick the smartest ones. To find out the truth is very hard," he challenged.

"And then?" said Miss Dana in a fluttery voice.

"Then they, and you, if you will . . ."

"Me?" She straightened. "I am a schoolteacher, Mr. Russell. Won't the police . . . ?"

"Not before dark."

"What are *you* going to be doing?"

"Dirtier work."

She bit her lip. "It's nosey. It's . . . not done."

"No," he agreed. "You may lose your job."

She wasn't a bad-looking young woman. Her eyes were fine. Her brow was serious, but there was the ghost of a dimple in her cheek. Her hands moved. "Oh, well, I can always take up beauty culture or something. What are the questions?" She had a pad of paper and a pencil half out of her purse, and looked alert and efficient.

Now, as the gang huddled, there was a warm sense of conspiracy growing. "Going to be the dickens of a job," Russell warned them. And he outlined some questions. "Now, don't let anybody fool you into taking a sloppy answer," he concluded. "Ask how they know. Get real evidence. But don't go to Matlin's—I'll go there."

"I'm not afraid of him." Freddy's nostrils flared.

"I think I stand a better chance of getting the answers," said Russell coolly. "Aren't we after the answers?"

Freddy swallowed. "And if it turns out . . . ?"

"It turns out the way it turns out," said Russell, rumpling the tow head. "Choose your henchmen. Tough, remember."

"Phil. Ernie." The kids who were left out wailed as the three small boys and their teacher, who wasn't a lot bigger, rose from the ground.

"It'll be tough, Mr. Russell," Miss Dana said grimly. "Whoever you are, thank you for getting me into this."

"I'm just a stranger," he said gently, looking down at her face. "But you are a friend and a teacher." Pain crossed her eyes. "You'll be teaching now, you know."

Her chin went up. "Okay kids. I'll keep the paper and pencil. Freddy, wipe your face. Stick your shirt in, Phil. Now, let's organize . . ."

It was nearly nine o'clock when the boys and the teacher, looking rather exhausted, came back to the Judge's house. Russell, whose face was grave, reached for the papers in her hands.

"Just a minute," said Miss Dana. "Judge, we have some questions."

Ernie Allen bared all his heap of teeth and stepped forward. "Did you see Bones today?" he asked with the firm skill of repetition. The Judge nodded. "How many times and when?"

"Once. Er . . . shortly before noon. He crossed my yard, going east."

The boys bent over the pad. Then Freddy's lips opened hard. "How do you know the time, Judge Kittinger?"

"Well," said the Judge, "hm . . . let me think. I was looking out the window for my company and just then he arrived."

"Five minutes of one, sir," Mike said.

Freddy flashed around. "What makes you sure?"

"I looked at my watch," said Russell. "I was taught to be exactly five minutes early when I'm asked to a meal." There was a nodding among the boys, and Miss Dana wrote on the pad.

"Then I was mistaken," said the Judge, thoughtfully. "It was shortly before one. Of course."

Phil Bourchard took over. "Did you see anyone go into Matlin's driveway or back lot?"

"I did not."

"Were you out of doors or did you look up that way?"

"Yes, I . . . When we left the table. Mike?"

"At two-thirty, sir."

"How do you know that time for sure?" asked Freddy Titus.

"Because I wondered if I could politely stay a little longer." Russell's eyes congratulated Miss Lillian Dana. She had made them a team, and on it, Freddy was the How-do-you-know-for-sure Department.

"Can you swear," continued Phil to the Judge, "there was nobody at all around Matlin's back lot then?"

"As far as my view goes," answered the Judge cautiously.

Freddy said promptly, "He couldn't see much. Too many trees. We can't count that."

They looked at Miss Dana and she marked on the pad. "Thank you. Now, you have a cook, sir? We must question her."

"This way," said the Judge, rising and bowing.

Russell looked after them and his eyes were velvet again. He met the Judge's twinkle. Then he sat down and ran an eye quickly over some of the sheets of paper, passing each on to his host.

Startled, he looked up. Lillian Dana, standing in the door, was watching his face.

"Do you think, Mike . . . ?"

A paper drooped in the Judge's hand.

"We can't stop," she challenged.

Russell nodded, and turned to the Judge. "May need some high brass, sir." The Judge rose. "And tell me, sir, where Matlin plays golf. And the telephone number of the Salvage League. No, Miss Dana, we can't stop. We'll take it where it turns."

"We must," she said.

It was nearly ten when the neighbors began to come in. The Judge greeted them soberly. The Chief of Police arrived. Mrs. Somers, looking grim and uprooted in a crêpe dress, came. Mr. Matlin, Mrs. Page, Mr. and Mrs. Daugherty, a Mr. and Mrs. Baker, and Diane Bourchard who was sixteen. They looked curiously at the tight little group, the boys and their blonde teacher.

Last of all to arrive was young Mr. Russell, who slipped in from the dark veranda, accepted the Judge's nod, and called the meeting to order.

"We have been investigating the strange death of a dog," he began. "Chief Anderson, while we know your department would have done so in good time, we also know you are busy, and some of us," he glanced at the dark window pane, "couldn't wait. Will you help us now?"

The Chief said, genially, "That's why I'm here, I guess." It was the Judge and his stature that gave this meeting any standing. Naïve, young, a little absurd it might have seemed had not the old man sat so quietly attentive among them.

"Thank you, sir. Now, all we want to know is what happened to the dog." Russell looked about him. "First, let us demolish the tramp." Mrs. Page's feathers ruffled. Russell smiled at her. "Mrs. Page saw a man go down Matlin's drive this morning. The Salvage League sent a truck to pick up rags and papers which at ten forty-two was parked in front of the Daughertys'. The man, who seemed poorly dressed in his working clothes, went to the tool room behind Matlin's garage, as he had been instructed to. He picked up a bundle and returned to his truck. Mrs. Page," purred Mike to her scarlet face, "the man was there. It was only your opinion about him that proves to have been, not a lie, but an error."

He turned his head. "Now, we have tried to trace the dog's day and we have done remarkably well, too." As he traced it for them, some faces began to wear at least the ghost of a smile, seeing the little dog frisking through the neighborhood. "Just before one," Mike went on, "Bones ran across the Judge's yard to the Allens' where the kids were playing ball. Up to this time no one saw Bones *above* Greenwood Lane or *up* Hannibal Street. But Miss Diane Bourchard, recovering from a sore throat, was not in school today. After lunch, she sat on her porch directly across from Mr. Matlin's back lot. She was waiting for school to be out, when she expected her friends to come by.

"She saw, not Bones, but Corky, an animal belonging to Mr. Daugherty, playing in Matlin's lot at about two o'clock. I want your opinion. If poisoned bait had been lying there at two, would Corky have found it?"

"Seems so," said Daugherty. "Thank God Corky didn't." He bit his tongue. "Corky's a show dog," he blundered.

"But Bones," said Russell gently, "was more like a friend. That's why we care, of course."

"It's a damned shame!" Daugherty looked around angrily.

"It is," said Mrs. Baker. "He was a friend of mine, Bones was."

"Go on," growled Daugherty, "What else did you dig up?"

"Mr. Matlin left for his golf at eleven thirty. Now, you see, it looks as if Matlin couldn't have left poison behind him."

"I most certainly did not," snapped Matlin. "I have said so. I will not stand for this sort of innuendo. I am not a liar. You said it was a conference . . ."

Mike held the man's eye. "We are simply trying to find out what happened to the dog," he said. Matlin fell silent.

"Surely you realize," purred Mike, "that, human frailty being what it is, there may have been other errors in what we were told this afternoon. There was at least one more.

"Mr. and Mrs. Baker," he continued, "worked in their garden this afternoon. Bones abandoned the ball game to visit the Bakers' dog, Smitty. At three o'clock, the Bakers, after discussing the time carefully, lest it be too late in the day, decided to bathe Smitty. When they caught him, for his ordeal, Bones was still there. . . . So, you see, Miss May Matlin, who says she saw Bones lying by the sidewalk *before three o'clock*, was mistaken."

Matlin twitched. Russell said sharply, "The testimony of the Bakers is extremely clear." The Bakers, who looked alike, both brown outdoor people, nodded vigorously.

"The time at which Mr. Matlin returned is quite well established. Diane saw him. Mrs. Daugherty, next door, decided to take a nap, at five after three. She had a roast to put in at four thirty. Therefore, she is sure of the time. She went upstairs and from an upper window, she, too, saw Mr. Matlin come home. Both witnesses say he drove his car into the garage at three ten, got out, and went around the building to the right of it—*on the weedy side.*"

Mr. Matlin was sweating. His forehead was beaded. He did not speak.

Mike shifted papers. "Now, we know that the kids trooped up to Phil Bourchard's kitchen at about a quarter of three. Whereas Bones, realizing that Smitty was in for it, and shying away from soap and water like any sane dog, went up Hannibal Street at three o'clock sharp. He may have known in some doggy way where Freddy was. Can we see Bones loping up Hannibal Street, going *above* Greenwood Lane?"

"We can," said Daugherty. He was watching Matlin. "Besides, he was found above Greenwood Lane soon after."

"No one," said Mike slowly, "was seen in Matlin's back lot, except Matlin. Yet, almost immediately after Matlin was there, the little dog died."

"Didn't Diane . . . ?"

"Diane's friends came at three-twelve. Their evidence is not reliable." Diane blushed.

"This . . . this is intolerable!" croaked Matlin. "Why *my* back lot?"

Daugherty said, "There was no poison lying around my place, I'll tell you that."

"How do you know?" begged Matlin. And Freddy's eyes, with the smudges under them, followed to Russell's face. "Why not in the street? From some passing car?"

Mike said, "I'm afraid it's not likely. You see, Mr. Otis Carnavon was stalled at the corner of Hannibal and Lee. Trying to flag a push. Anything thrown from a car on that block, he ought to have seen."

"Was the poison quick?" demanded Daugherty. "What did he get?"

"It was quick. The dog could not go far after he got it. He got cyanide."

Matlin's shaking hand removed his glasses. They were wet.

"Some of you may be amateur photographers," Mike said. "Mr. Matlin, is there cyanide in your cellar darkroom?"

"Yes, but I keep it . . . most meticulously . . ." Matlin began to cough.

When the noise of his spasm died, Mike said, "The poison was embedded in ground meat which analyzed, roughly, half-beef and the rest pork and veal, half and half." Matlin encircled his throat with his fingers. "I've checked with four neighborhood butchers and the dickens of a time I had," said Mike. No one smiled. Only Freddy looked up at him with solemn sympathy. "Ground meat was delivered to at least five houses in the vicinity. Meat that *was* one-half beef, one-quarter pork, one-quarter veal, was delivered at ten this morning to Matlin's house."

A stir like an angry wind blew over the room. The Chief of Police made some shift of his weight so that his chair creaked.

"It begins to look . . ." growled Daugherty.

"Now," said Russell sharply, "we must be very careful. One more thing. The meat had been seasoned."

"Seasoned!"

"With salt. And with . . . thyme."

"Thyme," groaned Matlin.

Freddy looked up at Miss Dana with bewildered eyes. She put her arm around him.

"As far as motives are concerned," said Mike quietly, "I can't discuss them. It is inconceivable to me that any man would poison a dog." Nobody spoke. "However, where are we?" Mike's voice seemed to catch Matlin just in time to keep him from falling off the chair. "We don't know yet what happened to the dog." Mike's voice rang. "Mr. Matlin, will you help us to the answer?"

Matlin said thickly, "Better get those kids out of here."

Miss Dana moved, but Russell said, "No. They have worked hard for the truth. They have earned it. And if it is to be had, they shall have it."

"You know?" whimpered Matlin.

Mike said, "I called your golf club. I've looked into your trash incinerator. Yes, I know. But I want you to tell us."

Daugherty said, "Well? Well?" And Matlin covered his face.

Mike said, gently, "I think there was an error. Mr. Matlin, I'm afraid, did poison the dog. But he never meant to, and he didn't know he had done it."

Matlin said, "I'm sorry . . . It's . . . I can't . . . She means to do her best. But she's a terrible cook. Somebody gave her those . . . those herbs. Thyme . . . thyme in everything. She fixed me a lunch box. I . . . couldn't stomach it. I bought my lunch at the club."

Mike nodded.

Matlin went on, his voice cracking. "I never . . . You see, I didn't even know it was meat the dog got. She said . . . she told me the dog was already dead."

"And of course," said Mike, "in your righteous wrath, you never paused to say to yourself, 'Wait, what *did* happen to the dog?'"

"Mr. Russell, I didn't lie. How could I know there was thyme in it? When I got home, I had to get rid of the hamburger she'd fixed for me—I didn't want to hurt her feelings. She tries . . . tries so hard . . ." He sat up suddenly. "*But what she tried to do today,*" he said, with his eyes almost out of his head, "*was to poison me!*" His bulging eyes roved. They came to Freddy. He gasped. He said, "Your dog saved my life!"

"Yes," said Mike quickly, "Freddy's dog saved your life. You see, your step-daughter would have kept trying."

People drew in their breaths. "The buns are in your incinerator," Mike said. "She guessed what happened to the dog, went for the buns, and hid them. She was late, you remember, getting to the disturbance. And she did lie."

Chief Anderson rose.

"Her mother . . ." said Matlin frantically, "her mother . . ."

Mike Russell put his hand on the plump shoulder. "Her mother's been in torment, tortured by the rivalry between you. Don't you think her mother senses something wrong?"

Miss Lillian Dana wrapped Freddy in her arms. "Oh, what a wonderful dog Bones was!" She covered the sound of the other voices. "Even when he died, he saved a man's life. Oh, Freddy, he was a wonderful dog."

And Freddy, not quite taking everything in yet, was released to simple sorrow and wept quietly against his friend . . .

When they went to fetch May Matlin, she was not in the house. They found her in the Titus's back shed. She seemed to be looking for something.

Next day, when Mr. and Mrs. Titus came home, they found that although the little dog had died, their Freddy was all right. The Judge, Russell, and Miss Dana told them all about it.

Mrs. Titus wept. Mr. Titus swore. He wrung Russell's hand. ". . . for stealing the gun . . ." he babbled.

But the mother cried, ". . . for showing him, for teaching him. . . . Oh, Miss Dana, oh, my dear!"

The Judge waved from his veranda as the dark head and the blonde drove away.

"I think Miss Dana likes him," said Ernie Allen.

"How do you know for sure?" said Freddy Titus.

THE STRIPPER
Anthony Boucher
Detective: Sister Ursula

MUCH LIKE the word "genius," the term "Renaissance Man" has been over-used through the years, but it is entirely reasonable to use that appellation for William Anthony Parker White (1911-1968), better known under the pseudonyms he used for his career as a writer of both mystery and science fiction, Anthony Boucher and H. H. Holmes. Under his real name, as well as under his pseudonyms, he established a reputation as a first-rate critic of opera and literature, including general fiction, mystery, and science fiction. He also was an accomplished editor, anthologist, playwright, and an eminent translator of French, Spanish, and Portuguese, becoming the first to translate Jorge Luis Borges into English.

He wrote prolifically in the 1940s, producing at least three scripts a week for such popular radio programs as *Sherlock Holmes*, *The Adventures of Ellery Queen*, and *The Case Book of Gregory Hood*. He also wrote numerous science fiction and fantasy stories, reviewed books in those genres as H. H. Holmes for the *San Francisco Chronicle* and *Chicago Sun-Times*, and produced notable anthologies in the science fiction, fantasy, and mystery genres.

All of Boucher's mystery novels were published in the 1930s and

1940s, beginning with *The Case of the Seven of Calvary* (1937), which was followed by four novels featuring Los Angeles private detective Fergus O'Breen, including *The Case of the Crumpled Knave* (1939) and *The Case of the Baker Street Irregulars* (1940). As H. H. Holmes, he wrote two novels in which an unlikely detective, Sister Ursula of the Sisters of Martha Bethany, assists Lieutenant Marshall of the Los Angeles Police Department: *Nine Times Nine* (1940) and *Rocket to the Morgue* (1942), which was selected for the Haycraft-Queen Definitive Library of Detective-Crime Mystery Fiction.

As Boucher (rhymes with "voucher"), he served as the long-time mystery reviewer of *The New York Times* (1951-1968, with eight hundred fifty-two columns to his credit) and *Ellery Queen's Mystery Magazine* (1957-1968). He was one of the founders of the Mystery Writers of America in 1946. The annual World Mystery Convention is familiarly known as the Bouchercon in his honor, and the Anthony Awards are also named for him.

"The Stripper" was originally published under his H. H. Holmes pseudonym in the January 1947 issue of *Ellery Queen's Mystery Magazine*.

The Stripper
by Anthony Boucher

HE WAS called Jack the Stripper because the only witness who had seen him and lived (J. F. Flugelbach, 1463 N. Edgemont) had described the glint of moonlight on bare skin. The nickname was inevitable.

Mr. Flugelbach had stumbled upon the fourth of the murders, the one in the grounds of City College. He had not seen enough to be of any help to the police; but at least he had furnished a name for the killer heretofore known by such routine cognomens as "butcher," "werewolf," and "vampire."

The murders in themselves were enough to make a newspaper's

fortune. They were frequent, bloody, and pointless, since neither theft nor rape was attempted. The murderer was no specialist, like the original Jack, but rather an eclectic, like Kürten the Düsseldorf Monster, who struck when the mood was on him and disregarded age and sex. This indiscriminate taste made better copy; the menace threatened not merely a certain class of unfortunates but every reader.

It was the nudity, however, and the nickname evolved from it, that made the cause truly celebrated. Feature writers dug up all the legends of naked murderers—Courvoisier of London, Durrant of San Francisco, Wallace of Liverpool, Borden of Fall River—and printed them as sober fact, explaining at length the advantages of avoiding the evidence of bloodstains.

When he read this explanation, he always smiled. It was plausible, but irrelevant. The real reason for nakedness was simply that it felt better that way. When the color of things began to change, his first impulse was to get rid of his clothing. He supposed that psychoanalysts could find some atavistic reason for that.

He felt the cold air on his naked body. He had never noticed that before. Noiselessly he pushed the door open and tiptoed into the study. His hand did not waver as he raised the knife.

The Stripper case was Lieutenant Marshall's baby, and he was going nuts. His condition was not helped by the constant allusions of his colleagues to the fact that his wife had once been a stripper of a more pleasurable variety. Six murders in three months, without a single profitable lead, had reduced him to a state where a lesser man might have gibbered, and sometimes he thought it would be simpler to be a lesser man.

He barked into phones nowadays. He hardly apologized when he realized that his caller was Sister Ursula, that surprising nun who had once planned to be a policewoman and who had extricated him from several extraordinary cases. But that was just it; those had been extraordinary, freak locked-room problems, while this was the horrible epitome of ordinary, clueless, plotless murder. There was no room in the Stripper case for the talents of Sister Ursula.

He was in a hurry and her sentences hardly penetrated his mind until he caught the word "Stripper." Then he said sharply, "So? Backtrack please, Sister. I'm afraid I wasn't listening."

"He says," her quiet voice repeated, "that he thinks he knows who the Stripper is, but he hasn't enough proof. He'd like to talk to the police about it; and since he knows I know you, he asked me to arrange it, so that you wouldn't think him just a crank."

"Which," said Marshall, "he probably is. But to please you, Sister . . . What did you say his name is?"

"Flecker. Harvey Flecker. Professor of Latin at the University."

Marshall caught his breath. "Coincidence," he said flatly. "I'm on my way to see him now."

"Oh. Then he did get in touch with you himself?"

"Not with me," said Marshall. "With the Stripper."

"God rest his soul . . ." Sister Ursula murmured.

"So. I'm on my way now. If you could meet me there and bring his letter—"

"Lieutenant, I know our order is a singularly liberal one, but still I doubt if Reverend Mother—"

"You're a material witness," Marshall said authoritatively. "I'll send a car for you. And don't forget the letter." Sister Ursula hung up and sighed. She had liked Professor Flecker, both for his scholarly wit and for his quiet kindliness. He was the only man who could hold his agnostic own with Father Pearson in disputatious sophistry, and he was also the man who had helped keep the Order's soup-kitchen open at the depth of the depression.

She took up her breviary and began to read the office for the dead while she waited for the car.

"It is obvious," Professor Lowe enunciated, "that the Stripper is one of the three of us."

Hugo Ellis said, "Speak for yourself." His voice cracked a little, and he seemed even younger than he looked.

Professor de'Cassis said nothing. His huge hunchback body crouched in the corner and he mourned his friend.

"So?" said Lieutenant Marshall. "Go on, Professor."

"It was by pure chance," Professor Lowe continued, his lean face alight with logical satisfaction, "that the back door was latched last night. We have been leaving it unfastened for Mrs. Carey since she lost her key; but Flecker must have forgotten that fact and inadvertently reverted to habit. Ingress by the front door was impossible, since it was not only secured by a spring lock but also bolted from within. None of the windows shows any sign of external tampering. The murderer presumably counted upon the back door to make plausible the entrance of an intruder; but Flecker had accidentally secured it, and that accident," he concluded impressively, "will strap the Tripper."

Hugo Ellis laughed, and then looked ashamed of himself.

Marshall laughed too. "Setting aside the Spoonerism, Professor, your statement of the conditions is flawless. This house was locked tight as a drum. Yes, the Stripper is one of the three of you." It wasn't amusing when Marshall said it.

Professor de'Cassis raised his despondent head. "But why?" His voice was guttural. "Why?"

Hugo Ellis said, "Why? With a madman?"

Professor Lowe lifted one finger as though emphasizing a point in a lecture. "Ah, but is this a madman's crime? There is the point. When the Stripper kills a stranger, yes, he is mad. When he kills a man with whom he lives . . . may he not be applying the technique of his madness to the purpose of his sanity?"

"It's an idea," Marshall admitted. "I can see where there's going to be some advantage in having a psychologist among the witnesses. But there's another witness I'm even more anxious to—" His face lit up as Sergeant Raglan came in. "She's here, Rags?"

"Yeah," said Raglan. "It's the sister. Holy smoke, Loot, does this mean this is gonna be another screwy one?"

Marshall had said *she* and Raglan had said *the sister*. These facts may serve as sufficient characterization of Sister Felicitas, who had accompanied her. They were always a pair, yet always spoken of in the singular. Now Sister Felicitas dozed in the corner where the hunchback crouched, and Marshall read and reread the letter which seemed like the posthumous utterance of the Stripper's latest victim:

My dear Sister:

I have reason to fear that someone close to me is Jack the Stripper.

You know me, I trust, too well to think me a sensationalist striving to be a star witness. I have grounds for what I say. This individual, whom I shall for the moment call "Quasimodo" for reasons that might particularly appeal to you, first betrayed himself when I noticed a fleck of blood behind his ear—a trifle, but suggestive. Since then I have religiously observed his comings and goings, and found curious coincidences between the absence of Quasimodo and the presence elsewhere of the Stripper.

I have not a conclusive body of evidence, but I believe that I do have sufficient to bring to the attention of the authorities. I have heard you mention a Lieutenant Marshall who is a close friend of yours. If you will recommend me to him as a man whose word is to be taken seriously, I shall be deeply obliged.

I may, of course, be making a fool of myself with my suspicions of Quasimodo, which is why I refrain from giving you his real name. But every man must do what is possible to rid this city a negotio perambulante in tenebris.

Yours respectfully,
Harvey Flecker

"He didn't have much to go on, did he?" Marshall observed. "But he was right. God help him. And he may have known more than he cared to trust to a letter. He must have slipped somehow and let Quasimodo see his suspicions. . . . What does that last phrase mean?"

"Lieutenant! And you an Oxford man!" exclaimed Sister Ursula.

"I can translate it. But what's its connotation?"

"It's from St. Jerome's Vulgate of the ninetieth psalm. The Douay version translates it literally: *of the business that walketh about in the dark;* but that doesn't convey the full horror of that nameless prowling *negotium.* It's one of the most terrible phrases I know, and perfect for the Stripper."

"Flecker was a Catholic?"

"No, he was a resolute agnostic, though I have always had hopes that Thomist philosophy would lead him into the Church. I almost think he refrained because his conversion would have left nothing to argue with Father Pearson about. But he was an excellent Church Latinist and knew the liturgy better than most Catholics."

"Do you understand what he means by Quasimodo?"

"I don't know. Allusiveness was typical of Professor Flecker; he delighted in British crossword puzzles, if you see what I mean. But I think I could guess more readily if he had not said that it might particularly appeal to me . . ."

"So? I can see at least two possibilities—"

"But before we try to decode the Professor's message, Lieutenant, tell me what you have learned here. All I know is that the poor man is dead, may he rest in peace."

Marshall told her. Four university teachers lived in this ancient (for Southern California) two-story house near the Campus. Mrs. Carey came in every day to clean for them and prepare dinner. When she arrived this morning at nine, Lowe and de'Cassis were eating breakfast and Hugo Ellis, the youngest of the group, was out mowing the lawn. They were not concerned over Flecker's absence. He often worked in the study till all hours and sometimes fell asleep there.

Mrs. Carey went about her work. Today was Tuesday, the day for changing the beds and getting the laundry ready. When she had finished that task, she dusted the living room and went on to the study.

The police did not yet have her story of the discovery. Her scream had summoned the others, who had at once called the police and, sensibly, canceled their classes and waited. When the police arrived, Mrs. Carey was still hysterical. The doctor had quieted her with a hypodermic, from which she had not yet revived.

Professor Flecker had had his throat cut and (Marshall skipped over this hastily) suffered certain other butcheries characteristic of the Stripper. The knife, an ordinary kitchen-knife, had been left by the body as usual. He had died instantly, at approximately one in the morning, when each of the other three men claimed to be asleep.

More evidence than that of the locked doors proved that the Stripper was an inmate of the house. He had kept his feet clear of the blood which bespattered the study, but he had still left a trail of small drops which revealed themselves to the minute police inspection—blood which had bathed his body and dripped off as he left his crime.

This trail led upstairs and into the bathroom, where it stopped. There were traces of watered blood in the bathtub and on one of the towels—Flecker's own.

"Towel?" said Sister Ursula. "But you said Mrs. Carey had made up the laundry bundle."

"She sends out only sheets and such—does the towels herself."

"Oh." The nun sounded disappointed.

"I know how you feel, Sister. You'd welcome a discrepancy anywhere, even in the laundry list. But that's the sum of our evidence. Three suspects, all with opportunity, none with an alibi. Absolutely even distribution of suspicion, and our only guidepost is the word *Quasimodo*. Do you know any of these three men?"

"I have never met them, Lieutenant, but feel as though I knew them rather well from Professor Flecker's descriptions."

"Good. Let's see what you can reconstruct. First, Ruggiero de'Cassis, professor of mathematics, formerly of the University of Turin, voluntary exile since the early days of Fascism."

Sister Ursula said slowly, "He admired de'Cassis, not only for his first-rate mind, but because he seemed to have adjusted himself so satisfactorily to life despite his deformity. I remember he said once, 'De'Cassis has never known a woman, yet every day he looks on Beauty bare.'"

"On Beauty . . . ? Oh yes. Millay. *Euclid alone* . . . All right. Now Marvin Lowe, professor of psychology, native of Ohio, and from what I've seen of him a prime pedant. According to Flecker . . . ?"

"I think Professor Lowe amused him. He used to tell us the latest Spoonerisms; he swore that flocks of students graduated from the University believing that modern psychology rested on the researches of two men named Frung and Jeud. Once Lowe said that his favorite book was Max Beerbohm's *Happy Hypocrite*; Professor Flecker insisted that was because it was the only one he could be sure of pronouncing correctly."

"But as a man?"

"He never said much about Lowe personally; I don't think they were intimate. But I do recall his saying, 'Lowe, like all psychologists, is the physician of Greek proverb.'"

"Who was told to heal himself? Makes sense. That speech mannerism certainly points to something a psychiatrist could have fun with. All right. How about Hugo Ellis, instructor in mathematics, native of Los Angeles?"

"Mr. Ellis was a child prodigy, you know. Extraordinary mathematical feats. But he outgrew them, I almost think deliberately. He made himself into a normal young man. Now he is, I gather, a reasonably good young instructor—just run of the mill. An adult with the brilliance which he had as a child might be a great man. Professor Flecker turned the French proverb around to fit him: 'If youth could, if age knew . . .'"

"So. There they are. And which," Marshall asked, "is Quasimodo?"

"Quasimodo . . ." Sister Ursula repeated the word, and other words seemed to follow it automatically. *"Quasimodo geniti infantes . . ."* She paused and shuddered.

"What's the matter?"

"I think," she said softly, "I know. But like Professor Flecker, I fear making a fool of myself—and worse, I fear damning an innocent man. . . . Lieutenant, may I look through this house with you?"

He sat there staring at the other two and at the policeman watching them. The body was no longer in the next room, but the blood was. He had never before revisited the scene of the crime; that notion was the nonsense of legend. For that matter he had never known his victim.

He let his mind go back to last night. Only recently had he been willing to do this. At first it was something that must be kept apart, divided from his normal personality. But he was intelligent enough to realize the danger of that. It could produce a seriously schizoid personality. He might go mad. Better to attain complete integration, and that could be accomplished only by frank self-recognition.

It must be terrible to be mad.

"Well, where to first?" asked Marshall.

"I want to see the bedrooms," said Sister Ursula. "I want to see if Mrs. Carey changed the sheets."

"You doubt her story? But she's completely out of the—All right. Come on."

Lieutenant Marshall identified each room for her as they entered it. Harvey Flecker's bedroom by no means consorted with the neatness of his mind. It was a welter of papers and notes and hefty German works on Latin philology and puzzle books by Torquemada and Caliban and early missals and codices from the University library. The bed had been changed and the clean upper sheet was turned back. Harvey Flecker would never soil it.

Professor de'Cassis's room was in sharp contrast—a chaste monastic cubicle. His books—chiefly professional works, with a sampling of Leopardi and Carducci and other Italian poets and an Italian translation of Thomas à Kempis—were neatly stacked in a case, and his papers were out of sight. The only ornaments in the room were a crucifix and a framed picture of a family group, in clothes of 1920.

Hugo Ellis's room was defiantly, almost parodistically the room of a normal, healthy college man, even to the University banner over the bed. He had carefully avoided both Flecker's chaos and de'Cassis's austerity; there was a precisely calculated normal litter of pipes and letters and pulp magazines. The pin-up girls seemed to be carrying normality too far, and Sister Ursula averted her eyes.

Each room had a clean upper sheet.

Professor Lowe's room would have seemed as normal as Ellis's, if less spectacularly so, if it were not for the inordinate quantity of books. Shelves covered all wall space that was not taken by door, window, or bed. Psychology, psychiatry, and criminology predominated; but there was a selection of poetry, humor, fiction for any mood.

Marshall took down William Roughead's *Twelve Scots Trials* and said, "Lucky devil! I've never so much as seen a copy of this before." He smiled at the argumentative pencilings in the margins. Then as he went to replace it, he saw through the gap that there was a second row of books behind. Paperbacks. He took one out and put it back hastily. "You wouldn't want to see that, Sister. But it might fit into that case we were proposing about repressions and word-distortions."

Sister Ursula seemed not to heed him. She was standing by the bed and said, "Come here."

Marshall came and looked at the freshly made bed.

Sister Ursula passed her hand over the mended but clean lower sheet. "Do you see?"

"See what?"

"The answer," she said.

Marshall frowned. "Look, Sister—"

"Lieutenant, your wife is one of the most efficient housekeepers I've ever known. I thought she had, to some extent, indoctrinated you. Think. Try to think with Leona's mind."

Marshall thought. Then his eyes narrowed and he said, "So . . ."

"It is fortunate," Sister Ursula said, "that the Order of Martha of Bethany specializes in housework."

Marshall went out and called downstairs. "Raglan! See if the laundry's been picked up from the back porch."

The Sergeant's voice came back. "It's gone, Loot. I thought there wasn't no harm—"

"Then get on the phone quick and tell them to hold it."

"But what laundry, Loot?"

Marshall muttered. Then he turned to Sister Ursula. "The men won't know of course, but we'll find a bill somewhere. Anyway, we won't need that till the preliminary hearing. We've got enough now to settle Quasimodo."

He heard the Lieutenant's question and repressed a startled gesture. He had not thought of that. But even if they traced the laundry, it would be valueless as evidence without Mrs. Carey's testimony . . .

He saw at once what had to be done.

They had taken Mrs. Carey to the guest room, that small downstairs bedroom near the kitchen which must have been a maid's room when this was a large family house. There were still police posted outside the house, but only Raglan and the Lieutenant inside.

It was so simple. His mind, he told himself, had never been functioning more clearly. No nonsense about stripping this time; this was not for pleasure. Just be careful to avoid those crimson jets. . . .

The Sergeant wanted to know where he thought he was going. He told him.

Raglan grinned. "You should've raised your hand. A teacher like you ought to know that."

He went to the back porch toilet, opened and closed its door without going in. Then he went to the kitchen and took the second-best knife. The best had been used last night.

It would not take a minute. Then he would be safe and later when the body was found what could they prove? The others had been out of the room too.

But as he touched the knife it began to happen. Something came from the blade up his arm and into his head. He was in a hurry, there was no time—but holding the knife, the color of things began to change.

He was half-naked when Marshall found him.

Sister Ursula leaned against the jamb of the kitchen door. She felt sick. Marshall and Raglan were both strong men, but they needed help to subdue him. His face was contorted into an unrecognizable mask like a demon from a Japanese tragedy. She clutched the crucifix of the rosary that hung at her waist and murmured a prayer to the Archangel Michael. For it was not the physical strength of the man that frightened her, nor the glint of his knife, but the pure quality of incarnate evil that radiated from him and made the doctrine of possession a real terror.

As she finished her prayer, Marshall's fist connected with his jaw and he crumpled. So did Sister Ursula.

"I don't know what you think of me," Sister Ursula said as Marshall drove her home. (Sister Felicitas was dozing in the backseat.) "I'm afraid I couldn't ever have been a policewoman after all."

"You'll do," Marshall said. "And if you feel better now, I'd like to run over it with you. I've got to get my brilliant deductions straight for the press."

"The fresh air feels good. Go ahead."

"I've got the sheet business down pat, I think. In ordinary middle-class households you don't change both sheets every week; Leona never does, I remembered. You put on a clean upper sheet, and the old upper becomes the lower. The other three bedrooms each had one clean sheet—the upper. His had two—upper and lower; therefore his upper sheet had been stained in some unusual way and had to be changed. The hasty bath, probably in the dark, had been careless, and there was some blood left to stain the sheet. Mrs. Carey wouldn't have thought anything of it at the time because she hadn't found the body yet. Right?"

"Perfect, Lieutenant."

"So. But now about Quasimodo . . . I still don't get it. He's the one it *couldn't* apply to. Either of the others—"

"Yes?"

"Well, who is Quasimodo? He's the Hunchback of Notre Dame. So it could mean the deformed de'Cassis. Who wrote Quasimodo? Victor Hugo. So it could be Hugo Ellis. But it wasn't either; and how in heaven's name could it mean Professor Lowe?"

"Remember, Lieutenant: Professor Flecker said this was an allusion that might particularly appeal to me. Now I am hardly noted for my devotion to the anticlerical prejudices of Hugo's *Notre-Dame de Paris*. What is the common meeting-ground of my interests and Professor Flecker's?"

"Church liturgy?" Marshall ventured.

"And why was your Quasimodo so named? Because he was born—or found or christened, I forget which—on the Sunday after Easter. Many Sundays, as you may know, are often referred to by the first word of their introits, the beginning of the proper of the Mass. As the fourth Sunday in Lent is called *Laetare* Sunday, or the third in Advent *Gaudete* Sunday. So the Sunday after Easter is known as *Quasimodo* Sunday, from its introit *Quasimodo geniti infantes* . . . 'As newborn babes.'"

"But I still don't see—"

"The Sunday after Easter," said Sister Ursula, "is more usually referred to as *Low* Sunday."

"Oh," said Marshall. After a moment he added reflectively, "*The Happy Hypocrite . . .*"

"You see that too? Beerbohm's story is about a man who assumes a mask of virtue to conceal his depravity. A schizoid allegory. I wonder if Professor Lowe dreamed that he might find the same happy ending."

Marshall drove on a bit in silence. Then he said, "He said a strange thing while you were out."

"I feel as though he were already dead," said Sister Ursula. "I want to say, 'God rest his soul.' We should have a special office for the souls of the mad."

"That cues into my story. The boys were taking him away and I said to Rags, 'Well, this is once the insanity plea justifies itself. He'll never see the gas chamber.' And he turned on me—he'd quieted down by then—and said, 'Nonsense, sir! Do you think I would cast doubt on my sanity merely to save my life?'"

"Mercy," said Sister Ursula. At first Marshall thought it was just an exclamation. Then he looked at her face and saw that she was not talking to him.

POSTICHE
Mignon G. Eberhart
Detective: Susan Dare

OFTEN DESCRIBED as the Mary Higgins Clark of her day, Mignon Good Eberhart (1899-1996) was once one of America's most success-ful and beloved mystery writers. She enjoyed a career that spanned six decades and produced sixty books, beginning with *The Patient in Room 18* (1929) and concluding with *Three Days for Emeralds* (1988).

Her first five books featured Sarah Keate, a middle-aged spinster, nurse, and amateur detective who works closely with Lance O'Leary, a promising young police detective in an unnamed Midwestern city. This unlikely duo functions effectively, despite Keate's penchant for stumbling into dangerous situations from which she must be rescued. She is inquisitive and supplies O'Leary with valuable information.

Equally unlikely is the fact that five films featuring Nurse Keate and O'Leary were filmed over a three-year period in the 1930s. *While the Patient Slept* (1935) featured Aline MacMahon as Nurse Keate and Guy Kibbee as O'Leary. *The Murder of Dr. Harrigan* (1936) starred Kay Linaker in the lead role, renamed Nurse Sally Keating and now much younger. *Murder by an Aristocrat* (1936) has Marguerite Churchill as Keating, and *The Great Hospital Mystery* (1937) features a much older Jane Darwell, before Warner Brothers-First National decided to go younger again with a lovely Ann Sheridan starring in both *The Patient in Room 18* (1938) and *Mystery House* (1938).

Eberhart's other series detective is Susan Dare who, like her creator, is a mystery writer. Young, attractive charming, romantic, and gushily emotional, she has a habit of stumbling into real-life murders.

"Postiche" was originally published in the August 1935 issue of *The Delineator.*

Postiche
By Mignon G. Eberhart

Postiche: A pretentious imitation, particularly used of an inartistic addition to an otherwise perfect work of art.—Encyclopædia Britannica.

THE WIGGENHORN house could never have been a pleasant place: its slate roof was too heavy and dark; its turrets too many, its windows too high and too narrow. It was still less so on the cold, windy March afternoon when Susan Dare dismissed the taxi that had brought her from the train, and put her hand upon the gate.

Susan pressed the bell and thought of Jim's words to her over the telephone. "Go ahead, if you must, Susie," he'd said. "But if it looks like trouble, you get out. You take too many chances, my girl." He'd paused there, and then said in an offhand way: "Where'd you say the place is? Just outside Warrington? And what's the name of the people?" She'd told him, and had an impression that he'd written it.

The door opened. A plump little maid took Susan's bag and invited her to enter.

The interior of the house was exactly what one would expect. There was a great deal of heavy, darkly upholstered furniture; stiff curtains which looked dusty and a musty smell tinged with camphor.

She had only a glimpse of the hall, however, for she was ushered at once into a hideous drawing-room and from a jungle of armchairs a woman arose. She was a large woman, very fat, with a jolly smile, several chins, eyes that were almost hidden in folds of flesh and lightish, untidy hair. There was an open box of chocolates on the table beside her.

"Miss Dare, I suppose," she said in an asthmatic voice. "I was expecting you. I am Miss Wiggenhorn. Miriam Wiggenhorn. Do sit down. Will you have tea?"

There was no tea in sight, so Susan said no, and thought Miss Wiggenhorn looked disappointed. "Now then, Miss Dare, I daresay you want to know exactly why I asked you to come here. I heard of you, you see, from John Van Dusen, our family lawyer. I believe he is acquainted with a woman for whom you did—er—something of the kind. A Mrs. Lasher." She picked up some embroidery hoops and then paused to glance quickly at Susan over them. Or at least, so Susan thought.

"Yes."

"Yes. Well, at any rate, when things—owing to the confusion—to my own wish rather"—she floundered, threading a needle with care, and said: "So John said call in Miss Dare. Let her look around."

"Perhaps you'd better tell me just what it is about. I have only your note asking me to come. I ought to tell you that I'm not a detective, but a writer of mystery stories. And that I'm not at all sure of being able to help you."

"I think that's quite sufficient. I mean—Mrs. Lasher—Mr. Van Dusen—you see, Miss Dare, this is the trouble." She made a careful and intricate stitch, took a breath and said: "My uncle, Keller Wiggenhorn, died a few days ago. He was buried yesterday. And I want to make sure he—died a natural death."

"You mean you think he was murdered?"

"Oh, dear, no."

"Then what do you mean?"

Mirian Wiggenhorn ate a chocolate cream thoughtfully. Then she said: "I think I'd better tell you the whole story. I'll tell it briefly."

And denuded of Miss Wiggenhorn's panting breaths and hesitation

it was certainly a brief enough story. Keller Wiggenhorn had been ail-
ing for some time, owing to a serious heart weakness. Had been so ill
in fact that for some three months he'd been obliged to have the care
of a trained nurse. He had died suddenly, when alone. The doctor
was not surprised; it was to be expected, he said. The nurse was not
surprised although she regretted that she had not been with her patient when he was taken with the last and fatal attack. No one had
known it even, although it had happened during the daytime. But
the nurse had been out in the garden, taking her rightful air and
exercise. Durrie had been in town ("Durrie?" said Susan. "My brother," said Miss Wiggenhorn. "Younger than I. We have lived with my
uncle for many years.")—Durrie had been in town; the cook busy in
the kitchen, and Miss Wiggenhorn herself had been in the kitchen.
"Putting up pickled peaches," said Miss Wiggenhorn. "Uncle was
very fond of them."

Only the maid might have known of his fatal attack, and she had
not. For he had apparently merely felt faint at first and had called to
the girl as she passed his door to hand him his bottle of smelling salts.
The girl had done so, had asked if he wanted anything else, had been
assured that he didn't. He was lying, she'd said, on a sort of couch,
drawn up to the windows so he could read. He had made no complaint, seemed no worse than usual. The girl had gone on about her
work downstairs.

There were no sounds. He hadn't rung the bell on the table beside him.

It was perhaps an hour after that that the maid returned and found
he was dead.

Miss Wiggenhorn paused again and Susan waited. There was nothing, certainly, in the recital so far to suggest the thing that Miss Wiggenhorn had implied and then denied.

"But you see," said Miriam Wiggenhorn. "He died in great pain
and struggle."

"Struggle!" said Susan sharply.

"The pillows were tossed about, his clothing disheveled, there were—marks on his throat."

It was very still. In the stillness someone walked heavily across the floor above and stopped.

"The doctor said it was all right. That with that particular trouble he was likely to gasp for breath at the last. He signed a certificate at once. Mind you, Miss Dare, I'm not saying there was murder done."

"Whom do you suspect?" said Susan bluntly.

Miriam Wiggenhorn did not reply directly. Instead she put down her embroidery with an air of decision and turned to face Susan.

"I only want you to stay here for a few days. To consider the thing. I want him to have died naturally, of course. But I cannot forget the—look of things. The marks on his throat. The doctor says he made them himself—clutching—you see?—for air. I don't suspect anyone. There is no one to suspect. Durrie and I. A cook who has been with us for years. A maid who is—too stupid in the first place; and has no motive."

"The nurse?"

"The nurse was devoted to her patient. And he to her. She is a sweet, charming young woman. As you will see."

"Did anyone profit directly by your uncle's death?"

"You mean money and property? Yes, of course. He left his property and money—all his possessions, equally divided between Durrie and me. We were like children to him. He was only a moderately wealthy man. His will permits us to live on in exactly the same manner. There's no motive at all."

"But still you feel he was murdered?"

"I feel that I want to be sure he was not. That is all."

There were footsteps overhead again and then someone was running down the stairway in the hall beyond. Miss Wiggenhorn said: "There's Durrie now."

"Do they—your family—know why I am here?" asked Susan.

"Oh, yes," said Miriam Wiggenhorn readily, and Durrie entered the room.

He was certainly much younger than his sister; young and slender with light-brown hair that had a crisp wave which any woman might have envied, light gray-blue eyes and a handsome profile which just escaped being pretty. He looked Susan over from under thick blond eyelashes and said, "How do you do," shortly.

"Rosina's out for a walk," said Miriam. "Were you looking for her?"

"No," he said quickly. "Not at all. That is—have you seen the book I was reading?"

"What book?" asked Miriam. In the midst of the little distraction of explaining and searching Durrie looked up. "You write, don't you, Miss Dare?"

"Yes," said Susan prepared to be modest. It wasn't necessary. He said "Humph" with definite disfavor, took up a book from another table and went away.

"Dinner's at seven," said Miss Wiggenhorn. "I'll take you to your room."

Left to herself in an unaired guest room, Susan sat down and surveyed the worn red roses of a Brussels carpet blankly.

Marks on a dead man's throat. A doctor's certificate. No motives. No murder. Yet she was there.

She rose and went to the window. Nottingham lace curtains did not obscure the depressing view of a bare, cold March garden. As she looked, however, a woman came into view, walking with her head bent against the wind. She wore a dark cape which, when the wind blew, showed glimpses of a scarlet lining, and paused at a fountain as if waiting for something—paused and looked up suddenly at the house. Despite the gathering gloom Susan could see the outline of her face; a darkly beautiful face with a rich, full mouth. Rosina that would be. The nurse. A sweet and charming young woman, Miriam had said.

Quite suddenly another figure was beside the nurse, coming swiftly from some shrub-masked path. It was Durrie, with no hat on and the collar of his coat turned up around his ears. He spoke to the woman briefly, they both turned to look directly upward at Susan's window and almost immediately moved away. They couldn't have seen her, of course; there was no light in her room. She pulled down the shade, and rang briskly for the maid.

Miss Wiggenhorn had said, leaving her, to question and explore as she liked.

And the little maid, Susan thought, had been prepared, for she answered her questions directly and fully and eyed her with a timorous look.

It was all exactly as Miss Wiggenhorn had already told her. The maid had heard Mr. Wiggenhorn call her, had entered the room and handed him his smelling salts.

"But didn't you think that perhaps he was having or about to have an attack?"

The maid hadn't. "He always liked to have things near him; his books, his spectacles; a glass of water; his smelling salts. I never thought anything about it."

"What did you do then?"

"I asked if there was anything else. The water glass was empty and he said to fill it and I did."

"Who found him? I mean after he was dead."

The girl's face paled a little but her eyes did not blink.

"I did. Dreadful, he looked. Everything was tossed about. Glass on the floor. Books—bottle with all the smelling salts spilled out of it. It looked as if he'd grabbed hold of the table cover and just jerked the whole thing off at once. He must have struggled—for a moment or two. I didn't hear anything at all. But then we'd shut the doors everywhere."

"Why? Was that customary?"

"I mean the doors to the back part of the house. Miss Miriam was making pickled peaches in the kitchen and the smell was all over the house. You know—vinegar and spices. So strong it was sort of sickening. The nurse said to shut the door of his bedroom."

"The nurse? What is her name?"

"Miss Hunt. Miss Rosina Hunt."

There was certainly something the girl wanted to tell—her plump face was bursting with it.

"I suppose Miss Hunt will be leaving soon?"

"She can't leave too soon," said the girl. "Not that she's not treated me well enough. But she's too bossy."

"Bossy?"

"Snappy—as if she owned the place. And stubborn! Even with Miss Miriam. After all, it's Miss Miriam's house. Hers and Mr. Durrie's."

"Mr. Durrie is not married?"

"No, ma'am. Not him. Though he was engaged to be married once. But it didn't last long."

Susan said abruptly: "Will you show me the room in which Mr. Wiggenhorn died, please."

But at the end of a good half hour spent in that chilly, huge bedroom Susan was little wiser than when she had entered it.

In the hall she met Miriam Wiggenhorn.

"Oh, you've been in his room?"

"Yes."

"That was right—John Van Dusen will be here to dinner. If there's anything—"

"There's nothing," said Susan, "yet."

Dinner. So she was to see the lawyer who had suggested sending for her. And the nurse would be there too. Rosina.

Miriam, now in cherry silk, was in the drawing-room when, half an hour later, Susan went down. With her was the lawyer, John Van Dusen, a spare, gray little man of fifty or so, who lifted his eyebrows, bowed to Susan and looked as if he were stuffed with sawdust.

And almost immediately Durrie came into the room, and then the nurse. And if the lawyer looked as if he were stuffed with sawdust, then the nurse looked as if she were charged with some high explosive. But she kept her beautiful dark eyes lowered and her red, rich mouth silent.

The dining room was dimly lighted. The food was very rich and very heavy and there was no conversation. The lawyer talked a little of politics and lifted his eyebrows a great deal; Durrie said nothing and looked at the nurse; the nurse looked at the table cloth and Miriam looked at nobody and ate steadily.

After dinner Susan had vaguely expected a talk with the lawyer. Instead they played Parcheesi. Played it till ten o'clock.

There was somewhere in the house a clock which struck on a gasping, breathless note not unlike Miriam's panting voice. When it struck ten John Van Dusen rose, the Parcheesi board disappeared, the nurse murmured and vanished.

"Good night, Miriam. Good night, Durrie. A pleasant evening. Good night, Miss Dare." The little lawyer paused and looked at Susan as if he had just become conscious of her presence. "Oh, yes," he said. "Miss Dare. So good of you to come. Not of course that there's any— er—reason for it. It really is absurd—the whole idea. Miriam is aware of my feeling, but she insisted—"

"Now, John," panted Miriam good-naturedly, "don't blame me for this. And don't trip on the step—it's likely to be slippery. Go with him to his car, Durrie."

Durrie obeyed.

Miriam looked at Susan.

"Well, my dear," she said expectantly. "How is it going? What did you think of John? He's a dear old fellow. But timid. Very timid. Wouldn't admit a murder if he saw it with his own eyes."

"Why is the nurse still here?" asked Susan.

"Rosina? Oh, I asked her to stay on for a little. During Uncle's long illness and her extreme devotion to him we became very fond of her."

The hall door opened and closed again and they could hear Durrie locking it.

"Well—how about some cake or sandwiches before you go to sleep. No? Very well. Just ring the bell if you do want anything."

Susan was still shuddering when she reached her room; her hostess's interest in food was, to say the least, inordinate.

And it was ubiquitous. Susan tossed and turned and between times dreamed of enormous boxes of chocolate creams pursuing her. Once, quite late, a sound of some kind in the hall roused her so thoroughly that she rose and opened her door cautiously and peered into the shadows of the night-lighted hall. There was, however, nothing there.

But she was still wide awake and tense when she heard it again. Or at least she heard a faint sound which was very like the creaking of the steps of a stairway. This time she reached the door softly and managed to open it without, she thought, being detected. And her care had its reward for she saw, coming very quietly from the landing of the stairs, the nurse. Rosina. She was wearing something long and dark and her face was hidden so that Susan saw only her thick, smooth black hair. But as she passed under the light she turned suddenly and cast a sharp strange look at Miriam Wiggenhorn's door. A look so strange and pale and fiery, so full of malevolence, that Susan felt queer and shaken long after the nurse had glided away.

But there was no reason to suspect murder. She told Miriam Wiggenhorn that the next morning.

She did not add that there was something hidden, something secret and ugly, going on in the house. She said merely that she had thus far found no reason to suspect murder.

Miss Wiggenhorn took it with bland detachment and asked her, still blandly, to stay on a few days. She would welcome proof of Keller Wiggenhorn's death being natural; she wanted Susan to have plenty of time. Susan said in that case she would like to see both the lawyer and the doctor and forestalled an offer on Miriam's part to have them summoned. She would go to their offices, said Susan firmly, and Miriam embroidered a flower and then said Durrie would take her in his car.

It was then that Susan risked a direct question about the nurse. "I saw her last night coming very quietly up the stairway. What would she be doing on the first floor so late? Do you know?"

"How late?"

"I don't know exactly. I suppose only around midnight."

Miriam Wiggenhorn pondered very briefly and offered a—to her—sound explanation.

"I suppose she had gone down to the kitchen for a glass of milk," she said. "Or for something to eat. I hope you aren't going to involve little Rosina in this, Miss Dare."

"But there's only you and your brother and Rosina who had the opportunity," said Susan brutally. "That is, if you except the cook and housemaid."

"I suppose so," said Miriam Wiggenhorn. "Well—I'll ask Durrie to take you to see John. And the doctor."

She did so. Durrie looked sullen but consented, and said, during the six-mile drive into Warrington, not one word.

And neither the doctor nor the lawyer yielded anything to Susan's inquiries. Except that the lawyer again rather nervously put the responsibility for calling Susan upon Miriam's plump shoulders.

In the end Susan, still with a silent and sullen Durrie, returned to the Wiggenhorn house no wiser than when she had left. They approached it this time along an old drive leading to a porte-cochère at a side door. Through the shrubs Susan caught glimpses of the garden, and, once, of a kind of summer-house, except that it was much more substantial than most summer-houses are. Durrie caught her look and said: "My studio."

"Studio? Oh, you paint, then?"

"Well, yes and no. I sort of dabble around at this and that." He hesitated and then said suddenly: "Look here, Miss Dare, I don't know what on earth's got into Miriam. Uncle wasn't murdered. Why, there's no one who would want to murder Uncle. It's a perfectly senseless notion. I wish—I wish you'd tell her so and leave."

"And there was no outsiders in the house, anyway," said Susan. "Except the nurse and—"

"Rosina don't do it! That's impossible. Why, she—she—I tell you she couldn't have done it. She thought the world of Uncle. And he of her."

"Will Rosina be leaving soon?"

"I suppose so. Just for a time. Until we can be married."

"Oh—"

"Yes."

"Did your uncle approve of your engagement?" asked Susan after a moment.

The reply was not what she expected.

"Yes," said Durrie. "He thought it was fine. Here you are, Miss Dare."

He opened the door for her. She lingered to watch as he walked around the car which he left standing in the drive and disappeared in the direction the summer-house.

Susan went thoughtfully into the hideous drawing-room. Rosina, immaculate in her white uniform, was there reading, and she lifted her fine eyes to give Susan one long, smoldering look. She was not disposed to be communicative.

Yes, she had liked Mr. Wiggenhorn very much. Yes, it was too bad he died alone; she felt very badly about that.

"But it takes them that way. It can't be helped. But it wasn't murder," she added with sudden, vehement scorn. "If he was murdered, it was an absolutely perfect crime. So perfect that it fooled me and the doctor, and I'm not easily fooled."

Susan was very thoughtful during a dreary, silent lunch. But it was not until late afternoon that, during a solitary, slow walk up and down the damp garden paths, one small phrase out of all the things that had been said to her began to emphasize itself. Was dispelled and returned.

Began to assume rather curious proportions. Under its insistency she finally let her fancy go and built up, with that as a premise, a curious fabric of murder. Or rather it built itself up, queerly, almost instantly, with the most terrifying logic.

It couldn't be. There were reasons why it couldn't be.

Yet—well, who would know? No one. Who could tell her what she must know? Come now, Susie, she could hear Jim saying: let's get down to brass tacks. How *could* it have been done?

The house was still quiet when at length she returned to it. She summoned the little housemaid to her own room again. "I want you to tell me again, exactly how you found Mr. Wiggenhorn."

The girl shut her eyes and twisted her white apron.

"Well, he was there on the couch. That's the first thing I saw, because he was all twisted—looked so queer, you know. Somehow I knew right away he was dead. I screamed and everybody—that is, Miss Wiggenhorn and cook and then the nurse—came running."

"And he had pulled off the cover of the table—"

"Oh, yes, and everything was spilled. Glass and water and—"

"Did you straighten the room?"

"Yes, ma'am. Right away. While Miss Wiggenhorn was telephoning for the doctor."

"What did you pick up?"

The girl's eyes opened widely. "Why, the—empty water glass. The bottle of smelling salts—"

"Was it open? I mean had Mr. Wiggenhorn used it?"

"Oh, yes, the stopped was out and it had fallen on its side."

"Then you gathered up the crystals of salts that had fallen out?"

"No, ma'am," said the girl. "The bottle must have been empty. There wasn't anything in it at all. Except a sort of mist—"

"Mist!" said Susan violently.

"Well—steam. As if it had had hot water in it—you know. Only the bottle was empty."

"I see," said Susan after a moment. "What did you do with it?"

"Why, I—I put it on the table. And straightened up the table and wiped up the water that had spilled from the glass—"

"Wait. There was nothing in the glass?"

"No, ma'am. It had fallen on its side too. I took it and washed it and put it back on the table."

She waited for further questions. Finally Susan said: "Was there any unusual odor in the room?"

The girl thought and then shook her head decisively. "No, ma'am. I didn't notice anything. Not even smelling salts—but then, the bottle was empty. But we were all excited—everybody running around—putting up windows."

"Opening windows? Who?"

But she didn't know exactly. "Besides," she said, "the smell of the vinegar and spices was all over the house. Suffocating, it was."

"It must have been. Did you replace the stopper in the smelling-salts bottle?"

She was dubious. Then remembered: "Yes. When I cleaned the room the next day. It had rolled under the couch."

"Do you clean Mr. Durrie's studio?" asked Susan abruptly.

"Oh, no," said the girl. "He's got bottles and glass things in there. And he won't let me clean it. Miss Miriam does it. Only Miss Miriam and the nurse are allowed to go into the studio. And if you want smells," she added with vehemence, "that's the place to get them. He says it's chemical experiments. Me and the cook think it's dreadful."

"Oh," said Susan. I've got to go, thought Susan, blindly. I've got to leave. I've got to get out of here now. At once. Will they try to stop me? And I have no proof.

The girl was looking worried.

"What's the matter, miss? Have I done anything wrong?"

"No, no," said Susan sharply. "It's all right. Do your parents live near here?"

"Two miles away."

"You'd better go to them at once. Walk. Make some excuse. Don't tell anyone you have talked to me. But go."

"G-go"—stammered the girl looking frightened. "Now?"

Somehow, tersely, Susan convinced her and watched her scuttle anxiously downstairs. (Besides she would be a valuable witness.) And still there was no proof. And no time to be lost.

The house was silent all around her. The hall empty, but shadowy and narrow. Which was Rosina's room?

She found it after opening doors to several cold, darkened bed-rooms. The nurse's red-lined cape was across a chair. Her books on a table: powder and creams and bottles quite evidently belonging to the nurse and not to Miriam, on the dressing table. In an adjoining bath-room were other things: a bathing cap, bath salts, sponge, tooth paste. She was exploring a large jar of bath powder with a cautious forefinger when there was a small rustle and Rosina herself stood in the doorway, eyes blazing.

"What are you doing in my things?"

"Searching," said Susan with false airiness.

"Searching! What for? I've nothing to conceal. I wish you'd get out of here."

"Nothing," said Susan, "would suit me better. Look here, when are you planning to be married?"

Rosina blinked.

"I don't know. Next summer. Why?"

"Why not immediately?"

"Why, I—we haven't—"

"Is there anything to prevent an immediate marriage?"

"Why—no! Certainly not!"

"Could you be married next week?"

"Y-yes. Yes, of course."

"Tomorrow?"

"Yes."

Susan permitted herself to look incredulous. "Are you sure?" she said very softly.

For a long moment the nurse's fine black eyes blazed into Susan's. Then she said furiously:

"Certainly. It's no affair of yours, but you might like to know, since you are so officious, that that is exactly what I'm going to do. I shall be married, Miss Snoopy Dare, tomorrow."

They stepped out into the hall and Rosina banged her door and, furious, went downstairs. Susan waited and then returned once more to the same room.

She looked around it again. There were remarkably few places of concealment. None, indeed, except the old-fashioned mahogany wardrobe. She looked at it with disfavor, but finally opened one of the heavy mirrored doors and stepped up into it. The few dresses offered little concealment. And there was only one way out. And Jim had said something about danger. But she didn't think of all that until she had settled herself to wait.

Not an easy wait. For the space was narrow and cramped, the air not too good in spite of the small opening she had left to enable her to see into the room, and a sense of danger, like a small red signal, became more and more marked. Danger in that muffled, orderly house. Danger—danger.

Minutes dragged on and Susan's muscles were numb and cramped. Suppose no one came. Suppose Rosina had decided on another course. But she wouldn't. And they knew, too, that Susan's own departure was imminent. Susan's eyes were blurred from staring too long and too fixedly at that crack of light. She closed them wearily.

And it was then that someone entered the room. Entered it so stealthily, so furtively that Susan felt only the faint jar of footsteps on the old floor.

Her heart pounded in her throat and her eyes were glued again to that crack.

And too late she realized that the wardrobe itself might be the objective.

Suppose the door should suddenly, silently open—suppose the very torrent of her thoughts betrayed, telepathically, her hiding place. Suppose—something passed across Susan's range of vision and obscured for an instant that crack of light.

Obscured it. And then was gone as silently, as swiftly, as it had come. But not too swiftly for recognition.

It was a long ten minutes before Susan dared move and open the door and, cautiously, emerge from her hiding place.

It was not difficult to find what she sought. The pungent odor of bath salts guided her. The jar was closed again, but it had been opened and disturbed.

She was cautious, too, in returning to her own room.

Now then, to get away. At once. Without fail.

Would they let her leave? She tossed her things in her bag and closed it; put on her coat. Knotted a yellow scarf with trembling hands and pulled her small brown hat at a jaunty angle over her light-brown hair. She looked pale and frightened. And was. But they had told her to go; at least Durrie had.

On the stairway she could hear their voices coming from the drawing-room.

Susan braced herself and entered.

And she need not have brace herself for it was all very simple and easy. They agreed that if Miss Dare felt that she could do no more and wished to go, she must go. They were very grateful to her. Her advice had relieved them greatly (this only from Miriam).

It was all very easy and very simple. Except that she didn't leave.

For something was wrong with the car.

"*Wrong with the car?*" panted Miriam. "Why, you were driving it only this morning."

"I know," said Durrie sulkily. "The thing won't start. I don't know what's wrong. You'll have to wait till morning, I guess, Miss Dare. There's only one night train in to Chicago. It leaves at six."

"A taxi"—said Susan with stiff lips.

"Too late," said Durrie, looking at his watch. "It's five-thirty now and the roads are a fright. You can't possibly make it."

Miriam looked up from her embroidery hoops. "It looks as if you'll have to spend another night with us, Miss Dare. We are very happy, indeed, to have you."

Susan's bag dropped and her heart with it. She had a sudden, sharp pang of longing for Jim. "Very well," she said after a moment. "But—a theater engagement—I'll telephone—"

There was an instant of complete silence. Then Miriam said, panting: "Show her the telephone, Durrie. It's there in the hall, Miss Dare."

They were listening, all of them, while she called Chicago and then a familiar number. But Jim was not there. "Will you give him a message, please," Susan said. "Tell him Miss Dare can't keep her engagement for the theater tonight. That she's"—she hesitated and then made curious use of a conventional phrase. "Tell him," she said, "that she's unavoidably detained."

But if they thought the use curious they did not say so.

Jim would understand her message; they had had no theater engagement. But there was no way of knowing when he would return and find it.

Was there anything really wrong with the car? And what would they say when they discovered that the little housemaid had gone home?

They said nothing of it. Nothing at all. The cook, enormous in a white apron, served the meal. What did they know? Somehow Susan managed to get food past a stricture in her throat.

Later they played parcheesi again.

"Tired, Miss Dare?" said Rosina once when Susan had glanced surreptitiously at her watch. And Miriam, holding dice in her fat, ringed hand, said:

"Are you perfectly sure you have nothing to tell us, Miss Dare? Your view of Uncle's death, I mean? Does it coincide in every way with what we know of it?"

Susan had to speak without hesitation. "I'm afraid I've discovered nothing that wasn't already known. But I'll think it over carefully; sometimes it takes a little while for things to become clear in one's mind."

Miriam tossed the dice and Durrie took his turn. He said calmly: "Is that why you sent the girl away?"

The question fell into absolute silence. Long afterward Susan was to remember the way Rosina's strong, wide, white hand closed upon the dice and held them rigidly. And her own swift, queer recollection of the empty room upstairs. The room where a kind old man had been cruelly murdered.

She couldn't have spoken. And Durrie, all at once white and strange, cried: "You thought you'd fasten it on Rosina. But she didn't kill him. She—"

"*Durrie*," said Miriam. "*Don't you know that only Rosina could have done it.*"

Durrie leaped to his feet. Rosina did not move and neither did Miriam.

And in the silence they all heard the sudden squealing of the brakes of an automobile at the side of the house.

"*Jim*," thought Susan. "Oh, let it be Jim—"

It was. Durrie went to the door and let him in. He gave one look at Susan and said very pleasantly that he'd come to take her home.

There was a bad moment when Miriam Wiggenhorn raised an objection.

"But you have only begun the investigation, Miss Dare. This is most distressing—most inconclusive—"

Jim said crisply: "Miss Dare will put any evidence she has into your hands in due form—"

It puzzled them a little. And in the instant of perplexity Jim thrust Susan out the door and closed it smartly behind them.

The engine of his car was running. Thirty seconds later they had turned into the public road and the Wiggenhorn house was a dark, brooding bulk behind them. "J-Jim," said Susan shakily.

"Scared?"

"Terrified—"

His profile looked forbidding. He said grimly: "I got your message. Drove like hell. What have you been stirring up?"

"Oh," said Susan. "A man was murdered, and I know who killed him. Can you remember chemistry?"

The car swerved, recovered, and Jim muttered. Susan went on:

"What was the name of that gas that's so dangerous? To breathe, I mean. It's heavier than air and if left open passes into the air. And when you transfer it from one container to another you have to be so careful not to breathe it—it burns the lungs or something."

"Wait a minute. Let me pull myself together." He lighted a cigarette and thought for a moment. "I know—you can see the fumes above the test tube. Otherwise you can't detect its presence except by smell. And if the tube is on its side all the gas escapes into the air. I'll remember it in a minute—hydrogen—"

"Hydrogen chloride," said Susan.

"Somebody die of it?"

"I think so," said Susan. "I'm sure—but somebody else can do the proving. I won't. They'll have to start with an autopsy."

Jim said: "Begin at the beginning."

Susan did. It took a long time and Jim said nothing till she had finished.

Then he said: "I begin to see the outline. Rich old man subject to heart attacks, likely to die of one, but doesn't. Somebody wants him to die at once. Hydrogen chloride is introduced into a smelling-salts bottle; bottle is green and thus no one is likely to perceive its apparent emptiness or its actual content. Maid hands man smelling salts, when he is alone. He gets a good big sniff of it before he can stop himself—that's bad, Susan. Think of the horrible pain—the shock—he dies really of the shock; his heart can't stand it. Ordinarily I think a person might live for some hours, or even days, and be conscious. But the murderer counted on that bad heart and won. It looks like a natural death. Anyway it is a successful murder. Durrie has a studio where he seems to do chemical experiments. The nurse would know something of chemistry. But the murder would have been perfect if Miriam hadn't suspected something. Which one did it?"

"It's funny," said Susan, "that you used the word a perfect murder. That very word is what started me thinking. Perfect. Too perfect!"

"Huh," said Jim with vehemence.

"Too perfect. No one suspected it was murder. And that was the motive, you see. Murder had to be suspected."

"Murder had to be—sorry, Susie, but I don't see."

"All right. Look at this. Durrie is in love with the nurse; wants to marry her. *His uncle didn't object.* And there was no motive at all, remember, for murder—no money motive. No question of thwarted love. No motive at all except—m except that Rosina was a very willful young woman—and Miriam, no less willful, hated her."

"But Miriam approved the marriage."

"Oh, *did* she!" said Susan. "Then why were Rosina and Durrie obliged to steal meetings. In the garden at dusk. At midnight."

"How do you know Rosina had gone downstairs to see Durrie?"

"I didn't. But it's a good reason. Name a better one."

"Suppose she did," conceded Jim. "What then?"

"Miriam had ruled that house and Durrie in the smallest detail for years. She loved her rule—a previous engagement of Durrie's had been mysteriously broken off. The uncle was about to die anyway; here was a perfect plan to get rid of Rosina."

"Do you mean Miriam murdered the old man? But that doesn't make sense. She didn't gain by it."

"She did, Jim, if she could make Durrie think, in his heart, that it was murder. And that the newcomer, the nurse, was the only one who could have done it."

"You can't prove this, Susan, it's mere theory. How do you know it was Miriam?"

"You've said it yourself, Jim—there's a French term, postiche. It means a counterfeit, an inartistic addition to an otherwise perfect work of art. Well, the murder was perfect. *It was too perfect.* No one suspected it was murder. So Miriam had failed. Had failed unless she could get someone—someone without official standing—like me—to look into it; perhaps to discover some little thing, not too much (she was very sure of herself); but enough to make Durrie think *it might have been murder.* And that if it was murder, only Rosina could have done it. She didn't know exactly how much she could trust me to see or not to see. I think she meant to watch—to—to—gauge—me. If necessary to introduce a little evidence against the nurse, as she did. It's queer; her very words of praise for Rosina made me suspect the nurse. At first. She's very clever—Miriam Wiggenhorn."

"Then the housemaid was in danger from her—"

"The housemaid is a very valuable witness. And Miriam might have discovered that I had something of the true story from her. The real story. It wasn't just accident that Miriam was pickling peaches that afternoon, filling the house with a smell of vinegar that would mask any other smell. This isn't the season for putting up fruit. She had to pickle canned fruit. Besides there was the inartistic addition—"

"You mean her calling you and talking of murder when *nobody had suspected it was murder* shows that she thought of murder when, if she were innocent, she would have had no reason to suspect it. And that for some reason she was determined to suggest that it *was* murder."

"To suggest it anyway. The perfect murder, except for the inartistic addition. Postiche. And I," said Susan, "am it."

"But"—Jim paused and said in a helpless way: "All this is very nice. But angel, it's only theory. It isn't a bad idea, you know, to have proof."

"Oh, yes—proof. It's in my bag. Wrapped in a handkerchief and mixed with bath salts. But identifiable."

"What!"

"Smelling salts. When she emptied the bottle she kept the salts in case her investigation should need a little steering. Rosina, you see, has a fine temper. When I hinted there was something preventing their marriage as if I were suspicious about it, she flounced down to tell Durrie and Miriam that she wanted it to take place at once. Durrie agreed, of course. Rosina had much the stronger will. Miriam agreed, too—and came straight upstairs to plant the clue. Nobody in the house ever used smelling salts but Keller Wiggenhorn."

"Framing her."

"Exactly. I suppose she would have tried something more open, given time."

"How did you know it was Miriam?"

"Saw her."

"From where?" demanded Jim.

"N-never mind," said Susan in a small voice.

Jim stopped the car and looked at her intently. But when he spoke it was with an air of preoccupation. "There's guilt in your voice," he said absently. "But we'll skip it. Do you know, I have a queer sort of impulse. I'd like to—"

"To what?"

"To kiss you," said Jim unexpectedly, and did so.

THE CASE OF THE CRIMSON KISS
Erle Stanley Gardner
Detective: Perry Mason

In 1950, George Gallup published the results of a nation-wide survey on mystery fiction, called the "Whodunit Derby," to determine the country's favorite mystery writer. The author who came in as the #1 choice was Erle Stanley Gardner (1889-1970), mainly because of his immensely popular lawyer/detective, Perry Mason.

For the record, the other writers who received the most votes, in order, were:

#2 Arthur Conan Doyle

#3 Ellery Queen

#4 Edgar Allan Poe

#5 Agatha Christie

#6 S. S. Van Dine

#7 Mary Roberts Rinehart

#8 Rex Stout

#9 Dashiell Hammett

Much of Gardner's career is important and inspiring because of the sheer numbers. In the decade before the first novel about Perry Mason, *The Case of the Velvet Claws* (1933), he averaged approximately

1,200,000 published words a year—the equivalent of one 10,000-word novella every three days, or one full-length novel every two weeks— and he had a day job as a lawyer.

He dictated cases to his secretary and, in 1932, it finally occurred to him that he could dictate fiction, too, which greatly speeded up the writing process, enabling him to produce novels for the first time. *Velvet Claws* famously took about three-and-a-half days, though Gardner modestly said it was really four days, since he needed a half day to think up the plot.

"The Case of the Crimson Kiss" was originally published in the June 1948 issue of *The American Magazine*; it was first collected in *The Case of the Crimson Kiss: A Perry Mason Novelette and Other Stories* (New York, William Morrow, 1970).

The Case of the Crimson Kiss
by Erle Stanley Gardner

PREOCCUPIED WITH PROBLEMS of her own happiness, Fay Allison failed to see the surge of bitter hatred in Anita's eyes. So Fay, wrapped in the mental warmth of romantic thoughts, went babbling on to her roommate, her tongue loosened by the cocktail which Anita had prepared before their makeshift dinner.

"I'd known I loved him for a long time," she said, "but honestly, Anita, it never occurred to me that Dane was the marrying kind. He'd had that one unfortunate affair, and he'd always seemed so detached and objective about everything. Of course, underneath all that reserve he's romantic and tender. . . . Anita, I'm so lucky, I can hardly believe it's true."

Anita Bonsal, having pushed her dinner dishes to one side, toyed with the stem of her empty cocktail glass. Her eyes were pinpricks of black hatred which she was afraid to let Fay Allison see. "You've fixed a date?" she asked.

"Just as soon as Aunt Louise can get here. I want her to be with me. I—and, of course, I'll want you, too."

"When will Aunt Louise get here?"

"Tomorrow or next day, I think. I haven't heard definitely."

"You've written her?"

"Yes. She'll probably take the night plane. I mailed her my extra keys so she can come right on in whenever she gets here, even if we aren't home."

Anita Bonsal was silent, but Fay Allison wanted to talk. "You know how Dane is. He's always been sort of impersonal. He took you out at first as much as he did me, and then he began to specialize on me. Of course, you're so popular, you didn't mind. It's different with me. Anita, I was afraid to acknowledge even to myself how deeply I felt, because I thought it might lead to heartache."

"All my congratulations, dear."

"Don't you think it will work out, Anita? You don't seem terribly enthusiastic."

"Of course it will work out. It's just that I'm a selfish devil and it's going to make a lot of difference in my personal life—the apartment and all that. Come on; let's get the dishes done. I'm going out tonight and I suppose you'll be having company."

"No, Dane's not coming over. He's going through a ceremony at his bachelor's club—one of those silly things that men belong to. He has to pay a forfeit or something, and there's a lot of horseplay. I'm so excited I'm just walking on air."

"Well," Anita said, "I go away for a three-day weekend and a lot seems to happen around here. I'll have to start looking for another roommate. This apartment is too big for me to carry by myself."

"You won't have any trouble. Just pick the person you want. How about one of the girls at the office?"

Anita shook her head, tight-lipped.

"Well, of course, I'll pay until the fifteenth and then—"

"Don't worry about that," Anita said lightly. "I'm something of a lone wolf at heart. I don't get along too well with most women, but I'll find someone. It'll take a little time for me to look around. Most of the girls in the office are pretty silly."

They did the dishes and straightened up the apartment, Fay Allison talking excitedly, laughing with light-hearted merriment, Anita Bonsal moving with the swift, silent efficiency of one who is skillful with her hands.

As soon as the dishes had been finished and put away, Anita slipped into a long black evening dress and put on her fur coat. She smiled at Fay and said, "You'd better take some of the sleeping pills tonight, dear. You're all wound up."

Fay said, somewhat wistfully, "I am afraid I talked you to death, Anita. I wanted someone to listen while I built air castles. I—I'll read a book. I'll be waiting up when you get back."

"Don't," Anita said. "It'll be late."

Fay said wistfully, "You're always so mysterious about things, Anita. I really know very little about your friends. Don't you ever want to get married and have a home of your own?"

"Not me. I'm too fond of having my own way, and I like life as it is," Anita said, and slipped out through the door.

She walked down the corridor to the elevator, pressed the button, and when the cage came up to the sixth floor, stepped in, pressed the button for the lobby, waited until the elevator was halfway down, then pressed the *Stop* button, then the button for the seventh floor.

The elevator rattled slowly upward and came to a stop.

Anita calmly opened her purse, took out a key, walked down the long corridor, glanced swiftly back toward the elevator, then fitted the key to Apartment 702, and opened the door.

Carver L. Clements looked up from his newspaper and removed the cigar from his mouth. He regarded Anita Bonsal with eyes that showed his approval, but he kept his voice detached as he said, "It took you long enough to get here."

"I had to throw a little wool in the eyes of my roommate, and listen to her prattle of happiness. She's marrying Dane Grover."

Carver Clements put down the newspaper. "The hell she is!"

"It seems he went overboard in a burst of romance, and his attentions became serious and honorable," Anita said bitterly. "Fay has written her aunt, Louise Marlow, and as soon as she gets here they'll be married."

Carver Clements looked at the tall brunette. He said, "I had it figured out that you were in love with Dane Grover, yourself."

"So that's been the trouble with you lately!"

"Weren't you?"

"Heavens, no!"

"You know, my love," Clements went on, "I'd hate to lose you now."

Anger flared in her eyes. "Don't think you own me!"

"Let's call it a lease," he said.

"It's a tenancy-at-will," she flared. "And kindly get up when I come into the room. After all, you might show some manners."

Clements arose from the chair. He was a spidery man with long arms and legs, a thick, short body, a head almost bald, but he spent a small fortune on clothes that were skillfully cut to conceal the chunkiness of his body. He smiled, and said, "My little spitfire! But I like you for it. Remember, Anita, I'm playing for keeps. As soon as I can get my divorce straightened out."

"You and your divorce!" she interrupted. "You've been pulling that line—"

"It isn't a line. There are some very intricate property problems. They can't be handled abruptly. You know that."

She said, "I know that I'm tired of all this pretense. If you're playing for keeps, make me a property settlement."

"And have my wife's lawyers drag me into court for another examination of my assets after they start tracing the checks? Don't be silly."

His eyes were somber in their steady appraisal. "I like you, Anita. I can do a lot for you. I like that fire that you have. But I want it in your heart and not in your tongue. My car's in the parking lot. You go on down and wait. I'll be down in five minutes."

She said, "Why don't you take me out as though you weren't ashamed of me?"

"And give my wife the opportunity she's looking for? Then you *would* have the fat in the fire. The property settlement will be signed within five or six weeks. After that I'll be free to live my own life in my own way. Until then—until then, my darling, we have to be discreet in our indiscretions."

She started to say something, checked herself, and stalked out of the apartment.

Carver Clements's automobile was a big, luxurious sedan equipped with every convenience; but it was cold sitting there, waiting.

After ten minutes, which seemed twenty, Anita grew impatient. She flung open the car door, went to the entrance of the apartment house, and angrily pressed the button of 702.

When there was no answer, she knew that Clements must be on his way down, so she walked back out. But Clements didn't appear.

Anita used her key to enter the apartment house. The elevator was on the ground floor. She made no attempt at concealment this time, but pressed the button for the seventh floor, left the elevator, strode down the corridor, stabbed her key into the metal lock of Clements's apartment, and entered the room.

Carver L. Clements, dressed for the street, was lying sprawled on the floor.

A highball glass lay on its side, two feet from his body. It had apparently fallen from his hand, spilling its contents as it rolled along the carpet. Clements's face was a peculiar hue, and there was a sharp, bitter odor which seemed intensified as she bent toward his froth-flecked lips. Since Anita had last seen him, he had quite evidently had a caller. The print of half-parted lips flared in gaudy crimson from the front of his bald head.

With the expertness she had learned from a course in first-aid,

Anita pressed her finger against the wrist, searching for a pulse. There was none.

Quite evidently, Carver L. Clements, wealthy playboy, yachtsman, broker, gambler for high stakes, was dead.

In a panic, Anita Bonsal looked through the apartment. There were all too many signs of her occupancy—nightgowns, lingerie, shoes, stockings, hats, even toothbrushes and her favorite tooth paste.

Anita Bonsal turned back toward the door and quietly left the apartment. She paused in the hallway, making certain there was no one in the corridor. This time she didn't take the elevator, but walked down the fire stairs, and returned to her own apartment. . . .

Fay Allison had been listening to the radio. She jumped up as Anita entered.

"Oh, Anita, I'm so glad! I thought you wouldn't be in until real late. What happened? It hasn't been a half-hour."

"I developed a beastly headache," Anita said. "My escort was a trifle intoxicated, so I slapped his face and came home. I'd like to sit up and have you tell me about your plans, but I do have a headache, and you must get a good night's sleep tonight. You'll need to be looking your best tomorrow."

Fay laughed. "I don't want to waste time sleeping. Not when I'm so happy."

"Nevertheless," Anita said firmly, "we're going to get to bed early. Let's put on pajamas and have some hot chocolate. Then we'll sit in front of the electric heater and talk for just exactly twenty minutes."

"Oh, I'm so glad you came back!" Fay said.

"I'll fix the drink," Anita told her. "I'm going to make your chocolate sweet tonight. You can start worrying about your figure tomorrow."

She went to the kitchen, opened her purse, took out a bottle of barbiturate tablets, emptied a good half of the pills into a cup, carefully ground them up into powder, and added hot water until they were dissolved.

When she returned to the living-room, carrying the two steaming cups of chocolate frothy with melted marshmallows floating on top, Fay Allison was in her pajamas.

Anita Bonsal raised her cup. "Here's to happiness, darling."

After they had finished the first cup of chocolate, Anita talked Fay into another cup, then let Fay discuss her plans until drowsiness made the words thick, the sentences detached.

"Anita, I'm *so* sleepy all of a sudden. I guess it's the reaction from having been so keyed up. I. . . darling, it's all right if I. . . You don't care if I. . . ."

"Not at all, dear," Anita said, and helped Fay into bed, tucking her in carefully. Then she gave the situation careful consideration.

The fact that Carver Clements maintained a secret apartment in that building was known only to a few of Clements's cronies. These people knew of Carver Clements's domestic difficulties and knew why he maintained this apartment. Fortunately, however, they had never seen Anita. That was a big thing in her favor. Anita was quite certain Clements's death hadn't been due to a heart attack. It had been some quick-acting, deadly poison. The police would search for the murderer.

It wouldn't do for Anita merely to remove her things from that apartment, and, besides, that wouldn't be artistic enough. Anita had been in love with Dane Grover. If it hadn't been for that dismal entanglement with Carver Clements. . . However, that was all past now, and Fay Allison, with her big blue eyes, her sweet, trusting disposition, had turned Dane Grover from a disillusioned cynic into an ardent suitor.

Well, it was a world where the smart ones got by. Anita had washed the dishes. Fay Allison had dried them. Her fingerprints would be on glasses and on dishes. The management of the apartment house very considerately furnished dishes identical in pattern, so it needed only a little careful work on her part. The police would find Fay Allison's nightgowns in Carver Clements's secret apartment. They would find glasses that had Fay's fingerprints on them. And when they went to question Fay Allison, they would find she had taken an overdose of sleeping pills.

Anita would furnish the testimony that would make it all check into a composite, sordid pattern. A girl who had been the mistress of a rich playboy, then had met a younger and more attractive man who had offered her marriage. She had gone to Carver Clements and wanted to check out, but with Carver Clements one didn't simply check out. So Fay had slipped the fatal poison into his drink, and then had realized she was trapped when Anita returned home unexpectedly and there had been no chance for Fay to make a surreptitious removal of her wearing apparel from the upstairs apartment. Anita would let the police do the figuring. Anita would be horrified, simply stunned, but, of course, cooperative.

Anita Bonsal deliberately waited three hours until things began to quiet down in the apartment house, then she took a suitcase and quietly went to work, moving with the smooth efficiency of a woman who has been accustomed to thinking out every detail.

When she had finished, she carefully polished the key to Apartment 702 so as to remove any possible fingerprints, and dropped it in Fay Allison's purse. She ground up all but six of the remaining sleeping tablets and mixed the powder with the chocolate which was left in the canister.

After Anita put on pajamas she took the remaining six tablets, washed off the label with hot water, and tossed the empty bottle out of the back window of the apartment. Then she snuggled down into her own twin bed and switched off the lights.

The maid was due to come at eight the next morning to clean up the apartment. She would find two still figures, one dead, one drugged.

Two of the tablets constituted the heaviest prescribed dose. The six tablets Anita had taken began to worry her. Perhaps she had really taken too many. She wondered if she could call a drug store and find out if— A moment later she was asleep. . . .

Louise Marlow, tired from the long airplane ride, paid off the taxi-cab in front of the apartment house.

The cab driver helped her with her bags to the entrance door. Louise Marlow inserted the key which Fay Allison had sent her, smiled her thanks to the driver, and picked up her bags.

Sixty-five years old, white-headed, steely-eyed, square of shoulder and broad of beam, she had a salty philosophy of her own. Her love was big enough to encompass those who were dear to her with a protecting umbrella. Her hatred was bitter enough to goad her enemies into confused retreat.

With casual disregard for the fact that it was now one o'clock in the morning, she marched down the corridor to the elevator, banged her bags into the cage, and punched the button for the sixth floor.

The elevator moved slowly upward, then shuddered to a stop. The door slid slowly open and Aunt Louise, picking up her bags, walked down the half-darkened corridor.

At length she found the apartment she wanted, inserted her key, opened the door, and groped for a light switch. She clicked it on, and called, "It's me, Fay!"

There was no answer.

Aunt Louise dragged her bags in, pushed the door shut, called out cheerfully, "Don't shoot," and then added by way of explanation, "I picked up a cancellation on an earlier plane, Fay."

The continued silence bothered her. She moved over to the bedroom.

"Wake up, Fay. It's your Aunt Louise!"

She turned on the bedroom light, smiled down at the two sleepers, said, "Well, if you're going to sleep right through everything, I'll make up a bed on the davenport and say hello to you in the morning."

Then something in the color of Fay Allison's face caused the keen eyes to become hard with concentration.

Aunt Louise went over and shook Fay Allison, then turned to Anita Bonsal and started shaking her.

The motion finally brought Anita back to semiconsciousness from drugged slumber. "Who is it?" she asked thickly.

"I'm Fay Allison's Aunt Louise. I got here ahead of time. What's happened?"

Anita Bonsal knew in a drowsy manner that this was a complicating circumstance that she had not foreseen, and despite the numbing effect of the drug on her senses, managed to make the excuse which was to be her first waking alibi.

"Something happened," she said thickly. "The chocolate . . . We drank chocolate and it felt like . . . I can't remember . . . can't remember . . . I want to go to sleep."

She let her head swing over on a limp neck and became a dead weight in Louise Marlow's arms.

Aunt Louise put her back on the bed, snatched up a telephone directory, and thumbed through the pages until she found the name *Perry Mason, Attorney.*

There was a night number: Westfield 6-5943.

Louise Marlow dialed the number.

The night operator on duty at the switchboard of the Drake Detective Agency, picked up the receiver and said, "Night number of Mr. Perry Mason. Who is this talking, please?"

"This is Louise Marlow talking. I haven't met Perry Mason but I know his secretary, Della Street. I want you to get in touch with her and tell her that I'm at Keystone 9-7600. I'm in a mess and I want her to call me back here just as quick as she can. . . Yes, that's right! You tell her it's Louise Marlow talking and she'll get busy. I think I may need Mr. Mason before I get done; but I want to talk with Della right now."

Louise Marlow hung up and waited.

Within less than a minute she heard the phone ring, and Della Street's voice came over the line as Aunt Louise picked up the receiver.

"Why, Louise Marlow, whatever are *you* doing in town?"

"I came in to attend the wedding of my niece, Fay Allison," Aunt Louise said. "Now, listen, Della. I'm at Fay's apartment. She's been drugged and I can't wake her up. Her roommate, Anita Bonsal, has also been drugged. Someone's tried to poison them!

"I want to get a doctor who's good, and who can keep his mouth shut. Fay's getting married tomorrow. Someone's tried to kill her, and I propose to find out what's behind it. If anything should get into the newspapers about this, I'll wring someone's neck. I'm at the Mandrake Arms, Apartment 604. Rush a doctor up here, and then you'd better get hold of Perry Mason and—"

Della Street said, "I'll send a good doctor up right away, Mrs. Marlow. You sit tight. I'm getting busy."

When Aunt Louise answered the buzzer, Della Street said, "Mrs. Marlow, this is Perry Mason. This is 'Aunt Louise,' Chief. She's an old friend from my home town."

Louise Marlow gave the famous lawyer her hand and a smile. She kissed Della, said, "You haven't changed a bit, Della. Come on in."

"What does the doctor say?" Mason asked.

"He's working like a house afire. Anita is conscious. Fay is going to pull through, all right. Another hour and it would have been too late."

"What happened?" Mason asked.

"Someone dumped sleeping medicine in the powdered chocolate, or else in the sugar."

"Any suspicions?" Mason asked.

She said, "Fay was marrying Dane Grover. I gather from her letters he's a wealthy but shy young man who had one bad experience with a girl years ago and had turned bitter and disillusioned, or thought he had.

"I got here around one o'clock, I guess. Fay had sent me the keys. As soon as I switched on the light and looked at Fay's face I knew that something was wrong. I tried to wake her up and couldn't. I finally shook some sense into Anita. She said the chocolate did it. Then I called Della. That's all I know about it."

"The cups they drank the chocolate from?" Mason asked. "Where are they?"

"On the kitchen sink—unwashed."

"We may need them for evidence," Mason said.

"Evidence, my eye!" Louise Marlow snorted. "I don't want the police in on this. You can imagine what'll happen if some sob sister spills a lot of printer's ink about a bride-to-be trying to kill herself."

"Let's take a look around," Mason said.

The lawyer moved about the apartment. He paused as he came to street coats thrown over the back of a chair, then again as he looked at the two purses.

"Which one is Fay Allison's?" he asked.

"Heavens, I don't know. We'll have to find out," Aunt Louise said.

Mason said, "I'll let you two take the lead. Go through them carefully. See if you can find anything that would indicate whether anyone might have been in the apartment shortly before they started drinking the chocolate. Perhaps there's a letter that will give us a clue, or a note."

The doctor, emerging from the bedroom, said, "I want to boil some water for a hypo."

"How are they coming?" Mason asked, as Mrs. Marlow went to the kitchen.

"The brunette is all right," the doctor said, "and I think the blonde will be soon."

"When can I question them?"

The doctor shook his head. "I wouldn't advise it. They are groggy, and there's some evidence that the brunette is rambling and contradictory in her statements. Give her another hour and you can get some facts."

The doctor, after boiling water for his hypo, went back to the bedroom.

Della Street moved over to Mason's side and said in a low voice,

"Here's something I don't understand, Chief. Notice the keys to the apartment house are stamped with the numbers of the apartments. Both girls have keys to this apartment in their purses. Fay Allison also has a key stamped 702. What would she be doing with the key to another apartment?"

Mason's eyes narrowed for a moment in speculation. "What does Aunt Louise say?"

"She doesn't know."

"Anything else to give a clue?"

"Not the slightest thing anywhere."

Mason said, "Okay, I'm going to take a look at 702. You'd better come along, Della."

Mason made excuses to Louise Marlow: "We want to look around on the outside," he said. "We'll be back in a few minutes."

He and Della took the elevator to the seventh floor, walked down to Apartment 702, and Mason pushed the bell button.

They could hear the sound of the buzzer in the apartment, but there was no sound of motion inside.

Mason said, "It's a chance we shouldn't take, but I'm going to take a peek, just for luck."

He fitted the key to the door, clicked back the lock, and gently opened the door.

The blazing light from the living-room streamed through the open door, showed the body lying on the floor, the drinking glass which had rolled from the dead fingers.

The door from an apartment across the hall jerked open. A young woman with disheveled hair, a bathrobe around her, said angrily, "After you've pressed a buzzer for five minutes at this time of the night you should have sense enough to—"

"We have," Mason interrupted, pulling Della Street into the apartment and kicking the door shut behind them.

Della Street, clinging to Mason's arm, saw the sprawled figure on the floor, the crimson lipstick on the forehead, looked at the overturned chair by the table, the glass which had rolled along the carpet, spilling part of its contents, at the other empty glass standing on the table.

"Careful, Della, we mustn't touch anything."

"Who is he?"

"Apparently he's People's Exhibit A. Do you suppose the nosy dame in the opposite apartment is out of the hall by this time? We'll have to take a chance anyway." He wrapped his hand with his handkerchief, turned the knob on the inside of the door, and pulled it silently open.

The door of the apartment across the hall was closed.

Mason warned Della Street to silence with a gesture. They tiptoed out into the corridor, pulling the door closed behind them.

As the door clicked shut, the elevator came to a stop at the seventh floor. Three men and a woman came hurrying down the corridor.

Mason's voice was low, reassuring: "Perfectly casual, Della. Just friends departing from a late card game."

They caught the curious glances of the four people, and moved slightly to one side until the quartet had passed.

"Well," Della Street said, "they'll certainly know us if they ever see us again. The way that woman looked me over!"

"I know," Mason said, "but we'll hope that—oh—oh! They're going to 702!"

The four paused in front of the door. One of the men pressed the buzzer button.

Almost immediately the door of the opposite apartment jerked open. The woman with the bathrobe shrilled, "I'm suffering from insomnia. I've been trying to sleep, and this—" She broke off as she saw the strangers.

The man who had been pressing the button grinned and said in a booming voice, "We're sorry, ma'am. I only just gave him one short buzz."

"Well, the other people who went in just before you made enough commotion."

"Other people in here?" the man asked. He hesitated a moment, then went on, "Well, we won't bother him if he's got company."

Mason pushed Della Street into the elevator and pulled the door shut.

"What in the world do we do now?" Della Street asked.

"Now," Mason said, his voice sharp-edged with disappointment, "we ring police headquarters and report a possible homicide. It's the only thing we can do."

There was a phone booth in the lobby. Mason dropped a nickel, dialed police headquarters, and reported that he had found a corpse in Apartment 702 under circumstances indicating probable suicide.

While Mason was in the phone booth, the four people came out of the elevator. There was a distinct aroma of alcohol as they pushed their way toward the door. The woman, catching sight of Della Street standing beside the phone booth, favored her with a feminine appraisal which swept from head to foot.

Mason called Louise Marlow in Apartment 604. "I think you'd better have the doctor take his patients to a sanitarium where they can have complete quiet," he said.

"He seems to think they're doing all right here."

"I distrust doctors who *seem* to think," Mason said. "I would suggest a sanitarium immediately."

Louise Marlow was silent for a full three seconds.

"I think the patients should have *complete quiet*," Mason said.

"Damn it," Louise Marlow sputtered. "When you said it the first time I missed it. The second time I got it. You don't have to let your needle get stuck on the record! I was just trying to figure it out."

Mason heard her slam down the phone at the other end of the line.

Mason grinned, hung up the phone, put the key to 702 in an envelope, addressed the envelope to his office, stamped it, and dropped it in the mailbox by the elevator.

Outside, the four persons in the car were having something of an argument. Apparently there was some sharp difference of opinion as to what action was to be taken next, but as a siren sounded they reached a sudden unanimity of decision. They were starting the car as the police radio car pulled in to the curb. The siren blasted a peremptory summons.

One of the radio officers walked over to the other car, took possession of the ignition keys, and ushered the four people up to the door of the apartment house.

Mason hurried across the lobby to open the locked door.

The officer said, "I'm looking for a man who reported a body."

"That's right. I did. My name's Mason. The body's in 702."

"A body!" the woman screamed.

"Shut up," the radio officer said.

"But we know the— Why, we told you we'd been visiting in 702— We—"

"Yeah, you said you'd been visiting a friend in 702, name of Carver Clements. How was he when you left him?"

There was an awkward silence; then the woman said, "We really didn't get in. We just went to the door. The woman across the way said he had company, so we left."

"Said he had company?"

"That's right. But I think the company had left. It was these two here."

"We'll go take a look," the officer said. "Come on."

Lieutenant Tragg, head of the Homicide Squad, finished his examination of the apartment and said wearily to Mason, "I presume by this time you've thought up a good story to explain how it all happened."

Mason said, "As a matter of fact, I don't know this man from Adam. I had never seen him alive."

"I know," Tragg said sarcastically; "you wanted him as a witness to an automobile accident and just happened to drop around in the wee, small hours of the morning.

"But," Tragg went on, "strange as it may seem, Mason, I'm interested to know how you got in. The woman who has the apartment across the corridor says you stood there and rang the buzzer for as long as two minutes. Then she heard the sound of a clicking bolt just as she opened her door to give you a piece of her mind."

Mason nodded gravely. "I had a key."

"A key! The hell you did! Let's take a look at it."

"I'm sorry; I don't have it now."

"Well, now," Tragg said, "isn't that interesting! And where did you get the key, Mason?"

Mason said, "The key came into my possession in a peculiar manner. I found it."

"Phooey! That key you have is the dead man's key. When we searched the body we found that stuff on the table there. There's no key to this apartment on him."

Mason sparred for time, said, "And did you notice that despite the fact there's a jar of ice cubes on the table, a bottle of whiskey, and a siphon of soda, the fatal drink didn't have any ice in it?"

"How do you know?" Tragg asked.

"Because when this glass fell from his hand and the contents spilled over the floor, it left a single small spot of moisture. If there had been ice cubes in the glass they'd have rolled out for some distance and then melted, leaving spots of moisture."

"I see," Tragg said sarcastically, "and then, having decided to commit suicide, the guy kissed himself on the forehead and—"

He broke off as one of the detectives, walking down the hallway, said, "We've traced that cleaning mark, Lieutenant."

The man handed Tragg a folded slip of paper.

Tragg unfolded the paper. "Well, I'll be—"

Mason met Tragg's searching eyes with calm steadiness.

"And I suppose," Tragg said, "you're going to be surprised at this one: Miss Fay Allison, Apartment 604, in this same building, is the person who owns the coat that was in the closet. Her mark from the dry cleaner is on it. I think, Mr. Mason, we'll have a little talk with Fay Allison, and just to see that you don't make any false moves until we get there, we'll take you right along with us. Perhaps you already know the way."

As Tragg started toward the elevator, a smartly dressed woman in the late thirties or early forties stepped out of the elevator and walked down the corridor, looking at the numbers over the doors.

Tragg stepped forward. "Looking for something?"

She started to sweep past him.

Tragg pulled back his coat, showed her his badge.

"I'm looking for Apartment 702," she said.

"Whom are you looking for?"

"Mr. Carver Clements, if it's any of your business."

"I think it is," Tragg said. "Who are you and how do you happen to be here?"

She said, "I am Mrs. Carver L. Clements, and I'm here because I was informed over the telephone that my husband was secretly maintaining an apartment here."

"And what," Tragg asked, "did you intend to do?"

"I intend to show him that he isn't getting away with anything," she said. "You may as well accompany me. I feel certain that—"

Tragg said, "702 is down the corridor, at the corner on the right. I just came from there. Your husband was killed some time between seven and nine o'clock tonight."

Dark brown eyes grew wide with surprise. "You—you're sure?"

Tragg said, "Someone slipped him a little cyanide in his whiskey and soda. I don't suppose you'd know anything about that?"

She said slowly, "If my husband is dead—I can't believe it. He hated me too much to die. He was trying to force me to make a property settlement, and in order to make me properly submissive, he'd put me through a softening-up process, a period during which I didn't have money enough even to dress decently."

"In other words," Tragg said, "you hated his guts."

She clamped her lips together. "I didn't say that!"

Tragg grinned and said, "Come along with us. We're going down to an apartment on the sixth floor. After that I'm going to take your fingerprints and see if they match up with those on the glass which contained the poison."

Louise Marlow answered the buzzer. She glanced at Tragg, then at Mrs. Clements.

Mason, raising his hat, said with the grave politeness of a stranger, "We're sorry to bother you at this hour, but—"

"I'll do the talking," Tragg said.

The formality of Mason's manner was not lost on Aunt Louise. She said, as though she had never seen him before, "Well, this is a strange time—"

Tragg pushed his way forward. "Does Fay Allison live here?"

"That's right," Louise Marlow beamed at him. "She and another girl, Anita Bonsal, share the apartment. They aren't here now, though."

"Where are they?" Tragg asked.

She shook her head. "I'm sure I couldn't tell you."

"And who are you?"

"I'm Louise Marlow, Fay's aunt."

"You're living with them?"

"Heavens, no. I just came up tonight to be here for—for a visit with Fay."

"You said, I believe, that they are not here now?"

"That's right."

Tragg said, "Let's cut out the shadow-boxing and get down to brass tacks, Mrs. Marlow. I want to see both of those girls."

"I'm sorry, but the girls are both sick. They're in the hospital. It's just a case of food poisoning. Only—"

"What's the doctor's name?"

"Now, you listen to me," Louise Marlow said. "I tell you, these girls are too sick to be bothered and—"

Lieutenant Tragg said, "Carver L. Clements, who has an apartment on the floor above here, is dead. It looks like murder. Fay Allison had evidently been living up there in the apartment with him and—"

"What are you talking about!" Louise Marlow exclaimed indignantly. "Why, I—"

"Take it easy," Tragg said. "Her clothes were up there. There's a cleaner's mark that has been traced to her."

"Clothes!" Louise Marlow snorted. "Why, it's probably some junk she gave away somewhere, or—"

"I'm coming to that," Lieutenant Tragg said patiently. "I don't want to do anyone an injustice. I want to play it on the up-and-up. Now, then, there are fingerprints in that apartment, the fingerprints of a woman on a drinking glass, on the handle of a toothbrush, on a tube of tooth paste. I'm not going to get tough unless I have to, but I want to get hold of Fay Allison long enough to take a set of fingerprints. You try holding out on me, and see what the newspapers have to say tomorrow."

Louise Marlow reached an instant decision. "You'll find her at the Crestview Sanitarium," she said, "and if you want to make a little money, I'll give you odds of a hundred to one that—"

"I'm not a betting man," Tragg said wearily. "I've been in this game too long."

He turned to one of the detectives and said, "Keep Perry Mason and his charming secretary under surveillance, and away from a telephone until I get a chance at those fingerprints. Okay, boys, let's go."

Paul Drake, head of the Drake Detective Agency, pulled a sheaf of notes from his pocket as he settled down in the big clients' chair in Mason's office.

"It's a mess, Perry," he said.

"Let's have it," Mason said.

Drake said, "Fay Allison and Dane Grover were going to get married today. Last night Fay and Anita Bonsal, who shares the apartment with her, settled down for a nice, gabby little hen party. They made chocolate. Fay had two cups; Anita had one. Fay evidently got about twice the dose of barbiturate that Anita did. Both girls passed out.

"Next thing Anita knew, Louise Marlow, Fay's aunt, was trying to wake her up. Fay Allison didn't recover consciousness until after she was in the sanitarium.

"Anyhow, Tragg went out and took Fay Allison's fingerprints. They check absolutely with those on the glass. What the police call the murder glass is the one that slipped from Carver Clements's fingers and rolled around the floor. It had been carefully wiped clean of all fingerprints. Police can't even find one of Clements's prints on it. The other glass on the table had Fay's prints. The closet was filled with her clothes. She was living there with him. It's a fine mess.

"Dane Grover is standing by her, but I personally don't think he can stand the gaff much longer. When a man's engaged to a girl and the newspapers scream the details of her affair with a wealthy playboy all over the front pages, you can't expect the man to appear exactly nonchalant. The aunt, Louise Marlow, tells me he's being faced with terrific pressure to repudiate the girl, to break the engagement and take a trip.

"The girls insist it's all part of some sinister over-all plan to frame them, that they were drugged, and all that, but how could anyone have planned it that way? For instance, how could anyone have known they were going to take the chocolate in time to—?"

"The chocolate was drugged?" Mason asked.

Drake nodded. "They'd used up most of the chocolate, but the small amount left in the package is pretty well doped with barbiturate.

"The police theory," Drake went on, "is that Fay Allison had been playing house with Carver Clements. She wanted to get married. Clements wouldn't let her go. She slipped him a little poison. She intended to return and get her things out of the apartment when it got late enough so she wouldn't meet someone in the corridor if she came walking out of 702 with her arms full of clothes. Anita, who had gone out, unexpectedly returned, and that left Fay Allison trapped. She couldn't go up and get her things out of the apartment upstairs without disturbing Anita. So she tried to drug Anita and something went wrong."

"That's a hell of a theory," Mason said.

"Try and get one that fits the case any better," Drake told him. "One thing is certain—Fay Allison was living up there in that Apartment 702. As far as Dane Grover is concerned, that's the thing that will make him throw everything overboard. He's a sensitive chap, from a good family. He doesn't like having his picture in the papers. Neither does his family."

"What about Clements?"

"Successful businessman, broker, speculator. Also a wife who was trying to hook him for a bigger property settlement than Clements wanted to pay. Clements had a big apartment where he lived officially. This place was a playhouse. Only a few people knew he had it. His wife would have given a lot of money to have found out about it."

"What's the wife doing now?"

"Sitting pretty. They don't know yet whether Clements left a will, but she has her community property rights, and Clements's books will be open for inspection now. He'd been juggling things around pretty much, and now a lot of stuff is going to come out—safe-deposit boxes and things of that sort."

"How about the four people who met us in the hall?"

"I have all the stuff on them here," Drake said. "The men were Richard P. Nolin, a sort of partner in some of Clements's business; Manley L. Ogden, an income tax specialist; Don B. Ralston, who acted as dummy for Clements in some business transactions; and

Vera Payson, who is someone's girl-friend, but I'm darned if I can find out whose.

"Anyhow, those people knew of the hideout apartment and would go up there occasionally for a poker game. Last night, as soon as the dame across the hall said Clements had company, they knew what that meant, and went away. That's the story. The newspapers are lapping it up. Dane Grover isn't going to stay put much longer. You can't blame him. All he has is Fay Allison's tearful denial. Louise Marlow says we have to do something fast."

Mason said, "Tragg thinks I had Carver Clements's key."

"Where *did* you get it?"

Mason shook his head.

"Well," Drake said, "Carver Clements didn't have a key."

Mason nodded. "That is the only break we have in the case, Paul. We know Clements's key is missing. No one else does, because Tragg won't believe me when I tell him Clements hadn't given me his key."

Drake said, "It won't take Tragg long to figure the answer to that one. If Clements didn't give you the key, only one other person could have given it to you."

Mason said, "We won't speculate too much on that, Paul."

"I gathered we wouldn't," Drake said dryly. "Remember this, Perry, you're representing a girl who's going to be faced with a murder rap. You may be able to beat that rap. It's circumstantial evidence. But, in doing it, you'll have to think out some explanation that will satisfy an embarrassed lover who's being pitied by his friends and ridiculed by the public."

Mason nodded. "We'll push things to a quick hearing in the magistrate's court on a preliminary examination. In the meantime, Paul, find out everything you can about Carver Clements's background. Pay particular attention to Clements's wife. If she had known about that apartment—"

Drake shook his head dubiously. "I'll give it a once-over, Perry, but if she'd even known about that apartment, that would have been all she needed. If she could have raided that apartment with a photographer and had the deadwood on Carver Clements, she'd have boosted her property settlement another hundred grand and walked out smiling. She wouldn't have needed to use any poison."

Mason's strong, capable fingers were drumming gently on the edge of the desk. "There has to be *some* explanation, Paul."

Drake heaved himself wearily to his feet. "That's right," he said without enthusiasm, "and Tragg thinks he has it."

Della Street, her eyes sparkling, entered Mason's private office and said, "He's here, Chief."

"Who's here?" Mason asked.

She laughed. "Don't be like that. As far as this office is concerned, there is only one *he*."

"Dane Grover?"

"That's right."

"What sort?"

"Tall, sensitive-looking. Wavy, dark brown hair, romantic eyes. He's crushed, of course. You can see he's dying ten thousand deaths every time he meets one of his friends. Gertie, at the switchboard, can't take her eyes off of him."

Mason grinned, and said, "Let's get him in, then, before Gertie either breaks up a romance or dies of unrequited love."

Della Street went out, returned after a few moments, ushering Dane Grover into the office.

Mason shook hands, invited Grover to a seat. Grover glanced dubiously at Della Street. Mason smiled. "She's my right hand, Grover. She takes notes for me, and keeps her thoughts to herself."

Grover said, "I suppose I'm unduly sensitive, but I can't stand it when people patronize me or pity me."

Mason nodded.

"I've had them do both ever since the papers came out this morning."

Again, Mason's answer was merely a nod.

"But," Grover went on, "I want you to know that I'll stick."

Mason thought that over for a moment, then held Grover's eyes. "For how long?"

"All the way."

"No matter what the evidence shows?"

Grover said, "The evidence shows the woman I love was living with Carver Clements as his mistress. The evidence simply can't be right. I love her, and I'm going to stick. I want you to tell her that, and I want you to know that. What you're going to have to do will take money. I'm here to see that you have what money you need—all you want, in fact."

"That's fine," Mason said. "Primarily, what I need is a little moral support. I want to be able to tell Fay Allison that you're sticking, and I want some facts."

"What facts?"

"How long have you been going with Fay Allison?"

"A matter of three or four months. Before then I was—well, sort of squiring both of the girls around."

"You mean Anita Bonsal?"

"Yes. I met Anita first. I went with her for a while. Then I went with both. Then I began to gravitate toward Fay Allison. I thought I was just making dates. Actually, I was falling in love."

"And Anita?"

"She's like a sister to both of us. She's been simply grand in this whole thing. She's promised me that she'll do everything she can."

"Could Fay Allison have been living with Carver Clements?"

"She had the physical opportunity, if that's what you mean."

"You didn't see her every night?"

"No."

"What does Anita say?"

"Anita says the charge is ridiculous."

"Do you know of any place where Fay Allison could have had access to cyanide of potassium?"

"That's what I wanted to tell you about, Mr. Mason. Out at my place the gardener uses it. I don't know just what for, but—well, out there the other day, when he was showing Fay around the place—"

"Yes, yes," Mason said impatiently, as Grover paused; "go on."

"Well, I know the gardener told her to be very careful not to touch that sack because it contained cyanide. I remember she asked him a few questions about what he used it for, but I wasn't paying much attention. It's the basis of some sort of spray."

"Has your gardener read the papers?"

Grover nodded.

"Can you trust him?"

"Yes. He's very loyal to all our family. He's been with us for twenty years."

"What's his name?"

"Barney Sheff. My mother—well, rehabilitated him."

"He'd been in trouble? In the pen?"

"That's right. He had a chance to get parole if he could get a job. Mother gave him the job."

"I'm wondering if you have fully explored the possibilities of orchid growing."

"We're not interested in orchid growing. We can buy them and—"

"I wonder," Mason said in exactly the same tone, "if you have fully investigated the possibilities of growing orchids."

"You mean—Oh, you mean we should send Barney Sheff to—"

"Fully investigated the possibilities of growing orchids," Mason said again.

Dane Grover studied Mason silently for a few seconds. Then abruptly he rose from the chair, extended his hand, and said, "I wanted you to understand, Mr. Mason, that I'm going to stick. I brought you some money. I thought you might need it." He carelessly tossed an envelope on the table. And with that he turned and marched out of the office.

Mason reached for the envelope Grover had tossed on his desk. It was well filled with hundred-dollar bills.

Della Street came over to take the money. "When I get so interested in a man," she said, "that I neglect to count the money, you know I'm becoming incurably romantic. How much, Chief?"

"Plenty," Mason said.

Della Street was counting it when the unlisted telephone on her desk rang. She picked up the receiver, and heard Drake's voice on the line. "Hi, Paul," she said.

"Hi, Della. Perry there?"

"Yes."

"Okay," Drake said wearily, "I'm making a progress report. Tell him Lieutenant Tragg nabbed the Grover gardener, a chap by the name of Sheff. They're holding him as a material witness, seem to be all worked up about what they've discovered. Can't find out what it is."

Della Street sat motionless at the desk, holding the receiver.

"Hello, hello," Drake said; "are you there?"

"I'm here," Della said. "I'll tell him." She hung up the phone.

It was after nine o'clock that night when Della Street, signing the register in the elevator, was whisked up to the floor where Perry Mason had his offices. She started to look in on Paul Drake, then changed her mind and kept on walking down the long, dark corridor, the rapid tempo of her heels echoing back at her from the night silence of the hallway.

She rounded the elbow in the corridor, and saw that lights were on in Mason's office.

The lawyer was pacing the floor, thumbs pushed in the armholes of his vest, head shoved forward, wrapped in such concentration that he did not even notice the opening of the door.

The desk was littered with photographs. There were numerous sheets of the flimsy which Paul Drake used in making reports.

Della stood quietly in the doorway, watching the tall, lean-waisted man pacing back and forth. Granite-hard of face, the seething action of his restless mind demanded a physical outlet, and this restless pacing was just an unconscious reflex.

After almost a minute Della Street said, "Hello, Chief. Can I help?"

Mason looked up at her with a start. "What are you doing here?"

"I came up to see if there was anything I could do to help. Had any dinner?" she asked.

He glanced at his wrist watch, said, "Not yet."

"What time is it?" Della Street asked.

He had to look at his wrist watch again in order to tell her. "Nine forty."

She laughed. "I knew you didn't even look the first time you went through the motions. Come on, Chief; you've got to go get something to eat. The case will still be here when you get back."

"How do we know it will?" Mason said. "I've been talking with Louise Marlow on the phone. She's been in touch with Dane Grover and she knows Dane Grover's mother. Dane Grover says he'll stick. How does *he* know what he'll do? He's never faced a situation like this. His friends, his relatives, are turning the knife in the wound with their sympathy. How can he tell whether he'll stick?"

"Just the same," Della Street insisted, "I think he will. It's through situations such as this that character is created."

"You're just talking to keep your courage up," Mason said. "The guy's undergoing the tortures of the damned. He can't help but be influenced by the evidence. The woman he loves on the night before the wedding trying to free herself from the man who gave her money and a certain measure of security."

"Chief, you simply *have* to eat."

Mason walked over to the desk. "Look at 'em," he said; "photographs! And Drake had the devil's own time obtaining them. They're copies of the police photographs—the body on the floor, glass on the table, an overturned chair, a newspaper half open by a reading chair—an apartment as drab as the sordid affair for which it was used. And somewhere in those photographs I've got to find the clue that will establish the innocence of a woman, not only innocence of murder, but of the crime of betraying the man she loved."

Mason leaned over the desk, picked up the magnifying glass which was on his blotter, and started once more examining the pictures. "Hang it, Della," he said, "I think the thing's here somewhere. That glass on the table, a little whiskey and soda in the bottom, Fay Allison's fingerprints all over it. Then there's the brazen touch of that crimson kiss on the forehead."

"Indicating a woman was with him just before he died?"

"Not necessarily. That lipstick is a perfect imprint of a pair of lips. There was no lipstick on his lips, just there on the forehead. A shrewd man could well have smeared lipstick on his lips, pressed them against Clements's forehead after the poison had taken effect, and so directed suspicion away from himself. This could easily have happened if the man had known some woman was in the habit of visiting Clements in that apartment.

"It's a clue that so obviously indicates a woman that I find myself getting suspicious of it. If there were only something to give me a starting point. If only we had more time."

Della Street walked over to the desk. She said, "Stop it. Come and get something to eat. Let's talk it over."

"Haven't you had dinner?"

She smiled, and shook her head. "I knew you'd be working, and that if someone didn't rescue you, you'd be pacing the floor until two or three o'clock in the morning. What's Paul Drake found out?"

She picked up the sheets of flimsy, placed them together, and anchored everything in place with a paper-weight. "Come on, Chief."

But he didn't really answer her question until after he had relaxed in one of the booths in their favorite restaurant. He pushed back the plates containing the wreckage of a thick steak, and poured more coffee, then said, "Drake hasn't found out much—just background."

"What, for instance?"

Mason said wearily, "It's the same old seven and six. The wife, Marline Austin Clements, apparently was swept off her feet by the sheer power of Carver Clements's determination to get her. She overlooked the fact that after he had her safely listed as one of his legal chattels, he used that same acquisitive, aggressive tenacity of purpose to get other things he wanted. Marline was left pretty much alone."

"And so?" Della asked.

"And so," Mason said, "in the course of time, Carver Clements turned to other interests. Hang it, Della, we have one thing to work on, only one thing—the fact that Clements had no key on his body.

"You remember the four people who met us in the corridor. They had to get in that apartment house some way. Remember the outer door was locked. Any of the tenants could release the latch by pressing the button of an electric release. But if the tenant of some apartment didn't press the release button, it was necessary to have a key in order to get in.

"Now, then, those four people got in. How? Regardless of what they say now, one of them must have had a key."

"The missing key?" Della asked.

"That's what we have to find out."

"What story did they give the police?"

"I don't know. The police have them sewed up tight. I've got to get one of them on the stand and cross-examine him. Then we'll at least have something to go on."

"So we have to try for an immediate hearing and then go it blind?"

"That's about the size of it."

"Was that key in Fay Allison's purse Clements's missing key?"

"It could have been. If so, either Fay was playing house or the key was planted. In that case, when was it planted, how, and by whom? I'm inclined to think Clements's key must have been on his body at the time he was murdered. It wasn't there when the police arrived. That's the one really significant clue we have to work on."

Della Street shook her head. "It's too deep for me, but I guess you're going to have to wade into it."

Mason lit a cigarette."Ordinarily I'd spar for time, but in this case I'm afraid time is our enemy, Della. We're going to have to walk into court with all the assurance in the world and pull a very large rabbit out of a very small hat."

She smiled. "Where do we get the rabbit?"

"Back in the office," he said, "studying those photographs, looking for a clue, and—" Suddenly he snapped to attention.

"What is it, Chief?"

"I was just thinking. The glass on the table in 702—there was a little whiskey and soda in the bottom of it, just a spoonful or two."

"Well?" she asked.

"What happens when you drink whiskey and soda, Della?"

"Why—you always leave a little. It sticks to the side of the glass and then gradually settles back."

Mason shook his head. His eyes were glowing now. "You leave ice cubes in the glass," he said, "and then after a while they melt and leave an inch or so of water."

She matched his excitement. "Then there was no ice in the woman's glass?"

"And none in Carver Clements's. Yet there was a jar of ice cubes on the table. Come on, Della; we're going back and *really* study those photographs!"

Judge Randolph Jordan ascended the bench and rapped court to order.

"People versus Fay Allison."

"Ready for the defendant," Mason said.

"Ready for the Prosecution," Stewart Linn announced.

Linn, one of the best of the trial deputies in the district attorney's office, was a steely-eyed individual who had the legal knowledge of an encyclopedia, and the cold-blooded mercilessness of a steel trap.

Linn was under no illusions as to the resourcefulness of his adversary, and he had all the caution of a boxer approaching a heavyweight champion.

"Call Dr. Charles Keene," he said.

Dr. Keene came forward, qualified himself as a physician and surgeon who had had great experience in medical necropsies, particularly in cases of homicide.

"On the tenth of this month did you have occasion to examine a body in Apartment 702 at the Mandrake Arms?"

"I did."

"What time was it?"

"It was about two o'clock in the morning."

"What did you find?"

"I found the body of a man of approximately fifty-two years of age, fairly well fleshed, quite bald, but otherwise very well preserved for a man of his age. The body was lying on the floor, head toward the door, feet toward the interior of the apartment, the left arm doubled up and lying under him, the right arm flung out, the left side of the face resting on the carpet. The man had been dead for several hours. I fix the time of death as having taken place during a period between seven o'clock and nine o'clock that evening. I cannot place the time of death any closer than that, but I will swear that it took place within those time limits."

"And did you determine the cause of death?"

"Not at that time. I did later."

"What was the cause of death?"

"Poisoning caused by the ingestion of cyanide of potassium."

"Did you notice anything about the physical appearance of the man's body?"

"There was a red smear on the upper part of the forehead, apparently caused by lips that had been heavily coated with lipstick and then pressed against the skin in a somewhat puckered condition. It was as though some woman had administered a last kiss."

"Cross-examine," Linn announced.

"No questions," Mason said.

"Call Benjamin Harlan," Linn said.

Benjamin Harlan, a huge, lumbering giant of a man, promptly proceeded to qualify himself as a fingerprint and identification expert of some twenty years' experience.

Stewart Linn, by skillful, adroit questions, led him through an account of his activities on the date in question. Harlan found no latent fingerprints on the glass which the Prosecution referred to as the "murder glass," indicating this glass had been wiped clean of prints, but there were prints on the glass on the table which the Prosecution referred to as the "decoy glass," on the toothbrush, on the tube of tooth paste, and on various other articles. These latent fingerprints had coincided with the fingerprints taken from the hands of Fay Allison, the defendant.

Harlan also identified a whole series of photographs taken by the police showing the position of the body when it was discovered, the furnishings in the apartment, the table, the overturned chair, the so-called murder glass, which had rolled along the floor, the so-called decoy glass on the table, which bore unmistakably the fresh fingerprints of Fay Allison, the bottle of whiskey, the bottle of soda water, the jar containing ice cubes.

"Cross-examine," Linn said triumphantly.

Mason said, "You have had some twenty years' experience as a fingerprint expert, Mr. Harlan?"

"Yes, sir."

"Now, you have heard Dr. Keene's testimony about the lipstick on the forehead of the dead man?"

"Yes, sir."

"And that lipstick, I believe, shows in this photograph which I now hand you?"

"Yes, sir; not only that, but I have a close-up of that lipstick stain which I, myself, took. I have an enlargement of that negative, in case you're interested."

"I'm very much interested," Mason said. "Will you produce the enlargement, please?"

Harlan produced the photograph from his brief-case, showing a section of the forehead of the dead man, with the stain of lips outlined clearly and in microscopic detail.

"What is the scale of this photograph?" Mason asked.

"Life size," Harlan said. "I have a standard of distances by which I can take photographs to a scale of exactly life size."

"Thank you," Mason said. "I'd like to have this photograph received in evidence"

"No objection," Linn said.

"And it is, is it not, a matter of fact that the little lines shown in this photograph are fully as distinctive as the ridges and whorls of a fingerprint?"

"Just what do you mean?"

"Isn't it a fact well known to identification experts that the little wrinkles which form in a person's lips are fully as individual as the lines of a fingerprint?"

"It's not a 'well-known' fact."

"But it *is* a fact?"

"Yes, sir, it is."

"So that by measuring the distance between the little lines which are shown on this photograph, indicating the pucker lines of the skin, it would be fully as possible to identify the lips which made this lipstick print as it would be to identify a person who had left a fingerprint upon the scalp of the dead man."

"Yes, sir."

"Now, you have testified to having made imprints of the defendant's fingers and compared those with the fingerprints found on the glass."

"Yes, sir."

"Have you made any attempt to take an imprint of her lips and compare that print with the print of the lipstick on the decedent?"

"No, sir," Harlan said, shifting his position uneasily.

"Why not?"

"Well, in the first place, Mr. Mason, the fact that the pucker lines of lips are so highly individualized is not a generally known fact."

"But *you* knew it."

"Yes, sir."

"And the more skilled experts in your profession know it?"

"Yes, sir."

"Why didn't you do it, then?"

Harlan glanced somewhat helplessly at Stewart Linn.

"Oh, if the Court please," Linn said, promptly taking his cue from that glance, "this hardly seems to be cross-examination. The inquiry is wandering far afield. I will object to the question on the ground that it's incompetent, irrelevant, immaterial, and not proper cross-examination."

"Overruled," Judge Jordan snapped. "Answer the question!"

Harlan cleared his throat. "Well," he said, "I just never thought of it."

"Think of it now," Mason said. "Go ahead and take the imprint right now and right here. . . . Put on plenty of lipstick, Miss Allison. Let's see how your lips compare with those on the dead man's forehead."

"Oh, if the Court please," Linn said wearily, "this hardly seems to be cross-examination. If Mr. Mason wants to make Harlan his own witness and call for this test as a part of the defendant's case, that will be one thing; but this certainly isn't cross-examination."

"It may be cross-examination of Harlan's qualifications as an expert," Judge Jordan ruled.

"Oh, if the Court please! Isn't that stretching a technicality rather far?"

"Your objection was highly technical," Judge Jordan snapped. "It is overruled, and my ruling will stand. Take the impression, Mr. Harlan."

Fay Allison, with trembling hand, daubed lipstick heavily on her mouth. Then, using the make-up mirror in her purse, smoothed off the lipstick with the tip of her little finger.

"Go ahead," Mason said to Harlan; "check on her lips."

Harlan, taking a piece of white paper from his brief-case, moved down to where the defendant was sitting beside Perry Mason and pressed the paper against her lips. He removed the paper and examined the imprint.

"Go ahead," Mason said to Harlan; "make your comparison and announce the results to the Court."

Harlan said, "Of course, I have not the facilities here for making a microscopic comparison, but I can tell from even a superficial examination of the lip lines that these lips did not make that print."

"Thank you," Mason said. "That's all."

Judge Jordan was interested. "These lines appear in the lips only when the lips are puckered, as in giving a kiss?"

"No, Your Honor, they are in the lips all the time, as an examination will show, but when the lips are puckered, the lines are intensified."

"And these lip markings are different with each individual?"

"Yes, Your Honor."

"So that you are now prepared to state to the Court that despite the fingerprints of the defendant on the glass and other objects, her lips definitely could not have left the imprint on the dead man's forehead?"

"Yes, Your Honor."

"That's all," Judge Jordan said.

"Of course," Linn pointed out, "the fact that the defendant did not leave that kiss imprint on the man's forehead doesn't necessarily mean a thing, Your Honor. In fact, he may have met his death *because* the defendant found that lipstick on his forehead. The evidence of the fingerprints is quite conclusive that the defendant was in that apartment."

"The Court understands the evidence. Proceed with your case," Judge Jordan said.

"Furthermore," Linn went on angrily, "I will now show the Court that there was every possibility the print of that lipstick could have been deliberately planted by none other than the attorney for the defendant and his charming and very efficient secretary. I will proceed to prove that by calling Don B. Ralston to the stand."

Ralston came forward and took the stand, his manner that of a man who wishes he were many miles away.

"Your name is Don B. Ralston? You reside at 2935 Creelmore Avenue in this city?"

"Yes, sir."

"And you knew Carver L. Clements in his lifetime?"

"Yes."

"In a business way?"

"Yes, sir."

"Now, on the night—or, rather, early in the morning—of the 10th of this month, did you have occasion to go to Carver Clements's apartment, being Apartment Number 702 in the Mandrake Arms Apartments in this city?"

"I did, yes, sir."

"What time was it?"

"Around—well, it was between one and two in the morning—I would say around one thirty."

"Were you alone?"

"No, sir."

"Who was with you?"

"Richard P. Nolin, who is a business associate—or was a business associate—of Mr. Clements; Manley L. Ogden, who handled some of Mr. Clements's income tax work; and a Miss Vera Payson, a friend of—well, a friend of all of us."

"What happened when you went to that apartment?"

"Well, we left the elevator on the seventh floor, and as we were walking down the corridor, I noticed two people coming down the corridor toward us."

"Now, when you say 'down the corridor,' do you mean from the direction of Apartment 702?"

"That's right, yes, sir."

"And who were these people?"

"Mr. Perry Mason and his secretary, Miss Street."

"And did you actually enter the apartment of Carver Clements?"

"I did not."

"Why not?"

"When I got to the door of Apartment 702, I pushed the doorbell and heard the sound of the buzzer on the inside of the apartment. Almost instantly the door of an apartment across the hall opened, and a woman complained that she had been unable to sleep because of people ringing the buzzer of that apartment, and stated, in effect, that other people were in there with Mr. Clements. So we left immediately."

"Now, then, Your Honor," Stewart Linn said, "I propose to show that the two people referred to by the person living in the apartment across the hallway were none other than Mr. Mason and Miss Street, who had actually entered that apartment and were in there with the dead man and the evidence for an undetermined length of time."

"Go ahead and show it," Judge Jordan said.

"Just a moment," Mason said. "Before you do that, I want to cross-examine this witness."

"Cross-examine him, then."

"When you arrived at the Mandrake Arms, Mr. Ralston, the door to the street was locked, was it not?"

"Yes, sir."

"What did you do?"

"We went up to the seventh floor and—"

"I understand that, but how did you get in? How did you get past the entrance door? You had a key, didn't you?"

"No, sir."

"Then how *did* you get in?"

"Why *you* let us in."

"*I* did?"

"Yes."

"Understand," Mason said, "I am not now referring to the time you came up from the street in the custody of the radio officer. I am now referring to the time when you *first* entered that apartment house on the morning of the tenth of this month."

"Yes, sir. I understand. You let us in."

"What makes you say that?"

"Well, because you and your secretary were in Carver Clements's apartment, and—"

"You, yourself, don't *know* we were in there, do you?"

"Well, I surmise it. We met you just after you had left the apartment. You were hurrying down the hall toward the elevator."

Mason said, "I don't want your surmises. You don't even know I had been in that apartment. I want you to tell us how you got past the locked street door."

"We pressed the button of Carver Clements's apartment, and you— or, at any rate, someone—answered by pressing the button which released the electric door catch on the outer door. As soon as we heard the buzzing sound, which indicated the lock was released, we pushed the door open and went in."

"Let's not have any misunderstanding about this," Mason said. "Who was it pushed the button of Carver Clements's apartment?"

"I did."

"I'm talking now about the button in front of the outer door of the apartment."

"Yes, sir."

"And having pressed that button, you waited until the buzzer announced the door was being opened?"

"Yes, sir."

"How long?"

"Not over a second or two."

Mason said to the witness, "One more question: Did you go right up after you entered the house?"

"We—no, sir, not *right* away. We stopped for a few moments there in the lobby to talk about the type of poker we wanted to play. Miss Payson had lost money on one of these wild poker games where the dealer has the opportunity of calling any kind of game he wants, some of them having the one-eyed Jacks wild, and things of that sort."

"How long were you talking?"

"Oh, a couple of minutes."

"And then went right up?"

"Yes."

"Where was the elevator?"

"The elevator was on one of the upper floors. I remember we pressed the button and it took a little while to come down to where we were."

"That's all," Mason said.

Della Street's fingers dug into his arm. "Aren't you going to ask him about the key?" she whispered.

"Not yet," Mason said, a light of triumph in his eyes. "I know what happened now, Della. Give us the breaks, and we've got this case in the bag. First, make him prove we were in that apartment."

Linn said, "I will now call Miss Shirley Tanner to the stand."

The young woman who advanced to the stand was very different from the disheveled and nervous individual who had been so angry at the time Mason and Della Street had pressed the button of Apartment 702.

"Your name is Shirley Tanner, and you reside in Apartment 701 of the Mandrake Arms Apartments?"

"Yes, sir."

"And have for how long?"

She smiled, and said, "Not very long. I put in three weeks apartment hunting and finally secured a sublease on Apartment 701 on the afternoon of the eighth. I moved in on the ninth, which explains why I was tired almost to the point of hysterics."

"You had difficulty sleeping?"

"Yes."

"And on the morning of the tenth did you have any experiences which annoyed you—experiences in connection with the ringing of the buzzer in the apartment next door?"

"I most certainly did, yes, sir."

"Tell us exactly what happened."

"I had been taking sleeping medicine from time to time, but for some reason or other this night I was so nervous the sleeping medicine didn't do me any good. I had been unpacking, and my nerves were all keyed up. I was physically and mentally exhausted but I was too tired to sleep.

"Well, I was trying to sleep, and I think I had just got to sleep when I was awakened by a continual sounding of the buzzer in the apartment across the hall. It was a low, persistent noise which became very irritating in my nervous state."

"Go on," Linn said. "What did you do?"

"I finally got up and put on a robe and went to the door and flung it open. I was terribly angry at the very idea of people making so much noise at that hour of the morning. You see those apartments aren't too soundproof and there is a ventilating system over the doors of the apartments, The one over the door of 702 was apparently open and I had left mine open for night-time ventilation. And then I was angry at myself for getting so upset over the noise. I knew it would prevent me from sleeping at all, which is why I lay still for what seemed an interminable time before I opened the door."

Linn smiled. "And you say you *flung* open the door?"

"Yes, sir."

"What did you find?"

"Two people across the hall."

"Did you recognize them?"

"I didn't know them at the time but I know them now."

"Who were they?"

She pointed a dramatic finger a Perry Mason. "Mr. Perry Mason, the lawyer for the defendant, and the young woman, I believe his secretary, who is sitting there beside him—not the defendant, but the woman on the other side."

"Miss Della Street," Mason said with a bow.

"Thank you," she said.

"And," Linn went on, "what did you see those people do?"

She said, "I saw them enter the apartment."

"Did you see how they entered the apartment—I mean, how did they get the door open?"

"They must have used a key. Mr. Mason was just pushing the door open and I—"

"No surmises, please," Linn broke in. "Did you actually see Mr. Mason using a key?"

"Well, I heard him."

"What do you mean?"

"As I was opening my door I heard metal rasping against metal, the way a key does when it scrapes against a lock. And then, when I had my door all the way open, I saw Mr. Mason pushing his way into 702."

"But you only know he must have had a key because you heard the sound of metal rubbing against metal?"

"Yes, and the click of the lock."

"Did you say anything to Mr. Mason and Miss Street?"

"I most certainly did, and then I slammed the door and went back and tried to sleep. But I was so mad by that time I couldn't keep my eyes closed."

"What happened after that?"

"After that, when I was trying to sleep—I would say just a few seconds after that—I heard that buzzer again. This time I was good and mad."

"And what did you do?"

"I swung open the door and started to give these people a piece of my mind."

"People?" Linn asked promptingly.

"There were four people standing there. The Mr. Ralston, who has just testified, two other men, and a woman. They were standing there at the doorway, jabbing away at the button, and I told them this was a sweet time to be calling on someone and making a racket, and that anyway the gentleman already had company, so if he didn't answer his door, it was because he didn't want to."

"Did you at that time see Mr. Mason and Miss Street walking down the corridor?"

"No. I did not. I had my door open only far enough to show me the door of Apartment 702 across the way."

"Thank you," Linn said. "Now, you distinctly saw Mr. Mason and Miss Street enter that apartment?"

"Yes."

"And close the door behind them?"

"Yes."

"Cross-examine!" Linn said triumphantly.

Mason, taking a notebook from his pocket, walked up to stand beside Shirley Tanner. "Miss Tanner," he said, "are you certain that you heard me rub metal against the keyhole of that door?"

"Certain," she said.

"My back was toward you?"

"It was when I first opened my door, yes. I saw your face, however, just after you went in the door. You turned around and looked at me over your shoulder."

"Oh, we'll stipulate," Linn said, with an exaggerated note of weariness in his voice, "that the witness couldn't see through Mr. Mason's back. Perhaps learned counsel was carrying the key in his teeth."

"Thank you," Mason said, turning toward Linn. Then, suddenly stepping forward, he clapped his notebook against Shirley Tanner's face.

The witness screamed and jumped back.

Linn was on his feet "What are you trying to do?" he shouted.

Judge Jordan pounded with his gavel. "Mr. Mason!" he reprimanded. "That is contempt of court!"

Mason said, "Please let me explain, Your Honor. The Prosecution took the lip-prints of my client. I feel that I am entitled to take the lip-prints of this witness. I will cheerfully admit to being in contempt of court, in the event I am wrong, but I would like to extend this imprint of Shirley Tanner's lips to Mr. Benjamin Harlan, the identification expert, and ask him whether or not the print made by these lips is not the same as that of the lipstick kiss which was found on the dead forehead of Carver L. Clements."

There was a tense, dramatic silence in the courtroom.

Mason stepped forward and handed the notebook to Benjamin Harlan.

From the witness stand came a shrill scream of terror. Shirley Tanner tried to get to her feet. Her eyes were wide and terrified, her face was the color of putty.

She couldn't make it. Her knees buckled. She tried to catch herself then fell to the floor. . . .

It was when order was restored in the courtroom that Perry Mason exploded his second bombshell.

"Your Honor," he said, "either Fay Allison is innocent or she is guilty. If she is innocent, someone framed the evidence which would discredit her. And if someone did frame that evidence, there is only one person who could have had access to the defendant's apartment, one person who could have transported glasses, toothbrushes, and tooth paste containing Fay Allison's fingerprints, one person who could have transported clothes bearing the unmistakable stamp of ownership of the defendant in this case. . . . Your Honor I request that Anita Bonsal be called to the stand."

There was a moment's silence.

Anita Bonsal, there in the courtroom, felt suddenly as though she had been stripped stark naked by one swift gesture. One moment, she had been sitting there, attempting to keep pace with the swift rush of developments. The next moment, everyone in the courtroom was seeking her out with staring, prying eyes.

In her sudden surge of panic, Anita did the worst thing she could possibly have done: She ran.

They were after her then, a throng of humanity, motivated only by the mass instinct to pursue that which ran for cover.

Anita dashed to the stairs, went scrambling down them, found herself in another hallway in the Hall of Justice. She dashed the length of that hallway, frantically trying to find the stairs. She could not find them.

An elevator offered her welcome haven.

Anita fairly flung herself into the cage.

"What's the hurry?" the attendant asked.

Shreds of reason were beginning to return to Anita's fear-racked mind. "They're calling my case," she said. "Let me off at—"

"I know," the man said, smiling. "Third floor. Domestic Relations Court."

He slid the cage to a smooth stop at the third floor. "Out to the left," he said. "Department Twelve."

Anita's mind was beginning to work now. She smiled at the

elevator attendant, walked rapidly to the left, pushed open a door, and entered the partially filled courtroom. She marched down the center aisle and calmly seated herself in the middle seat in a row of benches.

She was now wrapped in anonymity. Only her breathlessness and the pounding of her pulses gave indication that she was the quarry for which the crowd was now searching.

Then slowly the triumphant smile faded from her face. The realization of the effect of what she had done stabbed her consciousness. She had admitted her guilt. She could flee now to the farthest corners of the earth, but her guilt would always follow her.

Perry Mason had shown that she had not killed Carver Clements, but he had also shown that she had done something which in the minds of all men would be even worse. She had betrayed her friend. She had tried to ruin Fay Allison's reputation. She had attempted the murder of her own roommate by giving her an overdose of sleeping tablets.

How much would Mason have been able to prove? She had no way of knowing. But there was no need for him to prove anything now. Her flight had given Mason all the proof he needed.

She must disappear, and that would not be easy. By evening her photograph would be emblazoned upon the pages of every newspaper in the city. . . .

Back in the courtroom, almost deserted now except for the county officials who were crowding around Shirley Tanner, Mason was asking questions in a low voice.

There was no more stamina left in Shirley Tanner than in a wet dishrag. She heard her own voice answering the persistent drone of Mason's searching questions.

"You knew that Clements had this apartment in 702? . . . You deliberately made such a high offer that you were able to sublease

Apartment 701? . . . You were suspicious of Clements and wanted to spy on him?"

"Yes," Shirley said, and her voice was all but inaudible, although it was obvious that the court reporter, standing beside her, was taking down in his notebook all she said.

"You were furious when you realized that Carver Clements had *another* mistress and that all his talk to you about waiting until he could get his divorce was merely bait which you had grabbed?"

Again she said, "Yes." There was no strength in her any more to think up lies.

"You made the mistake of loving him," Mason said. "It wasn't his money you were after, and you administered the poison. How did you do it, Shirley?"

She said, "I'd poisoned the drink I held in my hand I knew it made Carver furious when I drank, because whiskey makes me lose control of myself, and he never knew what I was going to do when I was drunk.

"I rang his bell, holding that glass in my hand. I leered at him tipsily when he opened the door, and walked on in. I said, 'Hello, Carver darling. Meet your next-door neighbor,' and I raised the glass to my lips.

"He acted just as I knew he would. He was furious. He said, 'You little devil, what're you doing here? I've told you I'll do the drinking for both of us.' He snatched the glass from me and drained it."

"What happened?" Mason asked.

"For a moment, nothing," she said. "He went back to the chair and sat down. I leaned over him and pressed that kiss on his head. It was a goodbye kiss. He looked at me frowned; then suddenly he jumped to his feet and tried to run to the door but he staggered and fell face forward."

"And what did you do?"

"I took the key to his apartment from his pocket so I could get back in to fix things the way I wanted and get possession of the glass, but I was afraid to be there while he was—dying."

Mason nodded. "You went back to your own apartment, and then, after you had waited a few minutes and thought it was safe to go back, you couldn't, because Anita Bonsal was at the door?"

She nodded, and said, "She had a key. She went in. I supposed, of course, she'd call the police and that they'd come at any time. I didn't dare to go in there then. Finally, I decided the police weren't coming after all. It was past midnight then."

"So then you went back in there? You were in there when Don Ralston rang the bell. You—"

"Yes," she said. "I went back into that apartment. By that time I had put on a bathrobe and pajamas and ruffled my hair all up. If anyone had said anything to me, if I had been caught, I had a story all prepared to tell them, that I had heard the door open and some-one run down the corridor, that I had opened my door and found the door of 702 ajar, and I had just that minute looked in to see what had happened."

"All right," Mason said; "that was your story. What did you do?"

"I went in and wiped all my fingerprints off that glass on the floor. Then the buzzer sounded from the street."

"What did you do?"

She said, "I saw someone had fixed up the evidence just the way I had been going to fix it up. A bottle of whiskey on the table, a bottle of soda, a jar of ice cubes."

"So what did you do?"

She said, "I was rattled, I guess, so I just automatically pushed the button which released the downstairs door catch. Then I ducked back into my own apartment, and hadn't any more than got in when I heard the elevator stop at the seventh floor. I couldn't understand that, because I knew these people couldn't possibly have had time enough to get up to the seventh floor in the elevator. I waited, listening, and heard you two come down the corridor. As soon as the buzzer sounded in the other apartment, I opened the door to chase you away, but you were actually entering the apartment, so I had to make a quick excuse, that the sound of the buzzer had wakened me. Then I jerked the door shut. When the four people came up, I thought you were still in the apartment, and I had to see what was happening."

"How long had you known him?" Mason asked.

She said sadly, "I loved him. I was the one that he wanted to marry when he left his wife. I don't know how long this other romance had been going on. I became suspicious, and one time when I had an opportunity to go through his pockets, I found a key stamped, 'Mandrake Arms Apartment, Number 702.' Then I thought I knew, but I wanted to be sure. I found out who had Apartment 701 and made a proposition for a sublease that couldn't be turned down.

"I waited and watched. This brunette walked down the corridor and used *her* key to open the apartment. I slipped out into the corridor and listened at the door. I heard him give her the same old line he'd given me so many times, and I hated him. I killed him—and I was caught."

Mason turned to Stewart Linn and said, "There you are, young man. There's your murderess, but you'll probably never be able to get a jury to think it's anything more than manslaughter."

A much chastened Linn said, "Would you mind telling me how you figured this out, Mr. Mason?"

Mason said, "Clements's key was missing. Obviously he must have had it when he entered the apartment. Therefore, the murderer must have taken it from his pocket. Why? So he or she could come back. And if what Don Ralston said was true, *someone* must have been in the apartment when he rang the bell from the street, someone who let him in by pressing the buzzer.

"What happened to that someone? I must have been walking down the corridor within a matter of seconds after Ralston had pressed the button on the street door. Yet I saw no one leaving the apartment. *Obviously, then, the person who pressed the buzzer must have had a place to take refuge in a nearby apartment!*

"Having learned that a young, attractive woman had only that day taken a lease on the apartment opposite, the answer became so obvious it ceased to be a mystery."

Stewart Linn nodded thoughtfully. "It all fits in," he said.

Mason picked up his brief-case, smiled to Della Street. "Come on, Della," he said. "Let's get Fay Allison and—"

He stopped as he saw Fay Allison's face. "What's happened to *your* lipstick?" he asked.

And then his eyes moved over to take in Dane Grover, who was standing by her, his face smeared diagonally across the mouth with a huge, red smear of lipstick.

Fay Allison had neglected to remove the thick coating of lipstick which she had put on when Mason had asked Benjamin Harlan, the identification expert, to take an imprint of her lips. Now, the heavy mark where her mouth had been pressed against the mouth of Dane Grover gave a note of incongruity to the entire proceedings.

On the lower floors a mob of eagerly curious spectators were baying like hounds upon the track of Anita Bonsal. In the court-room the long, efficient arm of the law was gathering Shirley Tanner into its grasp, and there, amidst the machinery of tragedy, the romance of Fay Allison and Dane Grover picked up where it had left off. . . .

It was the gavel of Judge Randolph Jordan that brought them back to the grim realities of justice.

"The Court," announced Judge Jordan, "will dismiss the case against Fay Allison. The Court will order Shirley Tanner into custody, and the Court will suggest to the Prosecutor that a complaint be issued for Anita Bonsal, upon such charge as may seem expedient to the office of the District Attorney. And the Court does hereby extend its most sincere apologies to the defendant, Fay Allison. And the Court, personally wishes to congratulate Mr. Perry Mason upon his brilliant handling of this matter."

There was a moment during which Judge Jordan's stern eyes rested upon the lipstick-smeared countenance of Dane Grover. A faint smile twitched at the corners of His Honor's mouth.

The gavel banged once more.

"The Court," announced Judge Randolph Jordan, "is adjourned."

THE ENCHANTED GARDEN
H. F. Heard
Detective: Mr. Mycroft

THE ENGLISH social historian and author of science and mystery fiction Henry Fitzgerald Heard (1889-1971) was born in London, studied at Cambridge University, then turned to writing essays and books on historical, scientific, religious, mystical, cultural, and social subjects, signing them Gerald Heard, the name under which all his nonfiction appeared. He moved to the United States in 1937 to head a commune in California, and later appeared as a character in several Aldous Huxley novels, notably as William Propter, a mystic, in *After Many a Summer Dies the Swan* (1939).

A Taste for Honey (1941) introduced Mr. Mycroft, a tall, slender gentleman who had retired to Sussex to keep bees. The story is told by Sydney Silchester, a reclusive man who loves honey, which he obtains from Mr. and Mrs. Heregrove, the village beekeepers, until he discovers the lady's body, black and swollen from bee stings. After the coroner's inquest, Silchester turns to Mr. Mycroft for a fresh supply of honey and receives a warning about Heregrove's killer bees.

Robert Bloch, the author of *Psycho* (1959) and many other novels and stories, and Anthony Marriott adapted the novel for a truly awful contemporary screenplay titled *The Deadly Bees* (1966). For an episode of television's *The Elgin Hour*, Alvin Sapinsley wrote the script for "Sting of Death," which starred Boris Karloff as Mr. Mycroft; it aired on February 22, 1955.

Mr. Mycroft appeared in two additional novels by Heard: *Reply Paid* (1942) and *The Notched Hairpin* (1949). Among Heard's other science fiction and mystery novels, perhaps his best-known work is the short story "The President of the United States of America, Detective," which won the first prize in *Ellery Queen's Mystery Magazine*'s contest in 1947.

"The Enchanted Garden" was originally published in the March 1949 issue of *Ellery Queen's Mystery Magazine*.

The Enchanted Garden
By H. F. Heard

NATURE'S A queer one,' said Mr. Squeers," I remarked.

"I know what moves you to misquote Dickens," was Mr. Mycroft's reply.

Here was a double provocation: first, there was the injury of being told that the subject on which one was going to inform someone was already known to him, and secondly, there was the insult that the happy literary quotation with which the information was to be introduced was dismissed as inaccurate. Still it's no use getting irritated with Mr. Mycroft. The only hope was to lure his pride onto the brink of ignorance.

"Then tell me," I remarked demurely, "what I have just been reading?"

"The sad, and it is to be feared, fatal accident that befell Miss Hetty Hess who is said to be extremely rich, and a 'colorful personality' and 'young for her years'—the evidence for these last two statements being a color photograph in the photogravure section of the paper which establishes that her frock made up for its brevity only by the intense viridity of its green color."

I am seldom untruthful deliberately, even when considerably non-plussed; besides it was no use: Mr. Mycroft was as usual one move ahead. He filled in the silence with: "I should have countered that naturalists are the queer ones."

I had had a moment to recover, and felt that I could retrieve at least a portion of my lost initiative. "But there's no reason to link the accident with the death. The notice only mentions that she had had a fall a few weeks previously. The cause of death was 'intestinal stasis'."

"Cause!" said Mr. Mycroft. He looked and sounded so like an old raven as he put his head on one side and uttered "caws," that I couldn't help laughing.

"Murder's no laughing matter!" he remonstrated.

"But surely, *cher maître*, you sometimes are unwilling to allow that death can ever be through natural causes!"

"Cause? There's sufficient cause here."

"*Post hoc, propter hoc*," I was glad to get off one of my few classic tags. "Because a lady of uncertain years dies considerably *after* a fall from which her doctor vouched there were no immediate ill effects, you would surely not maintain that it was *on account* of the fall that the rhythm of her secondary nervous system struck and stopped for good? And even if it was, who's to blame?"

"Cause." At this third quothing of the Raven I let my only comment be a rather longer laugh—and waited for my lecture. Mr. Mycroft did not fail me. He went on: "I'll own I know nothing about causality in the outer world, for I believe no one does really. But I have spent my life, not unprofitably, in tracing human causality. As you're fond of Dickens, I'll illustrate from Copperfield's Mr. Dick. The *causes* of King Charles's head coming off may have been due to four inches of iron going through his neck. I feel on safer ground when I say it was due to his failing to get on with his parliament. You say Miss Hess died naturally—that is to say (1) her death, (2) her accident a fortnight before, and (3) the place where that accident took place, all have only a chance connection. Maybe your case would stand were I not watching *another* line of causality."

"You mean a motive?"

"Naturally."

"But motives aren't proof! Or every natural death would be followed by a number of unnatural ones—to wit, executions of executors and legatees!"

"I don't know whether I agree with your rather severe view of human nature. What I do know is that when a death proves to be far too happy an accident for someone who survives, then we old sleuths start with a trail which often ends with our holding proofs that not even a jury can fail to see."

"Still," I said, "suspicion can't always be right!"

What had been no more than an after-lunch sparring-match suddenly loomed up as active service with Mr. Mycroft's, "Well, the police agree with you in thinking that there's no proof, and with me in suspecting it *is* murder. That's why I'm going this afternoon to view the scene of the accident, unaccompanied—unless, of course, you would care to accompany me?"

I may sometimes seem vain but I know my uses. So often I get a ringside seat because, as Mr. Mycroft has often remarked, my appearance disarms suspicion.

"We are headed," Mr. Mycroft resumed as we bowled along in our taxi, "for what I am creditably informed is in both senses of the word a gem of a sanctuary—gem, because it is both small and jewelled."

We had been swaying and sweeping up one of those narrow rather desolate canyons in southern California through which the famous "Thirteen suburbs in search of a city" have thrust corkscrew concrete highways. The lots became more stately and secluded, the houses more embowered and enwalled, until the ride, the road, and the canyon itself all ended in a portico of such Hispano-Moorish impressiveness that it might have been the entrance to a veritable Arabian Nights Entertainments. There was no one else about, but remarking, "This is Visitors' Day," Mr. Mycroft alit, told our driver to wait, and strolled up to the heavily grilled gate. One of the large gilt nails which bossed the gate's carved timbers had etched round it in elongated English so as to pretend to be Kufic or at least ordinary Arabic the word PRESS. And certainly it was as good as its word. For not only did the stud sink into the gate, the gate followed suit and sank into the arch, and we strolled over the threshold into as charming an enclosure as I have ever seen. The gate closed softly behind us. Indeed, there was nothing to suggest that we weren't in an enchanted garden. The ground must have risen steeply on either hand. But you didn't see any ground—all manner of hanging vines and flowering shrubs rose in festoons, hanging in garlands, swinging in delicate sprays. The crowds of blossom against the vivid blue sky, shot through by the sun, made the place intensely vivid. And in this web of color, like quick bobbins, the shuttling flight of humming-birds was everywhere. The place was, in fact, alive with birds. But not a single human being could I see.

Birds are really stupid creatures and their noises, in spite of all the poetry that has been written about them, always seem to me tiring. Their strong point is, of course, plumage. I turned to Mr. Mycroft and remarked that I wished the Polynesian art of making cloaks of birds' feathers had not died out. He said he preferred them alive but that he believed copies of the famous plumage-mantles could now be purchased for those who liked to appear in borrowed plumes.

"This, I understand," continued Mr. Mycroft, "is supposed to be the smallest and choicest of all the world's bird sanctuaries. It is largely reserved for species of that mysterious living automaton, the hummingbird," and as was the way with the old bird himself, in a moment he seemed to forget why we were there. First, he scanned the whole place. The steep slopes came down till only a curb-path of marble divided the banks of flowers from a floor of water. At the farther end of this was a beautiful little statue holding high a lance, all of a lovely, almost peacock-green hue. And from this lance rose a spray of water, a miniature fountain. This little piece of art seemed to absorb him and as he couldn't walk on the water and examine it, he took binoculars from his pocket and scanned it with loving care. Then his mind shifted and slipping the glasses back in his pocket, he gave the same interest to the birds. His whole attention now seemed to be involved with these odd little bird-pellets. Hummingbirds are certainly odd. To insist on flying all the time you are drinking nectar from the deep flask of a flower always seems to me a kind of *tour de force* of pointless energy. In fact, it really fatigues me a little even to watch them. But the general plan of the place was beautiful and restful: there was just this narrow path of marble framing the sheet of water and this wall of flowers and foliage. The path curved round making an oval and at the upper end, balancing the fine Moorish arch through which we had entered, there rose a similar horseshoe arch, charmingly reflected in the water above which it rose. It made a bridge over which one could pass to reach the marble curb on the other side of the water.

"A bower," remarked Mr. Mycroft. He loitered along, cricking back his neck farther and farther to watch the birds perched on sprays right against the sky. He had now taken a pen from his pocket and was jotting down some ornithological observation. Poor old dear, he never could enjoy but must always be making some blot of comment on the bright mirror of—well, what I mean is that I was really taking it in and he was already busy manufacturing it into some sort of dreary information. And poor Miss Hess, she too must wait till he came back to her actual problem, if indeed there was one.

I watched him as he stepped back to the very edge of the marble curb so that he might better view a spray of deep purple bougainvillea at which a hummingbird was flashing its gorget. Yes, it would have been a pretty enough bit of color contrast, had one had a color camera to snap it, but I had seen a sign on the gate outside asking visitors not to take photographs. So I watched my master. And having my wits about me I suddenly broke the silence. "Take care!" I shouted. But too late. Mr. Mycroft had in his effort to see what was too high above him stepped back too far. The actual edge of the marble curb must have been slippery from the lapping of the ripples. His foot skidded. He made a remarkable effort to recover. I am not hard-hearted but I could not help tittering as I saw him—more raven-like than ever— flap his arms to regain his balance. And the comic maneuver served perfectly—I mean it still gave me my joke and yet saved him from anything more serious than a loss of gravity. His arms whirled. Pen and paper scrap flew from his hands to join some hummingbirds but the Mycroft frame, under whose overarching shadow so many great criminals had cowered, collapsed not gracefully but quite safely just short of the water.

I always carry a cane. It gives poise. The piece of paper and even the pen—which was one of those new "light-as-a-feather" plastic things— were bobbing about on the surface. Of course, Mr. Mycroft who was a little crestfallen at such an absent-minded slip, wouldn't let me help him up. In fact he was up before I could have offered. My only chance of collecting a "Thank-you" was to salvage the flotsam that he had so spontaneously "cast upon the waters." I fished in both the sopped sheet and the pen, and noticed that Mr. Mycroft had evidently not had time to record the precious natural-history fact that he had gleaned before his lack of hindsight attention parted the great mind and the small sheet. Nor when I handed him back his salvaged apparatus did he do so; instead he actually put both pen and sopped sheet into his pocket. "Shaken," I said to myself; "there's one more disadvantage of being so high up in the clouds of speculation."

As we continued on our way along the curb and were approaching the horseshoe Moorish arch-bridge, Mr. Mycroft began to limp. My real fondness for him made me ask, "Have you strained anything?"

Mr. Mycroft most uncharacteristically answered, "I think I will rest for a moment."

We had reached the place where the level marble curb, sweeping round the end of the pond, rose into the first steps of the flight of stairs that ran up the back of the arch. These stairs had a low, fretted rail. It seemed to me that it might have been higher for safety's sake, but I suppose that would have spoiled the beauty of the arch, making it look too heavy and thick. It certainly was a beautiful piece of work and finished off the garden with charming effectiveness. The steps served Mr. Mycroft's immediate need well enough, just because they were so steep. He bent down and holding the balustrade with his left hand, lowered himself until he was seated. So he was in a kind of stone chair, his back comfortably against the edge of the step above that one on which he sat. And as soon as he was settled down, the dizziness seemed to pass, and his spirits obviously returned to their old bent. He started once more to peek about him. The irrelevant vitality of being interested in anything mounted once again to its usual unusual intensity.

After he had for a few moments been swinging his head about in the way that led to his fall—the way a new-born baby will loll, roll, and goggle at the sky—he actually condescended to draw me into the rather pointless appreciations he was enjoying. "You see, Mr. Silchester, one of their breeding boxes." He pointed up into the foliage, which here rose so high that it reared a number of feet above the highest pitch of the arch.

"Surely," I asked, for certainly it is always safer with Mr. Mycroft to offer information armored in question form, "surely breeding boxes are no new invention?"

Mr. Mycroft's reply was simply, "No, of course not," and then he became vague.

I thought: Now he'll start making notes again. But no, poor old pride-in-perception was evidently more shaken by his fall than I'd thought. I felt a real sympathy for him, as I stood at a little distance keeping him under observation but pretending to glance at the scene which, though undoubtedly pretty, soon began to pall for really it had no more sense or story about it than a kaleidoscope. Poor old thing, I repeated to myself, as out of the corner of my eye, I saw him let that big cranium hang idly. But the restless, nervous energy still fretted him. Though his eyes were brooding out of focus, those long fingers remained symptomatic of his need always to be fiddling and raveling with something. How important it is, I reflected, to learn young how to idle well. Now, poor old dear, he just can't rest. Yes, Britain can still teach America something: a mellow culture knows how to meander; streams nearer their source burst and rush and tumble.

The Mycroft fingers were running to and fro along the curb of the step against which he was resting his back. I thought I ought to rouse him. He must be getting his fingernails into a horrid condition as they aimlessly scraped along under that ledge and the very thought even of someone rasping and soiling his nails sets my teeth on edge.

My diagnosis that the dear old fellow was badly shaken was confirmed when I suggested, "Shall we be getting on?" and he answered, "Certainly." And I must say that I was trebly pleased when, first, Mr. Mycroft took my extended hand to pull him to his feet, then accepted my arm as we went up the bridge and down its other side, and once we were outside the gate let me hold the door of the cab open for him. At that moment from an alcove in the gate-arch popped a small man with a book. Would we care to purchase any of the colored photographs he had for sale, and would we sign the visitors' book? I bought a couple and said to Mr. Mycroft, "May I sign Mr. Silchester and friend?"—for this was a ready way for him to preserve his anonymity, when he remarked, "I will sign," and in that large stately hand the most famous signature was placed on the page.

As we swirled down the canyon, Mr. Mycroft gave his attention to our new surroundings. Suddenly he exclaimed, "Stop!" The cab bumped to a standstill. The spot he had chosen was certainly a contrast to our last stop. Of course, once outside the houses of the rich, this countryside is pretty untidy. We had just swished round one of those hairpin curves all these canyon roads make as they wiggle down the central cleft. The cleft itself was in slow process of being filled by the cans and crocks that fall from the rich man's kitchen. Something, disconcerting to a sane eye even at this distance, had caught Mr. Mycroft's vulture gaze. Even before the cab was quite still, he was out and went straight for the garbage heap. I need not say that not only did I stay where I was, I turned away. For that kind of autopsy always makes me feel a little nauseated. Mr. Mycroft knows my reasonable limits. He had not asked me to go with him and when he came back he spared me by not displaying his trophy, whatever it might be. I caught sight of him stuffing a piece of some gaudy colored wrapping-paper into his pocket as he climbed into the seat beside me, but I was certainly more anxious not to notice than he to conceal.

Nor, when we reached home, did Mr. Mycroft become any more communicative. Indeed, he went straight to his study and there, no doubt, unloaded his quarry. He did not, as a matter of fact, put in an appearance till dinner. Nor did the dinner rouse him. I can hardly blame him for that. For I, too, was a little abstracted and so have to confess that I had ordered a very conventional repast, the kind of meal that you can't remember five minutes after you have ordered it or five minutes after it has been cleared away—a dinner so lacking in art that it can arouse neither expectation nor recollection.

Truth to tell, I was not a little disconcerted at the tameness of our "adventure." Mr. M. had as good as told me that he would disclose a plot and a pretty ugly one, but all we had seen was a charming enough stage, set for comedy rather than tragedy. And not a soul in view, far less a body.

The only incident, and surely that was tamely comic and I had to enjoy even that by myself, was Mr. Mycroft's skid. Indeed, as we sat on in silence I was beginning to think I might say something—perhaps a little pointed—about pointless suspicion. But on looking across at Mr. M. who was sitting dead still at the other side of the table, I thought the old fellow looked more than a little tired. So I contented myself with the feeling that his fall had shaken him considerably more than he chose to allow.

But as I rose to retire, after reading my half-chapter of Jane Austen—for me an unfailing sedative—the old fellow roused himself.

"Thank you for your company, Mr. Silchester. Quite a fruitful day." Perhaps he saw I was already "registering surprise." For he added, "I believe we sowed and not only reaped this afternoon but if you will again give me your company, we will go tomorrow to gather the harvest."

"But I thought today was Visitors' Day?"

"Oh," he carelessly remarked, "I expect the proprietor will be glad of callers even the day after. The place was quite deserted, wasn't it? Maybe he's thinking of closing it. And that would be a pity before we had seen all that it may have to offer."

Well, I had enjoyed the little place and was not averse to having one more stroll round it. So, as it was certain we should go anyhow, I agreed with the proviso, "I must tell you that though I agree the place is worth a second visit for its beauty, nevertheless I am still convinced that to throw a cloud of suspicion over its innocent brightness might almost be called professional obsessionalism."

I was rather pleased at that heavy technical-sounding ending and even hoped it might rouse the old man to spar back. But he only replied, "Excellent, excellent. That's what I hoped you'd think and say. For that, of course, is the reaction I trust would be awakened in any untrained—I mean, normal mind."

The next afternoon found us again in the garden, I enjoying what was there and Mr. M. really liking it as much as I did but having to spin all over its brightness the gossamer threads of his suspicions and speculations. The water was flashing in the sun, the small spray-fountain playing, birds dancing—yes, the place was the nicest *mise-en-scène* for a meditation on murder that anyone could ask. Again we had the place to ourselves. Indeed, I had just remarked on the fact to Mr. M. and he had been gracious enough to protrude from his mystery mist and reply that perhaps people felt there might still be a shadow over the place, when a single other visitor did enter. He entered from the other end. I hadn't thought there was a way in from that direction but evidently behind the bridge and the thicket there must have been.

He strolled down the same side of the small lake as we were advancing up. But I didn't have much chance to study him for he kept on turning round and looking at the bridge and the fountain. I do remember thinking what a dull and ugly patch his dreary store suit made against the vivid living tapestries all around us. The one attempt he made to be in tune was rather futile: he had stuck a bright red hibiscus flower in his button-hole. And then that thought was put out of my mind by an even juster judgment. Mr. M. was loitering behind—sometimes I think that I really do take things in rather more quickly than he—at least, when what is to be seen is what is meant to be seen. He pores and reflects too much even on the obvious. So it was I who saw what was going forward and being of a simple forthright nature took the necessary steps at once. After all, I did not feel that I had any right to be suspicious of our host who was certainly generous and as certainly had been put in a very unpleasant limelight by police and press. My duty was to see that what he offered so freely to us should not be abused or trespassed on. As the man ahead turned round again to study the fountain and the arch I saw what he was doing. He had a small color camera pressed against him and was going to take a photo of the fountain and the bridge. Now, as we knew, visitors were asked expressly not to do this. So I stepped forward and tapped him on the shoulder, remarking that as guests of a public generosity we should observe the simple rule requested of us. He swung round at my tap. My feelings had not been cordial at first sight, his action had alienated them further, and now a close-up clinched the matter. His hat was now pushed back and showed a head of billiard-baldness; his eyes were weak and narrowed-up at me through glasses, rimless glasses that like some colorless fly perched on his nose—that hideous sight-aid called rightly a *pince-nez*.

Suddenly his face relaxed. It actually smiled, and he said, "That is really very kind of you. It is a pity when the rule is not kept for it does deprive the pension house for pets of a little income—almost all that one can spare for that excellent work. I am grateful, grateful." I was taken aback, even more so with the explanation. "I have the responsibility for this place. Owing to a very ungenerous press campaign we are not getting the visitors we used to. So I thought I would take a few more photos for the sales-rack at the gate. Yes, I am the owner of this little place, or as I prefer to say, the trustee of it in the joint interests of the public and philanthropy. May I introduce myself?—I am Hiram Hess, Jr."

After my *faux pas* I stumbled out some kind of apology.

"Please don't make any excuse. I only wish all my guests felt the same way in our common responsibility," he replied. "Indeed, now that you have done me one kindness, you embolden me to ask for another. I believe that the public has been scared away and this seems a heaven-sent opportunity."

All this left me somewhat in the dark. I am not averse to being treated as an honored guest and murmured something about being willing to oblige. Then I remembered Mr. M. and that I was actually taking the leading part in a scene and with the "mystery character" to whom he had in fact introduced me. I turned round and found Mr. M. at my heels. I think I made the introduction well and certainly the two of them showed no signs of not wishing to play the parts in which I was now the master of ceremonies. Mr. Hess spoke first: "I was just about to ask your friend. . ."—"Mr. Silchester," I prompted—"whether he would add another kindness. I was told only yesterday by a friend that natural history photos sell better if they can be combined with human interest of some sort. Of course when I was told that, I saw at once he was right. It must be, musn't it?" Mr. M. made a "Lord Burleigh nod."

"I am glad you agree. So I suggested that I might ask a movie star to pose. But my friend said No, I should get a handsome young man whose face has not been made wearisome to the public and that would give a kind of mystery element to the photo. People would ask, 'In what movie did that face appear?'" I own that at this personal reference—I am a Britisher, you know—I felt a little inclined to blush.

"And," hurried on Mr. Hess, "now, the very day after I am told what to do, I am offered the means to do it!"

Frankness has always been my forte. Like many distinguished and good-looking people, I like being photographed and these new colored ones are really most interesting. "I would be most happy to oblige," I said, and turned to see how Mr. M. would react to my taking the play out of his hands. Of course this odd little man couldn't be a murderer. I'm not a profound student of men but that was now perfectly clear to me. Mr. M. merely treated us to another of his "Lord Burleigh nods" and then, "While you are posing Mr. Silchester, may I walk about?"

"Please look upon the place as your own," left Mr. M. free to stroll away and he seemed quite content to use his fieldglasses looking at the birds and blooms.

"Now," said Mr. Hess, all vivacity and I must confess, getting more likable every moment, "my idea is that we put the human interest, if I may so describe my collaborator, right in the middle of the scene. You will be the focus round which the garden is, as it were, draped." Then he paused and exclaimed, "Why, of course, that's the very word—why didn't I think of it before? I wonder whether you would be kind enough to agree—it would make the picture really wonderful."

Again I was a little at a loss, but the small man's enthusiasm was quite infectious. "How can I help further?" I asked.

"Well, it was the word drape that shot the idea into my head, darting like one of these sweet birdkins. Don't you think, Mr. Silchester, that men's clothes rather spoil the effect here?"

He looked down on his own little store suit and smiled. It was true enough but a sudden qualm shook my mind. The thought of stripping and posing, with Mr. Mycroft in the offing—well, I felt that awkward blush again flowing all over me. Whether my little host guessed my confusion or not, his next words put me at ease. "Do you think that you'd consent to wear just for the photo a robe I have?"

My relief that I was not to be asked to disrobe but to robe made me say, "Of course, of course," and without giving me any further chance to qualify my consent, off hurried little Hess. He was not gone more than a couple of minutes—not enough time for me to go back to where Mr. Mycroft was loitering near the gate at the other end of the pool—before once again he appeared, but nearly hidden even when he faced me. For what he was holding in his arms and over his shoulder was one of those Polynesian feather cloaks of which I had remarked to Mr. Mycroft that I thought they were one of the finest of all dresses ever made by man.

"Of course," Hess said, "this isn't one of the pieces that go to museums. I always hoped that somehow I would make a picture of this place in which this cloak would play the leading part."

All the while he said this he was holding out the lovely wrap for me to examine and as he finished he lightly flung the robe over my shoulder. "Oh, that's it, that's it!" he said, standing back with his head on one side like a bird. And looking down, I could not help thinking that I too was now like a bird and, to be truthful, a very handsome one.

So, without even casting a look behind me to see if Mr. Mycroft was watching and perhaps smiling, I followed Mr. Hess as he led the way, saying over his shoulder, heaped with the Polynesian robe, "I said right in the center and I mean to keep my word." It was clear what he meant, for already he was mounted on the steps of the horseshoe-arch bridge and was going up them. Yes, I was to be the *clou* of the whole composition. When we reached the very apex of the arch, he held out the cloak to me, remarking, "You will find it hangs better if you'll just slip off your coat." I agreed and obeyed. I had already laid aside my cane. He was evidently quite an artist and was determined to pose me to best possible effect. He tried a number of poses and none seemed to him good enough. "I have it!" he finally clicked out. "Oh, the thing gets better and better! Why you aren't in the movies . . . But of course after this . . . photogenic—why, it's a mild word! I'm not asking for anything theatrical—only an accent, as it were—just the natural inevitable drama, one might say. The cloak itself sets the gesture. You see, the sun is high above and you are the center of this pool of flowers and birds. And so we would get perfect action, perfect face lighting, and perfect hang of drapery if you would just stretch up your arms to the sun and let the light pour on your face. You stand here, with your back to the garden—its high-priest offering all its life to the sun."

While the little man had been saying this, he had been arranging the robe to make it hang well, tucking it in at my feet. "The shoes mustn't show, you know," he said, as he stooped like a little bootblack and arranged my train; then he shifted my stance until he had me close to the balustrade, for only there could he get the light falling full on my upturned face. One couldn't help falling in with his fancy—it was infectious. I rolled up my sleeves so that now, as I stood looking into the sun, I confess I could not help feeling the part. I forgot all about my old spider, Mr. Mycroft. I was one with nature, transformed by the robe which covered every sign of the civilized man on me, and by my setting. Mr. Hess darted back to the other side of the arch, up which we had come, and began—I could see out of the corner of my upturned eye—to focus his camera.

And then he seemed to spoil it all. After some delay he became uncertain. Finally, he came back up to me. "It's magnificent. I've never had the chance to take such a photo. But that's what so often happens with really great opportunities and insights into art and high beauty, isn't it?"

I was more than a little dashed. "Do you mean that you have decided not to take the photo?" I asked. Perhaps there was a touch of resentment in my voice. After all, I had been to a great deal of inconvenience; I had lent myself to a very unusual amount of free model work and laid myself open to Mr. Mycroft's wry humor which would be all the more pointed if the photo was never taken.

"No—Oh, of course not!" But the tone had so much reservation in it that I was not in the slightest reassured, and even less so when he showed his hand, for then I was certain he had just thought up a none-too-unclever way of getting out of the whole business. "But as I've said, and as I know you know, whenever one glimpses a true

summit of beauty one catches sight of something even more remarkable beyond."

I snapped out, "Am I to presume that on reconsideration you would
prefer not a high light but a foil, not myself but my old sober friend
down by the gate?"

I had been growing quite resentful. But my resentment changed to
outrage at the absurdity of his answer. It was a simple "Yes." Then seeing me flush, he hurriedly added, "I do believe that majestic old figure
would make a perfect foil to yours."

Of course, this was an amend of sorts, but of a very silly sort. For
could the man be such a fool as to think that while I might be generous and accommodating to a fault, my old friend would fall in with
this charade?

"I think," I said with considerable dignity, beginning to draw the
robe away from my shoulders, "that when you want models, Mr. Hess,
you had better pay for them."

But my arm got no further than halfway down the coat-sleeve.
For my eyes were held. Looking up at the sun makes you a little dizzy and your sight blotchy, but there was no doubt what I was seeing.
That silly little Hess had run along the curb and as I watched was
buttonholing Mr. Mycroft. I didn't wait to struggle into my jacket
but running down the steps went to where they stood together by
the exit. I couldn't hear what was being said but was sure I guessed.
Yet, in a moment, I was again at a loss. For instead of Mr. Mycroft
turning down the grotesque offer, beckoning to me, and going out
of the gate, Mr. M. was coming toward me, and he and Hess were
talking quite amicably. Of course, I could only conclude that Hess
had been spinning some new kind of yarn but all I could do was to
go right up to them and say, "Perhaps you will be good enough to
tell me what you have arranged!"

I was still further bewildered when it was Mr. M. who answered,
"I think Mr. Hess's idea is excellent. If the picture is to be the success
which he hopes, it should have contrast and, if I may put it in that way,

significance—a picture with a story. Wasn't that your telling phrase, Mr. Hess?"

Hess beamed: "Precisely, precisely! Mr. Mycroft is so instantly intuitive." And the little fellow looked Mr. M. up and down with a mixture of surprise and complacency that I found very comic and sedative to my rightly ruffled feelings. Still I was quite in the dark as to what had happened to make the three of us so suddenly and so unexpectedly a happy family with—of all people—Mr. M. as the matchmaker. Hess, however, was bubbling over to tell me:

"Do forgive me, rushing off like that. So impulsive. But that's the way I am—'stung with the sudden splendor of a thought.' You see, that was the way I was with you, wasn't I? And I know you're an artist too and so you must know that when one idea comes, generally an even brighter one comes rushing on its heels," he tittered. "I was also a bit frightened, I must confess," he ran on. "What if Mr. Mycroft had refused? I knew if I asked you, you'd say he would; and of course you'd have been right. So I just rushed on to my fate, risked losing the whole picture—the best so often risks the good, doesn't it?"

While the little fellow had been pouring out this excited rigmarole, he had been leading us back to the bridge and as Mr. M. followed without any kind of unwillingness, I fell in too. After all, it looked as though we were going to get the photo. As we reached the steps it was Mr. M. who forestalled Hess just as Hess was about to give us some directions. "You would like us, wouldn't you, to pose on the other side of the bridge-top?"

"Yes, that's it—just where I had Mr. Silchester."

I took up my position, picking up the robe, putting down my jacket. Hess arranged the fall of the robe as before. I must admit he was neat at that sort of thing. He moved me to exactly the spot I had held, asked me once more to raise my bared arms to the sun and throw back my head—"Just like a priest of Apollo," was his phrase, a phrase which I didn't quite like Mr. M. hearing. And even when Hess remarked to Mr. Mycroft, "with Mr. Silchester it's an inevitable piece of casting, isn't it?"—Mr. M. replied only, "Yes, quite a pretty piece of casting." I could only imagine that now Mr. Mycroft saw that the little fellow was obviously as harmless as a hummingbird—and about as brainless.

But Hess couldn't stay content with one triumph; he must try to crown it with another. "And you, Mr. Mycroft, you too are going to be perfectly cast," and he chuckled.

"I am ready to fall in with any of your plans for philanthropy," was Mr. Mycroft's answer. The pomposity might have been expected but the agreeability was certainly one more shock of surprise.

"Now," and the little man had put down his camera and was fussing like a modiste round a marchioness client whom she was fitting for a ball dress, "now, Mr. Silchester is set and ready. You, Mr. Mycroft, would you please just sit here, just behind him, on the balustrade. You see, my idea has about it something of what great artists call inevitability! The group casts itself—it's a great piece of moving sculpture. Here is Mr. Silchester gazing with stretched-out arms at the glorious orb of day, his face flooded with its splendor, the very symbol of youth accepting life—life direct, warm, pulsing, torrential . . ." As he ran on like this I began to have a slight crick in my neck, and with one's head thrown back my head began to throb a little and my eyes got quite dizzy with the sunlight. "Now, please, Mr. Silchester," said the voice at my feet, "hold the pose for just a moment more while I place Mr. Mycroft," and I heard our little artist in *tableau vivant* cooing to Mr. Mycroft. "And you, you see, are the wisdom of age, grey, wise, reflective, a perfect contrast, looking down into the deep waters of contemplation."

Evidently Mr. Mycroft fell in with all this, even to having himself shifted until he was right behind me. I remember I was a little amused at the thought of Mr. Mycroft being actually put at my feet and, more, that there I stood with the leading role and with my back to him—he who was so used to being looked up to. Perhaps it was this thought that gave one more stretch to the tiring elastic of my patience. And in a moment more evidently Mr. Mycroft's cooperation had been so full that Hess was content. The little fellow ran back down the steps of the other side of the bridge and I could just see from the corner of my rather swimming eyes that he had picked up his camera and was going to shoot us. But again he was taken with a fussy doubt. He ran back to us. We were still too far apart. He pushed us closer till my calves were actually against Mr. Mycroft's shoulder blades.

"The composition is perfect in line and mass," murmured Hess, "it is a spot of high-lighting color that's wanted and right near the central interest, the upturned, sun-flooded face. Mr. Silchester, please don't move an inch. I have the very thing here."

I squinted down and saw the little fellow flick out from his button-hole the hibiscus blossom which he was wearing. I saw what was coming. The beautiful Samoans did always at their feasts wear a scarlet hibiscus set behind the ear so that the blossom glowed alongside their eye. In silence I submitted as Hess fitted the flower behind my left ear and arranged the long trumpet of the blossom so that it rested on my cheek bone. Then at last he was content, skipped back to his camera, raised it on high, focussed. . . . There was a click—I am sure I heard that. And I'm equally sure there was a buss, or twang. And then involuntarily I clapped my hands to my face and staggered back to avoid something that was dashing at my eye. I stumbled heavily backwards against Mr. Mycroft, felt my balance go completely, the cloak swept over my head and I plunged backwards and downwards into the dark.

My next sensation was that I was being held. I hadn't hit anything. But I was in as much pain as though I had. For one of my legs was caught in some kind of grip and by this I was hanging upside down. For suddenly the bell-like extinguisher in which I was pending dropped away—as when they unveil statues—and I was exposed. Indeed, I could now see myself in the water below like a grotesque narcissus, a painfully ludicrous pendant.

How had I managed to make such a grotesque stumble? I could only suppose that the long gazing at the sun had made me dizzy and then some dragon-fly or other buzzing insect had darted at me—probably at that idiotic flower—which in spite of my fall still stuck behind my ear. That had made me start and I had overturned. For though the flower held its place, the cloak was gone and now lay mantling the surface of the pond some six feet below me.

These observations, however, were checked by another dose of even more severe pain. I was being hauled up to the balustrade above me by my leg and the grip that paid me in foot by foot was Mr. Mycroft's sinewy hands. When my face came up far enough for me to see his, his was quite without expression. He did have the kindness to say, "Sun dizziness, of course," and then over his shoulder where I next caught sight of the anxious face of little Hess, "Don't be alarmed. I caught him just in time. I fear, however, that your valuable cloak will not be the better for a wetting."

The little fellow was full of apologies. While this went on Mr. Mycroft had helped me into my jacket, given me my cane and led me, still shaken, to the gate, accompanied all the way by a very apologetic Hess. When we were there Mr. Mycroft closed the incident quietly. "Don't apologize, Mr. Hess. It was a brilliant idea, if the execution fell a little below expectation," and then putting his hand up to my ear, "I am sure you would like this flower as a souvenir of an eventful day. I hope the picture-with-a-meaning will develop."

As we swirled away in a taxi, every sway of the car made me nearly sick. When we were home Mr. Mycroft broke the silence: "I have a call to make and one or two small things to arrange."

Mr. Mycroft didn't come back till dinner was actually being put on the table and he too looked as fresh as snow, after a hot shower and a clean change of linen, I felt. He was kind, too, about the meal. The avocado-and-chive paste served on hot crackers he praised by the little joke that the paste showed symbolically how well my suavity and his pungency really blended. The Pacific lobster is a creature of parts but it needs skill to make it behave really *à la Thermidor,* and I was pleased that the chef and I had made my old master confess that he would not know that it was not a Parisian *langouste.* The chicken *à la King* he smilingly said had something quite regal about it while the *bananes flambées* he particularly complimented because I had made them out of a locally grown banana which, because it is more succulent than the standard varieties, lends itself to better blending with alcohol. Indeed, he was so pleased that while the coffee was before us he asked whether I'd like to hear the end of the story in which I had played so important a part. Of course I admitted that nothing would give me more pleasure. But I was more than usually piqued when he said quietly, "Let me begin at the end. As we parted I said I was going to make a call. It has been answered as I wished. Do not fear that we shall have to visit the bird sanctuary again. It is closed—permanently. Now for my story. It seemed for both of us to be marked by a series of silly little misadventures. First, it was my turn to fall and you kindly helped me. Then, on our second call, it was your turn to endure the humiliation of an upset. But each served its purpose."

"But what did you gain from skidding on our first visit?" I asked.

"This," said Mr. Mycroft, rising and taking from the mantelshelf, where I had seen him place his fountain pen when he sat down to dinner, the little tube.

"That was only a recovery, not a gain," I said.

"No," he replied, "it garnered something when it fell. To misquote—as both of us like doing—'Cast your pen upon the waters and in a few moments it may pick up more copy than if you'd written for a week with it!'"

My "What do you mean?" was checked as he carefully unscrewed the top.

"See those little holes," he said, pointing to small openings just under the shoulder of the nib; then he drew out the small inner tube. It wasn't of rubber—it was of glass and was full of fairly clear water.

"This is water—water from the pond in the bird sanctuary. It looks like ordinary pond-water. As a matter of fact, it contains an unusually interesting form of life in it."

I began to feel a faint uneasiness.

"Oh, don't be alarmed. It is safely under screw and stopper now and is only being kept as Exhibit A—or, if you like it better, a stage-property in a forthcoming dramatic performance which will be Act Three of the mystery play in which you starred in Act Two, Scene Two."

"But I don't quite see . . ." was met by Mr. Mycroft more graciously than usual with, "There's really no reason why you should. I couldn't quite see myself, at the beginning. Yes, I do indeed admire such richness of double-dyed thoroughness when I come across it. It is rare for murderers to give one such entertainment, so elaborate and meticulous. They usually shoot off their arrows almost as soon as it enters their heads that they can bring down their bird and without a thought of how it may strike a more meditative mind afterward. But this man provided himself with a second string of rather better weave than his first."

Well, when Mr. Mycroft gets into that kind of strain it is no use saying anything. So I swallowed the I.D.S. formula that was again rising in my throat and waited.

"You remember, when you helped me to my feet and the pen had been salvaged, that with your aid we completed the round of the little lake. But when we had gone no farther than the beginning of the high-backed bridge, I felt I must rest. Do you recall what I did then?"

Could I recall! Naturally, for that was the very incident that had confirmed my suspicion that Mr. Mycroft was really shaken. I answered brightly:

"You sat, I can see it now, and for a moment you appeared to be dazed. And while you rested, as the beautiful old song, "The Lost Chord," expresses it, your 'fingers idly wandered.' But I noticed that they must be getting dirty, because, whether you knew it or not, they were feeling along under the jutting edge of the slab that made the step against which your back was resting."

"Admirable. And the quotation is happy, for my fingers were idly wandering (to go on with the old song) over the 'keys'!"

Mr. Mycroft cocked his old head at me and went on gaily, "And may I add that I am not less pleased that you thought the old man was so shaken that he really didn't know what he was doing! For that is precisely the impression that I had to give to another pair of eyes watching us from nearby cover. Well, after that little rest and glance about at those sentimental birdy-homes, the breeding boxes, I told you we could go home. And now may I ask you three questions?" I drew myself up and tried to sharpen my wits. "First," said my examiner, "did you observe anything about the garden generally?"

"Well," I replied, "I remember you called my attention to the little Nereid who held a spear from which the jet of the small fountain sprang?"

"Yes, that's true and indeed in every sense of the word, to the point. But did you notice something about—I will give you a clue—the flowers?"

"There were a lot of them!"

"Well, I won't hold you to that longer. I couldn't make out myself whether it had any significance. Then in the end I saw the light—yes, the light of the danger signal! Does that help you?"

"No," I said, "I remain as blind as a bat to your clue."

"Then, secondly, if the flowers failed to awake your curiosity, what about the birds?"

"Again, a lot of them and I did like that minah bird with its charmingly anaemic hostess voice."

"No, that was off the trail. I'll give you another clue—what about the breeding boxes?"

"Well, they're common enough little things, aren't they?"

"All right," he replied with cheerful patience, "now for my last question. When we were coming back do you remember any special incident?"

Then I did perk up. "Yes, of course—the contrast stuck in my mind. After being bathed in all that beauty we passed a dump corner and you got out and hunted for curios in the garbage."

"And brought back quite a trophy," said the old hunter as he pulled something out of his pocket, remarking "Exhibit B."

And then, do you know, my mind suddenly gave a dart—I do things like that every now and then. The thing he had pulled out and placed on the table was only a piece of cellophane or celluloid. It was also of a very crude and common red. It was the color that made my mind take its hop, a hop backwards. "I don't know what that dirty piece of road-side flotsam means but I now recall something about the garden—there wasn't a single red flower in it!"

Mr. Mycroft positively beamed. His uttered compliment was of course the "left-handed" sort he generally dealt me. "Mr. Silchester, I have always known it. It is laziness, just simple laziness, that keeps you from being a first-rate observer. You can't deny that puzzles interest you, but you can't be bothered to put out your hand and pluck the fruit of insight crossed with foresight."

I waved the tribute aside by asking what the red transparency might signify.

"Well," he said, "it put an idea into your head by what we may call a negative proof. Now, go one better and tell me something about it, itself, from its shape."

"Well, it's sickle-shaped, rather like a crescent moon. No," I paused, "no, you know I never can do anything if I strain. I have to wait for these flashes."

"All right," he said, "we will humor your delicate genius. But I will just say that it is a beautiful link. The color and the shape—yes, the moment I saw it lying there like a petal cast aside, my mind suddenly took wings like yours." He stopped and then remarked, "Well, the time has come for straight narrative. We have all the pieces of the board, yourself being actually the queen. It only remains to show you how the game was played. First, a tribute to Mr. Hess not as a man but as a murderer—an artist, without any doubt. Here are the steps by which he moved to his first check and how after the first queen had been taken—I refer to his aunt and her death—he was himself checkmated.

"You have noted that the garden has no red flowers and I have also suggested that the breeding box by the bridge interested me. About the water from the pond I have been frank and will shortly be franker. So we come to our second visit. It was then that our antagonist played boldly. How often have I had occasion to remind you that murderers love living over again the deaths they dealt, repeating a kill. That was Mr. Hess's wish. Of course, it wasn't pure love of art—he certainly knew something about me." Mr. Mycroft sighed, "I know you don't believe it, but I don't think you can imagine how often and how strongly a detective wishes to be unknown. To recognize you must remain unrecognized." He smiled again.

"Now note: You go up to him and ask him not to take photos. He shows first a startled resentment at your impudence, then a generous courtesy as proprietor for your interference on his behalf. Next, a sudden happy thought—how well you would look as part of the picture he was planning. He dresses you up, taking care to place you in a position in which you'll trip and fall. Now he has the middle link in his chain. But you were merely a link. You see, his real plan is to get me down too. He could, you will admit, hardly have hoped to lure me to act as model for a sun worshipper. But put you in that role and then he might persuade me to get into the picture also. Then, when you went over backwards, you would pull me into the pond as well."

"But," I said, "we should have had no more than a bad wetting."

"I see you are going to call for all my proofs before you will yield to the fact that we were really in the hands of a man as sane as all careful murderers are. You remember that charming little statuette which so took my fancy when we first visited the garden? It was of bronze. Not one of those cheap cement objects that people buy at the road-side and put in their gardens. It is a work of art, a museum-piece."

"It had patinated very nicely," I remarked, just to show I could talk *objet d'art* gossip as well as the master.

"I'm glad you observed that," he replied. "Yes, bronze is a remarkable material and worthy of having a whole Age named after it. More remarkable, indeed, than iron, for though iron has a better edge, it won't keep if constantly watered."

"What are you driving at?" For now I was getting completely lost in the old spider's spinning.

"That pretty little sham spear from which the water sprayed wasn't sham at all. It was a real spear, or shall we say, a giant hollow-needle. Because it was bronze it would keep its point unrusted. The only effect the water would have—and that would add to its lethal efficacy— would be to give it a patina. Further, I feel sure from the long close look I was able to give when we were being posed for our plunge, the blade of the spear had been touched up with a little acetic acid. That would no doubt corrode the fine edge a little but would make it highly poisonous—though not to the life in the pool."

"Why are you so interested in the pond-life?" I asked.

Mr. Mycroft picked up the small tube which he had removed from the fountain pen and which was now standing on a small side-table. "You'll remember, I said this pippet contains an interesting form of life—a very powerful form, if not itself poisoned. So powerful that, like most power-types, it tends to destroy others, yes, far higher types. This is really a remarkably fecund culture of a particularly virulent strain of typhoid bacillus."

I drew back. I don't like things like that near where I eat.

"Oh, it is safe enough so long as you don't drink it." I gasped. "So, you see, that was his plan. But, thoughtful man that he was, it was only his second string. He was a very thorough worker and had two concealed tools. If you fall over a bridge headlong and just underneath you is a Nereid holding a charming little wand, there is a good chance that you will fall, like the heroic Roman suicides, on your spear and so end yourself; and if the spear has round its socket some poison, the wound is very likely to give you blood-poisoning. But of course you may miss the point. People falling through the air are apt to writhe which may alter quite considerably the point at which they make their landing, or in this case, their watering. Well, thoughtful Mr. Hess realized how much human nature will struggle against gravitational fate—so he provided himself with a wider net. For when people fall headlong over a bridge, the natural reaction of panic is to open the mouth. So when they strike the water, they inevitably swallow a mouthful. And a little of this brew goes a long way."

"Now, now," I broke in, "I don't think any jury will send the nephew to join the aunt on that evidence."

"Why not?" was Mr. Mycroft's unexpectedly quiet rejoinder.

"First," I said, picking off the points on my fingers just as Mr. Mycroft sometimes does when closing a case, "granted this tube does contain typhoid germs, they may have been in this water from natural pollution. Proof that Hess poisoned the water cannot be sustained. Secondly, let me call the attention of judge and jury to the fact that when Miss Hess died a fortnight after her slight ducking, she did not die of typhoid. The cause of death was 'intestinal stasis.' Typhoid kills by a form of dysentery. Emphatically, that condition is polar to stasis."

"You are quite right," rejoined Mr. Mycroft, "the old-fashioned typhoid used to kill as you have described. But, would you believe it, the typhus germ has had the cunning to reverse his tactics completely. I remember a friend of mine telling me some years ago of this, and he had it from the late Sir Walter Fletcher, an eminent student of Medical Research in Britain. It stuck in my mind: the typhoid victim can now die with such entirely different symptoms that the ordinary doctor, unless he has quite other reasons to detect the presence of the disease, does not even suspect that his patient has died of typhoid, and with the best faith in the world fills in the death certificate never suggesting the true cause. "Yes," he went on meditatively, "I have more than once noticed that when a piece of information of that sort sticks in my mind, it may be prophetic. Certainly in this case it was."

I felt I might have to own defeat on that odd point when Mr. Mycroft remarked, "Well, let's leave Miss Hess and the medical side alone for a moment. Let's go back to the garden. I referred to you as the middle link. I have to be personal and even perhaps put myself forward. Mr. Hess was not averse to murdering you—if that was the only way of murdering me. We see how he maneuvered you to pose and then having got you in place, he set out to get me. You would stagger back, knock me off my perch, and both of us would plunge into the poisonous water, and one might be caught on the poisonous point. It was beautifully simple, really."

"You have got to explain how he would know that I would suddenly get dizzy, that a dragonfly or something would buzz right into my eyes and make me stagger."

"Quite easy—I was just coming to that. That was the first link in the chain. Now we can bring everything together and be finished with that really grim garden. Please recall the thing you noticed."

"No red flowers," I said dutifully and he bowed his acknowledgment.

"Next, the two things which you couldn't be expected to puzzle over. The breeding box which you did see but did not understand, and the undercurb of the step which even I didn't see but felt with my hand. That breeding box had the usual little doorway or round opening for the nesting bird to enter by, but to my surprise the doorway had a door and the door was closed. Now, that's going too far in pet-love sentimentality and although very cruel people are often very kind to animals, that kind of soapy gesture to birdmother comfort seemed to me strange—until I noticed, on the under-side of the next box, a small wheel. When I felt under the jamb of the step, I found two more such wheels—flanged wheels, and running along from one to the other, a black thread. Then when I knew what to look for, I could see the same black thread running up to the wheel fixed in the bird-box. I couldn't doubt my deduction any longer. That little door could be opened if someone raised his foot slightly and trod on the black thread that ran under the step curb.

"Now, one doesn't have to be a bird fancier to know that birds don't want to breed in boxes where you shut them up with a trap-door. What then could this box be for? You do, however, have to be something of a bird specialist to know about hawking and hummingbirds. The main technique of the former is the hood. When the bird is hooded it will stay quietly for long times on its perch. Cut off light and it seems to have its nervous reactions all arrested. Could that box be a hood not merely for the head of a bird but for *an entire bird?* Now we must switch back, as swoopingly as a hummingbird, to Miss Hess. You remember the description?"

It was my turn to be ready. I reached round to the paper rack and picked out the sheet that had started the whole adventure. I read out, "The late Miss Hess, whose huge fortune has gone to a very quiet recluse nephew whose one interest is birds, was herself a most colorful person and wonderfully young for her years." I added, "There's a colored photo of the colorful lady. She's wearing a vivid green dress. Perhaps that's to show she thought herself still in her salad days?"

"A good suggestion," replied Mr. Mycroft generously, "but I think we can drive our deductions even nearer home. Of course, I needed first-hand information for that. But I had my suspicions before I called."

"Called where?"

"On the doctor of the late lady. He was willing to see me when I could persuade him that his suspicions were right and that his patroness had really been removed by foul means. Then he told me quite a lot about the very odd person she was. She was shrewd in her way. She kept her own doctor and she paid him handsomely and took the complementary precaution of not remembering him in her will. Yes, he had every reason for keeping her going and being angry at her being gone. She was keen on staying here and not only that but on keeping young. But her colorfulness in dress was something more, he told me, than simply 'mutton dressing itself up to look like lamb.' She was color-blind and like that sort—the red-green colorblindness—she was very loath to admit it. That bright green dress of the photo pretty certainly seemed to her bright red."

I was still at a loss and let the old man see it.

"Now comes Hess's third neat piece of work. Note these facts: the aunt is persuaded to come to the garden—just to show that the nephew has turned over a new page and is being the busy little bird lover—sure way to keep in the maiden lady's good graces. He takes her round." Suddenly Mr. Mycroft stopped and picked up the celluloid red crescent. "Many color-blind persons have eyes that do not like a glare. The thoughtful nephew, having led auntie round the garden, takes her up the bridge to view the dear little birdie's home. She has to gaze up at it and he has thoughtfully provided her with an eye-shade—green to her, red to him, and red to something else. "Certain species of hummingbirds are particularly sensitive to red—all animals, of course, preferred to any other color. When young these particular hummingbirds have been known to dash straight at any object that is red and thrust their long bill toward it, thinking no doubt it is a flower. They will dart at a tomato held in your hand. Well, the aunt is gazing up to see the birdie's home; she's at the top of the bridge, just where you stood. Nephew has gone on, sure that aunt is going to follow. He is, in fact, now down by that lower step. He just treads on the concealed black thread. The door flies open, the little feathered bullet which had been brooding in the dark sees a flash of light and in it a blob of red. The reflex acts also like a flash. It dashes out right at Miss Hess's face. Again a reflex. This time it is the human one. She staggers back, hands to face—not knowing what has swooped at her—the flight of some of these small birds is too quick for the human eye. Of course she falls, takes her sup of the water, goes home shaken, no doubt not feeling pleased with nephew but not suspicious. After a fortnight we have a condition of stasis. The sound, but naturally not very progressive doctor, sees no connection. The police and public are also content. Nevertheless, she dies."

"And then?" I said, for I was on tiptoe of interest now.

"Well, Hess couldn't put a red eye-hood over your eyes, hoping you'd think it green and so make you a mark for his bird-bullet. So he put a hibiscus behind your ear. Each fish must be caught with its own bait, though the hook is the same. His effort with us was even more elaborate than with his aunt. What a pity that artists can't be content with a good performance but must always be trying to better it! Well, the bird sanctuary is closed and with it the sanctuary of a most resourceful murderer."

5-4=MURDERER
Baynard Kendrick
Detective: Captain Duncan Maclain

BAYNARD (HARDWICK) Kendrick (1894-1977) was born in Philadelphia and graduated from the Episcopal Academy in 1912. In 1914, he became the first American to join the Canadian Infantry, signing up one hour after World War I was declared; he served as a sergeant in England for the duration of the war.

During WWII, he instructed blind veterans, receiving a special plaque from General Omar Bradley to honor his work. Although fully sighted, he had a life-long interest in the blind and was one of the organizers of the Blinded Veterans Association, its only sighted advisor, and Honorary Chairman of its Board of Directors. After jobs with various companies in Florida, Philadelphia, and New York, he became a full-time writer in 1932 and settled in Florida.

Kendrick was one of the founders of the Mystery Writers of America, bearing membership card #1, serving as its first president in 1945, and receiving its Grand Master Award in 1967.

While producing numerous short stories for the pulps, notably the series of fourteen stories about Miles Standish Rice that he wrote for the prestigious *Black Mask*, the most distinguished of all detective fiction magazines, he is remembered today for his novels about Captain Duncan Maclain, a blinded WWI veteran who becomes a private eye, assisted by his friend and partner, Spud Savage, but even more by his two dogs, Schnucke and Dreist.

The first Maclain novel, *The Last Express* (1937), was filmed by Universal in 1938 with Edward Arnold, who also starred in *The Hidden Eye* (1945), an original film script in which Maclain battles Nazi spies. The 1971-1972 television series *Longstreet* that starred James Franciscus as a blind detective, was based on the Maclain series.

"5-4=Murderer" was originally published in the January 1953 issue of *Ellery Queen's Mystery Magazine*.

5-4=Murderer

By Baynard Kendrick

THIRTY-FIVE YEARS OF BLINDNESS, and twenty-one years as a private investigator, had driven home one unassailable truth to Captain Duncan Maclain. He lived in a world of blackness, but it was lighted with hearing, touch, taste, and smell. To disregard any notion conveyed to his mind by those four keen senses working together, no matter how foolish it seemed for the moment, was to court trouble, and sometimes to invite death . . .

It lacked five minutes of midnight when Maclain got out of the heavy truck that had picked him up hitch-hiking three miles away on 17-E, plodding carefully along with his left foot on the macadam and his right on the grassy shoulder. The friendly driver hadn't guessed he was blind, but had felt Maclain's urgency to reach a telephone.

"That's Nick's Diner over there." People were always uselessly pointing out places to Duncan Maclain. "This is the junction of 303 and 17-E. I'd pull up closer but I bogged there once. You can't put these trucks where you can put a car."

"Thanks a million," said Duncan Maclain.

The truck rolled off. Twenty minutes before, a December storm in the southland had broken with a freezing wind and an icy deluge. Using a stick he had cut in the woods as an emergency cane, the captain stepped out swiftly toward the smell of the diner, strong on the breeze through the pouring rain.

He was miserable, and strung as taut as an overtuned wire. A long-distance call from Philip Barstow, the state's attorney, had brought the captain without Schnucke, his Seeing-Eye dog, from New York to Red Platte that morning by plane. They'd driven thirty miles out to Barstow's one-room hunting cabin, and hunted quail all day. Barstow was one of the captain's oldest friends, and he was never surprised at Maclain's ability to knock down three out of five singles, shooting merely at the sound.

There had been trouble and graft in the State Police, according to Phil Barstow, and the Crime Commission had started a probe on four recent unsolved shootings and on the unrestrained gambling in the vicinity. Colonel William Yerkes, in charge of the State Police, had finally asked Barstow to call in Duncan Maclain. A blind man interested in criminology, looking over the workings of the department, could accomplish more than any sighted investigator, in Yerkes's estimation.

Then, sitting over highballs after dinner in the hunting camp, Phil Barstow had toppled out of his chair, seized with a sudden heart attack just as he started to explain. He had given the captain Yerkes's private telephone number, 3-2111, and that was about all.

It was the start of a vivid grueling nightmare for Duncan Maclain. He had made Phil Barstow as comfortable as he could, and then left the camp in a panic. Working with his braille hunting-case compass, and following the sand woods-road with a foot in one six-inch deep rut, he had by some miracle of direction made the state road, 17-E, by 11:30.

His cigarettes, holder, and lighter were on the table when Barstow fell. His wallet, with identification card and money, was in a pocket of his hunting jacket hanging on the cabin wall. A search of his hunting pants and the pockets of the ancient woollen shirt he wore rewarded him with a badly rumpled handkerchief and a single dime. That, at least, was a break, for when he reached a phone he could make his call.

Exactly ninety-six steps from the truck his improvised cane struck an artificial hedge in front of the diner. The captain found an opening a little to his right, took two steps up, and briefly stood listening before he went in.

It might have been a cough he'd heard, or the clearing of a throat. It might have been imagination carried to his overstrung nerves and tired body on the driving rain and rising wind. Whatever it was, it conveyed a feeling of being watched. His listening brought no recurrence. He shrugged and dismissed it as he opened the door and went in.

Nobody spoke and he heard no breathing. He took two steps forward and found the counter. Muffled sounds of running water and the clatter of dishes drifted in toward him—from a pantry, probably, with a swinging-door entrance in back of the counter.

He followed thirteen stools to the right and found a cigarette machine partly blocking a window. A hinged flap there gave a passage through the counter.

He retraced his steps to where he had started and walked on down to the other end, twelve stools more. There he found a telephone booth.

He went inside and shut the door and sat for a space holding on to his dime. A call to Colonel Yerkes would solve everything—get a police car to pick him up at Nick's Diner and dispatch an ambulance to the camp for Phil. It would also do something else—tie Duncan Maclain and Yerkes inextricably together. Maclain was supposed to be looking over the department on his own as Barstow's friend. He wasn't supposed to know the colonel, and didn't. The uncanny judgment that had made the captain what he was, told him in every fiber that to call the colonel was wrong.

He put in his dime, dialed the operator, and asked for the Chief, saying he wanted to report an emergency call.

When he hung up he felt certain an ambulance would get to the camp for Phil and that the Red Platte Hotel would send a car for him. He had explained everything to the chief operator. There was always one great light burning steadily through the blackness, the friendliness of all the world to people who couldn't see.

His dime had even been returned. It would buy a cup of coffee. He put it in his pocket and sat for a space with his forehead wrinkled.

Life was full of patterns to Duncan Maclain and the pattern of the phone booth seemed somehow awry. His hand went over the dial box and paused on top. A double bell was there. That seemed natural enough, although different from the type of dial box he knew in New York. But under the shelf where the telephone sat he found two more boxes fastened to the phone-booth wall. Each of the boxes had bells on top—bells of different shape, designed to give a different sound. It was those boxes that had been cramping him since he first sat down, pressing up against his knee.

He came out, found a stool near the phone booth, and sat down; then he called out, quite loudly, "Hello, is there anybody here?"

"Who do you think I am?" a voice demanded from behind the counter farther down. "Do you think I'm deaf or can't you see?"

"The last one's right," said Duncan Maclain. "I'm blind."

"Well, whatta ya know!"

Steps came toward him in back of the counter. He was conscious of an odor of pomade and clothes long impregnated with cooking. Someone breathed on him—a short man from the location of his head, and heavy, judging from the weight of his steps as he walked along the duckboards in back of the counter. The captain was suddenly conscious of his two-day growth of beard, his damp ragged shirt, and tousled hair.

"You must be that blind guy who goes hunting with Phil Barstow."

"That's right." The captain held out his hand. "I'm Duncan Maclain."

"Well, whatta ya know! I'm Nick Gherigis. I own the joint."

A pudgy hand, freshly wiped but not too dry of dishwater, shook the captain's, confirming his estimation of Nick's height and girth by its feel.

"Phil's been stopping in here for over ten years now. Where is he?"

The captain told Nick what had happened.

"Well, whatta ya know!" said Nick Gherigis. "My old lady's got a bum ticker, too. We live out in back. She's having to take it easy. Usually she helps, but right now all the work is on me. I'd drive you back to the camp now, but I don't like to leave her."

"I feel sure the ambulance will get there," Maclain told him.

"It'll get there for Barstow. He's the big wheel around here. You hungry?"

"Plenty."

"I'll fix you up some ham and eggs."

"I only have a dime with me."

"Skip it," Nick said. "Phil will pay me if you don't." He hesitated briefly. "Hell, I suppose if you can shoot a bird you can eat ham and eggs without me feeding you."

The captain said, "I usually manage to find my mouth."

The telephone rang in the booth.

"Shall I answer that for you?" Maclain got up from his stool.

Nick said, "Let it ring. The joint's closed. It's ten past 12. If you'll excuse me a minute I think the old lady's calling me."

Over the intermittent ringing the captain heard the swish of a swinging door. He could follow Nick for a few quick steps. The phone bell rang again and at its pause he felt quite certain that out in the pantry Nick had closed another door.

Maclain sat down on a stool right by the booth. A quick thought struck him that someone might be calling him at Nick's—from the hospital or hotel. Cursing his own stupidity, he reached in the booth without leaving the stool, found the receiver, and put it to his ear.

Nick's voice came over the telephone, trembling in intensity: "A hundred a week is cleaning me now. I'll blow the works before I'll double it. Kate don't know nothing, but I'm leaving her a list that'll jail everyone in the whole damn state if anything happens to me. Now go to hell!"

When the swinging door swished as Nick came back, the captain was sitting with his elbows on the counter.

There was a tinkle of keys, the snip of a lock, and the unmistakable ring of a bell and slide of a drawer as the cash register opened. A clink of change followed, and the crisp dry rustle of currency. Then came the tap of bills being straightened on edge against the top of the counter.

Nick went back through the swinging door. An instant later something clanged.

An atmosphere of menace had suddenly seeped into the diner. The captain was as sensitive to the coming of trouble as he was to the brewing of a storm. Nick was frightened. His voice and words had told all that on the extension of the pay phone. Now, after locking the cash register up for the night, he'd opened it again and removed all the money to hide it somewhere in the pantry.

"I hope he'll trust me for some cigarettes," muttered Maclain.

Nick came back, shut the cash register drawer, and said, "It's a helluva night. If that car don't show from the hotel, you'd better stay here. There's an extra little room at the back. It ain't much, but it's dry. I'll fix your eats."

Gas popped under a grill, ignited from the pilot light that Nick turned on. It was followed by the soft slap of a piece of ham tossed on the grill. The captain heard the crack of eggs against the edge of a bowl, and a second later, a comforting sizzle.

The captain nerved himself, as if for a great ordeal. "I left my cigarettes at the camp—with all my money. I hate to impose on your kindness, but I was wondering—"

"Name your brand," Nick said.

Then it happened.

Accompanied by a gust of wind, someone came through the diner door, about ten stools from where Maclain was sitting. In a voice that was high with terror, a woman screamed from behind the swinging door: "Nicky, don't shoot! Don't kill anyone!"

A gun went off, firing three times. The muffled footsteps of slippered feet stumbled off in the pantry.

Nick went down, slithering more than falling, collapsing forever with the feeble dead flap of his pudgy hand against the counter.

The captain sat like a man of bronze, his cup half-raised. Any second the gun would go off again and his own career would be finished.

Unhurried footsteps walked away—toward the other end of the diner where the cigarette machine stood. The captain listened, counting, and let a sound-etched photograph developed in his brain of a man about the size of Nick, with an overcoat rapping against his legs.

The captain remembered the hinged counter-flap. He heard it raised, and he could feel the vibrations as the man swung it over and dropped it against the counter.

He counted the footsteps along the duckboards and jumped involuntarily at the sound of the bell and the opening of the cash drawer.

For three long seconds he listened to heavy and muffled breathing, as the man stared in the drawer. The captain knew then why the man hadn't shot him.

The man was masked with something covering his nose and mouth—a handkerchief perhaps. He couldn't know Maclain was blind, but he didn't care; he couldn't be recognized.

The clank of metal sounded from the duckboards near where the captain figured Nick lay. "He's disposed of the gun beside his victim," the captain thought, and wondered why.

The heavy footsteps retraced their course, paused for a second inside the door, then went on out.

For thirty seconds the captain waited, tense and listening. There had been no sound of a car.

He set his coffee cup down and began to function again. When he knew his way, he could move much faster than most sighted people. He went to the end of the counter and through the opening almost on a run. Then he grew more cautious. He felt along, with his fingers brushing shelves of condiments and canned goods, until he reached the swinging door. As he had already pictured, a large round porthole of glass was set in the door.

The woman who had screamed was undoubtedly Mrs. Gherigis. She must have seen the gunman through the window in the door. The captain figured swiftly that she couldn't have seen Nick standing in front of the grill out of range of vision.

Why had she screamed, "Nicky, don't shoot! Don't kill anyone!"?

The captain snapped his fingers in sudden understanding. The masked killer must have been wearing some of Nick's clothes. Mrs. Gherigis didn't know her husband had been shot—she had thought *he* was the killer!

"Of whom?"

Obviously the man, whoever he was, who was shaking Nick down.

The aroma of the cooking ham and eggs grew sharper, mixed with the smell of the simmering coffee.

If Duncan Maclain knew any fear, it was that of fire. With even greater caution, he located the gas knob and turned off the grill.

His foot touched Nick's head. The captain knelt and let his perceptive fingers roam lightly over Nick's body. The gunman was an expert and he had shot to kill, wasting nothing. All three bullets had hit, one in Nick's stomach, one in his mouth, and one in his eye.

Water was gurgling softly in the Monel-metal sink, under the counter close by the captain's head. He cleansed the blood from his fingers.

Anxious now to check the accuracy of his hearing, he felt around Nick's body until he found the gun. With his hand resting on it, he froze.

The swinging door had opened gently behind him, but that wasn't the sound that held him rigid. It was the unmistakable click of a hammer as someone cocked a .38 revolver.

"Mrs. Gherigis?" a man's voice called out.

The captain made no move to turn.

"You there! Don't bother to look around—just leave that automatic where it is. Stand up slowly and put your hands behind you. I'm Corporal Walsh of the state police and I've got you covered."

The captain obeyed. The chill of steel on his wrists was cold as Walsh snapped handcuffs on. He felt himself frisked by an expert hand that relieved him of his pocket knife and laid it on the counter. The frisking seemed to throw Maclain off balance and he leaned against Walsh to right himself. Walsh was tall and thin, and he pushed the captain angrily away.

Then Walsh yelled, "Burzak—come in here!"

A blast of icy wind struck the captain as another man came in.

Seconds ticked by, then Burzak asked, "Isn't that the guy that got off the truck?"

"The same," said Walsh. "Get Lieutenant Corman personally on the phone and tell him exactly what happened—that we were parked down there on 303 at the crossroads, saw this man get off the truck, and were watching the place when we heard the shots. We drove up with our lights off and nailed him."

"Efficiently, too," muttered Duncan Maclain. "I was so busy checking my marvelous powers of hearing that I didn't hear you fellows come."

The captain's braille-watch said five to one. The two police cars, with Lieutenant Corman and his three technicians from Homicide, had rolled up twenty minutes before. The captain had heard them brake to a stop.

Corman was thickset, quiet, efficient, and deadly. It hadn't been very difficult to identify himself to Corman. The lieutenant had checked by phone with the hospital and found that an ambulance was on its way to Barstow. Then he had checked with the Red Platte Hotel and learned that they had not yet been able to send a car out to Nick's because of the storm. "Cancel it," Corman told them smoothly. "We'll bring him in."

"Dead or alive," thought Maclain.

Corman had then ordered the captain's handcuffs taken off and had grown quite friendly.

The captain sat on a stool, with Corman next to him, between him and the door, and listened to the pop of another flashlight bulb. The measurements, photographing, and finger-printing were almost finished. The ambulance and intern would arrive any minute to cart Nick away.

"Mrs. Gherigis killed her husband," said Duncan Maclain. "Make a ten-minute tour of the place with me and I'll show you how."

"That's a hot one," said Burzak from farther down. "The lieutenant just got through talking to her in back. She says you were the only one in the diner. She was looking through that glass in the swinging door and saw you shoot the gun."

"Which narrows it down to her word against mine," said Maclain. "But she made one mistake—a big one—in picking me for a witness while she tried to look like a man. She thought I was a bum who had wandered in here and that my story would be disbelieved. What she over-looked was that I couldn't have shot him and couldn't even see her, because I'm totally blind."

Corman stood up. "I'll make a tour with you. If you can make that story stick, Maclain, it's the very first thing I've heard that sounds like sense."

There were two things in the pantry that interested Duncan Maclain—a big deep-freeze that clanged when the lid dropped down, and a closet. The closet door stood ajar and had a Yale lock on it. What caught Maclain up was the fact that the door was lined with heavy asbestos.

"There's nothing in there but supplies and beer," said Corman. "We've already looked around. Nick had it insulated against moisture."

Duncan Maclain was already inside the closet, his fingers traveling along the wall and back of the stacked-up cases of beer. The wires he was searching for led up in back of the shelves. He came out and checked the Yale lock again, making sure it was on the thumb latch and that even if the door were shut it would open without the key.

"When I search for things," said Duncan Maclain, "I first have to find where they aren't. That's what proves to me that my thinking is right." He hooked his fingers on Corman's arm. "The washroom seems to be the logical place. Let's look there."

Two coats and a hat were hanging in the washroom, with four of Nick's soiled aprons and two suits of his overalls. Corman stood in silence as the captain's fingers brushed them all. For twelve inches up from the bottom of the legs, one of the suits of white overalls was damp and muddy.

"Those were what Mrs. Gherigis wore when she did the shooting." The captain pointed to the hat and one of the overcoats and the muddy overalls. "They're damp and Nick hasn't been out of this place since the rain started. I think if you turn them over to your technicians, lieutenant, and check the sweatband in that hat, you can prove that's what Mrs. Gherigis had on."

"Well, I'll be—" said Corman. "I'll take them now."

"No, wait." The captain stretched out his hand. "Take me out and around in front. There's a hedge out there. I felt it coming in. I'll show you how she got in and out of the diner and yet was not seen by Walsh and Burzak in their car."

They came out of the washroom, and a couple of steps to the right Corman opened another door.

"There's a storm vestibule here," Corman said. He opened a second door, letting in a gust of wind and rain. "Wait here a second," Corman went on. "We'll get drowned in this. I'll get the slickers from Walsh's car." Corman went out.

The captain raised both his sensitive hands and swept them up and down along each side of the inner vestibule door. It was the logical place to put an electric meter, fuse box, and cutout switch for the diner. He grunted in satisfaction as he found them.

An automobile door slammed and Corman came back with two slickers. They put them on and went out into the rain.

He struck the fronds of the prickly hedge in front of the diner a few feet farther on. It ran from the end of the diner to the door. It was more than head-high and planted about eighteen inches out from the diner wall.

"Have you a flashlight, lieutenant?"

"Yes."

"Shine it in back of this hedge and see if there are any footprints."

"There's nothing but water," Corman said. "It's an inch deep, at least."

"Well, that's one up for Mrs. Gherigis," said Duncan Maclain. "Let's follow briefly what she did. You'll find when you make an investigation that Nick Gherigis had been paying out dough."

"To whom?" Corman rasped.

"To a dame," said the captain. "I have very keen ears. Mrs. Gherigis called Nick in while I was in the diner, and I heard them quarreling. He's been keeping a woman some place and it's been on her mind for a long time. Tonight was the finish.

"She went in back and got Nick's gun, put on his white overalls, hat, and coat in the washroom, came around here in back of this hedge, shot him, and went back the same way, leaving the clothes in the washroom. With only Nick and me and her in the diner, she felt sure you'd hang it on me—a bum."

"I'll buy it," Corman said suddenly. "Driving up here from the road with their lights off, Walsh and Burzak couldn't have seen her from the police car."

There was a swish of tires and a splashing of water as a heavy car turned from 17-E to stop in front of the diner.

Corman said, "We might as well go inside. The morgue wagon is here."

"Do you mind if I talk with Mrs. Gherigis?" the captain asked.

"Go ahead," said Corman.

The captain stood and listened while two men carrying a stretcher went in through the diner door. Corman went in with them.

When the granite of anger set in Maclain, he ceased to be a human being and turned into a machine. He was blind, but with the inexorable blindness of justice. He hated a killer, but in his code there were worse . . .

Maclain was part of the rain and the raging wind as he took the keys from Corman's car and the ambulance. There were none in the car that had brought the technicians, so the captain swiftly raised the hood of that car and jerked the distributor wires loose, disabling the machine. A moment later he sped around the diner and was down on all fours, crawling about to pat the ground beside and underneath Walsh's and Burzak's official car. Then he got to his feet, opened the door, and removed the keys.

Beside him, Burzak's gritty voice said suddenly, "What are you doing?"

"I was about to put your slicker back in," said Duncan Maclain.

"Wait till Walsh hears this one," Burzak said. "You lying bum, I knew that you could see!"

The captain hit him, one straight right, backed with one hundred and ninety pounds of fury. It landed just an inch and a half underneath the sound of Burzak's words.

He slid out of the dripping slicker and draped it over the fallen trooper, then stepped into the vestibule and pulled the main light-switch beside the door. His feet made no noise as he sped past the washroom, across the pantry, into the insulated closet.

There wasn't even the tiniest snip as he shut himself in by pushing up the button and releasing the Yale lock on the inside of the door. He brailled the closet with frantic speed and stopped with every sense alert at three big, round cans set together on a shelf before him.

They were fastened with little tin hasps, like those on a bread box.

The captain tried to lift a can and found it wouldn't move. He opened the hasp and raised the lid to stick in a probing finger. Sugar—but only on top! His finger had struck a metal bottom less than an inch and a half down.

He shut the top and twisted the can around. It was cut out at the back and set in a groove. He hadn't been wrong when he had traced the wires. He reached inside and lifted from its cradle the combination mouth-and-earpiece of a French-style telephone.

The dial signal clicked in his ear and settled to a buzzing sound. Maclain reached in through the opening and dialed 3-2111.

"Colonel Yerkes?"

"Yes. Who is it?" The colonel's voice sounded sleepy.

"It's Duncan Maclain. Phil Barstow's—"

"I know all about you." The voice was wide awake now. "I thought you were out at Barstow's camp."

"Do you know Nick's Diner?"

"Of course!"

"Fine," said Maclain. "Then get together six of your best men—ones you're positive you can trust. Arm them to the ears and get out here as fast as you can. Nick was shot an hour ago by one of your own troopers—Burzak—while Corporal Walsh was waiting outside in the car."

"Good Lord!" said Yerkes. "Why?"

"Nick was running a wire room, receiving and sending bets on the aces. He has an extension to the pay booth and two dial phones concealed in a sound-proof room off the pantry. I'm locked in and telephoning from it."

"Who else is at the diner?"

"Lieutenant Corman, three technicians, two men from the morgue, Walsh and Burzak, and Mrs. Gherigis," said Maclain. "None of them are leaving—I have all the car keys. At the moment they're probably hunting for me. I put out all the lights in the place and I had to knock Trooper Burzak cold when he started to move their police car."

"Can you hold it a minute?" Yerkes demanded. "I've got another phone here. I'm going to start out the riot car. Hang on!"

The colonel was back in a few moments. "Tell me briefly what happened and I'll be right along. The riot squad is already on its way."

"Phil had a heart attack," said Duncan Maclain. "I came here to get to a phone. An ambulance is on its way to pick up Phil.

"Walsh and Burzak were parked outside by the end of the diner, where I couldn't have seen them even if I had eyes. But they saw me come in. The telephone rang and Nick left to take the call in this closet, where I am now. He told me he'd heard his wife call. I thought somebody might be phoning me back about the ambulance for Phil, so I picked up the phone in the booth.

"Nick was on the extension and I overheard part of the call. He said that a hundred a week was cleaning him and he'd blow the works before he'd double it. He said he was leaving his wife a list that would jail them all."

"You don't know who he was talking to?"

"I don't," said Maclain. "Maybe Corman."

"What makes you think that?"

"It's an idea I got when Walsh told Burzak to get Lieutenant Corman personally and to tell him exactly what had happened—that they had been parked down there on 303 at the crossroads, had seen me get off the truck, had driven up with their lights off, and had nailed me. It sounded like an awful lot of yackety-yak to send in on a murder call."

"Do you have any proof, Captain Maclain?" Yerkes's voice was grim.

"Plenty, but I haven't much time to tell you—somebody has just started pounding on the door. I guess they've got the lights back on.

"Walsh and Burzak saw me come in, decided it was a good time to rub out Nick and hang it on someone they thought was only a bum. Right now I look like one. Burzak put on Nick's hat, coat, and overalls—he found them in the washroom inside the side entrance. Then he came around through the front, shot Nick, and took a look in the cash register. I think he wanted that list Nick had talked about, but Nick had cleaned out the cash drawer and hidden the stuff after the warning call.

"Burzak was scarcely out of the diner when Walsh came in and put me under a gun. It was the world's fastest piece of police work, Colonel.

"Anyway, Burzak had dressed up to look like Nick and had blasted him. Mrs. Gherigis saw a man through the window of the pantry door and thought it was Nick. She still doesn't know Nick's dead."

"You sound pretty sure, Maclain."

"Of course I'm sure; get this, Colonel: five of us were here. Nick was shot. Mrs. Gherigis couldn't have done it—she was back of a door and out of range of vision. I didn't, and Walsh is tall and thin—too tall to get Nick's things on and be mistaken for him by Nick's wife. Five minus four equals one—Burzak."

"Just a second, Captain Maclain. What evidence have you got?"

"I think you'll find Nick's list of names in the deep-freeze, Colonel—I heard the lid clang. Your laboratory can prove that Burzak had Nick's clothes on. . . I'd better hang up now—they're breaking the door."

"One more second," Yerkes pleaded. "Can you *prove* that Burzak and Walsh were there all the time—from *before* the murder?"

"I have to hurry, Colonel. Burzak's and Walsh's police car hasn't moved from right beside this diner since before 11:30 when it started to rain. Everything around here is soaking but it's bone dry under their car."

"I'll be right over," said Yerkes. "Is there anything I can bring you?"

"Cigarettes, Colonel," said Duncan Maclain, "I never did get any. And maybe just a wee drop of scotch. I'm dryer inside than the ground under Walsh's and Burzak's car."

THERE'S DEATH
FOR REMEMBRANCE
Frances and Richard Lockridge
Detectives: Pamela and Jerry North

INARGUABLY THE most famous, charming, and successful crime-fighting couple in all of detective fiction (skipping Nick and Nora Charles who, after all, appeared in only a single book), is Mr. and Mrs. North, the creations of Frances Louise Davis Lockridge (1896-1963) and her husband, Richard Orson Lockridge (1898-1982).

Richard Lockridge was a reporter in Kansas and then drama critic for the *New York Sun*. In the 1930s, he was a frequent contributor to *The New Yorker*, his short stories and articles winning him praise as the archetypical writer for that magazine. His series of non-mystery stories about a publisher and his wife were collected in *Mr. and Mrs. North* (1938).

When Frances Lockridge decided to write a detective story, she became bogged down and he suggested that he use his creations as the main characters. She devised the plot, he did the actual writing, and the result was *The Norths Meet Murder* (1940), the first of a series of twenty-seven detective novels than ended with *Murder by the Book* (1963) when Frances died.

The series garnered a great deal of critical praise for its humor, the portrayal of the Greenwich Village neighborhood in which the authors and the Norths lived, but it fell into formulaic plots that disenchanted some critics. Pam's penchant for fearlessly wandering into the villain's path and needing to be rescued in the last chapter irked more than a few readers. Jerry spends most of his time reading manuscripts for his mystery magazine while Pam takes care of the cats and stumbles across bodies, then looking for murderers.

The Norths came to Broadway in *Mr. and Mrs. North* (1941), a comic play by Owen Davis, which served as the basis for a 1942 motion picture of the same title that starred Gracie Allen and William Post, Jr. In the same year, a charming radio series also titled *Mr. and Mrs. North* made its debut and became an instant and enduring success. Barbara Britton and Richard Denning starred in the television series that ran for fifty-seven half-hour episodes (1952-1954).

"There's Death for Remembrance" was originally published in the November 16, 1955, issue of *This Week*; it has been frequently reprinted as "Pattern for Murder" and "Murder for Remembrance."

There's Death for Remembrance
By Frances & Richard Lockridge

FERN HARTLEY CAME TO NEW YORK to die, although that was far from her intention. She came from Centertown, in the Middle West, and died during a dinner party—given in her honor, at a reunion of schoolmates. She died at the bottom of a steep flight of stairs in a house on West Twelfth Street. She was a little woman and she wore a fluffy white dress. She stared at unexpected death through strangely bright blue eyes. . . .

There had been nothing to foreshadow so tragic an ending to the party—nothing, at any rate, on which Pamela North, who was one of the schoolmates, could precisely put a finger. It was true that Pam, as the party progressed, had increasingly felt tenseness in herself; it was also true that, toward the end, Fern Hartley had seemed to behave somewhat oddly. But the tenseness, Pam told herself, was entirely her own fault, and as for Fern's behavior—well, Fern *was* a little odd. Nice, of course, but—trying. Pam had been tried.

She had sat for what seemed like hours with a responsive smile stiffening her lips and with no comparable response stirring in her mind. It was from that, surely, that the tenseness—the uneasiness—arose. Not from anything on which a finger could be put. It's my own fault, Pam North thought. This is a reunion, and I don't reunite. Not with Fern, anyway.

It had been Fern on whom Pam had responsively smiled. Memories of old days, of schooldays, had fluttered from Fern's mind like pressed flowers from the yellowed pages of a treasured book. They had showered about Pam North, who had been Fern's classmate at Southwest High School in Centertown. They had showered also about Hortense Notson and about Phyllis Pitt. Classmates, too, they had been those years ago—they and, for example, a girl with red hair.

"—*red* hair," Fern Hartley had said, leaning forward, eyes bright with memory. "Across the aisle from you in Miss Burton's English class. Of *course* you remember, Pam. She went with the boy who stuttered."

I *am* Pamela North, who used to be Pamela Britton, Pam told herself, behind a fixed smile. I'm not an impostor; I did go to Southwest High. If only I could prove it by remembering something—anything. Any *little* thing.

"The teacher with green hair?" Pam North said, by way of experiment. "Streaks of, anyway? Because the dye—"

Consternation clouded Fern's bright eyes. "*Pam!*" she said. "That was another one entirely. Miss Burton was the one who—"

It had been like that from the start of the party—the party of three couples and Miss Fern Hartley, still of Centertown. They were gathered in the long living room of the Stanley Pitts's house—the gracious room which ran the depth of the small, perfect house—an old New York house, retaining the charm (if also something of the inconvenience) of the previous century.

As the party started that warm September evening, the charm was uppermost. From open casement windows at the end of the room there was a gentle breeze. In it, from the start, Fern's memories had fluttered.

And none of the memories had been Pam North's memories. Fern has total recall; I have total amnesia, Pam thought, while keeping the receptive smile in place, since one cannot let an old schoolmate down. Did the others try as hard? Pam wondered. Find themselves as inadequate to recapture the dear, dead days?

Both Hortense Notson and Phyllis Pitt had given every evidence of trying, Pam thought, letting her mind wander. Fern was now reliving a perfectly wonderful picnic, of their junior year. Pam was not.

Pam did not let the smile waver; from time to time she nodded her bright head and made appreciative sounds. Nobody had let Fern down; all had taken turns in listening—even the men. Jerry North was slacking now, but he had been valiant. His valor had been special, since he had never even been in Centertown. And Stanley Pitt had done his bit, too; of course, he was the host. Of course, Fern was the Pitts's house guest; what a lovely house to be a guest in, Pam thought, permitting her eyes briefly to accompany her mind in its wandering.

Stanley—what a distinguished-looking man he is, Pam thought—was with Jerry, near the portable bar. She watched Jerry raise his glass as he listened. Her own glass was empty, and nobody was doing anything about it. An empty glass to go with an empty mind, Pam thought, and watched Fern sip ginger ale. Fern never drank anything stronger. Not that she had anything against drinking. Of course not. But even one drink made her feel all funny.

"Well," Pam had said, when Fern had brought the subject up, earlier on. "Well, that's more or less the idea, I suppose. This side of hilarious, of course."

"You know," Fern said then, "you always did talk funny. Remember when we graduated and you—"

Pam didn't remember. Without looking away from Fern, or letting the smile diminish, Pam nevertheless continued to look around the room. How lovely Phyllis is, Pam thought—really is. Blonde Phyllis Pitt was talking to Clark Notson, blond also, and sturdy, and looking younger than he almost certainly was.

Clark had married Hortense in Centertown. He was older—Pam remembered that he had been in college when they were in high school. He had married her when she was a skinny, dark girl, who had had to be prouder than anyone else because her parents lived over a store and not, properly, in a house. And look at her now, Pam thought, doing so. Dark still—and slim and quickly confident, and most beautifully arrayed.

Well, Pam thought, we've all come a long way. (She nodded, very brightly, to another name from the past—a name signifying nothing.) Stanley Pitt and Jerry—neglecting his own wife, Jerry North was— had found something of fabulous interest to discuss, judging by their behavior. Stanley was making points, while Jerry listened and nodded. Stanley was making points one at a time, with the aid of the thumb and the fingers of his right hand. He touched thumbtip to successive fingertips, as if to crimp each point in place. And Jerry— how selfish could a man get—ran a hand through this hair, as he did when he was interested.

"Oh," Pam said. "Of course I remember *him*, Fern."

A little lying is a gracious thing.

What a witness Fern would make, Pam thought. Everything that had happened—beginning, apparently, at the age of two—was brightly clear in her mind, not muddy as in the minds of so many. The kind of witness Bill Weigand, member in good standing of the New York City Police Department, always hoped to find and almost never did—never had, that she could remember, in all the many investigations she and Jerry had shared since they first met Bill years ago.

Fern would be a witness who really remembered. If Fern, Pam thought, knew something about a murder, or where a body was buried, or any of the other important things which so often come up, she would remember it precisely and remember it whole. A good deal of sifting would have to be done, but Bill was good at that.

Idly, her mind still wandering, Pam hoped that Fern did not, in fact, know anything of buried bodies. It could, obviously, be dangerous to have so total a recall and to put no curb on it. She remembered, and this from association with Bill, how often somebody did make that one revealing remark too many. Pam sternly put a curb on her own mind and imagination. What could Fern—pleasant, bubbling Fern, who had not adventured out of Centertown, excepting for occasional trips like these—know of dangerous things?

Pam North, whose lips ached, in whose mind Fern's words rattled, looked hard at Jerry, down the room, at the bar. Get me out of this, Pam willed across the space between them. Get me out of this! It had been known to work or had sometimes seemed to work. It did not now. Jerry concentrated on what Stanley Pitt was saying. Jerry ran a hand through his hair.

"Oh, dear," Pam said, breaking into the flow of Fern's words, as gently as she could. "Jerry wants me for something. You know how husbands are."

She stopped abruptly, remembering that Fern didn't, never having had one. She got up—and was saved by Phyllis, who moved in. What a hostess, Pam thought, and moved toward Jerry and the bar. The idea of saying that to poor Fern, Pam thought. This is certainly one of my hopeless evenings. She went toward Jerry.

"I don't," she said when she reached him, "remember anything about anything. Except one teacher with green hair, and that was the wrong woman."

Jerry said it seemed very likely.

"There's something a little ghoulish about all this digging up of the past," Pam said. "Suppose some of it's still alive?" she added.

"Huh?" Jerry said.

He was told not to bother. And that Pam could do with a drink. Jerry poured, for them both, from a pitcher in which ice tinkled.

"Sometime," Pam said, "she's going to remember that one thing too many. That's what I mean. You see?"

"No," Jerry said, simply.

"Not everybody," Pam said, a little darkly, "wants everything remembered about everything. Because—"

Stanley Pitt, who had turned away, turned quickly back. He informed Pam that she had something there.

"I heard her telling Hortense—" Stanley Pitt said, and stopped abruptly, since Hortense, slim and graceful (and *so* beautifully arrayed) was coming toward them.

"How Fern doesn't change," Hortense said. "Pam, do you remember the boy next door?"

"I don't seem to remember anything," Pam said. "Not anything at all."

"You don't remember," Hortense said. "I don't remember. Phyllis doesn't. And with it all, she's so—sweet." She paused. "Or is she?" she said. "Some of the things she brings up—always doing ohs, the boy next door was. How does one do an oh?"

"Oh," Jerry said, politely demonstrating, and then, "Was he the one with green hair?" The others looked blank at that, and Pam said it was just one of the things she'd got mixed up, and now Jerry was mixing it worse. And, Pam said, did Hortense ever feel she hadn't really gone to Southwest High School at all and was merely pretending she had? Was an impostor?

"Far as I can tell," Hortense said, "I never lived in Centertown. Just in a small, one-room vacuum. Woman without a past." She paused. "Except," she said, in another tone, "Fern remembers me in great detail."

Stanley Pitt had been looking over their heads—looking at his wife, now the one listening to Fern. In a moment of silence, Fern's voice fluted. "Really, a dreadful thing to happen," Fern said. There was no context.

"Perhaps," Stanley said, turning back to them, "it's better to have no past than to live in one. Better all around. And safer."

He seemed about to continue, but then Clark Notson joined them. Clark did not, Pam thought, look like a man who was having a particularly good time. "Supposed to get Miss Hartley her ginger ale," he said. He spoke rather hurriedly.

Jerry, who was nearest the bar, said, "Here," and reached for the innocent bottle—a bottle, Pam thought, which looked a little smug and virtuous among the other bottles. Jerry used a silver opener, snapped off the bottle cap. The cap bounced off, tinkled against a bottle.

"Don't know your own strength," Clark said, and took the bottle and, with it, a glass into which Jerry dropped ice. "Never drinks anything stronger, the lady doesn't," Clark said, and bore away the bottle.

"And doesn't need to," Hortense Notson said, and drifted away. She could drift immaculately.

"She buys dresses," Pam said. "Wouldn't you know?"

"As distinct—?" Jerry said, and was told he knew perfectly well what Pam meant.

"Buys them for, not from," Pam said.

To this, Jerry simply said, "Oh."

It was then a little after eight, and there was a restless circulation in the long room. Pam was with Phyllis Pitt. Phyllis assured her that food would arrive soon. And hadn't old times come flooding back?

"Mm," Pam said. Pam was then with Clark Notson and, with him, talked unexpectedly of tooth paste. One never knows what will come up at a party. It appeared that Clark's firm made tooth paste. Stanley Pitt joined them. He said Clark had quite an operation there. Pam left them and drifted, dutifully, back to Fern, who sipped ginger ale. Fern's eyes were very bright. They seemed almost to glitter.

(But that's absurd, Pam thought. People's don't, only cats'.)

"It's so exciting," Fern said, and looked around the room, presumably at "it." "To meet you all again, and your nice husbands and—" She paused. "Only," she said, "I keep wondering. . ."

Pam waited. She said, "What, Fern?"

"Oh," Fern said. "Nothing dear. Nothing really. Do you remember—"

Pam did not. She listened for a time, and was relieved by Hortense, and drifted on again. For a minute or two, then, Pam North was alone and stood looking up and down the softly lighted room. Beyond the windows at the far end, lights glowed up from the garden below. The room was filled, but not harshly, with conversation—there seemed, somehow, to be more than the seven of them in it. Probably, Pam thought, memories crowded it—the red-haired girl, the stuttering boy.

Fern laughed. Her laughter was rather high in pitch. It had a little "hee" at the end. That little "hee," Pam thought idly, would identify Fern—be something to remember her by. As Jerry's habit of running his hand through his hair would identify him if, about all else, she suddenly lost her memory. (As I've evidently begun to do, Pam North thought.) Little tricks. And Fern puts her right index finger gently to the tip of her nose, presumably when she's thinking. Why, Pam thought, she did that as a girl, and was surprised to remember.

Her host stood in front of her, wondering what he could get her. She had, Pam told him, everything.

"Including your memories?" Stanley Pitt asked her. Pam noticed a small scar on his chin. But it wasn't, of course, the same thing as— as running a hand through your hair. But everybody has something, which is one way of telling them apart.

"I seem," Pam said, "a little short of memories."

"By comparison with Miss Hartley," Stanley said, "who isn't? A pipe line to the past. Can't I get you a drink?"

He could not. Pam had had enough. So, she thought, had all of them. Not that anybody was in the least tight. But still . . .

Over the other voices, that of Fern Hartley was raised. There was excitement in it. So it isn't alcohol, Pam thought, since Fern hadn't had any. It's just getting keyed up at a party. She looked toward Fern, who was talking, very rapidly, to Jerry. No doubt, Pam thought, about what I was like in high school. Not that there's anything he shouldn't know. But still . . .

Fern was now very animated. If, Pam thought, I asked whether anyone here was one cocktail up I'd—why, I'd say Fern. Fern, of all people. Or else, Pam thought, she has some exciting surprise.

It was now eight thirty. A maid appeared at the door, waited to be noticed, and nodded to Phyllis Pitt, who said, at once, "Dinner, everybody." The dining room was downstairs, on a level with the garden. "These old stairs," Phyllis said. "Everybody be careful."

The stairs were, indeed, very steep, and the treads very narrow. But there were handrails and a carpet. The stairway ended in the dining room, where candles glowed softly on the table, among flowers.

"If you'll sit—" Phyllis said, starting with Pam North. "And you and—" They moved to the places indicated. "And Fern—" Phyllis said, and stopped. "Why," she said, "where is—"

She did not finish, because Fern Hartley stood at the top of the steep staircase. She was a slight figure in a white dress. She seemed to be staring fixedly down at them, her eyes strangely bright. Her face was flushed and she made odd, uncertain movements with her little hands.

"I'm—" Fern said, and spoke harshly, loudly, and so that the word was almost a shapeless sound. "I'm—"

And then Fern Hartley, taking both hands from the rails, pitched headfirst down the staircase. In a great moment of silence, her body made a strange, soft thudding on the stairs. She did not cry out.

At the bottom of the red-carpeted stairs she lay quite still. Her head was at a hideous angle to her body—an impossible angle to her body. That was how she died.

Fern Hartley died of a broken neck. There was no doubt. Six people had seen her fall. Now she lay at the bottom of the stairs and no one would ever forget her soft quick falling down that steep flight. An ambulance surgeon confirmed the cause of her death and another doctor from up the street—called when it seemed the ambulance would never get there—confirmed it, too.

But after he had knelt for some time by the body the second doctor beckoned the ambulance surgeon and they went out into the hallway. Then the ambulance surgeon beckoned one of the policemen who had arrived with the ambulance, and the policeman went into the hall with them. After a few minutes, the policeman returned and asked, politely enough, that they all wait upstairs. There were, he said meaninglessly, a few formalities.

They waited upstairs, in the living room. They waited for more than two hours, puzzled and in growing uneasiness. Then a thinnish man of medium height, about whom there was nothing special in appearance, came into the room and looked around at them.

"Why, *Bill!*" Pam North said.

The thinnish man looked at her, and then at Jerry North, and said, "Oh." Then he said there were one or two points.

And then Pam said, "Oh," on a note strangely flat.

How one introduces a police officer, who happens to be an old and close friend, to other friends who happen to be murder suspects—else why was Bill Weigand there?—had long been a moot question with Pam and Jerry North. Pam said, "This is Bill Weigand, everybody. Captain Weigand. He's—he's a policeman. So there must be—" And stopped.

"All right, Pam," Bill Weigand said. Then, "You all saw her fall. Tell me about it." He looked around at them, back at Pam North. It was she who told him.

Her eyes had been "staring"? Her face flushed? Her movements

uncertain? Her voice hoarse? "Yes," Pam said, confirming each statement. Bill Weigand looked from one to another of the six in the room.
He received nods of confirmation. One of the men—tall, dark-haired
but with gray coming, a little older than the others—seemed about to
speak. Bill waited. The man shook his head. Bill got them identified
then. The tall man was Stanley Pitt. This was his house.

"But," Bill said, "she hadn't been drinking. The medical examiner
is quite certain of that." He seemed to wait for comment.

"She said she never did," Pam told him.

"So—" Bill said.

Then Hortense Notson spoke, in a tense voice. "You act," she said,
"as if you think one of us pushed her."

Weigand looked at her carefully. He said, "No. That didn't happen,
Mrs. Notson. How could it have happened? You were all in the dining
room, looking up at her. How could any of you have pushed her?"

"Then," Clark Notson said, and spoke quickly, with unexpected
violence. "Then why all this? She . . . what? Had a heart attack?"

"Possibly," Bill said. "But the doctors—"

Again he was interrupted.

"I've heard of you," Notson said, and leaned forward in his chair.
"Aren't you homicide?"

"Right," Bill said. He looked around again, slowly. "As Mr. Notson
said, I'm homicide." And he waited.

Phyllis Pitt—the pretty, the very pretty, light-haired woman—had
been crying. More than the rest, in expression, in movements, she
showed the shock of what had happened. "Those dreadful stairs," she
said, as if to herself. "Those dreadful stairs."

Her husband got up and went to her and leaned over her. He
touched her bright hair and said, very softly, "All right, Phyl. All right."

"Bill," Pam said. "Fern fell downstairs and—and died. What more
is there?"

"You all agree," Bill said, "that she was flushed and excited and
uncertain—as if she had been drinking. But she hadn't been drinking.

And . . . the pupils of her eyes were dilated. That was why she seemed to be staring. Because, you see, she couldn't see where she was going. So . . ." He paused. "She walked off into the air. I have to find out why. So what I want . . ."

It took him a long time to get what he wanted, which was all they could remember, one memory reinforcing another, of what had happened from the start of the dinner party until it ended with Fern Hartley, at the foot of the staircase, all her memories dead. Pam, listening, contributing what she could, could not see that a pattern formed—a pattern of murder.

Fern had seemed entirely normal—at least, until near the end. They agreed on that. She had always remembered much about the past and talked of it. Meeting old school friends, after long separation, she had seemed to remember everything—far more than any of the others.

"Most of it, to be honest, wasn't very interesting." That was Hortense Notson. Hortense looked at Pam, at Phyllis Pitt.

"She was so sweet," Phyllis said, in a broken voice.

"So—so interested herself." Pam said. "A good deal of it was pretty long ago, Bill."

Fern had shared her memories chiefly with the other women. But she had talked of the past, also, with the men.

"It didn't mean much to me," Stanley Pitt said. "It seemed to be all about Centertown, and I've never been in Centertown. Phyllis and I met in New York." He paused. "What's the point of this?" he said.

"I don't know," Bill Weigand told him. "Not yet. Everything she remembered seemed to be trivial? Nothing stands out? To any of you?"

"She remembered I had a black eye the first time she saw me," Clark Notson said. "Hortense and I—when we were going together—ran into her at a party. It was a long time ago. And I had a black eye, she said. I don't remember anything about it. I don't even remember the party, actually. Yes, I'd call it pretty trivial."

"My God," Stanley Pitt said. "*Is* there some point to this?"

"I don't know," Bill said again, and was patient. "Had you known Miss Hartley before, Mr. Pitt?"

"Met her for the first time yesterday," Stanley told him. "We had her to dinner and she stayed the night. Today I took her to lunch, because Phyl had things to do about the party. And—" He stopped. He shrugged and shook his head, seemingly at the futility of everything.

"I suppose," Jerry North said, "the point is—did she remember something that somebody—one of us—wanted forgotten?"

"Yes," Bill said. "It may be that."

Then it was in the open. And, with it in the open, the six looked at one another; and there was a kind of wariness in the manner of their looking. Although what on earth I've got to be wary about I don't know, Pam thought. Or Jerry, she added in her mind. She couldn't have told Jerry anything about me. Well, not anything important. At least not very . . .

"I don't understand," Phyllis said, and spoke dully. "I just don't understand at all. Fern just—just fell down those awful stairs."

It became like a game of tennis, with too many players, played in the dark. "Try to remember," Bill had told them; and it seemed they tried. But all they remembered was apparently trivial.

"There was something about a boy next door," Phyllis Pitt remembered. "A good deal older than she was—than we all were. Next door to Fern. A boy named—" She moved her hands helplessly. "I've forgotten. A name I'd never heard before. Something—she said something dreadful—happened to him. I suppose he died of something."

"No," Hortense Notson said. "She told me about him. He didn't die. He went to jail. He was always saying 'oh.'" She considered. "I think," she said, "he was named Russell something." She paused again. "Never in my life, did I hear so much about people I'd never heard of. Gossip about the past."

Stanley Pitt stood up. His impatience was evident.

"Look," he said. "This is my house, Captain. These people are my guests. Is any of this badgering getting you anywhere? And . . . where is there to get? Maybe she had a heart attack. Maybe she ate something that—" He stopped, rather abruptly; rather as if he had stumbled over something.

Weigand waited, but Pitt did not continue. Then Bill said they had thought of that. The symptoms—they had all noticed the symptoms— including the dilation of the pupils, might have been due to acute food poisoning. But she had eaten almost nothing during the cocktail period. The maid who had passed canapés was sure of that. Certainly she had eaten nothing the rest had not. And she had drunk only ginger ale, from a freshly opened bottle.

"Which," Bill said, "apparently you opened, Jerry."

Jerry North ran his right hand through his hair. He looked at Bill blankly.

"Of course you did," Pam said. "So vigorously the bottle cap flew off. Don't you—"

"Oh," Jerry said. Everybody looked at him. "Is that supposed—"

But he was interrupted by Pitt, still leaning forward in his chair. "Wait," Pitt said, and put right thumb and index finger together, firmly, as if to hold a thought pinched between them. They waited.

"This place I took her to lunch," Stanley said. "It's a little place— little downstairs place, but wonderful food. I've eaten there off and on for years. But . . . I don't suppose it's too damned sanitary. Not like your labs are, Clark. And the weather's been hot. And—" He seemed to remember something else and held this new memory between thumb and finger. "Miss Hartley ate most of a bowl of ripe olives. Said she never seemed to get enough of them. And . . . isn't there something that can get into ripe olives? That can poison people?" He put the heel of one hand to his forehead. "God," he said. "Do you suppose it was that?"

"You mean food poisoning?" Weigand said. "Yes—years ago people got it from ripe olives. But not recently, that I've heard of. New methods and—"

"The olives are imported," Pitt said. "From Italy, I think. Yes. Dilated pupils—"

"Right," Bill said. "And the other symptoms match quite well. You may—"

But now he was interrupted by a uniformed policeman, who brought him a slip of paper. Bill Weigand looked at it and put it in his pocket and said, "Right," and the policeman went out again.

"Mr. Notson," Bill said, "you're production manager of the Winslow Pharmaceutical Company, aren't you?"

Notson looked blank. He said, "Sure."

"Which makes all kinds of drug products?"

Notson continued to look blank. He nodded his head.

"And Mr. Pitt," Bill Weigand said. "You're—"

He's gone off on a tangent, Pam North thought, half listening. What difference can it make that Mr. Notson makes drugs—or that Mr. Pitt tells people how to run offices and plants better—is an "efficiency engineer"? Because just a few minutes ago, somebody said something really important. Because it was wrong. Because—Oh! Pam thought. It's on the tip of my mind. If people would only be quiet, so I could think. If Bill only wouldn't go off on these—

"All kinds of drugs," Bill was saying, from his tangent, in the distance. "Including preparations containing atropine?"

She heard Clark Notson say, "Yes. Sure."

"Because," Bill said, and now Pam heard him clearly—very clearly—"Miss Hartley had been given atropine. It might have been enough to have killed her, if she had not had quick and proper treatment. She'd had enough to bring on dizziness and double vision. So that, on the verge of losing consciousness, she fell downstairs and broke her neck. Well?"

He looked around.

"The ginger ale," Jerry said. "The ginger ale I opened. That . . . opened so easily. Was that it?"

"Probably," Bill said. "The cap taken off carefully. Put back on carefully. After enough atropine sulphate had been put in. Enough to stop her remembering." Again he looked around at them; and Pam looked, too, and could see nothing—except shock—in any face. There seemed to be fear in none.

"The doctors suspected atropine from the start," Bill said, speaking slowly. "But the symptoms of atropine poisoning are very similar to those of food poisoning—or ptomaine. If she had lived to be treated, almost any physician would have diagnosed food poisoning—particularly after Mr. Pitt remembered the olives—and treated for that. Not for atropine. Since the treatments are different, she probably would not have lived." He paused. "Well," he said, "what did she remember? So that there was death for remembrance?"

Phyllis Pitt covered her eyes with both hands and shook her head slowly, dully. Hortense Notson looked at Weigand with narrowed eyes and her husband with—Pam thought—something like defiance. Stanley Pitt looked at the floor and seemed deep in thought, to be planning each thought between thumb and finger, when Weigand turned from them and said, "Yes?" to a man in civilian clothes. He went to talk briefly with the man. He returned. He said the telephone was a useful thing; he said the Centertown police were efficient.

"The boy next door," Weigand said, "was named Russell Clarkson. He was some years—fifteen, about—older than Fern Hartley. Not a boy any more, when she was in high school, but still 'the boy next door.' He did go to jail, as you said, Mrs. Notson. He helped set up a robbery of the place he worked in. A payroll messenger was killed. Clarkson got twenty years to life. And—he escaped in two years, and was never caught. And—*he was a chemist*. Mr. Notson. As you are. Mr. *Clark* Notson."

Notson was on his feet. His face was very red and he no longer looked younger than he was. He said, "You're crazy! I can prove—" His voice rose until he was shouting across the few feet between himself and Weigand.

And then it came to Pam—came with a kind of violent clarity.

"Wait, Bill. *Wait!*" Pam shouted. "It wasn't 'ohs' at all. Not *saying* them. That's what was wrong."

They were listening. Bill was listening.

Then Pam pointed at Hortense. "You," she said, "the first time you said *doing* ohs. Not saying 'Oh.' You even asked how one *did* an oh. We thought it was the—the o-h kind of O. But—it was the *letter* O. And—*look at him now!* He's doing them now. *With his fingers.*"

And now she pointed at Stanley Pitt, who was forming the letter O with the thumb and index finger of his right hand; who now, violently, closed into fists his betraying hands. A shudder ran through his body. But he spoke quietly, without looking up from the floor.

"She hadn't quite remembered," he said, as if talking of something which had happened a long time ago. "Not quite." And he put the thumb and index finger tip to tip again, to measure the smallness of a margin. "But—she would have. She remembered everything. I've changed a lot and she was a little girl, but . . ."

He looked at his hands. "I've always done that, I guess," he said. He spread his fingers and looked at his hands. "Once it came up," he said, "there would be fingerprints. So—I had to try." He looked up, then, at his wife. "You see, Phyl, that I had to try?"

Phyllis covered her face with her hands.

After a moment Stanley Pitt looked again at his hands, spreading them in front of him. Slowly he began to bring together the fingertips and thumbtips of both hands; and he studied the movements of his fingers intently, as if they were new to him. He sat so, his hands moving in patterns they had never been able to forget, until Weigand told him it was time to go.

THE MONKEY MURDER
Stuart Palmer
Detective: Hildegarde Withers

CHARLES STUART Palmer (1905-1968), a descendent of colonists who settled in Salem, Massachusetts, in 1634, led a picaresque American life before becoming a successful writer, holding such jobs as iceman, sailor, publicity man, apple picker, newspaper reporter, taxi driver, poet, editor, and ghost-writer.

The Penguin Pool Murder (1931) introduced the popular spinster-sleuth Hildegarde Withers. Formerly a schoolteacher, the thin, angular, horse-faced snoop devoted her energy to aiding Inspector Oliver Piper of the New York City Police Department, driving him slightly crazy in the process. She is noted for her odd, even eccentric, choice of hats. Palmer stated that she was based on his high school English teacher, Miss Fern Hackett, and on his father.

There were thirteen more novels in the Miss Withers series, the last, *Hildegarde Withers Makes the Scene* (1969), being completed by Fletcher Flora after Palmer died. There also were three short story collections, with the first, *The Riddles of Hildegarde Withers* (1947), being selected as a *Queen's Quorum* title. It was followed by *The Monkey Murder and Other Hildegarde Withers Stories* (1950), and *People vs. Withers and Malone* (1963), in conjunction with Craig Rice, which also featured her series character, John J. Malone.

The film version of *The Penguin Pool Murder* was released in 1932 and spurred five additional comic mystery films, the first three featuring Edna May Oliver in a perfect casting decision, followed by Helen Broderick, and the last, *Forty Naughty Girls* (1937), with Zasu Pitts. Piper was played by James Gleason in all films.

The success of the series gained Palmer employment as a scriptwriter with thirty-seven mystery screenplays to his credit, mostly for such popular series as Bulldog Drummond, the Lone Wolf, and the Falcon.

"The Monkey Murder" was originally published in the January 1947 issue of *Ellery Queen's Mystery Magazine*; it was first collected in *The Monkey Murder and Other Hildegarde Withers Stories* (New York, Bestseller, 1950).

The Monkey Murder
By Stuart Palmer

AFTER-THEATER CROWDS were flowing sluggishly around Times Square, and then suddenly an eddy was formed by the halting of a pugnacious little Irishman, who stared back over his shoulder. "A fine thing!" observed Inspector Oscar Piper with some bitterness, "when murderers walk the streets and thumb their noses at the skipper of the homicide squad!"

"Oscar!" gasped Miss Hildegarde Withers, clutching her rakish bonnet and peering into the crowd. "Did he really? That nice, neat man?"

"That nice, neat man committed a nice, neat murder, and now he's going scot-free, and he—well, maybe he didn't actually thumb his nose but he smiled and tipped his hat. That was George Wayland, the wife-strangler, blast him!"

The old-maid schoolteacher firmly gripped her friend's arm, steering him down a side street and into a smoky little basement restaurant. She ordered a bottle of chianti and two plates of spaghetti with mushrooms, and then demanded to know what this was all about.

"You were up at Cape Cod when it happened," confessed the Inspector. "This fellow Wayland killed his wife for her money, trying to cloud the issue with a phony religious-cult background. The body of Janet Wayland, a good-looking, rich, and slightly silly dame of about thirty-eight, was found mother-naked in the back bedroom of a house she owned, up on East Sixty-fourth. The place had been vacant for a year—her husband had lived at a hotel while she was away—and there weren't any servants yet, but they had moved back in, anyway, a few days before. The woman was lying on a sort of sacrificial altar, tied hand and foot. The room was fixed up so that it looked like the nightmare of a Hollywood set-designer for B-budget horror pictures. And the idol above the altar was a big ugly stuffed monkey, its tail extending into a length of rawhide which had been soaked and then allowed to dry and tighten slowly around the woman's throat. You can look at the official photos if you have a strong enough stomach."

"Please leave my stomach out of this," Miss Withers said primly. "What a weird, unbelievable sort of murder!"

"That kind we usually crack wide open in a couple of days," the Inspector told her. "Usually the hard ones are easy. When we found out that Wayland stood to inherit more than two hundred grand from his wife, and that they'd been rifting—or at least that she had just returned from a year's marital vacation in California—that seemed to cinch it. To top that, we learned that Wayland had been seen, in his wife's absence, running around with a big sexy Swede secretary, a luscious piece. That was the clincher. We arrested Wayland for murder."

"But what went wrong? Wouldn't he talk?"

"He talked our arm off. Stuck to his story that he returned from a business trip to Albany and that as soon as he got in the house he smelled the incense and heard the music. There was an automatic pho-nograph playing one record over and over, right there in the murder room. Oriental music, by some Russian. . . ."

"Rimsky-Korsakoff? Probably 'The Young Prince and the Young Princess,' from *Scheherazade*." Miss Withers hummed a bit of it.

"Something like that. Anyway, he claimed that he had to break down the door of the room to get in. The neighbors heard a crash, just a minute before he rushed out yelling bloody murder. The door had actually been bolted on the inside—we can spot things like that—and the window was locked too. Janet Wayland had been dead for about two hours then, and he claimed he had just got in at Grand Central. He even had the right seat-stub, too—but he could have picked up one of those at the station without ever getting on a train. We figured he'd bolted the door and broken it in some time before the murder, and then set up the door and crashed it again to make the proper noise at the right time."

The schoolteacher frowned. "But Oscar—"

"Let me give you the rest of it. Wayland yelled for the lie-detector test as soon as we picked him up, but it came out haywire. He showed a guilty reaction to some of the key questions, but he gave the same reaction to three or four of the harmless ones—so that was that. We had to let him cool."

"And no doubt started to bear down on the lady in the case?"

Inspector Piper grinned. "You know our methods. We began to dig around, and we turned one of our lady-killing cops loose on the secretary. Inga Rasmussen worked as a secretary in the main office of the company where Wayland is a traveling salesman—he makes a couple of hundred a week peddling big mining machinery all over the country. Lieutenant Bartz gave the girl quite a play, but after a week he reported that as far as he could see there was nothing in it. She had only gone out with Wayland because she was new in town and didn't know anybody else. It had only been dinner and dancing anyhow, and while Wayland hadn't admitted having a wife out in California, he also didn't make any more than the usual polite passes in the taxicab on the way to take her home."

"I wouldn't even know about those," confessed Miss Withers with a faint note of regret in her voice. "But do go on."

"That's about it. We couldn't trap Wayland in any important lie. We couldn't trace any of the phony theatrical junk in the murder room, but traveling like he did, he could have picked it up here and there. He had motive and opportunity, so we piled up what evidence we had and then the district attorney refused to take it to the Grand Jury. His objection was that George Wayland, from everything we could find out about him, is such a simple, ordinary, unimaginative guy. He is Mister Average American—likes baseball, smokes popular cigarettes, reads the front page of the newspaper and then turns back to the comics. He goes to the movies to see Betty Grable and Ann Sheridan, he bets on Joe Louis and the Yankees, orders ham and eggs or steak in a restaurant, drinks beer or bourbon, and goes to church once a year on Easter. . . ."

"I don't follow," the schoolteacher interrupted. "Many murderers were average citizens. Look at Judd Gray, and Crippen—"

"Wait. According to the D.A., and I'm inclined to agree, the average citizen commits the average murder. He uses a gun or a knife if he's a man, a sash-weight or poison if he's a woman. I mean—"

"I know what you mean. Something more has gone into the composition of Janet Wayland's murder than two blockheads to kill and be killed, to paraphrase De Quincey. Something unlike Wayland—you admit he might commit a murder, but it wouldn't be the kind of murder this is, even though you're sure that somehow he did it anyway!"

Piper nodded. "The murder was out of character. Any good defense attorney could point out Wayland as the average man and then ask a jury if they believed he'd think of strangling anybody with the tail of an East-Indian monkey-god. That, plus the locked-room thing, would get him off, probably. See what I mean?"

"I do indeed. But where did Wayland get the idea?"

"Must have read it somewhere. But where? Yet he did it. I've been a cop long enough to smell a real *wrongo,* and he's one."

Miss Withers sipped the last of her wine, which she had liberally diluted with seltzer. "You seem to be upon the horns of a dilemma, Oscar. I'm not vain enough to think that I can perform any miracles at this late date, but I'd like to pay a call on the lady in the case, if you happen to have her address."

The Inspector picked up the check. "Go ahead," he told her. "But you'll find that angle was very thoroughly covered."

The next day was Sunday, and shortly after noon Miss Hildegarde Withers emerged from the subway at Sheridan Square, once the haunt of artists, writers, and madcaps, and nowadays trod by more prosaic though no doubt better-shod feet. The address was on Minetta Lane, which she located with some difficulty. She climbed to the top floor and leaned heavily upon the bell, with no results. Then she knocked. A female voice from within cried "Just a minute!" and then the door was opened by a tall, flushed girl in rumpled green silk lounging pajamas. "Yes?" she said, in a pleasant but somewhat flat middle-western accent. "What is it?"

"Miss Rasmussen? My name is Withers, Hildegarde Withers. Inspector Piper, down at headquarters, suggested that I call on you for a little chat. Completely unofficial, of course. I hope it's not an inconvenient time?"

"Not at all, come on in. You'll have to excuse the mess the place is in, but a girl friend of mine was here for breakfast, and I haven't straightened up yet. Sunday is my lazy day, you know."

The room was small, with high narrow windows, and had been cheerfully if somewhat artily furnished with rattan and chintz and cheap brassware. Inga indicated the couch. "Do sit down while I fix myself up, I won't be a minute."

If it was lipstick that the girl intended to put on, she was already wearing a smudge of it on the lobe of her left ear. Miss Withers sniffed disapprovingly, but all the same she was resolved that if she had any choice in her next reincarnation, she was going to insist on red-gold hair, apple-blossom skin, and eyes like drowned stars. She sat there quietly until Inga returned. "No doubt you think I'm a meddlesome character," the schoolteacher began, "but after all, a woman was murdered—"

Inga flashed: "If you're harping on the Wayland thing, I never saw Mrs. Wayland and I'm sorry I ever saw Mr. Wayland and I'm not going to be badgered about it any longer!"

Miss Withers nodded. She looked at the twin wet rings on the glass top of the coffee table, then poked at the edge of the divan cushion where had been spilled some thirty-five cents in change, a small jack-knife, and a silver cigarette lighter. Then she sniffed the air judicially. "Your girl friend smokes a pipe, doesn't she?"

Inga didn't answer, but her eyes flashed a brighter green. "Why don't you ask him to come out of the bedroom?" the schoolteacher continued quietly. "The three of us can have a nice heart-to-heart talk."

"Okay!" blazed the girl. She crossed the room with a stride like an Amazon's, and flung open the bedroom door. A man was standing there, a little foolishly, but Miss Withers saw with a start of surprise that it was not George Wayland. It was a young, very handsome police officer, in his shirt-sleeves.

"Gracious," she murmured. "If it isn't Lieutenant Bartz!"

The girl seized his arm and drew him into the room. "Tommy, make her stop asking questions and go away!"

The Lieutenant looked unhappy. "I don't see—"

"The murder of Janet Wayland is still in the open file, young man. And didn't the Inspector tell me that you had dropped this line of investigation?"

He smiled sheepishly. "I'm not on duty now, ma'am. We—we sorta got engaged, Inga and I. We can't do much about it now, though, on account of it isn't ethical for me to marry any suspect—I mean, anyone involved in a case, at least not until it's settled. You won't go telling Inspector Piper, will you?"

Miss Withers was beaming. "How perfectly romantic! So policemen do have their softer moments! I was beginning to wonder. The Inspector only proposed to me once, years ago, and he took that back before I could accept him." She congratulated them both.

"I hope now," Inga said, "you'll believe that I hardly knew that awful Wayland man. If the case could only be settled—"

Lieutenant Bartz put his arm around her. "Inga is just dying to cook my breakfasts every morning," he said. "And fight with me for the comic section."

"We'll have *two* papers!" Inga said fondly.

"And you'll sit there and tell me what you dreamed the night before." He turned. "Inga always has the cutest dreams."

"My father," Miss Withers advised him, "always said he would rather hear it rain on a tin roof than hear a woman tell her dreams. But young love—ah, me! And all that stands in the way is the specter of Mrs. Wayland, isn't it?"

"If you're going to try to take that case out of moth-balls," the Lieutenant offered, "I'd like to help in any way I can." Inga nodded too.

"Then let's put our heads together and figure out a way for me to pay a call on George Wayland," Miss Withers said. There was an immediate huddle, with the Lieutenant suggesting that she could say she was a newspaper reporter, and Inga offering the idea of Miss Withers claiming to be a member of some religious cult that the late Mrs. Wayland had belonged to, out in California.

"I'm afraid I'm not the type for a reporter, and Wayland is no doubt allergic to them anyway by this time. And I couldn't pass as a devoted follower of the *swami* anyway. . . ."

Lieutenant Bartz snapped his fingers. "I happen to know that Wayland is trying to cash in on his wife's property. The house is going to be listed for sale, so why not pretend you're a buyer?"

"Say no more, young man!" Miss Withers took her departure, but she was only halfway down the stairs when she heard the sound of young, impetuous feet, and Inga came up beside her wearing a raincoat.

"I'll walk with you as far as the corner," the girl offered. "I want to apologize for the way I talked when you first came in, and anyway I want to bring back some ice cream. Tommy loves *gelati*—that's the Italian ice cream that's so crisp and creamy."

The schoolteacher, a little touched, said that was all right. "Why didn't Tommy come too?"

"I set him to washing dishes," Inga confided. "You've got to get a man trained early the right way, I always say."

They walked on, and said another goodbye outside the little Neapolitan confectionery on the corner of the Square. "Be happy, my child," said Miss Withers. "You've had a very narrow escape."

Inga nodded slowly. "But I still can't believe Mr. Wayland did it! He was such a gentleman—and he *wasn't the type!*"

Miss Withers rode on uptown, then took the shuttle to Fifth and climbed aboard a north-bound bus. She got off at Sixty-fourth and walked east, wondering just what type George Wayland really was, and how he would receive her. The whole thing, as it turned out, was ridiculously easy, almost too easy in fact. Wayland himself answered the door when she rang the bell of the neat four-story brownstone, and seemed to have no reluctance whatever about showing the house to a prospective buyer with a very weak story.

His smile was easy and warming. Miss Withers guessed that he was around thirty-five, a little on the plump side but well-tanned and dressed with extreme neatness. He might easily have been the man behind the railing in her bank, the vestryman at church, or the one who helped her with her bundles on a Pullman.

Wayland talked a good deal, and a little fast, but that might or might not be a sign of nervousness. "Here's the living room," he was saying. "The furniture's for sale too, if you're interested."

Miss Withers was emphatically not interested in Italian Rennaissance with all its dust-catching heavy carvings, but she nodded pleasantly. The downstairs rooms all seemed furnished with more money than taste, the pictures being reproductions of such traditional works of art as *The Blue Boy*, *Age of Innocence*, and *The Horse Fair*. There were few books, and those were sets of Victorian novelists, in very good bindings.

On the second floor he displayed two front bedrooms, one obviously his own for there was an expensive leather toilet kit on the chest of drawers, silver brushes, and numerous bottles of cologne and shaving lotion nearby, and a heavy silk dressing-gown on the bed. Wayland led the way toward the rear, where one doorway gaped wide like a missing tooth.

Wayland paused for a moment. "This door," he said, "is to be replaced." He made no sign of entering, but Miss Withers sailed blithely past him. The room, however, showed no clues. It was completely bare, stripped down to the baseboards. The one window, opening above the sloping roof of the kitchen, had a heavy iron grille built into the original stone—nothing larger than a cat could have entered or left that way.

Miss Withers thought that she had never seen a less productive scene-of-the-crime. She followed Wayland to the third floor, where there was nothing much of interest, and then back down again. "Now we'll have a look at the cellar," the man said. And he opened a little door which led down out of the butler's pantry.

The air which rose from the cellar's depths was dank and musty and cold, yet with a trace of perfume. For the first time Miss Hildegarde Withers felt an unpleasant chill of apprehension. Upstairs was one thing, but going down into the semi-darkness of a basement with a man supposed to have killed one woman in this house already—

Her agile mind devised all sorts of excuses. She could say that she had to run along, that her friends were waiting, that the house was too large. . . .

"'One who never turned his back, but marched breast forward!'" she quoted. After all, Wayland was no more dangerous in one place than another. She started, a little gingerly, down the stairs.

Down below there was a great pile of paper cartons, some neatly tied with string and some open and overflowing. Miss Withers saw women's dresses, shoes, underwear, and all the rest of it—a pitiful exhibit.

"I've asked the Goodwill people to pick that stuff up," Wayland was saying. "Just some old clothes that I have no use for now." Miss Withers followed him obediently onward, gathering from her quick glimpse of the debris that the late Mrs. Wayland had been addicted to very high heels and to the scent of gardenia. She had also, from the look of her girdles, been very fat around the middle. Wayland was at this moment delivering a lecture about construction and termites and water-heaters, but the schoolteacher only nodded from time to time. She peered into the shadows underneath the stair, noticing a rough shelf on which had been neatly arranged a row of old magazines dating, she noted, as far back as 1934. Most of them seemed to deal with women's fashions, a few with travel, and there was a long row of pulps, in the adventure and outdoor category.

Wayland saw what had caught her eyes, and came back to lift one of the periodicals from the rack, blow the dust from it, and shake his head. "I was always going to re-read some of these. But I guess there's nothing deader than old magazines. . . ."

Miss Withers was forcibly reminded of something *much* deader, when her eyes fell upon the ruins of a paneled door which had been thrown into a corner. It certainly had been most thoroughly smashed, and the marks where the bolt had torn away were clearly visible. Behind this door Janet Wayland had been murdered. . . .

"There's one thing I may as well tell you," Wayland said. "It may queer the sale of the house. My wife died here, in fact she was murdered—"

"Yes, I know," said Miss Withers, backing away a little.

"Oh, then you *did* read the papers!"

She nodded. "But I'm not at all fidgety about such things. I imagine that if most old houses could talk, they'd have a tale of violence and tragedy to tell."

He nodded agreeably. "I never want to see the place again, of course. I'm anxious to sell it, and use the money in trying to trace down the murderer of my wife. The police are helpless, but I intend to try the big private agencies. . . ." He shook his head. "But of course that wouldn't interest you, except that I'm in a position to accept any halfway-reasonable offer for the house."

They went on back past the magazines, past the pitiful heap of the dead woman's clothing, and up the steep stair. "Well," said George Wayland, "that's the works. You've seen everything. *What do you think about it?*"

His eyes met hers directly, but they were wary, amused, and almost teasing. The schoolteacher suddenly realized what he was thinking. He hadn't for a moment been fooled about her being a possible purchaser. In some odd way, perhaps almost in spite of himself, he was letting her know that he had murdered his wife, that he was getting away with it, and that he dared her to say or do anything.

"Think it over," Wayland continued. "You don't have to make up your mind today." He laughed, and his laughter to Miss Withers seemed as hard and brittle as the breaking of wood—or the crackle of thorns under a pot. Somehow she managed to keep from screaming, to hold herself from bursting into panicky flight, until he had opened the front door for her once more. "Thank you for coming," said George Wayland. "And *do* remember me to your friend the Inspector."

The door closed, and Miss Withers scuttled down the street, her feathers ruffled, for all the world like a scandalized hen. "Laugh in my face, will he? The nerve of him!" A moment or so later she almost burst out laughing, realizing that her tone had almost exactly been that of the Inspector last night when he complained that Wayland had thumbed his nose at him.

But how had the man known who she was? He couldn't have remembered her from that chance encounter on the crowded street. Unless he had eyes in the back of his head, or was in league with the devil. Of course, according to one way of thinking, *all* murderers were in league with the devil. . . .

The Inspector dropped over, later that night, to find Miss Withers perched before her aquarium of tropical fish, so deeply immersed in that miniature world that she had to shake her head violently for a moment to get back to everyday. It was a sure sign that she was in mental turmoil.

She told him of her call on Inga Rasmussen, leaving out for the moment any mention of the Lieutenant, and also told him of her later venture into the house on East Sixty-fourth. "I see now what you mean about that man, Oscar," she admitted. "He killed her, and he's laughing!"

"He'll have something else to laugh about," the Inspector informed her wearily as he sank into a chair. "*The Dispatch*, it seems, is going to nail my hide to the wall in its Sunday section next week. They've dug up a lot of stuff on the Wayland murder, and they've stolen or faked some photos of the room. 'Police Powerless in Weird Love Cult Killing'—you know the sort of thing. It embarrasses the mayor, and he blasts at the Commissioner, and the Commish blasts at me. It's a hot seat to be sitting in. If Wayland would make just one mistake—"

"He doesn't look like a man who makes mistakes," Miss Withers said. "If only we could make one *for* him!" She provided the unhappy policeman with coffee and doughnuts, and insisted upon his smoking one of his fat green-brown perfectos, usually verboten in her vicinity. "Cheer up, Oscar. In a week, anything can happen!"

"Sure—I can break my leg," he said dismally.

"I might have an idea," she continued hopefully. "I do believe I feel one coming on!"

"Heaven save us from any more of your ideas," Piper said ungallantly. "I've got headaches enough as it is."

All the same, when the days of the week slipped by without any word from the lady who usually referred to herself as self-appointed gadfly to the police department, the Inspector began to get restive. He had postponed warning the powers upstairs about the forthcoming newspaper article, hoping against hope that something would happen. On Friday he called the press room downstairs, located the reporter who had tipped him off, and demanded to know what was the latest moment at which the article could be jerked. "It's put to bed at five o'clock tonight," he was told.

"Thanks," said the Inspector grimly, and then put in a call for Miss Withers. "Just wondered how you are, and what's new?" he opened.

"Oh, Oscar! One of my guppies is having young—or what *do* you call baby fish?"

"Puppies!" cried Inspector Oscar Piper, a little hysterically. "Guppies' puppies! Of all the—"

"No need to shout. By the way, I've been giving some thought to that other matter. Something you said the other night gave me an idea. Of course it all depends on one thing and another—"

"What things? I sit here on a hot stove, and you double-talk!"

"Oh, whether there is a pay-phone in the ice cream store, and what kind of a job they did for me out at the printing plant at Dunellen, New Jersey, and what time the Goodwill Industries truck gets around—"

He began to burble again, but she promised to call back, and hung up.

A few moments later Miss Withers's phone rang again. This time it was Lieutenant Bartz. "Just wondered if you were getting anywhere with your sleuthing," he said cheerily. "Anything I can do to help? I'm worried—"

"I'm sure you both are," Miss Withers said cryptically.

"That's right. Inga and I are very anxious, because if the case doesn't get settled, why then we can't get married."

"Exactly. Believe me, you'll be the first to know. Or almost the first, anyway." Miss Withers went back to her aquarium, where the female guppy was having trouble with her eleventh offspring. The vivip-arous mite finally had to be removed by a pair of tweezers, its mother wrapped in wet cotton and then replaced in the tank, whereupon she immediately produced numbers twelve and thirteen.

It was shortly after four o'clock when the schoolteacher received her long-awaited call. "This is Mac speakin'," came the querulous, un-steady voice of a lifelong alcoholic. "It's all set, ma'am. We made the pick-up this aft'noon."

"Well, thank heavens!" Miss Hildegarde Withers immediately seized her capacious handbag, her umbrella, and then jammed on a headpiece which looked, as the Inspector had once said, as if it had been designed by somebody who had heard of hats but never actually seen one.

Her trip downtown, and her entrance into the office of the Inspec-tor, were breathless. The little man looked up from his desk, which was littered with half-smoked cigars. "Come down to say goodbye, Hildegarde? Because Monday morning I expect to be sitting at a pre-cinct desk—"

"Nonsense, Oscar. You're not going to be *busted*, to use your own ungrammatical term. Because you're going out right now and arrest George Wayland for the murder of his wife."

"Oh, I am?" The Inspector snorted.

She nodded brightly. "And while you're there, go down in the cellar and pick up a copy of one of the magazines on the cellar shelf. It is, if I remember correctly, *Tropical Adventure Tales* for October, 1939, and there is something on page twenty-six that you simply must read. The district attorney will be interested in it later, but right now you must read it out loud to Mr. Wayland, after you have him here."

Inspector Piper stared at her, hard. "On the level?"

She nodded. "Cross my heart."

The Inspector hesitated, shrugged, and then suddenly went into action. As soon as he had left the office, Miss Withers picked up the telephone. "Inspector Piper wants you to locate Lieutenant Bartz," she said sweetly to the man at the police switchboard, "and ask him to come down at once . . . because there's good news for him!"

Then she calmly sat down, having sowed the wind, to await the whirlwind. The hands of the clock were at quarter to five when the cavalcade arrived—first the Inspector, then George Wayland fuming and spluttering between two uniformed patrolmen, and finally a pair of plainclothes detectives, one of whom bore a copy of a battered pulp magazine with a lurid cover.

Wayland saw Miss Withers, and bowed. "Now I begin to see—" he began bitterly.

"Not yet, but you will," the Inspector promised. "Sit down, Mr. Wayland, and I'll read you a bedtime story—out of a magazine which four witnesses saw me take out of your cellar. Let's see—page twenty-six—here it is." Piper cleared his throat. "*I peered through a tangle of vines past Ali, my trusty gun-bearer—*"

Wayland yawned. "What is this, Inspector? Isn't this cruel and in-human treatment or something?"

"*—past Ali, my trusty gun-bearer,*" continued Piper determinedly, "*and there by the flickering light of the jungle fires I saw the Witch-men dancing their ceremonial dance of death. Their bodies were painted in hid-eous, grotesque colors, and as they chanted they raised their arms to the vast looming statue of Hanuman, the monkey-god. . . .*"

Miss Withers noticed that Wayland had stopped yawning. In the background Lieutenant Bartz, with Inga clinging to his arm, came into the room and stopped stock-still near the door.

The Inspector's flat, Brooklynese tones contrasted strangely with the purple prose he was reading, but he held his audience spellbound all the same. "*Then I gave a shudderin' gasp of horror, for I could see Karen, her ivory-white almost nude body stretched out on the sack—the sacrificial block—so that she could move neither hand nor foot. Her pale lovely face was upraised to the idol, frozen wit' terror. The music rose to a cress—crescendo, pulsing in my veins. Swirls of incense from the stolen temple vessels rose around the tortured girl, but the worst was yet to come. No, no, this could not be! The Thing, the statue of Hanuman, the monkey-god was alive! Its tail was moving like a sinuous, hairy snake, moving down slowly to wrap itself around the throat of the helpless girl! To be continued in our next issue.'"*

Wayland had struggled to his feet. "It's a *lie!*" he screamed. "It's a frame-up! I never read that magazine—"

"You never *remembered* reading it—you never remembered where you got the idea for the murder, but you were unlucky enough to keep the proof that will send you to the Chair!" Piper held the magazine, spread open, in front of the prisoner. "In your own cellar, you mugg!"

The sweat was pouring from Wayland's round face, but he made one last feeble effort. "But the door—you admit I had to break down the door—"

"You broke it down *before* the murder was committed—and then set it up again so you could smash it at the right time, with witnesses listening!"

The fight was gone out of the man now. He held his head in his hands, sobbing a little. Miss Withers leaned over and whispered something to the Inspector. "What?" he cried.

"But, of course, Oscar. He couldn't have done it alone! Somebody had to—"

"No, no! I was alone!" cried Wayland. "Inga didn't—"

"Shut up, you fool!" Inga cried, tearing herself away from the young detective and hovering over Wayland like an avenging Fury. "You weak, sniveling fool! They've trapped you!" She stopped suddenly, biting her hand. The room was still.

"I was about to say," continued Miss Withers, "that somebody had to be on the inside of that room, to bolt the door for him so he could break it down. And what is more likely than that it should be the young lady who rushed out so fast to telephone a warning to him when she heard I was coming to snoop around?"

"Prove that in court!" Inga cried.

"Your mistake," Miss Withers advised her, "was made when you set your fiancé to washing the dishes so you could get out and make your phone call. No girl in her right mind would do a thing like that *before* she had the young man signed, sealed, and delivered."

Then everyone started talking at once. The Inspector took over, very swiftly and efficiently, at that point, and Wayland and Inga Rasmussen were hustled off down the hall in different directions. After a little while Piper returned to his office, mopping his forehead. Miss Withers sat there quite alone, reading *Tropical Adventure Tales.*

He nodded jubilantly. "They're both confessing a mile a minute, each trying to put the blame on the other one. Even if they repudiate the confessions later, we've got more than we need."

"Red-heads are hot-headed," Miss Withers observed. "I counted on that." She looked at her watch. "Five-thirty. I'm sorry there isn't time to stop that feature story."

"Huh? Oh, that won't matter. The editor will just look like a fool, panning us for a murder that was all washed up two days before." He looked around. "Where's young Bartz?"

"Gone to turn in his badge, for being made such a fool of. She never intended to marry him, but it was a wonderful cover-up for her while Wayland cashed in on their loot. And she had a direct pipe-line for information on what the police were doing on the case."

Piper grinned. "I'll let him sweat for a day or two, and then reprimand him and forget it. I think I'll call the boys in the press room and give them the story. You'll get credit, too—that was darn smart of you, memorizing the magazines in the cellar and then getting back copies and reading through all of them to uncover the inspiration for the murder." He looked up. "Hey, where you going?"

"I was just getting near the exit," Miss Withers said softly. "So I can make a run for it after I confess that the magazine was a *fake*. Oscar, I wrote that story myself, and paid to have it set in type and bound into a copy of an old pulp magazine similar to the ones in Wayland's cellar. I thought he wouldn't remember for sure—and you said if we could only prove where he got the idea—"

"Go on," commanded the Inspector grimly.

"So I knew the Goodwill people were going to pick up some stuff in Wayland's cellar, and I got in touch with a reformed bum who works for them—I used to give him dimes now and then—and he planted the magazine this afternoon!"

"Great Judas Priest!" whispered the Inspector.

"So we'll *never* know where Wayland actually did get the idea, but I happen to know that Inga likes to tell her dreams at the breakfast table. It might very well have been one of her nightmares—a nightmare that came true!"

She adjusted her hat so that it perched a little more precariously than before, and started out. "Come back here!" the Inspector commanded.

Miss Withers smiled feebly. "You're not furious with me?"

"Furious?" The Inspector was sheepish. "I feel like eating crow."

She beamed at him. "Make it chicken, and I'll rush home and put on the dotted Swiss and join you. Shall we say Fourchette's at eight?"

THE ADVENTURE OF
THE AFRICAN TRAVELER
Ellery Queen
Detective: Ellery Queen

As ANTHONY Boucher once wrote in *The New York Times*, Ellery Queen *is* the American detective story, the creator and defender of the fair play mystery puzzle.

In what remains one of the most brilliant marketing decisions of all time, the two Brooklyn cousins who collaborated under the pseudonym Ellery Queen, Frederic Dannay (born Daniel Nathan) (1905-1982) and Manfred B(ennington) Lee (born Manford Lepofsky) (1905-1971), also named their detective Ellery Queen. They reasoned that if readers forgot the name of the author, *or* the name of the character, they might remember the other. It worked, as Ellery Queen is counted among the handful of best known names in the history of mystery fiction.

Lee was a full collaborator on the fiction created as Ellery Queen, but Dannay on his own was also one of the most important figures in the mystery world. He founded *Ellery Queen's Mystery Magazine* in 1941 and it remains, more than seventy years later, the most significant periodical in the genre. He also formed one of the first great collections of detective fiction first editions, the rare contents leading to reprinted stories in the magazines and anthologies he edited, which are among the best ever produced, most notably *101 Years' Entertainment* (1941), which gets my vote as the greatest mystery anthology ever published.

Dannay also produced such landmark reference books as *Queen's Quorum* (1951), a listing and appreciation of the 106 (later expanded to 125) most important short story collections in the genre, and *The Detective Short Story* (1942), a bibliography of all the collections Dannay had identified up to the publication date. More than a dozen movies were based on Queen books, there were several radio and television shows as well as comics; it was not far-fetched to describe the ubiquitous Ellery Queen in the 1930s, 1940s, and 1950s as the personification of the American detective story.

"The Adventure of the African Traveler" was originally published in *The Adventures of Ellery Queen* (New York, Frederick A. Stokes, 1934).

The Adventure of the African Traveler
By Ellery Queen

MR. ELLERY Queen, wrapped loosely in English tweeds and reflections, proceeded—in a manner of speaking—with effort along the eighth-floor corridor of the Arts Building, that sumptuous citadel of the University. The tweeds were pure Bond Street, for Ellery was ever the sartorial fellow; whereas the reflections were Americanese, Ellery's ears being filled with the peculiar patois of young male and female collegians, and he himself having been Harvard, 'Teen.

This, he observed severely to himself as he lanced his way with the ferrule of his stick through a brigade of yelling students, was higher education in New York! He sighed, his silver eyes tender behind the lenses of his *pince-nez;* for, possessing that acute faculty of observation so essential to his business of studying criminal phenomena, he could not help but note the tea-rose complexions, the saucy eyes, and the osier figures of various female students in his path. His own Alma Mater, he reflected gloomily, paragon of the educational virtues that it was, might have been far better off had it besprinkled its muscular classes with nice-smelling co-eds like these—yes, indeed!

Shaking off these unprofessorial thoughts, Mr. Ellery Queen edged gingerly through a battalion of giggling girls and approached Room 824, his destination, with dignity.

He halted. A tall and handsome and fawn-eyed young woman was leaning against the closed door, so obviously lying in wait for him that he began, under the buckling tweeds, to experience a—good lord!—a trepidation. Leaning, in fact, on the little placard which read:

CRIMINOLOGY, APPLIED

MR. QUEEN

This was, of course, sacrilege. . . . The fawn-eyes looked up at him soulfully, with admiration, almost with reverence. What did a member of the faculty do in such a predicament? Ellery wondered with a muted groan. Ignore the female person, speak to her firmly—?

The decision was wrested from his hands and, so to speak, placed on his arm. The brigand grasped his left biceps with devotional vigor and said in fluty tones: "You're Mr. Ellery Queen, himself, aren't you?

"I *knew* you were. You've the nicest eyes. Such a queer color. Oh, it's going to be *thrilling*, Mr. Queen!"

"I beg your pardon."

"Oh, I didn't say, did I?" The hand, which he observed with some astonishment was preposterously small, released his tingling biceps. She said sternly, as if in some way he had fallen in her estimation: "And you're the famous detective. Hmm. Another illusion blasted. . . . Old Icky sent me, of course."

"Old *Icky?*"

"You don't know even that. Heavens! Old Icky is Professor Ickthorpe, B.A., M.A., Ph.D., and goodness knows what else."

"Ah!" said Ellery. "I begin to understand."

"And high time, too," said the young woman severely. "Furthermore, Old Icky is my father, do you see. . . . " She became all at once very shy, or so Ellery reasoned, for the black lashes with their impossible sweep dropped suddenly to veil eyes of the ultimate brownness.

"I do see, Miss Ickthorpe." Ickthorpe! "I see all too clearly. Because Professor Ickthorpe—ah—inveigled me into giving this fantastic course, because you are Professor Ickthorpe's daughter, you think you may wheedle your way into my group. Fallacious reasoning," said Ellery, and planted his stick like a standard on the floor. "I think not. No."

Her slipper-toe joggled his stick unexpectedly, and he flailed wildly to keep from falling. "Do come off your perch, Mr. Queen. . . . There! That's settled. Shall we go in, Mr. Queen? Such a nice name."

"But—"

"Icky has arranged things, bless him." "I refuse abso—"

"The Bursar has been paid his filthy lucre. I have my B.A., and I'm just dawdling about here working for my Master's. I'm really very intelligent. Oh, come on—don't be so professorish. You're much too nice a young man, and your *devastating* silv'ry eyes—"

"Oh, very well," said Ellery, suddenly pleased with himself. "Come along."

It was a small seminar room, containing a long table flanked with chairs. Two young men rose, rather respectfully, Ellery thought. They seemed surprised but not too depressed at the vision of Miss Ickthorpe, who was evidently a notorious character. One of them bounded forward and pumped Ellery's hand.

"Mr. Queen! I'm Burrows, John Burrows. Decent of you to pick me and Crane out of that terrific bunch of would-be manhunters." He was a nice young fellow, Ellery decided, with bright eyes and a thin intelligent, face.

"Decent of your instructors and record, Burrows, I'd say. . . . And you're Walter Crane, of course?"

The second young man shook Ellery's hand decorously, as if it were a rite; he was tall, broad, and studious-looking in a pleasant way. "I am, sir. Degree in chemistry. I'm really interested in what you and the Professor are attempting to do."

"Splendid. Miss Ickthorpe—rather unexpectedly—is to be the fourth member of our little group," said Ellery. "Rather unexpectedly! Well, let's sit down and talk this over."

Crane and Burrows flung themselves into chairs, and the young woman seated herself demurely, Ellery threw hat and stick into a corner, clasped his hands on the bare table, and looked at the white ceiling. One must begin. . . . "This is all rather nonsensical, you know, and yet there's something solid in it. Professor Ickthorpe came to me some time ago with an idea. He had heard of my modest achievements in solving crimes by pure analysis, and he thought it might be interesting to develop the faculty of detection by deduction in young university students. I wasn't so sure, having been a university student myself."

"We're rather on the brainy side these days," said Miss Ickthorpe.

"Hmm. That remains to be seen," said Ellery dryly. "I suppose it's against the rules, but I can't think without tobacco. You may smoke, gentlemen. A cigarette, Miss Ickthorpe?"

She accepted one absently, furnished her own match, and kept looking at Ellery's eyes. "Field work, of course?" asked Crane, the chemist.

"Precisely." Ellery sprang to his feet. "Miss Ickthorpe, *please* pay attention. . . . If we're to do this at all, we must do it right. . . . Very well. We shall study crimes out of the current news—crimes, it goes without saying, which lend themselves to our particular brand of detection. We start from scratch, all of us—no preconceptions, understand. . . . You will work under my direction, and we shall see what happens."

Burrows's keen face glowed. "Theory? I mean—won't you give us any principles of attack first—classroom lectures?"

"To hell with principles. I beg your pardon, Miss Ickthorpe. . . . The only way to learn to swim, Burrows, is to get into the Water. . . . There were sixty-three applicants for this confounded course. I wanted only two or three—too many would defeat my purpose; unwieldy, you know. I selected you, Crane, because you seem to have the "analytical mind to a reasonable degree, and your scientific training has developed your sense of observation. You, Burrows, have a sound academic background and, evidently, an excellent top-piece." The two young men blushed. "As for you, Miss Ickthorpe," continued Ellery stiffly, "you selected yourself, so you'll have to take the consequences. Old Icky or no Old Icky, at the first sign of stupidity out you go."

"An Ickthorpe sir, is never stupid."

"I hope—I sincerely hope—not. . . . Now, to cases. An hour ago, before I set out for the University, a flash came in over the Police Headquarters' wire. Most fortuitously, I thought, and we must be properly grateful. . . . Murder in the theatrical district—chap by the name of Spargo is the victim. A queer enough affair, I gathered, from the sketchy facts given over the tape. I've asked my father—Inspector Queen, you know—to leave the scene of the crime exactly as found. We go there at once."

"Bully!" cried Burrows. "To grips with Crime! This is going to be great. Shan't we have any trouble getting in, Mr. Queen?"

"None at all. I've arranged for each of you gentlemen to carry a special police pass, like my own; I'll get one for you later, Miss Ickthorpe. . . . Let me caution all of you to refrain from taking anything away from the scene of the crime—at least without consulting me first. And on no account allow yourselves to be pumped by reporters."

"A murder," said Miss Ickthorpe thoughtfully, with a sudden dampening of spirits.

"Aha! Squeamish already. Well, this affair will be a test-case for all of you. I want to see how your minds work in contact with the real thing. . . . Miss Ickthorpe, have you a hat or something?"

"Sir?"

"Duds, duds! You can't traipse in there this way, you know!"

"Oh!" she murmured, blushing. "Isn't a sport dress *au fait* at murders?" Ellery glared, and she added sweetly: "In my locker down the hall, Mr. Queen. I shan't be a moment."

Ellery jammed his hat on his head. "I shall meet the three of you in front of the Arts Building in five minutes. Five minutes, Miss Ickthorpe!" And, retrieving his stick, he stalked like any professor from the seminar room. All the way down the elevator, through the main corridor, on the marble steps outside, he breathed deeply. A remarkable day! he observed to the campus. A really remarkable day.

The Fenwick Hotel lay a few hundred yards from Times Square. Its lobby was boiling with policemen, detectives, reporters and, from their universal appearance of apprehension, guests. Mountainous Sergeant Velie, Inspector Queen's right-hand man, was planted at the door, a cement barrier against curiosity-seekers. By his side stood a tall, worried-looking man dressed somberly in a blue serge suit, white linen, and black bow-tie.

"Mr. Williams, the hotel manager," said the Sergeant.

Williams shook hands. "Can't understand it. Terrible mess. You're with the police?"

Ellery nodded. His charges surrounded him like a royal guard—a rather timid royal guard, to be sure, for they pressed close to him as if for protection. There was something sinister in the atmosphere. Even the hotel clerks and attendants, uniformly dressed in gray—suits, ties, shirts—wore strained expressions, like stewards on a foundering ship.

"Nobody in or out, Mr. Queen," growled Sergeant Velie. "Inspector's orders. You're the first since the body was found. These people okay?"

"Yes. Dad's on the scene?"

"Upstairs, third floor, Room 317. Mostly quiet now."

Ellery leveled his stick. "Come along, young 'uns. And don't—" he added gently, "don't be so nervous. You'll become accustomed to this sort of thing. Keep your heads up."

They bobbed in unison, their eyes a little glassy. As they ascended in a policed elevator, Ellery observed that Miss Ickthorpe was trying very hard to appear professionally *blasé*. Ickthorpe indeed! This should take the starch out of her. . . . They walked down a hushed corridor to an open door. Inspector Queen, a small birdlike gray little man with sharp eyes remarkably like his son's, met them in the doorway.

Ellery, suppressing a snicker at the convulsive start of Miss Ickthorpe, who had darted one fearful glance into the death-room and then gasped for dear life, introduced the young people to the Inspector, shut the door behind his somewhat reluctant charges, and looked about the bedroom.

Lying on the drab carpet, arms outflung before him like a diver, lay a dead man. His head presented a curious appearance: as if some one had upset a bucket of thick red paint over him, clotting the brown hair and gushing over his shoulders. Miss Ickthorpe gave vent to a faint gurgle which certainly was not appreciation. Ellery observed with morbid satisfaction that her tiny hands were clenched and that her elfin face was whiter than the bed near which the dead man lay sprawled. Crane and Burrows were breathing hard.

"Miss Ickthorpe, Mr. Crane, Mr. Burrows—your first corpse," said Ellery briskly. "Now, dad, to work. How does it stand?"

Inspector Queen sighed. "Name is Oliver Spargo. Forty-two, separated from his wife two years ago. Mercantile traveler for a big drygoods exporting house. Returned from South Africa after a year's stay. Bad reputation with the natives in the outlying settlements— thrashed them, cheated them; in fact, was driven out of British Africa by a scandal. It was in the New York papers not long ago. . . . Registered at the Fenwick here for three days—same floor, by the way— then checked out to go to Chicago. Visiting relatives." The Inspector grunted, as if this were something justifiably punished by homicide. "Returned to New York this morning by plane. Checked in at 9:30. Didn't leave this room. At 11:30 he was found dead, just as you see him, by the colored maid on this floor, Agatha Robins."

"Leads?"

The old man shrugged. "Maybe—maybe not. We've looked this bird up. Pretty hard guy, from the reports, but sociable. No enemies, apparently; all his movements since his boat docked innocent and accounted for. *And* a lady-killer. Chucked his wife over before his last trip across, and took to his bosom a nice blonde gal. Fussed with her for a couple of months, and then skipped out—and *didn't* take her with him. We've had both women on the pan."

"Suspects?"

Inspector Queen stared moodily at the dead traveler. "Well, take your pick. He had one visitor this morning—the blonde lady I just mentioned. Name of Jane Terrill—no sign of occupation. Huh! She evidently read in the ship news of Spargo's arrival two weeks ago; hunted him up, and a week ago, while Spargo was in Chicago, called at the desk downstairs inquiring for him. She was told he was expected back this morning—he'd left word. She came in at 11:05 this a.m., was given his room-number, was taken up by the elevator-boy. Nobody remembers her leaving. But she says she knocked and there was no answer, so she went away and hasn't been back since. Never saw him—according to her story."

Miss Ickthorpe skirted the corpse with painful care, perched herself on the edge of the bed, opened her bag and began to powder her nose. "And the wife, Inspector Queen?" she murmured. Something sparkled in the depths of her fawn-brown eyes. Miss Ickthorpe, it was evident, had an idea and was taking heroic measures to suppress it.

"The wife?" snorted the Inspector. "God knows. She and Spargo separated, as I said, and she claims she didn't even know he'd come back from Africa. Says she was window-shopping this morning."

It was a small featureless hotel room, containing a bed, a wardrobe closet, a bureau, a night-table, a desk, and a chair. A dummy fireplace with a gas-log; an open door which led to a bathroom—nothing more.

Ellery dropped to his knees beside the body, Crane and Burrows trooping after with set faces. The Inspector sat down and watched with a humorless grin. Ellery turned the body over; his hands explored the rigid members, stiff in *rigor mortis.*

"Crane, Burrows, Miss Ickthorpe," he said sharply. "Might as well begin now. Tell me what you see—Miss Ickthorpe, you first." She jumped from the bed and ran around the dead man; he felt her hot unsteady breath on the back of his neck. "Well, well? Don't you see *anything?* Good lord, there's enough here, I should think."

Miss Ickthorpe licked her red lips and said in a strangled voice: "He—he's dressed in lounging-robe, carpet-slippers and—yes, silk underwear beneath."

"Yes. And black silk socks and garters. And the robe and underwear bear the dealer's label: *Johnson's, Johannesburg, U.S.Afr.* What else?"

"A wrist-watch on his left wrist. I think"—she leaned over and with the shrinking tip of a finger nudged the dead arm—"Yes, the watch crystal is cracked. Why, it's set at 10:20!"

"Good," said Ellery in a soft voice. "Dad, did Prouty examine the cadaver?"

"Yes," said the Inspector in a resigned voice. "Spargo died some time between 11:00 and 11:30, Doc says. I figure—"

Miss Ickthorpe's eyes were shining. "Doesn't that mean—?"

"Now, now, Miss Ickthorpe, if you have an idea keep it to yourself. Don't leap at conclusions. That's enough for you. Well, Crane?"

The young chemist's brow was ridged. He pointed to the watch, a large gaudy affair with a leather wrist-strap. "Man's watch. Concussion of fall stopped the works. Crease in leather strap at the second hole, where the prong now fits; but there's also a crease, a deeper one, at the third hole."

"That's really excellent, Crane. And?"

"Left hand splattered and splashed with dried blood. Left palm also shows stain, but fainter, as if he had grabbed something with his bloody hand and wiped most of the blood off. There ought to be something around here showing a red smudge from his clutching hand. . . . "

"Crane, I'm proud of you. Was anything found with a blood-smear on it, dad?"

The Inspector looked interested. "Good work, youngster. No, El, nothing at all. Not even a smear on the rug. Must be something the murderer took away."

"Now, Inspector," chuckled Ellery, "this isn't *your* examination. Burrows, can you add anything?"

Young Burrows swallowed rapidly: "Wounds on the head show he was struck with a heavy instrument many times. Disarranged rug probably indicates a struggle. And the face—"

"Ah! So you've noticed the face, eh? What about the face?"

"Freshly shaved. Talcum powder still on cheeks and chin. Don't you think we ought to examine the bathroom, Mr. Queen?"

Miss Ickthorpe said peevishly: "I noticed that, too, but you didn't give me a chance. . . . The powder *is* smoothly applied, isn't it? No streaks, no heavy spots."

Ellery sprang to his feet. "You'll be Sherlock Holmeses yet. . . . The weapon, dad?"

"A heavy stone hammer, crudely made—some kind of African curio, our expert says. Spargo must have had it in his bag—his trunk hasn't arrived yet from Chicago."

Ellery nodded; on the bed lay an open pigskin traveling-bag. Beside it, neatly laid out, was an evening outfit: tuxedo coat, trousers, and vest; stiff-bosomed shirt; studs and cufflinks; a clean wing-collar; black suspenders; a white silk handkerchief. Under the bed were two pairs of black shoes, one pair brogues, the other patent-leather. Ellery looked around; something, it seemed, disturbed him. On the chair near the bed lay a soiled shirt, a soiled pair of socks, and a soiled suit of underwear. None exhibited bloodstains. He paused thoughtfully.

"We took the hammer away. It was full of blood and hair," continued the Inspector. "No fingerprints anywhere. Handle anything you want—everything's been photographed and tested for prints."

Ellery began to puff at a cigarette. He noticed that Burrows and Crane were crouched over the dead man, occupied with the watch. He sauntered over, Miss Ickthorpe at his heels.

Burrows's thin face was shining as he looked up. "Here's something!" He had carefully removed the timepiece from Spargo's wrist and had pried open the back of the case. Ellery saw a roughly circular patch of fuzzy white paper glued to the inside of the case, as if something had been rather unsuccessfully torn away. Burrows leaped to his feet. "That gives *me* an idea," he announced. "Yes, sir." He studied the dead man's face intently.

"And you, Crane?" asked Ellery with interest. The young chemist had produced a small magnifying-glass from his pocket and was scrutinizing the watchworks.

Crane rose. "I'd rather not say now," he mumbled. "Mr. Queen, I'd like permission to take this watch to my laboratory."

Ellery looked at his father; the old man nodded. "Certainly, Crane. But be sure you return it. . . . Dad, you searched this room thoroughly, fireplace and all?"

The Inspector cackled suddenly. "I was wondering when you'd get to that. There's something almighty interesting in that fireplace." His face fell and rather grumpily he produced a snuff-box and pinched some crumbs into his nostrils. "Although I'll be hanged if I know what it means."

Ellery squinted at the fireplace, his lean shoulders squaring; the others crowded around. He squinted again, and knelt; behind the manufactured gas-log, in a tiny grate, there was a heap of ashes. Curious ashes indeed, patently not of wood, coal, or paper. Ellery poked about in the débris—and sucked in his breath. In a moment he had dug out of the ashes ten peculiar objects: eight flat pearl buttons and two metal things, one triangular in outline, eye-like, the other hook-like—both small and made of some cheap alloy. Two of the eight buttons were slightly larger than the rest. The buttons were ridged, and in the depression in each center were four thread-holes. All ten objects were charred by fire.

"And what do you make of that?" demanded the Inspector.

Ellery juggled the buttons thoughtfully. He did not reply directly. Instead, he said to his three pupils, in a grim voice: "You might think about these. . . . Dad, when was this fireplace last cleaned?"

"Early this morning by Agatha Robins, the mulatto maid. Some one checked out of this room at seven o'clock, and she cleaned up the place before Spargo got here. Fireplace was clean this morning, she says."

Ellery dropped buttons and metal objects on the night-table and went to the bed. He looked into the open traveling-bag; its interior was in a state of confusion. The bag contained three four-in-hand neckties, two clean white shirts, socks, underwear, and handkerchiefs. All the haberdashery, he noted, bore the same dealer's tab—*Johnson's, Johannesburg, U.S.Afr.* He seemed pleased, and proceeded to the wardrobe closet. It contained merely a tweed traveling suit, a brown topcoat, and a felt hat.

He closed the door with a satisfied bang. "You've observed everything?" he asked the two young men and the girl.

Crane and Burrows nodded, rather doubtfully. Miss Ickthorpe was barely listening; from the rapt expression on her face, she might have been listening to the music of the spheres.

"Miss Ickthorpe!"

Miss Ickthorpe smiled dreamily. "Yes, Mr. Queen," she said in a submissive little voice. Her large brown eyes began to rove.

Ellery grunted and strode to the bureau. Its top was bare. He went through the drawers; they were empty. He started for the desk, but the Inspector said: "Nothing there, son. He hadn't time to stow anything away. Except for the bathroom, you've seen everything."

As if she had been awaiting the signal, Miss Ickthorpe dashed for the bathroom. She seemed very anxious indeed to explore its interior. Crane and Burrows hurried after her.

Ellery permitted them to examine the bathroom before him. Miss Ickthorpe's hands flew over the objects on the rim of the washbowl. There was a pigskin toilet-kit, open, draped over the marble; an uncleansed razor; a still damp shaving-brush; a tube of shaving cream; a small can of talcum; and a tube of tooth paste. To one side lay a celluloid shaving-brush container, its cap on the open kit.

"Can't see a thing of interest here," said Burrows frankly. "You, Walter?"

Crane shook his head. "Except that he must have just finished shaving before he was murdered, not a thing."

Miss Ickthorpe wore a stern and faintly exultant look. "That's because, like all men, you're blinder'n bats. . . . *I've* seen enough."

They trooped by Ellery, rejoining the Inspector, who was talking with some one in the bedroom. Ellery chuckled to himself. He lifted the lid of a clothes-hamper; it was empty. Then he picked up the cap of the shaving-brush container. The cap came apart in his fingers, and he saw that a small circular pad fitted snugly inside. He chuckled again, cast a derisive glance at the triumphant back of the heroic Miss Ickthorpe outside, replaced cap and tube, and went back into the bedroom.

He found Williams, the hotel manager, accompanied by a policeman, talking heatedly to the Inspector. "We can't keep this up forever, Inspector Queen," Williams was saying. "Our guests are beginning to complain. The night-shift is due to go on soon, I've got to go home myself, and you're making us stay here all night, by George. After all—"

The old man said: "Psih!" and cocked an inquiring eye at his son. Ellery nodded. "Can't see any reason for not lifting the ban, dad. We've learned as much as we can. . . . You young people!" Three pairs of eager eyes focused on him; they were like three puppies on a leash.

"Have you seen enough?" They nodded solemnly. "Anything else you want to know?"

Burrows said quickly: "I want a certain address."

Miss Ickthorpe paled. "Why, so do I! John, you mean thing!"

And Crane muttered, clutching Spargo's watch in his fist: "I want something, too—but I'll find it out right in this hotel!"

Ellery smoothed away a smile, shrugged, and said: "See Sergeant Velie downstairs—that Colossus we met at the door. He'll tell you anything you may want to know.

"Now, follow instructions. It's evident that the three of you have definite theories. I'll give you two hours in which to formulate them and pursue any investigations you may have in mind." He consulted his watch. "At 6:30, meet me at my apartment on West Eighty-seventh Street, and I'll try to rip your theories apart. . . . Happy hunting!"

He grinned dismissal. They scrambled for the door, Miss Ickthorpe's turban slightly awry, her elbows working vigorously to clear the way.

"And now," said Ellery in a totally different voice when they had disappeared down the corridor, "come here a moment, dad. I want to talk to you alone."

At 6:30 that evening Mr. Ellery Queen presided at his own table, watching three young faces bursting with sternly repressed news. The remains of a dinner, barely touched, strewed the cloth.

Miss Ickthorpe had somehow contrived, in the interval between her dismissal and her appearance at the Queens' apartment, to change her gown; she was now attired in something lacy and soft, which set off—as she obviously was aware—the whiteness of her throat, the brownness of her eyes, and the pinkness of her cheeks. The young men were preoccupied with their coffee cups.

"Now, class," chuckled Ellery, "recitations." They brightened, sat straighter and moistened their lips. "You've had, each of you, about two hours in which to crystallize the results of your first investigation. Whatever happens, I can't take credit, since so far I've taught you nothing. But by the end of this little confabulation, I'll have a rough idea of just what material I'm working with."

"Yes, sir," said Miss Ickthorpe.

"John—we may as well discard formality—what's *your* theory?"

Burrows said slowly: "I've more than a theory, Mr. Queen. I've the solution!"

"*A* solution, John. Don't be too cocky. And what," said Ellery, "is this solution of yours?" Burrows drew a breath from the depths of his boots. "The clue that led to my solution was Spargo's wrist-watch." Crane and the girl started. Ellery blew smoke and said encouragingly: "Go on."

"The two creases on the leather strap," replied Burrows, "were significant. As Spargo wore the watch, the prong was caught in the second hole, so that there was a crease *across* the second hole. Yet a deeper crease appeared across the *third* hole. Conclusion: the watch was habitually worn by a person with a smaller wrist. In other words, the watch was not Spargo's!"

"Bravo," said Ellery softly. "Bravo."

"Why, then, was Spargo wearing some one else's watch? For a very good reason, I maintain. The doctor had said Spargo died between 11:00 and 11:30. Yet the watch-hands had apparently stopped at 10:20. The answer to this discrepancy? That the murderer, finding no watch on Spargo, took her own watch, cracked the crystal and stopped the works, then set the hands at 10:20 and strapped it about Spargo's dead wrist. This would seem to establish the time of death at 10:20 and would give the murderer an opportunity to provide an alibi for that time, when all the while the murder actually occurred about 11:20. How's that?"

Miss Ickthorpe said tartly: "You say 'her.' But it's a man's watch, John—you forget that." Burrows grinned. "A woman can own a man's watch, can't she? Now whose watch was it? Easy. In the back of the case there was a circular patch of fuzzy paper, as if something had been ripped out. What made of paper is usually pasted in the back of a watch? A photograph. Why was it taken out? Obviously, because the murderer's face was in that photograph. . . . In the last two hours I followed this lead. I visited my suspect on a reportorial pretext and managed to get a look at a photograph-album she has. There I found one photograph with a circular patch cut out. From the rest of the photo it was clear that the missing circle contained the heads of a man and a woman. My case was complete!"

"Perfectly amazing," murmured Ellery. "And this murderess of yours is—?"

"Spargo's wife! . . . Motive—hate, or revenge, or thwarted love, or something."

Miss Ickthorpe sniffed, and Crane shook his head. "Well," said Ellery, "we seem to be in disagreement. Nevertheless a very interesting analysis, John. . . . Walter, what's yours?"

Crane hunched his broad shoulders. "I agree with Johnny that the watch did not belong to Spargo, that the murderer set the hands at 10:20 to provide an alibi; but I disagree as to the identity of the criminal. I also worked on the watch as the main clue. But with a vastly different approach.

"Look here." He brought out the gaudy timepiece and tapped its cracked crystal deliberately. "Here's something you people may not know. Watches, so to speak, breathe. That is, contact with warm flesh causes the air inside to expand and force its way out through the minute cracks and holes of the case and crystal. When the watch is laid aside, the air cools and contracts, and dust-bearing air is sucked into the interior."

"I always said I should have studied science," said Ellery. "That's a new trick, Walter. Continue."

"To put it specifically, a baker's watch will be found to contain flour-dust. A bricklayer's watch will collect brick-dust." Crane's voice rose triumphantly. "D'you know what I found in this watch? Tiny particles of a woman's face-powder!"

Miss Ickthorpe frowned. Crane continued in a deep voice: "And a very special kind of face-powder it is, Mr. Queen. Kind used only by women of certain complexions. What complexions? Negro brown! The powder came from a mulatto woman's purse! I've questioned her, checked her vanity-case, and although she denies it, I say that Spargo's murderess is Agatha Robins, the mulatto maid who 'found' the body!"

Ellery whistled gently. "Good work, Walter, splendid work. And of course from your standpoint she would deny being the owner of the watch anyway. That clears something up for *me*. . . . But motive?"

Crane looked uncomfortable. "Well, I know it sounds fantastic, but a sort of voodoo vengeance—reversion to racial type—Spargo had been cruel to African natives . . . it was in the papers. . . . "

Ellery shaded his eyes to conceal their twinkle. Then he turned to Miss Ickthorpe, who was tapping her cup nervously, squirming in her chair, and exhibiting other signs of impatience. "And now," he said, "we come to the star recitation. What have you to offer, Miss Ickthorpe? You've been simply saturated with a theory all afternoon. Out with it."

She compressed her lips, "You boys think you're clever. You, too, Mr. Queen—you especially. . . . Oh, I'll admit John and Walter have shown superficial traces of intelligence. . . . "

"*Will* you be explicit, Miss Ickthorpe?"

She tossed her head. "Very well. The watch had nothing to do with the crime at all!"

The boys gaped, and Ellery tapped his palms gently together. "*Very* good. I agree with you. Explain, please."

Her brown eyes burned, and her cheeks were very pink. "Simple!" she said with a sniff. "Spargo had arrived from Chicago only two hours before his murder. He had been in Chicago for a week and a half. Then for a week and a half he had been living *by Chicago time.* And, since Chicago time is *one hour earlier* than New York time, it merely means that *nobody* set the hands back; that they were standing at 10:20 when he fell dead, because he'd neglected to set his watch ahead on arriving in New York this morning!"

Crane muttered something in his throat, and Burrows flushed a deep crimson. Ellery looked sad. "I'm afraid the laurels so far go to Miss Ickthorpe, gentlemen. That happens to be correct. Anything else?"

"Naturally. I know the murderer, and it isn't Spargo's wife or that outlandish mulatto maid," she said exasperatingly. "Follow me. . . . Oh, this is so easy! . . . We all saw that the powder on Spargo's dead face had been applied very smoothly. From the condition of his cheeks and the shaving things in the bathroom it was evident that he'd shaved just before being murdered. But how does a man apply powder after shaving? How do *you* powder your face, Mr. Queen?" she shot at him rather tenderly.

Ellery looked startled. "With my fingers, of course." Crane and Burrows nodded.

"Exactly!" chortled Miss Ickthorpe. "And what happens? *I* know, because I'm a very observant person and, besides, Old Icky shaves every morning and I can't *help* noticing when he kisses me good-morning. Applied with the fingers on cheeks still slightly moist, the powder goes on in streaks, smudgy, heavier in some spots than others. But look at *my* face!" They looked, with varying expressions of appreciation. "You don't see powder streaks on *my* face, do you? Of course not! And why? Because I'm a woman, and a woman uses a powder-puff, and there isn't a single powder-puff in Spargo's bedroom or bathroom!"

Ellery smiled—almost with relief. "Then you suggest, Miss Ickthorpe, that the last person with Spargo, presumably his murderess, was a woman who watched him shave and then, with endearment perhaps, took out her own powder-puff and dabbed it over his face—only to bash him over the head with the stone hammer a few minutes later?"

"Well—yes, although I didn't think of it *that* way. . . . But—yes! And psychology points to the specific woman, too, Mr. Queen. A man's wife would never think of such an—an amorous proceeding. But a man's mistress would, and I say that Spargo's lady-love, Jane Terrill, whom I visited only an hour ago and who denies having powdered Spargo's face—she would!—killed him."

Ellery sighed. He rose and twitched his cigarette-stub into the fireplace. They were watching him, and each other, with expectancy. "Aside," he began, "from complimenting you, Miss Ickthorpe, on the acuteness of your knowledge of mistresses"—she uttered an outraged little gasp—"I want to say this before going ahead. The three of you have proved very ingenious, very alert; I'm more pleased than I can say. I do think we're going to have a cracking good class. Good work, all of you!"

"But, Mr. Queen," protested Burrows, "which one of us is right? Each one of us has given a different solution."

Ellery waved his hand. "Right? A detail, theoretically. The point is you've done splendid work—sharp observation, a rudimentary but promising linking of cause and effect. As for the case itself, I regret to say—you're all wrong!"

Miss Ickthorpe clenched her tiny fist. "I *knew* you'd say that! I think you're horrid. And I *still* think I'm right."

"There, gentlemen, is an extraordinary example of feminine psychology," grinned Ellery. "Now attend, all of you.

"You're all wrong for the simple reason that each of you has taken just one line of attack, one clue, one chain of reasoning, and completely ignored the other elements of the problem. You, John, say it's Spargo's wife, merely because her photograph-album contains a picture from which a circular patch with two heads has been cut away. That this might have been sheer coincidence apparently never occurred to you.

"You, Walter, came nearer the truth when you satisfactorily established the ownership of the watch as the mulatto maid's. But suppose Maid Robins had accidentally dropped the watch in Spargo's room at the hotel during his first visit there, and he had found it and taken it to Chicago with him? That's what probably happened. The mere fact that he wore her watch doesn't make her his murderess.

"You, Miss Ickthorpe, explained away the watch business with the difference-in-time element, but you overlooked an important item. Your entire solution depends on the presence in Spargo's room of a powder-puff. Willing to believe that no puff remained on the scene of the crime, because it suited your theory, you made a cursory search and promptly concluded no puff was there. But a puff *is* there! Had you investigated the cap of the celluloid tube in which Spargo kept his shaving-brush, you would have found a circular pad of powder-puff which toilet-article manufacturers in this effeminate age provide for men's traveling-kits."

Miss Ickthorpe said nothing; she seemed actually embarrassed.

"Now for the proper solution," said Ellery, mercifully looking away. "All three of you, amazingly enough, postulate a woman as the criminal. Yet it was apparent to me, after my examination of the premises, that the murderer *must have been a man.*" "A man!" they echoed in chorus.

"Exactly. Why did none of you consider the significance of those eight buttons and the two metal clips?" He smiled. "Probably because again they didn't fit your preconceived theories. But *everything* must fit in a solution. . . . Enough of scolding. You'll do better next time.

"Six small pearl buttons, flat, and two slightly larger ones, found in a heap of ashes distinctly not of wood, coal, or paper. There is only one common article which possesses these characteristics—a man's shirt. A man's shirt, the six buttons from the front, the two larger ones from the cuffs, the débris from the linen or broadcloth. Some one, then, had burned a man's shirt in the grate, forgetting that the buttons would not be consumed.

"The metal objects, like a large hook and eye? A shirt suggests haberdashery, the hook and eye suggests only one thing—one of the cheap bow-ties which are purchased ready-tied, so that you do not have to make the bow yourself."

They were watching his lips like kindergarten children. "You, Crane, observed that Spargo's bloody left hand had clutched something, most of the blood coming off the palm. But nothing smudged with blood had been found. . . . A man's shirt and tie had been burned. . . . Inference: In the struggle with the murderer, after he had already been hit on the head and was streaming blood, Spargo had clutched his assailant's collar and tie, staining them. Borne out too by the signs of struggle in the room.

"Spargo dead, his own collar and tie wet with blood, what could the murderer do? Let me attack it this way: The murderer must have been from one of three classes of people: a rank outsider, or a guest at the hotel, or an employee of the hotel. What had he done? He had burned his shirt and tie. But if he had been an outsider, he could have turned up his coat-collar, concealing the stains long enough to get out of the hotel—no necessity, then, to burn shirt and tie when time was precious. Were he one of the hotel guests, he could have done the same thing while he went to his own room. Then he must have been an employee.

"Confirmation? Yes. As an employee he would be forced to remain in the hotel, on duty, constantly being seen. What could he do? Well, he had to change his shirt and tie. Spargo's bag was open—shirt inside. He rummaged through—you saw the confusion in the bag—and changed. Leave his shirt? No, it might be traced to him. So, boys and girls, burning was inevitable. . . .

"The tie? You recall that, while Spargo had laid out his evening-clothes on the bed, there was no bow-tie there, in the bag, or anywhere else in the room. Obviously, then, the murderer took the bow-tie of the tuxedo outfit, and burned his own bow-tie with the shirt."

Miss Ickthorpe sighed, and Crane and Burrows shook their heads a little dazedly. "I knew, then, that the murderer was an employee of the hotel, a man, and that he was wearing Spargo's shirt and black or white bow-tie, probably black. But all the employees of the hotel wear gray shirts and gray ties, as we observed on entering the Fenwick. Except"—Ellery inhaled the smoke of his cigarette—"except one man. Surely you noticed the difference in his attire? . . . And so, when you left on your various errands, I suggested to my father that this man be examined—he seemed the best possibility. And, sure enough, we found on him a shirt and bow-tie bearing Johannesburg labels like those we had observed on Spargo's other haberdashery. I knew we should find this proof, for Sparg had spent a whole year in South Africa, and since most of his clothes had been purchased there, it was reasonable to expect that the stolen shirt and tie had been, too."

"Then the case was finished when we were just beginning," said Burrows ruefully.

"But—who?" demanded Crane in bewilderment.

Ellery blew a great cloud. "We got a confession out of him in three minutes. Spargo, that gentle creature, had years before stolen this man's wife, and then thrown her over. When Spargo registered at the Fenwick two weeks ago, this man recognized him and decided to revenge himself. He's at the Tombs right now—Williams, the hotel manager!"

There was a little silence. Burrows bobbed his head back and forth. "We've got a lot to learn," he said. "I can see that."

"Check," muttered Crane. "I'm going to like this course."

Ellery pshaw-pshawed. Nevertheless, he turned to Miss Ickthorpe who by all precedent should be moved to contribute to the general spirit of approbation. But Miss Ickthorpe's thoughts were far away. "Do you know," she said, her brown eyes misty, "you've never asked me my first name, Mr. Queen?"

PUZZLE FOR POPPY
Patrick Quentin
Detectives: Peter & Iris Duluth

Hugh Callingham Wheeler (1912-1987) and Richard Wilson Webb (1901-1970?) collaborated on the series featuring Peter and Iris Duluth, but both authors were part of a coterie of writers that mixed and matched on many other books published as by Q. Patrick, Patrick Quentin, and Jonathan Stagge. It was when Wheeler and Webb moved to the United States in the 1930s that they created the Duluth series, which changed their books from a recognizably British style to American in speech and tone.

Wheeler and Webb created the Patrick Quentin byline with *A Puzzle for Fools* (1936) which introduced Peter Duluth, a theatrical producer who stumbles into detective work by accident, and Iris Pattison, an actress suffering from melancholia who he meets at a sanitarium where he has gone to treat his alcoholism and eventually marries her. Iris is irresistibly curious about mysteries and draws her husband into helping her solve them.

The highly successful Duluth series of nine novels inspired two motion pictures, *Homicide for Three* (1948), starring Warren Douglas as Peter and Audrey Long as his wife Iris, and *Black Widow* (1954), with Van Heflin (Peter), Gene Tierney (Iris), Ginger Rogers,

George Raft, and Peggy Ann Garner. Webb dropped out of the collaboration in the early 1950s and Wheeler continued using the Quentin name but abandoned the Duluth series to produce stand-alone novels until 1965.

Oddly, all the Duluth novels were published using the Patrick Quentin nom de plume but the short stories were originally published as by Q. Patrick—until they, as well as non-series stories, were collected in *The Ordeal of Mrs. Snow and Other Stories* (1961), which was selected for *Queen's Quorum*.

"Puzzle for Poppy" was originally published in the February 1946 issue of *Ellery Queen's Mystery Magazine*; it was first collected in *The Puzzles of Peter Duluth* by Patrick Quentin (Norfolk, Virginia, Crippen & Landru, 2016).

Puzzle for Poppy
By Patrick Quentin

Yes, Miss Crump," snapped Iris into the phone. "No, Miss Crump. Oh, nuts, Miss Crump."

My wife flung down the receiver.

"Well?" I asked.

"She won't let us use the patio. It's that dog, that great fat St. Bernard. It mustn't be disturbed."

"Why?"

"It has to be alone with its beautiful thoughts. It's going to become a mother. Peter, it's revolting. There must be something in the lease."

"There isn't," I said.

When I'd rented our half of this La Jolla hacienda for my shore leave, the lease specified that all rights to the enclosed patio belonged to our eccentric cotenant. It oughtn't to have mattered, but it did because Iris had recently skyrocketed to fame as a movie star and it was impossible for us to appear on the streets without being mobbed.

For the last couple of days we had been virtually beleaguered in our apartment. We were crazy about being beleaguered together, but even Héloïse and Abelard needed a little fresh air once in a while.

That's why the patio was so important.

Iris was staring through the locked French windows at the forbidden delights of the patio. Suddenly she turned.

"Peter, I'll die if I don't get things into my lungs—ozone and things. We'll just have to go to the beach."

"And be torn limb from limb by your public again?"

"I'm sorry, darling. I'm terribly sorry." Iris unzipped herself from her housecoat and scrambled into slacks and a shirt-waist. She tossed me my naval hat. "Come, Lieutenant—to the slaughter."

When we emerged on the street, we collided head on with a man carrying groceries into the house. As we disentangled ourselves from celery stalks, there was a click and a squeal of delight followed by a powerful whistle. I turned to see a small girl who had been lying in wait with a camera. She was an unsightly little girl with sandy pigtails and a brace on her teeth.

"Geeth," she announced. "I can get two buckth for thith thnap from Barney Thtone. He'th thappy about you, Mith Duluth."

Other children, materializing in response to her whistle, were galloping toward us. The grocery man came out of the house. Passers-by stopped, stared and closed in—a woman in scarlet slacks, two sailors, a flurry of bobby-soxers, a policeman.

"This," said Iris grimly, "is the end."

She escaped from her fans and marched back to the two front doors of our hacienda. She rang the buzzer on the door that wasn't ours. She rang persistently. At length there was the clatter of a chain sliding into place and the door opened wide enough to reveal the face of Miss Crump. It was a small, faded face with a most uncordial expression.

"Yes?" asked Miss Crump.

"We're the Duluths," said Iris. "I just called you. I know about your dog, but . . ."

"Not *my* dog," corrected Miss Crump. "Mrs. Wilberframe's dog. The late Mrs. Wilberframe of Glendale who has a nephew and a niece-in-law of whom I know a great deal in Ogden Bluffs, Utah. At least, they *ought* to be in Ogden Bluffs."

This unnecessary information was flung at us like a challenge. Then Miss Crump's face flushed into sudden, dimpled pleasure.

"Duluth! Iris Duluth. You're *the* Iris Duluth of the movies?"

"Yes," said Iris.

"Oh, why didn't you tell me over the phone? My favorite actress! How exciting! Poor thing—mobbed by your fans. Of course you may use the patio. I will give you the key to open your French windows. Any time."

Miraculously the chain was off the door. It opened halfway and then stopped. Miss Crump was staring at me with a return of suspicion.

"You *are* Miss Duluth's husband?"

"Mrs. Duluth's husband," I corrected her. "Lieutenant Duluth."

She still peered. "I mean, you have proof?"

I was beyond being surprised by Miss Crump. I fumbled from my wallet a dog-eared snapshot of Iris and me in full wedding regalia outside the church. Miss Crump studied it carefully and then returned it.

"You must please excuse me. What a sweet bride! It's just that I can't be too careful—for Poppy."

"Poppy?" queried Iris. "The St. Bernard?"

Miss Crump nodded. "It is Poppy's house, you see. Poppy pays the rent."

"The dog," said Iris faintly, "pays the rent?"

"Yes, my dear. Poppy is very well-to-do. She is hardly more than a puppy, but she is one of the richest dogs, I suppose, in the whole world."

Although we entertained grave doubts as to Miss Crump's sanity, we were soon in swimming suits and stepping through our open French windows into the sunshine of the patio. Miss Crump introduced us to Poppy.

In spite of our former prejudices, Poppy disarmed us immediately. She was just a big, bouncing, natural girl unspoiled by wealth. She greeted us with great thumps of her tail. She leaped up at Iris, dabbing at her cheek with a long, pink tongue. Later, when we had settled on striped mattresses under orange trees, she curled into a big clumsy ball at my side and laid her vast muzzle on my stomach.

"Look, she likes you." Miss Crump was glowing. "Oh, I knew she would!"

Iris, luxuriating in the sunshine, asked the polite question. "Tell us about Poppy. How did she make her money?"

"Oh, she did not make it. She inherited it." Miss Crump sat down on a white iron chair. "Mrs. Wilberframe was a very wealthy woman. She was devoted to Poppy."

"And left her all her money?" I asked.

"Not quite all. There was a little nest egg for me. I was her companion, you see, for many years. But I am to look after Poppy. That is why I received the nest egg. Poppy pays me a generous salary too." She fingered nondescript beads at her throat. "Mrs. Wilberframe was anxious for Poppy to have only the best and I am sure I try to do the right thing. Poppy has the master bedroom, of course. I take the little one in front. And then, if Poppy has steak for dinner, I have hamburger." She stared intensely. "I would not have an easy moment if I felt that Poppy did not get the best."

Poppy, her head on my stomach, coughed. She banged her tail against the flagstones apologetically.

Iris reached across me to pat her. "Has she been rich for long?"

"Oh, no, Mrs. Wilberframe passed on only a few weeks ago." Miss Crump paused. "And it has been a great responsibility for me." She paused again and then blurted: "You're my friends, aren't you? Oh, I am sure you are. Please, please, won't you help me? I am all alone and I am so frightened."

"Frightened?" I looked up and, sure enough, her little bird face was peaked with fear.

"For Poppy." Miss Crump leaned forward. "Oh, Lieutenant, it is like a nightmare. Because I know. I just know they are trying to murder her!"

"They?" Iris sat up straight.

"Mrs. Wilberframe's nephew and his wife. From Ogden Bluffs, Utah."

"You mentioned them when you opened the door."

"I mention them to everyone who comes to the house. You see, I do not know what they look like and I do not want them to think I am not on my guard."

I watched her. She might have looked like a silly spinster with a bee in her bonnet. She didn't. She looked nice and quite sane, only scared.

"Oh, they are not good people. Not at all. There is nothing they would not stoop to. Back in Glendale, I found pieces of meat in the front yard. Poisoned meat, I know. And on a lonely road, they shot at Poppy. Oh, the police laughed at me. A car backfiring, they said. But I know differently. I know they won't stop till Poppy is dead." She threw her little hands up to her face. "I ran away from them in Glendale. That is why I came to La Jolla. But they have caught up with us. I know. Oh, dear, poor Poppy who is so sweet without a nasty thought in her head."

Poppy, hearing her name mentioned, smiled and panted.

"But this nephew and his wife from Ogden Bluffs, why should they want to murder her?" My wife's eyes were gleaming with a detective enthusiasm I knew of old. "Are they after her money?"

"Of course," said Miss Crump passionately. "It's the will. The nephew is Mrs. Wilberframe's only living relative, but she deliberately cut him off and I am sure I do not blame her. All the money goes to Poppy and—er—Poppy's little ones."

"Isn't the nephew contesting a screwy will like that?" I asked.

"Not yet. To contest a will takes a great deal of money—lawyers, fees and things. It would be much, much cheaper for him to kill Poppy. You see, one thing is not covered by the will. If Poppy were to die before she became a mother, the nephew would inherit the whole estate. Oh, I have done everything in my power. The moment the—er—suitable season arrived, I found a husband for Poppy. In a few weeks now, the—the little ones are expected. But these next few weeks . . ."

Miss Crump dabbed at her eyes with a small handkerchief. "Oh, the Glendale police were most unsympathetic. They even mentioned the fact that the sentence for shooting or killing a dog in this state is shockingly light—a small fine at most. I called the police here and asked for protection. They said they'd send a man around some time but they were hardly civil. So you see, there is no protection from the law and no redress. There is no one to help me."

"You've got us," said Iris in a burst of sympathy.

"Oh . . . oh . . ." The handkerchief fluttered from Miss Crump's face. "I knew you were my friends. You dear, dear things. Oh, Poppy, they are going to help us."

Poppy, busy licking my stomach, did not reply. Somewhat appalled by Iris's hasty promise but ready to stand by her, I said:

"Sure, we'll help, Miss Crump. First, what's the nephew's name?"

"Henry. Henry Blodgett. But he won't use that name. Oh, no, he will be too clever for that."

"And you don't know what he looks like?"

"Mrs. Wilberframe destroyed his photograph many years ago when he bit her as a small boy. With yellow curls, I understand. That is when the trouble between them started."

"At least you know what age he is?"

"He should be about thirty."

"And the wife?" asked Iris.

"I know nothing about her," said Miss Crump coldly, "except that she is supposed to be a red-headed person, a former actress."

"And what makes you so sure one or both of them have come to La Jolla?"

Miss Crump folded her arms in her lap. "Last night. A telephone call."

"A telephone call?"

"A voice asking if I was Miss Crump, and then—silence." Miss Crump leaned toward me. "Oh, now they know I am here. They know I never let Poppy out. They know every morning I search the patio for meat, traps. They must realize that the only possible way to reach her is to enter the house."

"Break in?"

Miss Crump shook her tight curls. "It is possible. But I believe they will rely on guile rather than violence. It is against that we must be on our guard. You are the only people who have come to the door since that telephone call. Now anyone else that comes to your apartment or mine, whatever their excuse . . ." She lowered her voice. "Anyone may be Henry Blodgett or his wife and we will have to outwit them."

A fly settled on one of Poppy's valuable ears. She did not seem to notice it. Miss Crump watched us earnestly and then gave a self-scolding cluck.

"Dear me, here I have been burdening you with Poppy's problems and you must be hungry. How about a little salad for luncheon? I always feel guilty about eating in the middle of the day when Poppy has her one meal at night. But with guests—yes, and allies—I am sure Mrs. Wilberframe would not have grudged the expense."

With a smile that was half-shy, half-conspiratorial, she fluttered away.

I looked at Iris. "Well," I said, "is she a nut or do we believe her?"

"I rather think," said my wife, "that we believe her."

"Why?"

"Just because." Iris's face wore the entranced expression which had won her so many fans in her last picture. "Oh, Peter, don't you see what fun it will be? A beautiful St. Bernard in peril. A wicked villain with golden curls who bit his aunt."

"He won't have golden curls any more," I said. "He's a big boy now."

Iris, her body warm from the sun, leaned over me and put both arms around Poppy's massive neck.

"Poor Poppy," she said. "Really, this shouldn't happen to a dog!"

The first thing happened some hours after Miss Crump's little salad luncheon while Iris and I were still sunning ourselves. Miss Crump, who had been preparing Poppy's dinner and her own in her apartment, came running to announce:

"There is a man at the door! He claims he is from the electric light company to read the meter. Oh, dear, if he is legitimate and we do not let him in, there will be trouble with the electric light company and if . . ." She wrung her hands. "Oh, what shall we do?"

I reached for a bathrobe. "You and Iris stay here. And for Mrs. Wilberframe's sake, hang on to Poppy."

I found the man outside the locked front door. He was about thirty with thinning hair and wore an army discharge button. He showed me his credentials. They seemed in perfect order. There was nothing for it but to let him in. I took him into the kitchen where Poppy's luscious steak and Miss Crump's modest hamburger were lying where Miss Crump had left them on the table. I hovered over the man while he located the meter. I never let him out of my sight until he had departed. In answer to Miss Crump's anxious questioning, I could only say that if the man had been Henry Blodgett he knew how much electricity she'd used in the past month—but that was all.

The next caller showed up a few minutes later. Leaving Iris, indignant at being out of things, to stand by Poppy, Miss Crump and I handled the visitor. This time it was a slim, brash girl with bright auburn hair and a navy-blue slack suit. She was, she said, the sister of the woman who owned the hacienda. She wanted a photograph for the newspapers—a photograph of her Uncle William who had just been promoted to Rear Admiral in the Pacific. The photograph was in a trunk in the attic.

Miss Crump, reacting to the unlikeliness of the request, refused entry. The red-head wasn't the type that wilted. When she started talking darkly of eviction, I overrode Miss Crump and offered to conduct her to the attic. The girl gave me one quick, experienced look and flounced into the hall.

The attic was reached by the back stairs through the kitchen. I conducted the red-head directly to her claimed destination. There were trunks. She searched through them. At length she produced a photograph of a limp young man in a raccoon coat.

"My Uncle William," she snapped, "as a youth."

"Pretty," I said.

I took her back to the front door. On the threshold she gave me another of her bold, appraising stares.

"You know something?" she said. "I was hoping you'd make a pass at me in the attic."

"Why?" I asked.

"So's I could tear your ears off."

She left. If she had been Mrs. Blodgett, she knew how to take care of herself, she knew how many trunks there were in the attic—and that was all.

Iris and I had dressed and were drinking daiquiris under a green and white striped umbrella when Miss Crump appeared followed by a young policeman. She was very pleased about the policeman. He had come, she said, in answer to her complaint. She showed him Poppy; she babbled out her story of the Blodgetts. He obviously thought she was a harmless lunatic, but she didn't seem to realize it. After she had let him out, she settled beamingly down with us.

"I suppose," said Iris, "you asked him for his credentials?"

"I . . ." Miss Crump's face clouded. "My dear, you don't think that perhaps he wasn't a real police . . .?"

"To me," said Iris, "everyone's a Blodgett until proved to the contrary."

"Oh, dear," said Miss Crump.

Nothing else happened. By evening Iris and I were back in our part of the house. Poppy had hated to see us go. We had hated to leave her. A mutual crush had developed between us.

But now we were alone again, the sinister Blodgetts did not seem very substantial. Iris made a creditable *Boeuf Stroganov* from yesterday's leftovers and changed into a lime green negligee which would have inflamed the whole Pacific Fleet. I was busy being a sailor on leave with his girl when the phone rang. I reached over Iris for the receiver, said "Hello," and then sat rigid listening.

It was Miss Crump's voice. But something was horribly wrong with it. It came across hoarse and gasping.

"Come," it said. "Oh, come. The French windows. Oh, please . . ."

The voice faded. I heard the clatter of a dropped receiver.

"It must be Poppy," I said to Iris. "Quick."

We ran out into the dark patio. Across it, I could see the light French windows to Miss Crump's apartment. They were half open, and as I looked Poppy squirmed through to the patio. She bounded toward us, whining.

"Poppy's all right," said Iris. "Quick!"

We ran to Miss Crump's windows. Poppy barged past us into the living room. We followed. All the lights were on. Poppy had galloped around a high-backed davenport. We went to it and looked over it.

Poppy was crouching on the carpet, her huge muzzle dropped on her paws. She was howling and staring straight at Miss Crump.

Poppy's paid companion was on the floor too. She lay motionless on her back, her legs twisted under her, her small, grey face distorted, her lips stretched in a dreadful smile.

I knelt down by Poppy. I picked up Miss Crump's thin wrist and felt for the pulse. Poppy was still howling. Iris stood, straight and white.

"Peter, tell me. Is she dead?"

"Not quite. But only just not quite. Poison. It looks like strychnine . . . ."

We called a doctor. We called the police. The doctor came, muttered a shocked diagnosis of strychnine poisoning and rushed Miss Crump to the hospital. I asked if she had a chance. He didn't answer. I knew what that meant. Soon the police came and there was so much to say and do and think that I hadn't time to brood about poor Miss Crump.

We told Inspector Green the Blodgett story. It was obvious to us that somehow Miss Crump had been poisoned by them in mistake for Poppy. Since no one had entered the house that day except the three callers, one of them, we said, must have been a Blodgett. All the Inspector had to do, we said, was to locate those three people and find out which was a Blodgett.

Inspector Green watched us poker-faced and made no comment. After he'd left, we took the companionless Poppy back to our part of the house. She climbed on the bed and stretched out between us, her tail thumping, her head flopped on the pillows. We didn't have the heart to evict her. It was not one of our better nights.

Early next morning, a policeman took us to Miss Crump's apartment. Inspector Green was waiting in the living room. I didn't like his stare.

"We've analyzed the hamburger she was eating last night," he said. "There was enough strychnine in it to kill an elephant."

"Hamburger!" exclaimed Iris. "Then that proves she was poisoned by the Blodgetts!"

"Why?" asked Inspector Green.

"They didn't know how conscientious Miss Crump was. They didn't know she always bought steak for Poppy and hamburger for herself. They saw the steak and the hamburger and they naturally assumed the hamburger was for Poppy, so they poisoned that."

"That's right," I cut in. "The steak and the hamburger were lying right on the kitchen table when all three of those people came in yesterday."

"I see," said the Inspector.

He nodded to a policeman who left the room and returned with three people—the balding young man from the electric light company, the redheaded vixen, and the young policeman. None of them looked happy.

"You're willing to swear," the Inspector asked us, "that these were the only three people who entered this house yesterday."

"Yes," said Iris.

"And you think one of them is either Blodgett or his wife?"

"They've got to be."

Inspector Green smiled faintly. "Mr. Burns here has been with the electric light company for five years except for a year when he was in the army. The electric light company is willing to vouch for that. Miss Curtis has been identified as the sister of the lady who owns this house and the niece of Rear Admiral Moss. She has no connection with any Blodgetts and has never been in Utah." He paused. "As for Officer Patterson, he has been a member of the police force here for eight years. I personally sent him around yesterday to follow up Miss Crump's complaint."

The Inspector produced an envelope from his pocket and tossed it to me. "I've had these photographs of Mr. and Mrs. Henry Blodgett flown from the files of the Ogden Bluffs *Tribune*."

I pulled the photographs out of the envelope. We stared at them. Neither Mr. or Mrs. Blodgett looked at all the sort of person you would like to know. But neither of them bore the slightest resemblance to any of the three suspects in front of us.

"It might also interest you," said the Inspector quietly, "that I've checked with the Ogden Bluffs police. Mr. Blodgett has been sick in bed for over a week and his wife has been nursing him. There is a doctor's certificate to that effect."

Inspector Green gazed down at his hands. They were competent hands. "It looks to me that the whole Blodgett story was built up in Miss Crump's mind—or yours." His grey eyes stared right through us. "If we have to eliminate the Blodgetts and these three people from suspicion, that leaves only two others who had the slightest chance of poisoning the hamburger."

Iris blinked. "Us?"

"You," said Inspector Green almost sadly.

They didn't arrest us, of course. We had no conceivable motive. But Inspector Green questioned us minutely and when he left there was a policeman lounging outside our door.

We spent a harried afternoon racking our brains and getting nowhere. Iris was the one who had the inspiration. Suddenly, just after she had fed Poppy the remains of the *Stroganov*, she exclaimed:

"Good heavens above, of course!"

"Of course, what?"

She spun to me, her eyes shining. "Barney Thtone," she lisped. "Why didn't we realize? Come on!"

She ran out of the house into the street. She grabbed the lounging policeman by the arm.

"You live here," she said. "Who's Barney Stone?"

"Barney Stone?" The policeman stared. "He's the son of the druggist on the corner."

Iris raced me to the drugstore. She was attracting quite a crowd. The policeman followed, too.

In the drugstore, a thin young man with spectacles stood behind the prescription counter.

"Mr. Stone?" asked Iris.

His mouth dropped open. "Gee, Miss Duluth. I never dreamed . . . Gee, Miss Duluth, what can I do for you? Cigarettes? An alarm clock?"

"A little girl," said Iris. "A little girl with sandy pigtails and a brace on her teeth. What's her name? Where does she live?"

Barney Stone said promptly: "You mean Daisy Kornfeld. Kind of homely. Just down the block. 712. Miss Duluth, I certainly . . ."

"Thanks," cut in Iris and we were off again with our ever growing escort.

Daisy was sitting in the Kornfeld parlor, glumly thumping the piano. Ushered in by an excited, cooing Mrs. Kornfeld, Iris interrupted Daisy's rendition of "The Jolly Farmer."

"Daisy, that picture you took of me yesterday to sell to Mr. Stone, is it developed yet?"

"Geeth no, Mith Duluth. I ain't got the developing money yet. Theventy-five thenth. Ma don't give me but a nickel an hour for practithing thith gothdarn piano."

"Here." Iris thrust a ten-dollar bill into her hand. "I'll buy the whole roll. Run get the camera. We'll have it developed right away."

"Geeth." The mercenary Daisy stared with blank incredulity at the ten-dollar bill.

I stared just as blankly myself. I wasn't being bright at all.

I wasn't much brighter an hour later. We were back in our apartment, waiting for Inspector Green. Poppy, all for love, was trying to climb into my lap. Iris, who had charmed Barney Stone into developing Daisy's films, clutched the yellow envelope of snaps in her hand. She had sent our policeman away on a secret mission, but an infuriating passion for the dramatic had kept her from telling or showing me anything. I had to wait for Inspector Green.

Eventually Iris's policeman returned and whispered with her in the hall. Then Inspector Green came. He looked cold and hostile. Poppy didn't like him. She growled. Sometimes Poppy was smart.

Inspector Green said: "You've been running all over town. I told you to stay here."

"I know." Iris's voice was meek. "It's just that I wanted to solve poor Miss Crump's poisoning."

"Solve it?" Inspector Green's query was skeptical.

"Yes. It's awfully simple really. I can't imagine why we didn't think of it from the start."

"You mean you know who poisoned her?"

"Of course." Iris smiled, a maddening smile. "Henry Blodgett."

"But . . ."

"Check with the airlines. I think you'll find that Blodgett flew in from Ogden Bluffs a few days ago and flew back today. As for his being sick in bed under his wife's care, I guess that'll make Mrs. Blodgett an accessory before the fact, won't it?"

Inspector Green was pop-eyed.

"Oh, it's my fault really," continued Iris. "I said no one came to the house yesterday except those three people. There was someone else, but he was so ordinary, so run-of-the-mill, that I forgot him completely."

I was beginning to see then. Inspector Green snapped: "And this run-of-the-mill character?"

"The man," said Iris sweetly, "who had the best chance of all to poison the hamburger, *the man who delivered it*—the man from the Supermarket."

"We don't have to guess. We have proof." Iris fumbled in the yellow envelope. "Yesterday morning as we were going out, we bumped into the man delivering Miss Crump's groceries. Just at that moment, a sweet little girl took a snap of us. This snap."

She selected a print and handed it to Inspector Green. I moved to look at it over his shoulder.

"I'm afraid Daisy is an impressionistic photographer," murmured Iris. "That hip on the right is me. The buttocks are my husband. But the figure in the middle—quite a masterly likeness of Henry Blodgett, isn't it? Of course, there's the grocery apron, the unshaven chin . . ."

She was right. Daisy had only winged Iris and me but with the grocery man she had scored a direct hit. And the grocery man was unquestionably Henry Blodgett.

Iris nodded to her policeman. "Sergeant Blair took a copy of the snap around the neighborhood groceries. They recognized Blodgett at the Supermarket. They hired him day before yesterday. He made a few deliveries this morning, including Miss Crump's, and took a powder without his pay."

"Well . . ." stammered Inspector Green. "Well . . ."

"Just how many charges can you get him on?" asked my wife hopefully. "Attempted homicide, conspiracy to defraud, illegal possession of poisonous drugs . . . . The rat, I hope you give him the works when you get him."

"We'll get him all right," said Inspector Green.

Iris leaned over and patted Poppy's head affectionately.

"Don't worry, darling. I'm sure Miss Crump will get well and we'll throw a lovely christening party for your little strangers . . . ."

Iris was right about the Blodgetts. Henry got the works. And his wife was held as an accessory. Iris was right about Miss Crump too. She is still in the hospital but improving steadily and will almost certainly be well enough to attend the christening party.

Meanwhile, at her request, Poppy is staying with us, awaiting maternity with rollicking unconcern.

It's nice having a dog who pays the rent.

FROM ANOTHER WORLD
Clayton Rawson
Detective: The Great Merlini

KNOWN TODAY as one of the greatest of all writers of impossible crimes, Clayton Rawson (1906-1971) also was one of America's most famous illusionists; he was a member of the American Society of Magicians and wrote on the subject frequently.

Born in Elyria, Ohio, he graduated from Ohio State University and worked as an illustrator for advertising agencies and magazines before turning to writing. He used his extensive knowledge of stage magic to create elaborate locked room and impossible crime novels and short stories.

Under his own name, all his fiction featured the Great Merlini, a professional magician and amateur detective who opened a magic shop in New York City's Times Square where he often is visited by his friendly rival, Inspector Homer Gavigan of the NYPD, when he is utterly baffled by a seemingly impossible crime. Merlini's adventures are recounted by freelance writer Ross Harte. There are only four Merlini novels, two of which have been adapted for motion pictures.

Miracles for Sale (1939) was based on Rawson's first novel, *Death from a Top Hat* (1938). In this film, the protagonist is named Mike

Morgan, played by Robert Young; it was directed by Tod Browning. The popular Mike Shayne series used Rawson's second book, *The Footprints on the Ceiling* (1939), as the basis for *The Man Who Wouldn't Die* (1942), with Lloyd Nolan starring as Shayne, who consults a professional magician for help. The other Merlini books are *The Headless Lady* (1940), *No Coffin for the Corpse* (1942), and *The Great Merlini* (1979), a complete collection of Merlini stories.

Under the pseudonym Stuart Towne, Rawson wrote four pulp novellas as Don Diavolo. The author was one of the four founding members of the Mystery Writers of America and created its motto: "Crime Does Not Pay—Enough."

"From Another World" was first published in the June 1948 issue of *Ellery Queen's Mystery Magazine*; it was first collected in *The Great Merlini* (Boston, Gregg Press, 1979).

From Another World
By Clayton Rawson

IT WAS undoubtedly one of the world's strangest rooms. The old-fashioned roll-top desk, the battered typewriter, and the steel filing cabinet indicated that it was an office. There was even a calendar memo-pad, a pen and pencil set, and an overflowing ashtray on the desk, but any resemblance to any other office stopped right there.

The desk top also held a pair of handcuffs, half a dozen billiard balls, a shiny nickel-plated revolver, one celluloid egg, several decks of playing cards, a bright green silk handkerchief, and a stack of unopened mail. In one corner of the room stood a large, galvanized-iron milk-can with a strait jacket lying on its top. A feathered devil mask from the upper Congo leered down from the wall above and the entire opposite wall was papered with a Ringling Bros. and Barnum & Bailey twenty-four sheet poster.

A loose-jointed dummy-figure of a small boy with pop-eyes and violently red hair lay on the filing cabinet together with a skull and a fish-bowl filled with paper flowers. And in the cabinet's bottom drawer, which was partly open and lined with paper, there was one half-eaten carrot and a twinkly-nosed, live white rabbit.

A pile of magazines, topped by a French journal, *l'Illusioniste*, was stacked precariously on a chair, and a large bookcase tried vainly to hold an even larger flood of books that overflowed and formed dusty stalagmites growing up from the floor—books whose authors would have been startled at the company they kept. Shaw's *Joan of Arc* was sandwiched between Rowan's *Story of the Secret Service* and the *Memoirs of Robert-Houdin*. Arthur Machen, Dr. Hans Gross, William Blake, Sir James Jeans, Rebecca West, Robert Louis Stevenson, and Ernest Hemingway were bounded on either side by Devol's *Forty Years a Gambler on the Mississippi* and Reginald Scot's *Discoverie of Witchcraft*.

The merchandise in the shop beyond the office had a similar surrealistic quality, but the inscription on the glass of the outer door, although equally strange, did manage to supply an explanation. It read: *Miracles For Sale*—THE MAGIC SHOP, *A. Merlini, Prop.*

And that gentleman, naturally, was just as unusual as his place of business. For one thing, he hadn't put a foot in it, to my knowledge, in at least a week. When he finally did reappear, I found him at the desk sleepily and somewhat glumly eyeing the unopened mail.

He greeted me as though he hadn't seen another human being in at least a month, and the swivel chair creaked as he settled back in it, put his long legs up on the desk, and yawned. Then he indicated the card bearing his business slogan—"Nothing Is Impossible"—which was tacked on the wall.

"I may have to take that sign down," he said lazily. "I've just met a theatrical producer, a scene designer, and a playwright all of whom are quite impossible. They came in here a week before opening night and asked me to supply several small items mentioned in the script. In one scene a character said, 'Begone!' and the stage directions read: 'The genie and his six dancing girl slaves vanish instantly.' Later an elephant, complete with howdah and princess, disappeared the same way. I had to figure out how to manage all that and cook up a few assorted miracles for the big scene in heaven, too. Then I spent thirty-six hours in bed. And I'm still half asleep." He grinned wryly and added, "Ross, if you want anything that is not a stock item, you can whistle for it."

"I don't want a miracle," I said. "Just an interview. What do you know about ESP and PK?"

"Too much," he said. "You're doing another magazine article?"

"Yes. And I've spent the last week with a queer assortment of characters, too—half a dozen psychologists, some professional gamblers, a nuclear physicist, the secretary of the Psychical Research Society, and a neurologist. I've got an appointment in half an hour with a millionaire, and after that I want to hear what you think of it."

"You interviewed Dr. Rhine at Duke University, of course."

I nodded. "Sure. He started it all. He says he's proved conclusively that there really are such things as telepathy, mind-reading, clairvoyance, X-Ray vision, and probably crystal-gazing as well. He wraps it all up in one package and calls it ESP—meaning Extra Sensory Perception."

"That," Merlini said, "is not the half of it. His psychokinesis, or PK for short, is positively miraculous—and frightening." The magician pulled several issues of the *Journal of Parapsychology* from the stack of magazines and upset the whole pile. "If the conclusions Rhine has published here are correct—if there really is a tangible mental force that can not only reach out and influence the movements of dice but exert its mysterious control over other physical objects as well—then he has completely upset the apple-cart of modern psychology and punctured a whole library of general scientific theory as well."

"He's already upset me," I said. "I tried to use PK in a crap game Saturday night. I lost sixty-eight bucks."

My skepticism didn't disturb Merlini. He went right on, gloomier than ever. "If Rhine is right, his ESP and PK have reopened the

Pandora's box in which science thought it had forever sealed Voodoo and witchcraft and enough other practices of primitive magic to make your hair stand on end. And you're growling about losing a few dollars—"

Behind me a hearty, familiar voice said, "I haven't got anything to worry about except a homicidal maniac who has killed three people in the last two days and left absolutely no clues. But can I come in?"

Inspector Homer Gavigan of the New York City Police Department stood in the doorway, his blue eyes twinkling frostily.

Merlini, liking the Cassandra role he was playing, said, "Sure, I've been waiting for you. But don't think that PK won't give you a splitting headache, too. All a murderer would have to do to commit the perfect crime—and a locked room one at that—would be to exert his psychokinetic mental force from a distance against the gun trigger." He pointed at the revolver on the desk. "Like this—"

Gavigan and I both saw the trigger, with no finger on it, move.

Bang!

The gun's report was like a thunderclap in the small room. I knew well enough that it was only a stage prop and the cartridge a blank, but I jumped a foot. So did Gavigan.

"Look, dammit!" the Inspector exploded, "how did you—"

The Great Merlini grinned. He was fully awake now and enjoying himself hugely. "No," he said, "that wasn't PK, luckily. Just ordinary run-of-the-mill conjuring. The Rising Cards and the Talking Skull are both sometimes operated the same way. You can have the secret at the usual catalog price of—"

Like most policemen Gavigan had a healthy respect for firearms and he was still jumpy. "I don't want to buy either of them," he growled. "Do we have a date for dinner—or don't we? I'm starved."

"We do," Merlini said, pulling his long, lean self up out of the chair and reaching for his coat. "Can you join us, Ross?"

I shook my head. "Not this time. I've got a date just now with Andrew Drake."

In the elevator Merlini gave me an odd look and asked, "Andrew Drake? What has he got to do with ESP and PK?"

"What doesn't he have something to do with?" I replied. "Six months ago, it was the Drake Plan to Outlaw War; he tried to take over UN singlehanded. Two months ago he announced he was setting up a fifteen-million dollar research foundation to find a cancer cure in six months. 'Polish it off like we did the atom bomb,' he says. 'Put in enough money, and you can accomplishing anything.' Now he's head over heels in ESP with some Yogi mixed in. 'Unleash the power of the human mind and solve all our problems.' Just like that."

"So that's what he's up to," Merlini said as we came out on to Forty-second Street, half a block from Times Square, to face a bitterly cold January wind. "I wondered."

Then, as he followed Gavigan into the official car that waited and left me shivering on the curb, he threw a last cryptic sentence over his shoulder.

"When Drake mentions Rosa Rhys," he said, "you might warn him that he's heading for trouble."

Merlini didn't know how right he was. If any of us had had any clairvoyant ability at all, I wouldn't have taken a cab up to Drake's; all three of us would have gone—in Gavigan's car and with the siren going full blast.

As it was, I stepped out all alone in front of the big Ninety-eighth Street house just off Riverside Drive. It was a sixty-year-old mansion built in the tortured style that had been the height of architectural fashion in the 80's but was now a smoke-blackened monstrosity as coldly depressing as the weather.

I nearly froze both ears just getting across the pavement and up the steps where I found a doctor with his finger glued—or frozen perhaps—to the bell push. A doctor? No, it wasn't ESP; a copy of the *A.M.A. Journal* stuck out his overcoat pocket, and his left hand carried the customary small black case. But he didn't have the medical man's usual clinical detachment. This doctor was jumpy as hell.

When I asked, "Anything wrong?" his head jerked around, and his pale blue eyes gave me a startled look. He was a thin, well-dressed man in his early forties.

"Yes," he said crisply. "I'm afraid so." He jabbed a long forefinger at the bell again just as the door opened.

At first I didn't recognize the girl who looked out at us. When I saw her by daylight earlier in the week, I had tagged her as in the brainy-but-a-bit-plain category, a judgment I revised somewhat now, considering what the Charles hair-do and Hattie Carnegie dress did for her.

"Oh, hello, doctor," she said. "Come in."

The doctor began talking even before he crossed the threshold. "Your father, Elinor—is he still in the study?"

"Yes, I think so. But what—"

She stopped because he was already gone, running down the hall toward a door at its end. He rattled the doorknob, then rapped loudly.

"Mr. Drake! Let me in!"

The girl looked puzzled, then frightened. Her dark eyes met mine for an instant, and then her high heels clicked on the polished floor as she too ran down the hall. I didn't wait to be invited. I followed.

The doctor's knuckles rapped again on the door. "Miss Rhys!" he called. "It's Dr. Garrett. Unlock the door!" There was no answer.

Garrett tried the doorknob once more, then threw his shoulder against the door. It didn't move.

"Elinor, do you have a key? We must get in there—quickly!"

She said, "No. Father has the only keys. Why don't they answer? What's wrong?"

"I don't know," Garrett said. "Your father phoned me just now. He was in pain. He said, '*Hurry! I need you. I'm—*'" The doctor hesitated, watching the girl; then he finished "'*—dying.*' After that—no answer." Garrett turned to me. "You've got more weight than I have. Think you can break this door in?"

I looked at it. The door seemed solid enough, but it was an old house and the wood around the screws that held the lock might give. "I don't know," I said. "I'll try."

Elinor Drake moved to one side and the doctor stepped behind me. I threw myself against the door twice and the second time felt it move a bit. Then I hit it hard. Just as the door gave way I heard the tearing sound of paper.

But before I could discover what caused that, my attention was held by more urgent matters. I found myself staring at a green-shaded desk lamp, the room's only source of light, at the overturned phone on the desk top, and at the sprawled shape that lay on the floor in front of the desk. A coppery highlight glinted on a letter-opener near the man's feet. Its blade was discolored with a dark wet stain.

Dr. Garrett said, "Elinor, you stay out," as he moved past me to the body and bent over it. One of his hands lifted Andrew Drake's right eyelid, the other felt his wrist.

I have never heard a ghost speak but the sound that came then was exactly what I would expect—a low, quivering moan shot with pain. I jerked around and saw a glimmer of white move in the darkness on my left.

Behind me, Elinor's whisper, a tense thread of sound, said, "Lights," as she clicked the switch by the door. The glow from the ceiling fixture overhead banished both the darkness and the spectre—but what remained was almost as unlikely. A chair lay overturned on the carpet, next to a small table that stood in the center of the room. In a second chair, slumped forward with her head resting on the tabletop, was the body of a young woman.

She was young, dark-haired, rather good-looking, and had an excellent figure. This latter fact was instantly apparent because—and I had to look twice before I could believe what I saw—she wore a brief, skin-tight, one-piece bathing suit. Nothing else.

Elinor's eyes were still on the sprawled shape on the floor. "Father. He's—dead?"

Garrett nodded slowly and stood up.

I heard the quick intake of her breath but she made no other sound. Then Garrett strode quickly across to the woman at the table.

"Unconscious," he said after a moment. "Apparently a blow on the head—but she's beginning to come out of it." He looked again at the knife on the floor. "We'll have to call the police."

I hardly heard him. I was wondering why the room was so bare. The hall outside and the living room that opened off it were furnished with the stiff, formal ostentation of the overly-rich. But Drake's study, by contrast, was as sparsely furnished as a cell in a Trappist monastery. Except for the desk, the small table, the two chairs, and a three-leaf folding screen that stood in one corner, it contained no other furniture. There were no pictures on the walls, no papers, and although there were shelves for them, no books. There wasn't even a blotter or pen on the desk top. Nothing but the phone, desk lamp—and, strangely enough, a roll of gummed paper tape.

But I only glanced at these things briefly. It was the large casement window in the wall behind the desk that held my attention—a dark rectangle beyond which, like a scattered handful of bright jewels, were the lights of Jersey and, above them, frosty pinpoints of stars shining coldly in a black sky.

The odd thing was that the window's center line, where its two halves joined, was criss-crossed by two-foot strips of brown paper tape pasted to the glass. The window was, quite literally, sealed shut. It was then that I remembered the sound of tearing paper as the lock had given way and the door had come open.

I turned. Elinor still stood there—motionless. And on the inside of the door and on the jamb were more of the paper strips. Four were torn in half, two others had been pulled loose from the wall and hung curled from the door's edge.

At that moment a brisk, energetic voice came from the hall. "How come you leave the front door standing wide open on the coldest day in—"

Elinor turned to face a broad-shouldered young man with wavy hair, hand-painted tie, and a completely self-assured manner. She said, "Paul!" then took one stumbling step and was in his arms.

He blinked at her. "Hey! What's wrong?" Then he saw what lay on the floor by the desk. His self-confidence sagged.

Dr. Garrett moved to the door. "Kendrick," he said, "take Elinor out of here. I'll—"

"No!" It was Elinor's voice. She straightened up, turned suddenly and started into the room.

But Paul caught her. "Where are you going?"

She tried to pull away from him. "I'm going to phone the police." Her eyes followed the trail of bloodstains that led from the body across the beige carpet to the overturned chair and the woman at the table. "She—killed him."

That was when I started for the phone myself. But I hadn't taken more than two steps when the woman in the bathing suit let out a hair-raising shriek.

She was gripping the table with both hands, her eyes fixed on Drake's body with the rigid unblinking stare of a figure carved from stone. Then, suddenly, her body trembled all over, and she opened her mouth again—But Garrett got there first.

He slapped her on the side of the face—hard.

It stopped the scream, but the horror still filled her round dark eyes and she still stared at the body as though it were some demon straight from hell.

"Hysteria," Garrett said. Then seeing me start again toward the phone, "Get an ambulance, too." And when he spoke to Paul Kendrick this time, it was an order. "And get Elinor out of here—quickly!"

Elinor Drake was looking at the girl in the bathing suit with wide, puzzled eyes. "She—she killed him. Why?"

Paul nodded. He turned Elinor around gently but swiftly and led her out.

The cops usually find too many fingerprints on a phone, none of them any good because they are superimposed on each other. But I handled the receiver carefully just the same, picking it up by one end. When Spring 7-1313 answered, I gave the operator the facts fast, then asked him to locate Inspector Gavigan and have him call me back. I gave Drake's number.

As I talked I watched Dr. Garrett open his black case and take out a hypodermic syringe. He started to apply it to the woman's arm just as I hung up.

"What's that, Doc?" I asked.

"Sedative. Otherwise she'll be screaming again in a minute."

The girl didn't seem to feel the needle as it went in.

Then, noticing two bright spots of color on the table, I went across to examine them closely and felt more than ever as though I had stepped straight into a surrealist painting. I was looking at two round- ed conical shapes each about two inches in length. Both were striped like candy canes, one in maroon against a white background, the other in thinner brilliant red stripes against an opalescent amber.

"Did Drake," I asked, "collect seashells, too?"

"No." Garrett scowled in a worried way at the shells. "But I once did. These are mollusks, but not from the sea. *Cochlostyla*, a tree snail. Habitat: The Philippines." He turned his scowl from the shells to me. "By the way, just who are you?"

"The name is Ross Harte." I added that I had had an appointment to interview Drake for a magazine article and then asked, "Why is this room sealed as it is? Why is this girl dressed only in—"

Apparently, like many medical men, Garrett took a dim view of reporters. "I'll make my statement," he said a bit stiffly, "to the police."

They arrived a moment later. Two uniformed prowl-car cops first, then the precinct boys and after that, at intervals, the homicide squad, an ambulance interne, a fingerprint man and photographer, the med- ical examiner, an assistant D.A. and later, because a millionaire rates more attention than the victim of a Harlem stabbing, the D.A. him- self, and an Assistant Chief Inspector even looked in for a few minutes.

Of the earlier arrivals the only familiar face was that of the Homicide Squad's Lieutenant Doran—a hardboiled, coldly efficient, no-nonsense cop who had so little use for reporters that I suspected he had once been bitten by one.

At Dr. Garrett's suggestion, which the interne seconded, the girl in the bathing suit was taken, under guard, to the nearest hospital. Then Garrett and I were put on ice, also under guard, in the living room. Another detective ushered Paul Kendrick into the room a moment later.

He scowled at Dr. Garrett. "We all thought Rosa Rhys was bad medicine. But I never expected anything like this. Why would she want to kill him? It doesn't make sense."

"Self-defense?" I suggested. "Could he have made a pass at her and—"

Kendrick shook his head emphatically. "Not that gal. She was making a fast play for the old man—and his money. A pass would have been just what she wanted." He turned to Garrett. "What were they doing in there—more ESP experiments?"

The doctor laid his overcoat neatly over the back of an ornate Spanish chair. His voice sounded tired and defeated. "No. They had gone beyond that. I told him that she was a fraud, but you know how Drake was—always so absolutely confident that he couldn't be wrong about anything. He said he'd put her through a test that would convince all of us."

"Of what?" I asked. "What was it she claimed she could do?"

The detective at the door moved forward. "My orders," he said, "are that you're not to talk about what happened until after the Lieutenant has taken your statements. Make it easy for me, will you?"

That made it difficult for us. Any other conversational subject just then seemed pointless. We sat there silent and uncomfortable. But somehow the nervous tension that had been in our voices was still there—a foreboding, ghostly presence waiting with us for what was to happen next.

A half hour later, although it seemed many times that long, Garrett was taken out for questioning, then Kendrick. And later I got the nod. I saw Elinor Drake, a small, lonely figure in the big hall, moving slowly up the wide stairs. Doran and the police stenographer who waited for me in the stately dining room with its heavy crystal chandelier looked out of place. But the Lieutenant didn't feel ill at ease; his questions were as coldly efficient as a surgeon's knife.

I tried to insert a query of my own now and then, but soon gave that up. Doran ignored all such attempts as completely as if they didn't exist. Then, just as he dismissed me, the phone rang. Doran answered, listened, scowled, and then held the receiver out to me. "For you," he said.

I heard Merlini's voice. "My ESP isn't working so well today, Ross. Drake is dead. I get that much. But just what happened up there, anyway?"

"ESP my eye," I told him. "If you were a mind-reader you'd have been up here long ago. It's a sealed room—in spades. The sealed room to end all sealed rooms."

I saw Doran start forward as if to object. "Merlini," I said quickly, "is Inspector Gavigan still with you?" I lifted the receiver from my ear and let Doran hear the "Yes" that came back.

Merlini's voice went on. "Did you say sealed room? The flash from headquarters didn't mention that. They said an arrest had already been made. It sounded like a routine case."

"Headquarters," I replied, "has no imagination. Or else Doran has been keeping things from them. It isn't even a routine sealed room. Listen: A woman comes to Drake's house on the coldest January day since 1812 dressed only in a bathing suit. She goes with him into his study. They seal the window and door on the inside with gummed paper tape. Then she stabs him with a paper knife. Before he dies, he knocks her out, then manages to get to the phone and send out an S.O.S.

"She's obviously crazy; she has to be to commit murder under those circumstances. But Drake wasn't crazy. A bit eccentric maybe, but not nuts. So why would he lock himself in so carefully with a homicidal maniac? If headquarters thinks that's routine I'll—" Then I interrupted myself. There was too much silence on the other end of the wire. "Merlini! Are you still there?"

"Yes," his voice said slowly, "I'm still here. Headquarters was much too brief. They didn't tell us her name. But I know it now."

Then, abruptly, I felt as if I had stepped off into some fourth-dimensional hole in space and had dropped on to some other nightmare planet.

Merlini's voice, completely serious, was saying, "Ross, did the police find a silver denarius from the time of the Caesars in that room? Or a freshly picked rose, a string of Buddhist prayer beads—perhaps a bit of damp seaweed—?"

I didn't say anything. I couldn't.

After a moment, Merlini added, "So—they did. What was it?"

"Shells," I said dazedly, still quite unconvinced that any conversation could sound like this. "Philippine tree snail shells. Why, in the name of—"

Merlini cut in hastily. "Tell Doran that Gavigan and I will be there in ten minutes. Sit tight and keep your eyes open—"

"Merlini!" I objected frantically, "if you hang up without—"

"The shells explain the bathing suit, Ross—and make it clear why the room was sealed. But they also introduce an element that Gavigan and Doran and the D.A. and the Commissioner are not going to like at all. I don't like it myself. It's even more frightening as a murder method than PK."

He hesitated a moment, then let me have both barrels.

"Those shells suggest that Drake's death might have been caused by even stranger forces—evil and evanescent ones—from another world!"

My acquaintance with a police inspector cut no ice with Doran; he ordered me right back into the living room.

I heard a siren announce the arrival of Gavigan's car shortly after, but it was a long hour later before Doran came in and said, "The Inspector wants to see all of you—in the study."

As I moved with the others out into the hall I saw Merlini waiting for me.

"It's about time," I growled at him. "Another ten minutes and you'd have found me D.O.A., too—from suspense."

"Sorry you had to cool your heels," he said, "but Gavigan is being difficult. As predicted, he doesn't like the earful Doran has been giving him. Neither do I." The dryly ironic good humor that was almost always in his voice was absent. He was unusually sober.

"Don't build it up," I said. "I've had all the mystery I can stand. Just give me answers. First, why did you tell me to warn Drake about Rosa Rhys?"

"I didn't expect murder, if that's what you're thinking," he replied. "Drake was elaborating on some of Rhine's original experiments aimed at discovering whether ESP operates more efficiently when the subject is in a trance state. Rosa is a medium."

"Oh, so that's it. She and Drake were holding a séance?"

Merlini nodded. "Yes. The Psychical Research Society is extremely interested in ESP and PK—it's given them a new lease on life. And I knew they had recommended Rosa, whom they had previously investigated, to Drake."

"And what about the Roman coins, roses, Buddhist prayer beads— and snail shells? Why the bathing suit and how does that explain why the room was sealed?"

But Doran, holding the study door open, interrupted before he could reply.

"Hurry it up!" he ordered.

Going into that room now was like walking onto a brightly lighted stage. A powerful electric bulb of almost floodlight brilliance had been inserted in the ceiling fixture and its harsh white glare made the room more barren and cell-like than ever. Even Inspector Gavigan seemed to have taken on a menacing air. Perhaps it was the black mask of shadow that his hat brim threw down across the upper part of his face; or it may have been the carefully intent way he watched us as we came in.

Doran did the introductions. "Miss Drake, Miss Potter, Paul Kendrick, Dr. Walter Garrett."

I looked at the middle-aged woman whose gayly frilled, altogether feminine hat contrasted oddly with her angular figure, her prim determined mouth, and the chilly glance of complete disapproval with which she regarded Gavigan.

"How," I whispered to Merlini, "did Isabelle Potter, the secretary of the Psychical Research Society, get here?"

"She came with Rosa," he answered. "The police found her upstairs reading a copy of Tyrrell's *Study of Apparitions*." Merlini smiled faintly. "She and Doran don't get along."

"They wouldn't," I said. "They talk different languages. When I interviewed her, I got a travelogue on the other world—complete with lantern slides."

Inspector Gavigan wasted no time. "Miss Drake," he began, "I understand the medical foundation for cancer research your father thought of endowing was originally your idea."

The girl glanced once at the stains on the carpet, then kept her dark eyes steadily on Gavigan. "Yes," she said slowly, "it was."

"Are you interested in psychical research?"

Elinor frowned. "No."

"Did you object when your father began holding séances with Miss Rhys?"

She shook her head. "That would only have made him more determined."

Gavigan turned to Kendrick. "Did you?"

"Me?" Paul lifted his brows. "I didn't know him well enough for that. Don't think he liked me much, anyway. But why a man like Drake would waste his time—"

"And you, doctor?"

"Did I object?" Garrett seemed surprised. "Naturally. No one but a neurotic middle-aged woman would take a séance seriously."

Miss Potter resented that one. "Dr. Garrett," she said icily, "Sir Oliver Lodge was not a neurotic woman, nor Sir William Crookes, nor Professor Zoëllner, nor—"

"But they were all senile," Garrett replied just as icily. "And as for ESP, no neurologist of any standing admits any such possibility. They leave such things to you and your society, Miss Potter—and to the Sunday supplements."

She gave the doctor a look that would have split an atom, and Gavigan, seeing the danger of a chain reaction if this sort of dialogue were allowed to continue, broke in quickly.

"Miss Potter. You introduced Miss Rhys to Mr. Drake and he was conducting ESP experiments with her. Is that correct?"

Miss Potter's voice was still dangerously radioactive. "It is. And their results were gratifying and important. Of course, neither you nor Dr. Garrett would understand—"

"And then," Garrett cut in, "they both led him on into an investigation of Miss Rhys's psychic specialty—apports." He pronounced the last word with extreme distaste.

Inspector Gavigan scowled, glanced at Merlini, and the latter promptly produced a definition. "An apport," he said, "from the French *apporter*, to bring, is any physical object supernormally brought into a séance room—from nowhere usually or from some impossible distance. Miss Rhys on previous occasions—according to the Psychical Society's *Journal*—has apported such objects as Roman coins, roses, beads, and seaweed."

"She is the greatest apport medium," Miss Potter declared somewhat belligerently, "since Charles Bailey."

"Then she's good," Merlini said. "Bailey was an apport medium whom Conan Doyle considered *bona fide*. He produced birds, oriental plants, small animals, and on one occasion a young shark eighteen inches long which he claimed his spirit guide had whisked instantly via the astral plane from the Indian Ocean and projected, still damp and very much alive, into the séance room."

"So," I said, "that's why this room was sealed. To make absolutely certain that no one could open the door or window in the dark and help Rosa by introducing—"

"Of course," Garrett added. "Obviously there could be no apports if adequate precautions were not taken. Drake also moved a lot of his things out of the study and inventoried every object that remained. He also suggested, since I was so skeptical, that I be the one to make certain that Miss Rhys carried nothing into the room on her person. I gave her a most complete physical examination—in a bedroom upstairs. Then she put on one of Miss Drake's bathing suits."

"Did you come down to the study with her and Drake?" Gavigan asked.

The doctor frowned. "No. I had objected to Miss Potter's presence at the séance and Miss Rhys countered by objecting to mine."

"She was quite right," Miss Potter said. "The presence of an unbeliever like yourself would prevent even the strongest psychic forces from making themselves manifest."

"I have no doubt of that," Garrett replied stiffly. "It's the usual excuse, as I told Drake. He tried to get her to let me attend but she refused flatly. So I went back to my office down the street. Drake's phone call came a half hour or so later."

"And yet"—Gavigan eyed the two brightly colored shells on the table—"in spite of all your precautions she produced two of these."

Garrett nodded. "Yes, I know. But the answer is fairly obvious now. She hid them somewhere in the hall outside on her arrival and then secretly picked them up again on her way in here."

Elinor frowned. "I'm afraid not, doctor. Father thought of that and asked me to go down with them to the study. He held one of her hands and I held the other."

Gavigan scowled. Miss Potter beamed.

"Did you go in with them?" Merlini asked.

She shook her head. "No. Only as far as the door. They went in and I heard it lock behind them. I stood there for a moment or two and heard Father begin pasting the tape on the door. Then I went back to my room to dress. I was expecting Paul."

Inspector Gavigan turned to Miss Potter. "You remained upstairs?"

"Yes," she replied in a tone that dared him to deny it. "I did."

Gavigan looked at Elinor. "Paul said a moment ago that your father didn't like him. Why not?"

"Paul exaggerates," the girl said quickly. "Father didn't dislike him. He was just—well, a bit difficult where my men friends were concerned."

"He thought they were all after his money," Kendrick added. "But at the rate he was endowing medical foundations and psychic societies—"

Miss Potter objected. "Mr. Drake did *not* endow the Psychic Society."

"But he was seriously considering it," Garrett said. "Miss Rhys—and Miss Potter—were selling him on the theory that illness is only a mental state due to a psychic imbalance—whatever that is."

"They won't sell me on that," Elinor said and then turned suddenly on Miss Potter, her voice trembling. "If it weren't for you and your idiotic foolishness Father wouldn't have been—killed." Then to Gavigan, "We've told all this before—to the Lieutenant. Is it quite necessary—"

The Inspector glanced at Merlini, then said, "I think that will be all for now. Okay, Doran, take them back. But none of them are to leave yet."

When they had gone, he turned to Merlini. "Well, I asked the questions you wanted me to, but I still think it was a waste of time. Rosa Rhys killed Drake. Anything else is impossible."

"What about Kendrick's cab driver?" Merlini asked. "Did your men locate him yet?"

Gavigan's scowl, practically standard operating procedure by now, grew darker. "Yes. Kendrick's definitely out. He entered the cab on the other side of town at just about the time Drake was sealing this room and he was apparently still in it, crossing Central Park, at the time Drake was killed."

"So," I commented, "he's the only one with an alibi."

Gavigan lifted his eyebrows. "The only one? Except for Rosa Rhys they *all* have alibis. The sealed room takes care of that."

"Yes," Merlini said quietly, "but the people with alibis also have motives while the one person who could have killed Drake has none."

"She did it," the Inspector answered. "So she's got a motive—and we'll find it."

"I wish I were as confident of that as you are," Merlini said. "Under the circumstances you'll be able to get a conviction without showing motive, but if you don't find one, it will always bother you."

"Maybe," Gavigan admitted, "but that won't be as bad as trying to believe what she says happened in this room."

That was news to me. "You've talked to Rosa?" I asked.

"One of the boys did," Gavigan said sourly. "At the hospital. She's already preparing an insanity defense."

"But why," Merlini asked, "is she still hysterical with fright? Could it be that she's scared because she really believes her story—because something like that really did happen in here?"

"Look," I said impatiently, "is it top secret or will somebody tell me what she says happened?"

Gavigan glowered at Merlini. "Are you going to stand there and tell me that you think Rosa Rhys actually believes—"

It was my question that Merlini answered. He walked to the table in the center of the room. "She says that after Drake sealed the window and door, the lights were turned off and she and Drake sat opposite each other at this table. His back was toward the desk, hers toward that screen in the corner. Drake held her hands. They waited. Finally she felt the psychic forces gathering around her—and then, out of nowhere, the two shells dropped onto the table one after the other.

Drake got up, turned on the desk light, and came back to the table. A moment later it happened."

The magician paused for a moment, regarding the bare, empty room with a frown. "Drake," he continued, "was examining the shells, quite excited and pleased about their appearance when suddenly, Rosa says, she heard a movement behind her. She saw Drake look up and then stare incredulously over her shoulder." Merlini spread his hands. "And that's all she remembers. Something hit her. When she came to, she found herself staring at the blood on the floor and at Drake's body."

Gavigan was apparently remembering Merlini's demonstration with the gun in his office. "If you," he warned acidly, "so much as try to hint that one of the people outside this room projected some mental force that knocked Rosa out and then caused the knife to stab Drake—"

"You know," Merlini said, "I half expected Miss Potter would suggest that. But her theory is even more disturbing." He looked at me. "She says that the benign spirits which Rosa usually evoked were overcome by some malign and evil entity whose astral substance materialized momentarily, killed Drake, then returned to the other world from which it came."

"She's a mental case, too," Gavigan said disgustedly. "They have to be crazy if they expect anyone to believe any such—"

"That," Merlini said quietly, "may be another reason Rosa is scared to death. Perhaps she believes it but knows you won't. In her shoes, I'd be scared, too." He frowned. "The difficulty is the knife."

Gavigan blinked. "The knife? What's difficult about that?"

"If I killed Drake," Merlini replied, "and wanted appearances to suggest that psychic forces were responsible, you wouldn't have found a weapon in this room that made it look as if I were guilty. I would have done a little de-apporting and made it disappear. As it is now, even if the knife was propelled supernaturally, Rosa takes the rap."

"And how," Gavigan demanded, "would you make the knife disappear if you were dressed, as she was, in practically nothing?" With sudden suspicion, he added, "Are you suggesting that there's a way she could have done that—and that you think she's not guilty because she didn't?"

Merlini lifted one of the shells from the table and placed it in the center of his left palm. His right hand covered it for a brief moment, then moved away. The shell was no longer there; it had vanished as silently and as easily as a ghost. Merlini turned both hands palms outward; both were unmistakably empty.

"Yes," he said, "she could have made the knife disappear—if she had wanted to. The same way she produced the two shells."

He made a reaching gesture with his right hand and the missing shell reappeared suddenly at his fingertips.

Gavigan looked annoyed and relieved at the same time. "So," he said, "you do know how she got those shells in here. I want to hear it. Right now."

But Gavigan had to wait.

At that moment a torpedo hit the water-tight circumstantial case against Rosa Rhys and detonated with a roar.

Doran, who had answered the phone a moment before, was swearing profusely. He was staring at the receiver he held as though it were a live cobra he had picked up by mistake.

"It—it's Doc Hess," he said in a dazed tone. "He just started the autopsy and thought we'd like to know that the point of the murder knife struck a rib and broke off. He just dug out a triangular pointed piece of—steel."

For several seconds after that there wasn't a sound. Then Merlini spoke.

"Gentlemen of the jury. Exhibit A, the paper knife with which my esteemed opponent, the District Attorney, claims Rosa Rhys stabbed Andrew Drake, is a copper alloy—and its point, as you can see, is quite intact. The defense rests."

Doran swore again. "Drake's inventory lists that letter opener, but that's all. There is no other knife in this room. I'm positive of that."

Gavigan jabbed a thick forefinger at me. "Ross, Dr. Garrett was in here before the police arrived. And Miss Drake and Kendrick."

I shook my head. "Sorry. There was no knife near the door and neither Elinor nor Paul came more than a foot into the room. Dr. Garrett examined Drake and Rosa, but I was watching him, and I'll testify that unless he's as expert at slight-of-hand as Merlini, he didn't pick up a thing."

Doran was not convinced. "Look, buddy. Unless Doc Hess has gone crazy too, there was a knife and it's not here now. So somebody took it out." He turned to the detective who stood at the door. "Tom," he said, "have the boys frisk all those people. Get a police woman for Miss Drake and Potter and search the bedroom where they've been waiting. The living room, too."

Then I had a brainstorm. "You know," I said, "if Elinor is covering up for someone—if three people came in here for the séance instead of two as she says—the third could have killed Drake and then gone out—with the knife. And the paper tape could have been. . ." I stopped.

"—pasted on the door *after* the murderer left?" Merlini finished. "By Rosa? That would mean she framed herself."

"Besides," Gavigan growled, "the boys fumed all those paper strips. There are fingerprints all over them. All Drake's."

Merlini said, "Doran, I suggest that you phone the hospital and have Rosa searched, too."

The Lieutenant blinked. "But she was practically naked. How in blazes could she carry a knife out of here unnoticed?"

Gavigan faced Merlini, scowling. "What did you mean when you said a moment ago that she could have got rid of the knife the same way she produced those shells?"

"If it was a clasp knife," Merlini explained, "she could have used the same method other apport mediums have employed to conceal small objects under test conditions."

"But dammit!" Doran exploded. "The only place Garrett didn't look was in her stomach!"

Merlini grinned. "I know. That was his error. Rosa is a regurgitating medium—like Helen Duncan in whose stomach the English investigator, Harry Price, found a hidden ghost—a balled-up length of cheesecloth fastened with a safety pin which showed up when he X-rayed her. X-rays of Rosa seem indicated, too. And search her hospital room and the ambulance that took her over."

"Okay, Doran," Gavigan ordered. "Do it."

I saw an objection. "Now you've got Rosa framing herself, too," I said. "If she swallowed the murder knife, why should she put blood on the letter opener? That makes no sense at all."

"None of this does," Gavigan complained.

"I know," Merlini answered. "One knife was bad. Two are much worse. And although X-rays of Rosa before the séance would have shown shells, I predict they won't show a knife. If they do, then Rosa needs a psychiatric examination as well."

"Don't worry," Gavigan said gloomily. "She'll get one. Her attorney will see to that. And they'll prove she's crazier than a bedbug without half trying. But if that knife isn't in her. . ." His voice died.

"Then you'll never convict her," Merlini finished.

"If that happens," the Inspector said ominously, "you're going to have to explain where that knife came from, how it really disappeared, and where it is now."

Merlini's view was even gloomier. "It'll be much worse than that. We'll also have an appearing and vanishing murderer to explain— someone who entered a sealed room, killed Drake, put blood on the paper knife to incriminate Rosa, then vanished just as neatly as any of Miss Potter's ghosts—into thin air."

And Merlini's prediction came true.

The X-ray plates didn't show the slightest trace of a knife. And it wasn't in Rosa's hospital room or in the ambulance. Nor on Garrett, Paul, Elinor Drake, Isabelle Potter—nor, as Doran discovered, on myself. The Drake house was a mess by the time the boys got through taking it apart—but no knife with a broken point was found anywhere. And it was shown beyond doubt that there were no trapdoors or sliding panels in the study; the door and window were the only exits.

Inspector Gavigan glowered every time the phone rang—the Commissioner had already phoned twice and without mincing words expressed his dissatisfaction with the way things were going.

And Merlini, stretched out in Drake's chair, his heels up on the desk top, his eyes closed, seemed to have gone into a trance.

"Blast it!" Gavigan said. "Rosa Rhys got that knife out of here somehow. She had to! Merlini, are you going to admit that she knows a trick or two you don't?"

The magician didn't answer for a moment. Then he opened one eye. "No," he said slowly, "not just yet." He took his feet off the desk and sat up straight. "You know," he said, "if we don't accept the theory of the murderer from beyond, then Ross must be right after all. Elinor Drake's statement to the contrary, there must have been a third person in this room when that séance began."

"Okay," Gavigan said, "we'll forget Miss Drake's testimony for the moment. At least that gets him into the room. Then what?"

"I don't know," Merlini said. He took the roll of gummed paper tape from the desk, tore off a two-foot length, crossed the room, and pasted it across the door and jamb, sealing us in. "Suppose I'm the killer," he said. "I knock Rosa out first, then stab Drake—"

He paused.

Gavigan was not enthusiastic. "You put the murder knife in your pocket, not noticing that the point is broken. You put blood on the paper knife to incriminate Rosa. And then—" He waited. "Well, go on."

"Then," Merlini said, "I get out of here." He scowled at the sealed door and at the window. "I've escaped from handcuffs, strait jackets, milk cans filled with water, packing cases that have been nailed shut.

I know the methods Houdini used to break out of safes and jail cells. But I feel like he did when a shrewd old turnkey shut him in a cell in Scotland one time and the lock—a type he'd overcome many times before—failed to budge. No matter how he tried or what he did, the bolt wouldn't move. He was sweating blood because he knew that if he failed, his laboriously built-up reputation as the Escape King would be blown to bits. And then. . ." Merlini blinked. "And then. . ." This time he came to a full stop, staring at the door.

Suddenly he blinked. "Shades of Hermann, Kellar, Thurston—and Houdini! So that's it!"

Grinning broadly, he turned to Gavigan. "We will now pass a miracle and chase all the ghosts back into their tombs. If you'll get those people in here—"

"You know how the vanishing man vanished?" I asked.

"Yes. It's someone who has been just as canny as that Scotch jailer—and I know who."

Gavigan said, "It's about time." Then he walked across the room and pulled the door open, tearing the paper strip in half as he did so.

Merlini, watching him, grinned again. "The method by which magicians let their audiences fool themselves—the simplest and yet most effective principle of deception in the whole book—and it nearly took me in!"

Elinor Drake's eyes still avoided the stains on the floor. Scott, beside her, puffed nervously on a cigarette, and Dr. Garrett looked drawn and tired. But not the irrepressible Potter. She seemed fresh as a daisy.

"This room," she said to no one in particular, "will become more famous in psychic annals than the home of the Fox sisters at Lilydale."

Quickly, before she could elaborate on that, Merlini cut in. "Miss Potter doesn't believe that Rosa Rhys killed Drake. Neither do I. But the psychic force she says is responsible didn't emanate from another World. It was conjured up out of nothing by someone who was— who had to be—here in this room when Drake died. Someone whom Drake himself asked to be here."

He moved into the center of the room as he spoke and faced them.

"Drake would never have convinced anyone that Rosa could do what she claimed without a witness. So he gave someone a key—someone who came into this room *before* Drake and Rosa and Elinor came downstairs."

The four people watched him without moving—almost, I thought, without breathing.

"That person hid behind that screen and then, after Rosa produced the apports, knocked her out, killed Drake, and left Rosa to face the music."

"All we have to do," Merlini went on, "is show who it was that Drake selected as a witness." He pointed a lean forefinger at Isabelle Potter. "If Drake discovered how Rosa produced the shells and realized she was a fraud, you might have killed him to prevent an exposure and save face for yourself and the Society; and you might have then framed Rosa in revenge for having deceived you. But Drake would never have chosen you. Your testimony wouldn't have convinced any of the others. No. Drake would have picked one of the skeptics—someone he was certain could never be accused of assisting the medium."

He faced Elinor. "You said that you accompanied Rosa and your father to the study door and saw them go in alone. We haven't asked Miss Rhys yet, but I think she'll confirm it. You couldn't expect to lie about that and make it stick as long as Rosa could and would contradict you."

I saw Doran move forward silently, closing in.

"And Paul Kendrick," Merlini went on, "is the only one of you who has an alibi that does not depend on the sealed room. That leaves the most skeptical one of the three—the man whose testimony would by far carry the greatest weight.

"It leaves you, Dr. Garrett. The man who is so certain that there are no ghosts is the man who conjured one up!"

Merlini played the scene down; he knew that the content of what he said was dramatic enough. But Garret's voice was even calmer. He shook his head slowly.

"I am afraid that I can't agree. You have no reason to assume that it must be one of us and no one else. But I would like to hear how you think I or anyone else could have walked out of this room leaving it sealed as it was found."

"That," Merlini said, "is the simplest answer of all. You walked out, but you didn't leave the room sealed. You see, *it was not found that way!*"

I felt as if I were suddenly floating in space.

"But look—" I began.

Merlini ignored me. "The vanishing murderer was a trick. But magic is not, as most people believe, only a matter of gimmicks and trapdoors and mirrors. Its real secret lies deeper than a mere deception of the senses; the magician uses a far more important, more basic weapon—the psychological deception of the mind. *Don't believe everything you see* is excellent advice; but there's a better rule: Don't believe everything you *think*."

"Are you trying to tell me," I said incredulously, "that this room wasn't sealed at all? That I just thought it was?"

Merlini kept watching Garrett. "Yes. It's as simple as that. And there was no visual deception at all. It was, like PK, entirely mental. You saw things exactly as they were, but you didn't realize that the visual appearance could be interpreted two ways. Let me ask you a question. When you break into a room the door of which has been sealed with paper tape on the inside, do you find yourself still in a sealed room?"

"No," I said, "of course not. The paper has been torn."

"And if you break into a room that had been sealed but from which someone has *already gone out*, tearing the seals—what then?"

"The paper," I said, "is still torn. The appearance is—"

"—*exactly the same!*" Merlini finished.

He let that soak in a moment, then continued. "When you saw the taped window, and then the torn paper on the door, you made a false assumption—you jumped naturally, but much too quickly, to a wrong conclusion. We all did. We assumed that it was you who had torn the paper—when you broke in. Actually, it was Dr. Garrett who tore the paper—when he went out!"

Garrett's voice was a shade less steady now. "You forget that Andrew Drake phoned me—"

Merlini shook his head, "I'm afraid we only have your own statement for that. You overturned the phone and placed Drake's body near it. Then you walked out, returned to your office where you got rid of the knife—probably a surgical instrument which you couldn't leave behind because it might have been traced to you."

Doran, hearing this, whispered a rapid order to the detective stationed at the door.

"Then," Merlini continued, "you came back immediately to ring the front-door bell. You said Drake had called you, partly because it was good misdirection; it made it appear that you were elsewhere when he died. But equally important, it gave you the excuse you needed to break in and find the body without delay—*before Rosa Rhys should regain consciousness and see that the room was no longer sealed!*"

I hated to do it. Merlini was so pleased with the neat way he was tying up all the loose ends. But I had to.

"Merlini," I said. "I'm afraid there is one little thing you don't know. When I smashed the door open, I heard the paper tape tear!"

I have seldom seen the Great Merlini surprised, but that did it. He couldn't have looked more astonished if lightning had struck him.

"You—you *what*?"

Elinor Drake said, "I heard it, too."

Garrett added, "And I."

It stopped Merlini cold for a moment, but only a moment.

"Then that's more misdirection. It has to be." He hesitated, then suddenly looked at Doran. "Lieutenant, get the doctor's overcoat, will you?"

Garrett spoke to the inspector. "This is nonsense. What possible reason could I have for—"

"Your motive was a curious one, doctor," Merlini said. "One that few murderers—"

Merlini stopped as he took the overcoat Doran brought in and removed from its pocket the copy of the AMA *Journal* I had noticed there earlier. He started to open it, then lifted an eyebrow at something he saw on the contents listing.

"I see," he said, and then read: *"A Survey of the Uses of Radioactive Tracers in Cancer Research* by Walter M. Garrett, M.D. So that's your special interest?" The magician turned to Elinor Drake. "Who was to head the $15-million foundation for cancer research, Miss Drake?"

The girl didn't need to reply. The answer was in her eyes as she stared at Garrett.

Merlini went on. "You were hidden behind the screen in the corner, doctor. And Rosa Rhys, in spite of all the precautions, successfully produced the apports. You saw the effect that had on Drake, knew Rosa had won, and that Drake was thoroughly hooked. And the thought of seeing all that money wasted on psychical research when it could be put to so much better use in really important medical research made you boil. Any medical man would hate to see that happen, and most of the rest of us, too.

"But we don't all have the coldly rational, scientific attitude you do, and we wouldn't all have realized so quickly that there was one very simple but drastic way to prevent it—murder. You are much too rational. You believe that one man's life is less important than the good his death might bring, and you believed that sufficiently to act upon it. The knife was there, all too handy, in your little black case. And so—Drake died. Am I right, doctor?"

Doran didn't like this as a motive. "He's still a killer," he objected. "And he tried to frame Rosa, didn't he?"

Merlini said, "Do you want to answer that, doctor?"

Garrett hesitated, then glanced at the magazine Merlini still held. His voice was tired. "You are also much too rational." He turned to Doran. "Rosa Rhys was a cheap fraud who capitalized on superstition. The world would be a much better place without such people."

"And what about your getting that job as the head of the medical foundation?" Doran was still unconvinced. "I don't supposed that had anything to do with your reasons for killing Drake?"

The doctor made no answer. And I couldn't tell if it was because Doran was right or because he knew that Doran would not believe him.

He turned to Merlini instead. "The fact still remains that the cancer foundation has been made possible. The only difference is that now two men rather than one pay with their lives."

"A completely rational attitude," Merlini said, "does have its advantages if it allows you to contemplate your own death with so little emotion."

Gavigan wasn't as cynical about Garrett's motives as Doran, but his police training objected. "He took the law into his own hands. If everyone did that, we'd all have to go armed for self-protection. Merlini, why did Ross think he heard paper tearing when he opened that door?"

"He did hear it," Merlini said. Then he turned to me. "Dr. Garrett stood behind you and Miss Drake when you broke in the door, didn't he?"

I nodded. "Yes."

Merlini opened the medical journal and riffled through it. Half a dozen loose pages, their serrated edges showing where they had been torn in half, fluttered to the floor.

Merlini said, "You would have made an excellent magician, doctor. Your deception was not visual, it was auditory."

"That," Gavigan said, "tears it."

Later I had one further question to ask Merlini.

"You didn't explain how Houdini got out of that Scottish jail, nor how it helped you solve the enigma of the unsealed door."

Merlini lifted an empty hand, plucked a lighted cigarette from thin air and puffed at it, grinning.

"Houdini made the same false assumption. When he leaned exhaustedly against the cell door, completely baffled by his failure to overcome the lock, the door suddenly swung open and he fell into the corridor. The old Scot, you see, hadn't locked it at all!"

GOOD-BYE, GOOD-BYE!
Craig Rice
Detective: John J. Malone

Born Georgiana Ann Randolph (1908-1957), Craig Rice's real-life mysteries were a match for her fiction. Because of her enormous popularity in the 1940s and 1950s (she was the first mystery writer to appear on the cover of *Time* magazine), she was often interviewed but was as forthcoming as a deep-cover agent for the Central Intelligence Agency. How her pseudonym was created is a question that remains unanswered sixty years after her premature death. Equally murky are questions about her marriages, the number of which remains a subject of conjecture. She was married a minimum of four times, and it is possible the number reached seven; that she had numerous affairs is not in dispute. She had three children.

Rice was born in Chicago, where she spent much of her life. Her parents took off for Europe when she was only three years old so she was raised by various family members. While working in radio and public relations, she sought a career in music, writing poetry, and general novels, with which she had no success, so she turned to writing detective novels with spectacular results.

Rice is perhaps best known for the John J. Malone series, though his fictional career began as a friend of a madcap couple, the handsome but dim press agent Jake Justus and his socially prominent bride-to-be, Helene Brand. Malone's "Personal File" usually contains a bottle of rye. Despite his seeming irresponsibility, Malone inspired great loyalty among his friends, including the Justuses, Maggie Cassidy, his long-suffering and seldom-paid secretary, and Captain Daniel von Flanagan of the Chicago homicide squad. The series began with *Eight Faces at Three* in 1939 and ran for a eleven novels. In addition to a total of seventeen novels under the Rice pseudonym, she also wrote *To Catch a Thief* (1943) as Daphne Sanders and three mysteries as Michael Venning.

"Good-bye, Good-bye!" was originally published in the June 1946 issue of *Ellery Queen's Mystery Magazine*; it was first collected in *The Name Is Malone* (New York, Pyramid, 1958).

Good-bye, Good-bye!
By Craig Rice

A WOMAN in the crowd gasped, almost screamed. Near her, a man in a gray topcoat covered his eyes with his hands. Half a block away an overdressed, overpainted, and very pretty girl sank to her knees on the concrete sidewalk and prayed. But most of the crowd stared upward in silence in half-horrified, half-delighted fascination.

On a narrow ledge twenty-two stories above the street, there was what seemed, from this distance, to be a small dark blob. The crowd knew that the blob was a girl in a mink coat, that she had been crouched on the ledge for hours, and that a minister, a policeman, and an eminent psychiatrist were pleading and reasoning with her through the open window.

John J. Malone was not one of the crowd. He was only trying to push his way through it to the entrance of the hotel, where a profitable

client was waiting for him, one who was ready to hand over a fat retainer before giving himself up on a burglary rap which John J. Malone
knew he could beat in five minutes even before a prejudiced jury.

The important business of collecting that retainer was one reason
why he didn't notice the crowd at first. A lone, crumpled five dollar bill
was in his right pants pocket, and he had a date with a very special and
very expensive blonde just half an hour from now. And this particular
client would pay the retainer in cash.

Malone was beginning to lose his temper with the crowd when he
suddenly realized that the space in front of the hotel was roped off.
That was when he looked up.

"Been there for hours," a man next to him murmured, almost
dreamily.

For a minute he stood there, horror-frozen. His mind took in what
was being said around him, even though he wasn't conscious of hearing it, and he became aware of the whole story—the fire department,
the police, the minister, and the psychiatrist.

There was a lump of ice where his stomach had been just a little
while ago. Life was so wonderful, even with the remains of yesterday's
warmed-over hangover, even with only five bucks in your pants and a
blonde waiting for you. If he could only explain that to the undecided
dark blob clinging to the ledge twenty-two stories above. *Undecided—!*
That was it. That was the key.

Suddenly he pushed his way, ruthlessly and almost blindly, through
the rest of the crowd, ran past the roped-off space where the fire department was holding life nets, past the frightened young cop who
tried to bar his way into the building, and through the deserted lobby.
He yelled for a boy to operate one of the empty elevators, finally got
attention by threatening to operate it himself, and was shot up to the
twenty-second floor.

It was easy to find the room. The door was open, spilling light into
the hall. A cop at the door said, "Malone—!" tried to stop him, and

was shoved aside. The minister, the eminent psychiatrist, and Detective Lieutenant Klutchetsky from the police department were shoved aside too.

At the window, he paused and drew a long, slow breath. Down the ledge from him was a white face and two terrified eyes. Malone spoke very softly and easily.

"Don't be afraid. You can get back here all right. Just creep along the ledge and keep your hands on the wall, and keep looking at me."

The dark figure stirred. She was not more than a few inches beyond the reach of his arm, but he knew better than to hold out a hand to her, yet.

"There's nothing to fear. Even if you should fall, they'll catch you with the nets. The worst that can happen to you is a skinned knee and a few bruises." Malone crossed his fingers for the bare-faced lie. "You're as safe as if you were in your own bed." It was the same tone he'd used innumerable times to nervous witnesses.

It was a full minute before the girl began to move, but when she did, it was in the direction of the window.

"Come on now," the little lawyer coaxed. "It's not so far. Only a bit of a ways now. Take it easy."

She managed about a foot and a half along the ledge, and stopped. He could see her face, and the terror on it, clearly now.

"You won't fall," Malone said. It was an almost heartbreaking effort to keep from reaching a hand to her.

Inside the room, and down on the sidewalk, the spectators were silent and breathless.

For just a moment it seemed to Malone that she'd smiled at him. No, it hadn't been a smile, just a relaxation of those frozen muscles around her mouth. How long had she been crouching on that ledge? He didn't dare guess.

Nor did he dare take his eyes from her face and look down, for fear her gaze would turn with his.

Inch by inch she moved toward the waiting window. Only a few feet away she hesitated, started to look down, and turned a shade more pale.

"For Pete's sake, hurry up," Malone said crossly. "It's colder than a Scandinavian Hell with this window open."

That did it. She actually did smile, and managed the last bit of window ledge, twenty-two stories up from the ground, like a little girl sliding on a cellar door. Finally Malone lifted her over the sill, and Klutchetsky, moving fast and breathing hard, slammed the window shut and locked it.

The eminent psychiatrist sank down on the nearest chair, his face a mottled gray. Klutchetsky and the uniformed cop stood glaring at her.

"You're a wicked, wicked girl," the minister began.

"Shut up," Malone told him absent-mindedly. He looked closely at the girl, who stood clutching the edge of the window frame for support.

She was small, and delicately built. Pale, distraught, and disheveled as she was, she was something very special. Her chalk-white and definitely dirty face was triangular in shape, and lovely. Her frightened eyes were brown and large, and ringed with long, dark lashes. Her tangled hair was honey blonde. Her mouth, naked of lipstick and with marks showing where teeth had almost bitten through a lower lip, was a pallid, wistful flower.

One more minute, Malone told himself, and he'd be writing poetry.

The mink coat was a magnificent one. The dusty rose dress under it came, Malone realized, from one of the very best shops. The torn and muddy stockings he recognized as silk. Jewels glittered at her slim wrists.

"As I live and breathe!" Malone said pleasantly, taking out a cigar and starting to unwrap it. "Doris Dawn!"

Doris Dawn drew her first long breath in many hours. She glanced around the ring of hostile faces, then flung herself into the security of Malone's warm and obvious friendliness. A faint color began to come back into her cheeks.

"You saved my life. I was out there—*forever*, trying to get enough nerve to crawl to a window. High places—they always—" The color faded again.

"You'd better put some makeup on," Malone growled. "You look terrible."

She almost smiled. She fumbled through her coat pockets, found a compact and lipstick, dropped them both through her trembling fingers. Malone picked them up for her. Pink Primrose lipstick, he noted approvingly. Exactly right for her pale skin.

He said, soothingly, "Relax. You're safe now."

"No. No, I'm not. That's it." She turned to Klutchetsky. "You're a policeman. *Do* something. Someone tried to kill me."

Klutchetsky and the eminent psychiatrist exchanged significant glances.

"Okay, sister," Klutchetsky said wearily. "Just come along quietly now."

Malone said, "Just a minute. Since when is it customary, in a case of attempted murder, to arrest the intended corpse?"

"Look, Malone," Klutchetsky said. He paused and sighed deeply. "We appreciate your help. Okay. Now suppose you let the police department handle its own problems in its own way."

"But I'm not a *problem*," the girl cried out. "*Someone*—"

"That's what you think," Klutchetsky told her. "Am I right, Doc?" He paused. The eminent psychiatrist nodded his head briskly.

"He tried to kill me," the girl gasped. "He will again. He put me out on that ledge and left me there. I was too scared to crawl back. I just held on. Until—"

"And who is this 'he,'" Klutchetsky interrupted skeptically, "and what does he look like?"

"I don't know. I've never seen him."

The police officer turned to the eminent psychiatrist. "See what I mean, Doc?" Again the psychiatrist nodded.

She began to sob, dry-eyed. She took a step toward Malone. "You believe me, don't you? Don't let them drag me away to—to a hospital. They're the police. Make them find him. Make them protect me."

"What I always say is," Malone murmured, lighting his cigar, "what do we pay taxes for?" He paused long enough to glare at the police officer and his aide. "But what you need is a good lawyer."

"Find me one!"

Malone smiled at her reassuringly. "I *have* found you one."

"Listen," Klutchetsky said. "This is the third time she's tried this. She's bats. Just ask Doctor Updegraff."

"A very interesting case," Doctor Updegraff purred. "Of course, after I have given it some study—"

"Nuts!" Malone said rudely.

"Precisely," the psychiatrist said.

Malone thought of a number of things he would like to do to Doctor Updegraff, all of them unkind, and most of them unmentionable. He thought, also, about the immediate problem. If Klutchetsky and Dr. Updegraff happened to be right, Doris Dawn would be better off in a hospital, and the sooner the better. On the other hand, if she was telling the truth—and Malone believed she was—she would be safer in jail, right now.

"As this young lady's lawyer," he began.

Klutchetsky said, "Now Malone. You heard what the doc here said. And maybe you remember this babe's mother."

"I do," Malone said, "I was secretly in love with her for years." He reflected that every impressionable male who'd been to the theater between 1925 and 1936 remembered Diana Dawn who'd committed suicide at the very height of her career.

"Okay," Klutchetsky said, "this babe takes poison, only she's found in time and luckily she didn't take much. Then she goes to work on her wrists with a razor blade, but she misses the right spot and anyhow a hotel maid finds her before she bled too much. Now she takes a room here under a phony name, and decides to jump."

The little lawyer was silent for a moment. Maybe, this time, Klutchetsky was right and he was wrong. Still—

"How about notes?" he asked. "Did she leave any?"

"Notes!" the police officer snorted, "what do you call these?" He waved an arm around the room.

Malone looked, and realized that the room was filled with mirrors. On every one of them was written, in lipstick, *Good-bye, Good-bye.* The letters were the color of dried blood. The bathroom door was a full-length mirror, and on it was scrawled, over and over "Good-bye, good-bye, good-bye, good-bye, good-bye—"

"I didn't write it!" Doris Dawn said.

Malone looked at her closely, then back at the dark red letters. He said to Klutchetsky, "I'm convinced."

The minister muttered something about the use of excessive make-up, the perils of the city, juvenile delinquency, and his next Sunday's sermon. Dr. Updegraff muttered something about the significance of the use of lipstick for a farewell message.

The girl gave a tragic little moan. "But I thought you'd help me!"

"Don't look now," Malone said, "but I am." He turned to Klutchetsky. "Better have the squad car go round to the alley. There must be a flock of reporters in the lobby by now. We'll go down the freight elevator."

Klutchetsky nodded his thanks, told the young cop to get headquarters on the phone, and said to Malone, "You'll have to show us the way. How come you always know where the freight elevators in hotels are, anyhow?"

"I have my secrets," Malone said coyly, "and all of them are sacred." He didn't add that, among those secrets, was the knowledge that the ledge outside the window was a good two and a half feet wide, and that it had a rim extending up for at least six inches.

One reason was that he didn't want to tell how he knew.

He held Doris Dawn firmly by the elbow as they walked to the door. Dr. Updegraff and the minister had volunteered, with willing helpfulness, indeed, even hopefulness, to stay behind and cope with the reporters. Malone had muttered something unpleasant about people who were their own press agents and thus kept honest, but starving, ex-newspapermen out of jobs.

Out in the alley, Klutchetsky thanked Malone for guiding them down the freight elevator, said good night, and ushered Doris Dawn into the back of the car. Malone promptly popped in beside her.

"Now wait a minute," Klutchetsky said, "You can't do this, Malone."

"I can," Malone said pleasantly, "I will and I am." He smiled. "Did you ever remember to tell your wife about that trip we took to the races while she was visiting her cousin in the east—" He paused.

"Oh, all right," the police officer growled. He slammed the car door shut and climbed in beside the uniformed driver.

As the car turned into Michigan Avenue, where the crowd was thinning and the fire department was packing up to leave, her hand crept into his like a cold, frightened kitten creeping into a feather bed.

"I didn't, you know," she whispered. "I couldn't have. There wasn't any reason. I've always had fun. I've always had everything. Until this started, I've always been happy."

"I know it," Malone whispered back. "I've heard you sing." He curled his fingers reassuringly around hers.

"But I don't want you to believe it because I say so and because you're sorry for me. I want you to believe it because something proves it to you. I want you to read my diary, and then you'll *really* know."

She reached into her pocket. "You trusted me, so I'm going to trust you. Here's the key to my house. It's 1117 Gay Street. You can remember that, can't you? The light switch is just to the right of the door, and the library is just to the left of the hall. There's a desk in the library and my diary is in the middle drawer, under an old telephone book. You've got to read it. And please don't mind there being a little dust everywhere because I've been too busy to do any dusting myself, and my housekeeper had to go to Clinton, Iowa, because her daughter-in-law had a baby."

Malone blinked. Doris Dawn, radio singing star, had spent agonizing hours on a window ledge twenty-two stories up from the street. She was in danger of being hustled into a psychopathic ward and if she were turned loose, she was probably in danger of being murdered. But she worried for fear he'd think her house needed dusting. It didn't make sense. But then, neither did Doris.

"Tell me," he said, "about this mysterious 'he'—"

"Honest," she said, "I never got a look at him. That first time—" The car was pulling up in front of headquarters. "It's all in the diary."

He squeezed her hand, tight. "Look. Don't answer any questions. Don't talk to any reporters. Refer everything to your lawyer. That's me. And don't be afraid."

A big sob of pity rose in his throat. She was so lovely, and so frightened. He wanted to put a comforting arm around her for just one moment. But Klutchetsky was already pulling open the car door.

"You'll be safe," he promised her. "I'll raise a little hell."

He raised so much hell that Doris Dawn was taken from headquarters in a police ambulance, two jumps ahead of the reporters, placed in a private hospital under an assumed name and with a police guard at the door. Indeed he was so efficient about his hell-raising that it was not until he was out on the sidewalk, in the cold spring rain, that he remembered overlooking a number of very important details.

One, he had neglected to tell Doris Dawn the name of her self-appointed lawyer. Two, he had neglected to learn the name of the private hospital, and the name under which she'd been registered.

He reflected that he'd probably have more trouble finding his client than she would have finding her lawyer. But those were the minor details.

The more important items were that, while appointing himself her lawyer, he'd forgotten to mention the delicate matter of a retainer. And worse than that, the original client he'd been on his way to see had certainly located another mouthpiece by this time.

Finally, the expensive blonde had never been known to wait for anyone more than half an hour. He was almost two hours late, by now.

Malone sighed unhappily and regretted having spent most of that lone five dollar bill buying magazines and candy for Doris Dawn at the newsstand, before the police ambulance took her away. Then he thought about Doris Dawn and decided he didn't regret it too much.

There was a grand total of eighty-seven cents in his pocket. The little lawyer ducked into the nearest corner bar and spent seventy-five cents of it on a gin and beer while he thought over all he knew about Doris Dawn.

Her mother, Diana Dawn, had been one of the most beautiful women of her, or any other, generation. Talented, too, though she hadn't needed to be. It was worth the price of a theater ticket just to look at her, she didn't have to utter one word or sing one note. She'd married a man as rich as she was beautiful, and been heart-broken when he was killed in a polo accident shortly after Doris was born.

Time had apparently healed wounds enough for her to marry again—this time, an actor. Malone fumbled through his memory for his name, finally found it. Robert Spencer. It seemed vaguely familiar to him, for some reason he couldn't quite place.

Diana Dawn Stuart Spencer had been married only a few months when her second husband had vanished from the face of the earth. Not long after, Diana herself had jumped from the end of Navy Pier into the cold waters of Lake Michigan, leaving alone in the world a small blonde daughter who inherited the Stuart fortune, was raised by a board of trustees, and burst upon the world at eighteen as Doris Dawn, singer, determined on making her own way in the world.

Malone put down his empty glass, sighed, and felt in his pockets. Two nickels, two pennies, and a telephone slug. He searched other pockets, not forgetting to investigate the lining of his coat and his trouser cuffs. Sometimes small change turned up unexpectedly. But not this time. He considered investing the two nickels in the slot machine, thought over the odds, and gave that up. He debated riding a street car to Joe the Angel's City Hall Bar and negotiating a small loan, then remembered Joe the Angel had gone to Gary, Indiana, to help celebrate a niece's wedding. He ended up by riding a State Street car to within a couple of blocks of 1117 Gay Street.

It was nearly midnight when he entered the tiny, perfect (though admittedly dusty) house Charles Stuart had built for his bride and left to his daughter, set in a small square of garden enclosed by a high brick wall. Less than half an hour later he was out in the garden with a spade he'd found in the back entry, shivering in the rain, and praying that he was on a fool's errand. Before one o'clock he was on the telephone in frantic search for Capt. Dan von Flanagan, of the Homicide Squad. By one-fifteen von Flanagan was there having brought, per Malone's request, two husky policemen with shovels, the morgue wagon, a basket, and a bottle of gin.

"I thought it was a joke," Malone said hoarsely, nursing his glass of gin. "I found her diary right where she said it would be." He nodded toward the little Chippendale desk. "I started to read it."

"Shame on you, Malone," von Flanagan said. "Reading a girl's diary." The big policeman looked uncomfortable and uneasy, perched on the edge of a delicate brocade chair. "What does it say?"

"It was her idea," Malone said. "Anyway, I wanted to read her version of those two—suicide attempts. And this paper fell out of it." He handed it to von Flanagan.

> *Dig, dig, dig.*
> *Under the willow tree in the garden.*

"It sounded like a couple of lines from a couple of popular songs. But I found a spade, and I dug."

"You must have been drunk," von Flanagan commented.

"Who, me?" Malone asked indignantly. He gulped the rest of his glass of gin, took out a cigar and lit it with only a slightly trembling hand.

"And don't be nervous," von Flanagan said. "You've seen skulls before."

"Who's nervous?" Malone demanded. He closed his eyes and remembered standing under a tree that dripped cold spring rain, bracing his feet in the mud and digging with a small inadequate shovel into the still half-frozen ground, until suddenly a white and fleshless face leered at him. A nearby door opened, and he jumped.

A policeman in an oilskin slicker and muddy boots said, "We found a'most all of him, 'cept a little bit of his left foot." He closed the door as he went out, and Malone closed his eyes. He opened the door again and said, "Looks like he was buried with all his clothes on, even his jewelry. Johnson's cleaning off his watch." He closed the door again. Malone sneezed.

"I hope you haven't caught cold," von Flanagan said solicitously.

"I never catch cold," Malone said. He finally got the cigar lit, reached for the gin bottle and said, "But just to be on the safe side—" He sneezed again. "About the diary. It was written by a very happy, very normal young girl who had everything to live for, including about half the money in the world. Up to the point where strange things began to happen to her." He reached for the little leather bound book and began to read aloud.

"A strange thing happened. Everything is very mixed up and I don't understand. I made myself a nightcap and went to bed early after the show, and woke up in a hospital. In between I sort of remember a lot of excitement and people running around, and being very sick and uncomfortable. They tried to tell me I took poison, but I know I didn't. They said I wrote "Good-bye, good-bye" in lipstick on the head of my bed, but by the time they let me come home it had been washed off so I couldn't tell if I wrote it or not. They found poison in my stomach but I know I hadn't taken any."

"She is nuts," von Flanagan commented.

"Wait a minute," Malone said. He went on. "I remember now that night there was a man in my room. He came to deliver a telegram only I never did see the telegram. I was in the bathtub so I put a robe on and opened the door a crack and told him to leave the telegram on the desk and shut the door when he went out. My nightcap was on the bed table. I wonder if someone is trying to poison me."

The little lawyer paused, refilled his glass, relit his cigar, and said, "After that, there's a note of uneasiness in the diary. The usual things—dates, parties, clothes—but a feeling of worry."

Von Flanagan scowled and said, "I remember a little about that. Someone called her maid and told her to hurry home, her employer was sick. Otherwise this babe might of died, though she didn't take much."

"Some time later," Malone said, "she wrote, '*Someone is trying to kill me.*'" He paused. "You'll remember this, too. She was found in a hotel room, registered under another name. The maid came in and found her in the bathroom, with her wrists cut." He paused once more and added, frowning, "She checked in, and did the slashing job *just before* the maid was due in that room on her regular rounds."

"Stupid of her," von Flanagan commented, "if she really wanted to—" he cleared his throat, "check in and check out. She should have known she'd be found in time."

"According to her diary," Malone told him, "a man telephoned her and told her that if she'd go to such-and-such a hotel, and register under such-and-such a name, he'd meet her there with some very important information about the long-missing Robert Spencer. She went there, answered the door, 'a man'—otherwise unidentified—forced her into the bathroom, slashed her wrists, and left her there unconscious. She told the police this story, and they laughed at her. The words *Good-bye, good-bye* were written on the bathroom mirror."

Von Flanagan shuffled his feet uncomfortably and said, "You gotta admit, Malone, it smells phony."

Malone ignored him. "From that point on, the diary is the story of a terrified girl who knows someone is trying to kill her. And yet," he put down his cigar, "I'll read you the last entry."

"I am terribly afraid, but I must know the truth. I have been promised that if I keep the appointment I will be told what happened to Robert Spencer. This I must know."

Malone closed the little diary gently and said, "The slip of paper directing me—or someone—to dig in the garden, under the tree, was found between those two pages." He picked up the remains of his cigar, decided it was past all hope of relighting, and began to unwrap a new one.

"She took poison," he said, "but not quite enough to kill her, and her maid was summoned home in time to have her rushed to a hospital. She registered at a hotel under a phony name and slashed her wrists—not badly—just before the hotel maid was due to come in."

"What are you trying to prove?" von Flanagan asked uneasily.

"Nothing. Except that 'the man' must have known that ledge was safe enough to push a baby carriage on. He thought she'd use her head and climb back in through her window, though he made sure someone would see her and call the police before she did. He obviously didn't know she had an abnormal fear of heights that would keep her frozen there, too scared to move and too sane to jump. Nor," he added modestly, "did he know that I'd arrive providentially."

"I don't know what you're getting at," von Flanagan said.

"Trouble is," Malone said, reaching for the gin bottle, "right now, neither do I."

Again the young policeman came to the door, even more mud on his boots and slicker. "We found a little of what's left of his clothes," he reported. "Looks like he's been there a *long* time. Got his wallet, his watch, and some other stuff. Looks like," he said, "he was some guy named Robert Spencer."

Malone lifted the gin bottle to his lips, and closed his eyes.

"It looks," the young policeman added, "like he might of been murdered. Anyway we found what must of been a bullet in what looks like it probably had been his stomach, once."

"Go away," Malone groaned. He put down the gin bottle and sneezed again.

"You're going to get pneumonia," von Flanagan said solicitously.

The little lawyer shook his head. "Not on my income."

"I better go back out," the young policeman said. "Johnson still thinks he can find the rest of that left foot." He slammed the door.

"Malone," von Flanagan said, "that note. Was it written in the same handwriting as the diary?"

Malone blew his nose and said "Yes," unhappily. That was one of the things that had been bothering him. Plus the fact that there was something maddeningly reminiscent about the wording of the note. "But," he added, "it wasn't written on a telephone pad." If he could only remember—

At this point another young policeman came in the room and said, "There's someone here inquiring about Miss Dawn. I thought I'd better speak to you. He says his name is Robert Spencer."

Malone covered his eyes with his hand and said, "This is too much!"

Von Flanagan said, "By all means, send him in."

"By *all* means," Malone repeated. "Maybe he can help find what's left of his own left foot." He sneezed again. He downed another drink of gin. Then, suddenly he remembered, Bob Spencer, actor. Appearing, right now, in a rather dreary and not too successful comedy. Robert Spencer had had a small son, parked somewhere with relatives, when he met and married Diana Dawn.

"There's someone with him," the policeman said. "A Mr. Apt."

"John Apt," Malone said. "He's an old-time theatrical agent. His friends call him Jack. Managed Diana Dawn, probably managed Robert Spencer, too—I don't know." He smothered the next sneeze.

Bob Spencer was tall, young, handsome and anxious-eyed. His first words were, "Is Doris all right? What's been happening to her?

Why are all these policemen at her house? Where is she? When can I see her?"

Jack Apt smiled at Malone, von Flanagan, and the young policeman. It was a friendly, ingratiating smile. He nodded a shoulder toward the young actor and said, "You pardon him, he is upset."

Nothing, Malone reflected, would ever upset Jack Apt. The diminutive agent had undoubtedly been born with a friendly smile and an imperturbable face and hadn't changed his expression in all his sixty-odd years. He had bright little eyes, a white, waxy skin, and a few wisps of silvery hair on his well-shaped skull. He wore a black Chesterfield that seemed too large for his tiny frame and carried, incredibly and appropriately, a black derby.

"I am greatly concerned," Jack Apt said. "I am the manager of Miss Dawn." He sat down on a straight-back chair and placed the derby neatly on his knees. "I would like your assurance, sir—"

"Where is she?" Bob Spencer demanded, his voice harsh with desperation.

"The young lady is quite safe," von Flanagan said coldly. "And what's it to you?"

"I'm in love with her," Bob Spencer said. "She's in love with me."

Malone looked at him and swallowed a sigh. He'd been cherishing a few very personal ideas about Doris Dawn. Now, he realized, he didn't have a chance.

"We're going to be married," Bob Spencer added.

The little lawyer sat up in surprise, but said nothing.

Jack Apt beamed. "Just like two little lovebirds. And then there will be no more difficulty about the money."

"Money?" Malone asked. It was one of his favorite subjects, right now more than ever.

"Never mind about the money," Bob Spencer said, *"Where is Doris?"*

"Never mind about Doris," Malone snapped. *"What* money?"

"Diana Dawn's will," Jack Apt explained. "She had a great deal of money. All of it from that unfortunate Mr. Stuart. She left it all to her second husband, Robert Spencer. Just before she died. Almost as though she had a premonition."

Malone scowled. "But Robert Spencer had disappeared before then."

"Quite right," Jack Apt said, nodding and smiling. "Therefore the will stated that until he was found, Doris Dawn would receive the income from the estate, and would have the use of this property for living purposes."

"*Found*," Malone quoted. "Did it specify—dead or alive?"

"No," Jack Apt said. He looked very innocent and mild, turning his derby round and round on his knee. "A very curious will, I admit. But Diana wanted it that way. Robert had his faults, but she was fond of him. He stole from her, lied to her, almost ruined her career, but she was fond of him right up to the end." Suddenly he didn't look quite as innocent, nor as mild. "There is a clause—if her daughter should die, before he returned or was found, the money would go to his heirs. Or—if her daughter married, before he returned or was found, the money would go to the daughter and her husband. A very complicated will, but then, Diana Dawn had a very complicated personality."

Young Bob Spencer obviously couldn't stand this any longer. He said, "But this isn't finding Doris. And she hasn't married anybody, and he—hasn't been found."

Just at that moment one of the young policemen came in and said, "Johnson just found the rest of the left foot. Looks like we got all of him now."

"*Him?*" Bob Spencer asked wildly. He stared around the room. "Where—is—Doris?"

"Right here," Doris Dawn's voice said.

Malone jumped, and turned around.

"Hello, Malone," a deep, masculine voice said. "Sorry we startled you."

She was still very pale, but her face had been washed and freshly made up. Her honey blonde hair was smooth over her shoulders. She wore a nurse's uniform and white shoes and stockings, but the dark mink coat was over the uniform.

Malone sneezed and said, "You're in a hospital. You're an illusion. Go away. Vanish. *Scat!*"

Jerry Kane laughed.

"And you, Kane," Malone said, breathing hard. "How did you get in here?"

"We came in through the back door," Kane said. "Very easy, since it's our own house."

"Our—?" the little lawyer exploded.

He glared at Jerry Kane. The gambler, racketeer, nightclub owner, and promoter was a big, rangy, yet strangely graceful man. His tanned face could be hard as nails, or it could be ingratiatingly friendly and smiling, and it had an old scar down one cheek. His business deals had always kept him inside the law—but just inside. He owned the night club in which Doris Dawn sang. His reputation with women was worse than Malone's.

The other occupants of the room had been momentarily struck speechless. Now, everyone spoke at once. All questions. All the same questions.

"I discovered," Doris Dawn said, "I had to get out of that hospital. I *had* to. Because there was a chance to find out—something. It was very easy, really. I bribed a nurse to call Jerry. He bribed the policeman by my door to go away. And he brought me a nurse's uniform, and all I had to do was put it on and walk out."

"And," the big man said, "before coming here we drove across the state line and were married. Meet Mrs. Kane."

Young Bob Spencer cried, "Doris!" in an anguished voice.

"You fool!" Jack Apt said.

She paid no attention. "This time, no one's going to stop me—finding out. It would be better, honestly, if you all just waited here for me." Suddenly a little gun flashed in her hand. "But don't try to stop me."

"Doris—baby—" Jerry Kane gasped. And then, "How the hell did you get my gun?"

"I took it out of your pocket," she said calmly. Her white little face was hard as ice. "If anyone tries to stop me or follow me, I'll shoot. No matter who. Even if it's Jerry, and I love Jerry. I always have." Suddenly she was gone.

Before anyone could move, little Jack Apt said, "Too bad you married her, Kane. Because she isn't going to inherit the money after all."

Kane swore bitterly and raced for the door. Suddenly everyone in the room was racing for the door. Malone caught up, out on the sidewalk, just as a car roared away down the street. Kane's car. With Doris driving. Other cars roared away. Bob Spencer's roadster. Two police cars.

Malone stood shivering. They'd never catch up with that car of Kane's, not even the squad car would. And here he was stranded, and only he knew where she was going.

Not a taxi in sight. None nearer than Chicago Avenue.

Chicago Avenue—a sudden thought struck him, he wheeled around and sprinted down the street. One block to State Street, three blocks to Chicago Avenue. He made it to the safety zone just as an east bound streetcar came clanging through the rain.

"Wet night," the conductor commented.

"Going to be wetter," Malone prophesied gloomily. He dropped the remaining nickel in the coin box and began searching his pockets for an imaginary two pennies. The streetcar had reached the turn into Lakeshore Drive when Malone found the telephone slug, handed it triumphantly to the conductor for change and was properly surprised and crestfallen when it was returned to him. He continued to search for the pennies right up to the moment when the now empty streetcar came to an abrupt halt at the end of the line.

"Guess I'll have to put you off here," the conductor said. "No fare, no ride."

Malone glanced through the window, saw the familiar outlines of Navy Pier, and said, "Only the brave deserve the fair." He reached into his vest pocket and said, "Have a cigar."

Jerry Kane's custom-built convertible was parked at the entrance to the pier. There were no other cars in sight. Malone sighed. This was something he was going to have to handle by himself.

He knew exactly where to go. Up the stairs on the left-hand side of the pier, and along the promenade. Dark and deserted now, and desolate in the rain. There was one certain point, just beyond the line of benches—he stared ahead through the wet blackness and saw no sign of a girl in a nurse's uniform. He began to run.

He reached the spot from which Diana Dawn had leaped to her death, years before, and looked over the railing. There was a blob of white on the black water. Malone peeled off his overcoat, kicked off his shoes, and jumped.

The water was icy cold. He caught his breath after one terrible moment, and swam in the direction of the white blob.

She was alive. She was struggling against the water. That gave him new strength. He held her head up for a minute and, by some miracle, managed to rid her of the dark mink coat that was pulling her down.

A boat was coming. A tiny canoe, dark against the darkness. Malone aimed for it, helping her. An oar came out from the canoe, and pushed—down.

There was a brief agony of being underwater and an even briefer remembrance of all the things that had made living so much fun. An almost unbearable roaring in his ears as he rose to the surface still holding her. A light that almost blinded him as he breathed air again.

A voice said, "Catch 'em before they go down again." Strong hands reached out and caught him by the armpits. One quick motion, and he was hauled into the motor boat that had made the almost unbearable roaring and had flashed its light in his face.

He longed to collapse into unconsciousness there on the deck, but first—he looked, and saw that she had been hauled on board, and was breathing. Then he managed, with his last strength, to point at the canoe.

He heard a shot. He pulled himself up enough to look over the edge of the boat. He saw the canoe, overturned, starting to settle and sink.

"You might have known I'd commandeer a shore boat," Jerry Kane said. "I knew where she'd go. After all, I've been in love with her for a long time."

Malone lay back against the set boards, thought the whole thing over, and finally said, "You know, I think I am getting a cold after all."

In the emergency room on the pier, Captain von Flanagan agreed that it was a shame young Bob Spencer—such a promising young actor, too—had perished in an attempt to rescue one of Chicago's favorite radio and stage entertainers, Miss Doris Dawn. Fortunately, Mr. Jerry Kane had come along in time to rescue Miss Dawn and Mr. John Joseph Malone, prominent Chicago attorney.

After the reporters and Doris Dawn and her new husband had gone, he said, "All right, Malone, what the hell happened?"

Malone snuggled into the blanket some kind soul had wrapped around him, sneezed, and said, "If Doris Dawn died, and the body of Robert Spencer were found, Robert Spencer's heir would inherit several million dollars. Bob Spencer, naturally, was the only heir. Being a young man of imagination, he decided it would be better for her to commit suicide than to be murdered in some ordinary way. There wouldn't be so many embarassing questions asked of the one person to benefit by her death."

He paused, sneezed twice, and went on, "But he also knew that it wasn't easy to make murder look like suicide. Especially to—" he paused again for a second or two—"very smart cops like von Flanagan here. Therefore, his prospective victim had to make several unsuccessful attempts at suicide." He sneezed once more. "My grandmother always said whiskey was the best thing to ward off a cold. Oh, thanks, pal. Very kind of you."

"I would of believed it," von Flanagan said slowly. "In fact, after those first coupla' tries—I mean, what looked like tries—if she'd of fell off that window ledge, with 'Good-bye, good-bye' wrote all over the mirrors, I'd of said suicide. And then when it looked like she jumped off of the pier, right at the place where her old lady jumped off years ago, after finding her step-pa's body and figuring out her old lady must of bumped him off and buried him there, and with her leaving a note saying right where he was—" He stopped, ran a handkerchief over his broad red face and said, "You know what I mean."

"I do," Malone said. "I know what you were supposed to think."

"But that note," von Flanagan said. "Why did she write it?"

"She didn't," Malone told him.

The police officer scowled. "It was in her handwriting. (Dig, dig, dig. And—under the willow tree in the garden.)"

"It was dictated to her," Malone said. He signed, and added, "You're not up on popular songs, von Flanagan. You check this with her and see if I'm not right. The murderer telephoned her and recommended a couple of songs that would be particularly good for her style of singing. He told her to write down the titles and get copies. She did. Then on his next visit he tore the leaf from the telephone pad and stuck it in her diary. Remember, she trusted him, and he probably had the run of the house."

Von Flanagan shook his head sadly. "The things some people will do!" He scratched the back of his neck.

"Remember, he had to have the body found," Malone said, "or else he couldn't inherit. This would have looked like her last suicide note. It would have built up her reason for the suicide—her remorse for her mother's having committed a murder. That must have been preying on her mind for years. That's why she was willing to keep all these appointments, because she was told she'd find out the truth."

"And what was the truth?" von Flanagan asked. "Why did her old lady bump off this guy?"

There was a second or two of silence. "Because," Malone said at last, "from all I've been able to learn, he was a no good son-of-a-bee who was wrecking her life and her career, and who should have been murdered years before." He wondered if it would do him any serious damage to smoke a cigar, decided he might as well try, reached in his pocket and encountered a repulsive, soggy mass of wet tobacco.

"Have one of mine," Jack Apt said quietly.

It was a fine Havana cigar. Malone accepted it with thanks, and privately wished it was one of his own favorite two-for-a-quarter brand.

"Only," von Flanagan said, "how did you know for sure she really hadn't meant to jump off that ledge?"

The little lawyer sneezed and sighed on the same breath, nearly strangling himself. "Because of the 'good-bye, good-bye,' written on the mirrors."

"I don't get it," von Flanagan said.

"You will," Malone told him, "if you'll think of Doris Dawn's coloring—and the color of lipstick that was used to write on the mirrors. No woman in her right mind would wear that shade with a skin like Doris's."

Von Flanagan rose and said admiringly, "I wish I knew how you find out such things."

"Even if I could trust you with the truth," Malone said, "you wouldn't believe it."

For a few minutes after von Flanagan had gone he sat hunched in his blankets, brooding. He'd found a murderer, he'd saved a life, he'd seen what looked like the beginning of a very happy marriage. But he still didn't have carfare home.

Suddenly Malone had enough of it—a bellyful. He turned and stared at Jack Apt. Apt stared back, uncomfortably. Then Malone said, "If I sit here much longer, I'll get double pneumonia and have to be shot full of penicillin. Besides, the whiskey's gone, this cigar stinks— come on, Apt, break down and spill the truth. Or shall I?"

Jack Apt said softly, "How did you know I murdered Robert Spencer?"

Malone sneezed again. "Cut it out, Apt. I may be all wet—but not in the brain. Add it up this way: you were Diana Dawn's manager. You must have been in love with her. Everyone who ever saw her was. You knew what he was doing to her—so you killed him. What you didn't know was that she loved him and that she would kill herself from anxiety over his disappearance."

"I killed him," Jack Apt said, "and I buried him. Young Bob Spencer wormed the truth about his burial place out of me. I didn't know the reason why he wanted to find it out. Perhaps you'd better call von Flanagan back here, and tell him."

Malone yawned and said, "von Flanagan gets on my nerves sometimes." He sneezed a double one this time. "It must have been hell for you all these years, after she killed herself. So why bring the cops in now?"

"It was hell," Jack Apt said, pulling on a pair of tan leather gloves. "It will continue to be. May I drive you anywhere, Malone?"

"No, thanks," Malone said. "I'll call a cab." He remembered his lack of cabfare. "Or maybe I'll walk."

The door opened and Maggie, his secretary, walked in. Her cheeks were pink and her eyes were blazing.

"I've been looking all over town for you. You owe me seven-and-a-half hours overtime. That burglar has decided he will have you enter a not-guilty plea. He waited hours for you, and then sent his retainer over by messenger. All in cash."

"Call me a cab," Malone said, "before pneumonia carries me off."

"And," Maggie said, "A girl has been calling you for hours. She just said to tell you she's That Blonde."

Malone leaped up, blankets falling to the floor. "Call her back and tell her I'll be there as soon as I change my clothes."

"But Mr. Malone," Maggie wailed, "you'll catch cold."

The little lawyer paused at the door. "Who, me? I never catch cold." He waved, said a cheerful "Good-bye, good-bye," and walked out whistling "The Willow Tree In The Garden."

LOCKED DOORS
Mary Roberts Rinehart
Detective: Hilda Adams

MARY ROBERTS Rinehart (1876-1958), the creator of what is generally known as the "Had-I-But-Known" school, regularly had her plucky heroines put themselves in situations from which they needed to be rescued. That school of detective story has often been parodied and maligned, but it was so well handled that Rinehart was, for decades, one of the most successful and beloved mystery writers in America, producing the first mystery novel ever to appear on the bestseller list, *The Man in Lower Ten* in 1909. She had written it first as a serial for the first pulp magazine, *Munsey's*. She later serialized her novel *The Circular Staircase* in the same pulp, but it was released in book form in 1908, a year before *The Man in Lower Ten* was issued as a book.

Probably her most successful work, she and Avery Hopwood adapted *The Circular Staircase* for the stage as *The Bat* in 1920, by which time she had become the highest-paid writer in America. The book had already served as the basis for a silent film, *The Circular Staircase* (1915) and then the play, which had some differences from the novel, inspired more than one film, including the silent *The Bat* (1926), and a sound version titled *The Bat Whispers* (1930).

Rinehart's most famous character is Hilda Adams, whose propensity for getting involved in crimes and mysteries garnered her the nickname "Miss Pinkerton" after Allan Pinkerton, the famous real-life detective. She was encouraged in her sleuthing endeavors by George Patton, a small-time country detective who goes on to become a police inspector. He is a recurring presence in the series and appears to be interested in deepening his relationship with the dedicated nurse; she calls it "nonsense," though there are numerous hints that she welcomes the attention and returns some of the attraction. She overhears private conversations, listens to people who are sick or wounded so not at their peak strength, and provides information to Patton. It is her stated conviction that she is betraying no trust and, since criminals act against society, then society must use every means at its disposal to bring them to justice.

Adams first appeared in "The Buckled Bag," published in the January 10 and January 17, 1914, issues of *The Saturday Evening Post*. After "Locked Doors" was published in 1925, the character was the eager detective in *Miss Pinkerton* (1932), *The Haunted Lady* (1942), and *Episode of the Wandering Knife* (1950).

"Locked Doors" was originally published in the omnibus *Mary Roberts Rinehart Mystery Book* (New York, Farrar & Rinehart, 1925).

Locked Doors
By Mary Roberts Rinehart

Chapter I: Dangerous Assignment

"You PROMISED," I reminded Mr. Patton, "to play with cards on the table."

"My dear young lady," he replied, "I have no cards! I suspect a game, that's all."

"Then—do you need me?"

The detective bent forward, his arms on his desk, and looked me over carefully.

"What sort of shape are you in? Tired?"

"No."

"Nervous?"

"Not enough to hurt."

"I want you to take another case, following a nurse who has gone to pieces," he said, selecting his words carefully. "I don't want to tell you a lot—I want you to go in with a fresh mind. It promises to be an extraordinary case."

"How long was the other nurse there?"

"Four days."

"She went to pieces in four days!"

"Well, she's pretty much unstrung. The worst is, she hasn't any real reason. A family chooses to live in an unusual manner, because they like it, or perhaps they're afraid of something. The girl was, that's sure. I had never seen her until this morning, a big, healthy-looking young woman; but she came in looking back over her shoulder as if she expected a knife in her back. She said she was a nurse from St. Luke's and that she'd been on a case for four days. She'd left that morning after about three hours' sleep in that time, being locked in a room most of the time, and having little but crackers and milk for food. She thought it was a case for the police."

"Who is ill in the house? Who was her patient?"

"There is no illness, I believe. The French governess had gone, and they wished the children competently cared for until they replaced her. That was the reason given her when she went. Afterward she—well, she was puzzled."

"How are you going to get me there?"

He gathered acquiescence from my question and smiled approval.

"Good girl!" he said. "Never mind how I'll get you there. You are the most dependable woman I know."

"The most curious, perhaps?" I retorted. "Four days on the case, three hours' sleep, locked in and yelling 'Police!' Is it out of town?"

"No, in the heart of the city, on Beauregard Square. Can you get some St. Luke's uniforms? They want another St. Luke's nurse."

I said I could get the uniforms, and he wrote the address on a card.

"Better arrive about five," he said.

"But—if they are not expecting me?"

"They will be expecting you," he replied enigmatically.

"The doctor, if he's a St. Luke's man—"

"There is no doctor."

It was six months since I had solved, or helped to solve, the mystery of the buckled bag for Mr. Patton. I had had other cases for him in the interval, cases where the police could not get close enough. As I said when I began this record of my crusade against crime and the criminal, a trained nurse gets under the very skin of the soul. She finds a mind surrendered, all the crooked little motives that have fired the guns of life revealed in their pitifulness.

Gradually I had come to see that Mr. Patton's point of view was right; that if the criminal uses every means against society, why not society against the criminal? At first I had used this as a flag of truce to my nurse's ethical training; now I flaunted it, a mental and moral banner. The criminal against society, and I against the criminal! And, more than that, against misery, healing pain by augmenting it sometimes, but working like a surgeon, for good.

I had had six cases in six months. Only in one had I failed to land my criminal, and that without any suspicion of my white uniform and rubber-soled shoes. Although I played a double game no patient of mine had suffered. I was a nurse first and a police agent second. If it was a question between turpentine compresses—stupes, professionally—and seeing what letters came in or went out of the house, the compress went on first, and cracking hot too. I am not boasting. That is my method, the only way I can work, and it speaks well for it that, as I say, only one man escaped arrest—an arson case where the factory owner hanged himself in the bathroom needle shower in the house he had bought with the insurance money, while I was fixing his breakfast tray. And even he might have been saved for justice had the cook not burned the toast and been obliged to make it fresh.

I was no longer staying at a nurses' home. I had taken a bachelor suite of three rooms and bath, comfortably downtown. I cooked my own breakfasts when I was off duty and I dined at a restaurant near. Luncheon I did not bother much about. Now and then Mr. Patton telephoned me and we lunched together in remote places where we would not be known. He would tell me of his cases and sometimes he asked my advice.

I bought my uniforms that day and took them home in a taxicab. The dresses were blue, and over them for the street the St. Luke's girls wear long cloaks, English fashion, of navy blue serge, and a blue bonnet with a white ruching and white lawn ties. I felt curious in it, but it was becoming and convenient. Certainly I looked professional.

At three o'clock that afternoon a messenger brought a small box, registered. It contained a St. Luke's badge of gold and blue enamel.

At four o'clock my telephone rang. I was packing my suitcase according to the list I keep pasted in the lid. Under the list, which was of uniforms, aprons, thermometer, instruments, a nurse's simple set of probe, forceps, and bandage scissors, was the word "box." This always went in first—a wooden box with a lock, the key of which was round my neck. It contained skeleton keys, a small black revolver of which I was in deadly fear, a pair of handcuffs, a pocket flashlight, and my badge from the chief of police. I was examining the revolver nervously when the telephone rang, and I came within an ace of sending a bullet into the flat below.

Did you ever notice how much you get out of a telephone voice? We can dissemble with our faces, but under stress the vocal cords seem to draw up tight and the voice comes thin and colorless. There's a little woman in the flat beneath—the one I nearly bombarded—who sings like a bird at her piano half the day, scaling vocal heights that make me dizzy. Now and then she has a visitor, a nice young man, and she disgraces herself, flats F, fogs E even, finally takes cowardly refuge in a wretched mezzo-soprano and cries herself to sleep, doubtless, later on.

The man who called me had the thin-drawn voice of extreme strain—a youngish voice.

"Miss Adams," he said, "this is Francis Reed speaking. I have called St. Luke's and they referred me to you. Are you free to take a case this afternoon?"

I fenced. I was trying to read the voice. "This afternoon?"

"Well, before night anyhow; as—as early this evening as possible."

The voice was strained and tired, desperately tired. It was not peevish. It was even rather pleasant.

"What is the case, Mr. Reed?"

He hesitated. "It is not illness. It is merely—the governess has gone and there are two small children. We want someone to give her undivided attention to the children."

"I see."

"Are you a heavy sleeper, Miss Adams?"

"A very light one." I fancied he breathed freer.

"I hope you are not tired from a previous case?" I was beginning to like the voice.

"I'm quite fresh," I replied almost gaily. "Even if I were not, I like children, especially well ones. I shan't find looking after them very wearying, I'm sure."

Again the odd little pause. Then he gave me the address on Beauregard Square, and asked me to be sure not to be late. "I must warn you," he added, "we are living in a sort of casual way. Our servants left us without warning. Mrs. Reed has been getting along as best she could. Most of our meals are being sent in."

I was thinking fast. No servants! A good many people think a trained nurse is a sort of upper servant. I've been in houses where they were amazed to discover that I was a college woman and, finding the two things irreconcilable, have openly accused me of having been driven to such a desperate course as a hospital training by an unfortunate love affair.

"Of course you understand that I will look after the children to the best of my ability, but that I will not replace the servants."

I fancied he smiled grimly.

"That of course. Will you ring twice when you come?"

"Ring twice?"

"The doorbell," he replied impatiently.

I said I would ring the doorbell twice.

The young woman below was caroling gaily, ignorant of the six-barreled menace over her head. I knelt again by my suitcase, but packed little and thought a great deal. I was to arrive before dusk at a house where there were no servants and to ring the doorbell twice. I was to be a light sleeper, although I was to look after two healthy children. It was not much in itself, but, taken in connection with the previous nurse's appeal to the police, it took on new possibilities.

At six I started out to dinner. It was early spring and cold, but quite light. At the first corner I saw Mr. Patton waiting for a streetcar, and at his quick nod I saw I was to get in also. He did not pay my fare or speak to me. It was a part of the game that we were never seen together except at the remote restaurant I mentioned before. The car thinned out and I could watch him easily. Far downtown he alighted and so did I. The restaurant was near. I went in alone and sat down at a table in a recess, and very soon he joined me. We were in the main dining-room but not of it, a sop at once to the conventions and to the necessity, where he was so well known, for caution.

"I got a little information—on—the affair we were talking of," he said as he sat down. "I'm not so sure I want you to take the case after all."

"Certainly I shall take it," I retorted with some sharpness. "I've promised to go."

"Tut! I'm not going to send you into danger unnecessarily."

"I am not afraid."

"Exactly. A lot of generals were lost in the Civil War because they were not afraid and wanted to lead their troops instead of saving themselves and their expensive West Point training by sitting back in a safe spot and directing the fight. Any fool can run into danger. It takes intellect to keep out."

I felt my color rising indignantly. "Then you brought me here to tell me I am not to go?"

"Will you let me read you two reports?"

"You could have told me that at the corner!"

"Will you let me read you two reports?"

"If you don't mind I'll first order something to eat. I'm to be there before dark."

"Will you let me—"

"I'm going, and you know I'm going. If you don't want me to represent you I'll go on my own. They want a nurse, and they're in trouble."

I think he was really angry. I know I was. If there is anything that takes the very soul out of a woman, it is to be kept from doing a thing she has set her heart on, because some man thinks it dangerous. If she has any spirit, that rouses it.

Mr. Patton quietly replaced the reports in his wallet and his wallet in the inside pocket of his coat, and fell to a judicial survey of the menu. But although he did not even glance at me he must have felt the determination in my face, for he ordered things that were quickly prepared and told the waiter to hurry.

"I have wondered lately," he said slowly, "whether the mildness of your manner at the hospital was acting, or the chastening effect of three years under an order book."

"A man always likes a woman to be a sheep."

"Not at all. But it is rather disconcerting to have a pet lamb turn round and take a bite out of one."

"Will you read the reports now?"

"I think," he said quietly, "they would better wait until we have eaten. We will probably both feel calmer. Suppose we arrange that nothing said before the oysters counts?"

I agreed, rather sulkily, and the meal went off well enough. I was anxious enough to hurry but he ate deliberately, drank his demitasse, paid the waiter, and at last met my impatient eyes and smiled.

"After all," he said, "since you are determined to go anyhow, what's the use of reading the reports? Inside of an hour you'll know all you need to know." But he saw that I did not take his teasing well, and drew out his pocketbook.

They were two typewritten papers clamped together.

They are on my desk before me now. The first one is endorsed:

Statement by Laura F. Bosworth, nurse, of St. Luke's Home for Graduate Nurses.

Miss Bosworth says:

I do not know just why I came here. But I know I'm frightened. That's the fact. I think there is something terribly wrong in the house of Francis M. Reed, 71 Beauregard Square. I think a crime of some sort has been committed. There are four people in the family, Mr. and Mrs. Reed and two children. I was to look after the children.

I was there four days and the children were never allowed out of the room. At night we were locked in. I kept wondering what I would do if there was a fire. The telephone wires are cut so no one can call the house, and I believe the doorbell is disconnected too. But that's fixed now. Mrs. Reed went round all the time with a face like chalk and her eyes staring. At all hours of the night she'd unlock the bedroom door and come in and look at the children.

Almost all the doors through the house were locked. If I wanted to get to the kitchen to boil eggs for the children's breakfast—for there were no servants, and Mrs. Reed was young and didn't know anything about cooking—Mr. Reed had to unlock about four doors for me.

If Mrs. Reed looked bad, he was dreadful—sunken eyed and white and wouldn't eat. I think he has killed somebody and is making away with the body.

Last night I said I had to have air, and they let me go out. I called up a friend from a pay-station, another nurse. This morning she sent me a special-delivery letter that I was needed on another case, and I got away. That's all; it sounds foolish, but try it and see if it doesn't get on your nerves.

Mr. Patton looked up at me as he finished reading.

"Now you see what I mean," he said. "That woman was there four days, and she is as temperamental as a cow, but in those four days her nervous system went to smash."

"Doors locked!" I reflected. "Servants gone; state of fear—it looks like a siege!"

"But why a trained nurse? Why not a policeman, if there is danger? Why anyone at all, if there is something that the police are not to know?"

"That is what I intend to find out," I replied. He shrugged his shoulders and read the other paper:

Report of Detective Bennett on Francis M. Reed, April 5, 1913:

Francis M. Reed is thirty-six years of age, married, a chemist at the Olympic Paint Works. He has two children, both boys. Has a small independent income and owns the house on Beauregard Square, which was built by his grandfather, General F. R. Reed. Is supposed to be living beyond his means. House is usually full of servants, and grocer in the neighborhood has had to wait for money several times.

On March twenty-ninth he dismissed all servants without warning. No reason given, but a week's wages instead of notice.

On March thirtieth he applied to the owners of the paint factory for two weeks' vacation. Gave as his reason nervousness and insomnia. He said he was "going to lay off and get some sleep." Has not been back at the works since. House under surveillance this afternoon. No visitors.

Mr. Reed telephoned for a nurse at four o'clock from a store on Eleventh Street. Explained that his telephone was out of order.

Mr. Patton folded up the papers and thrust them back into his pocket. Evidently he saw I was determined, for he only said:

"Have you got your revolver?"

"Yes."

"Do you know anything about telephones? Could you repair that one in an emergency?"

"In an emergency," I retorted, "there is no time to repair a telephone. But I've got a voice and there are windows. If I really put my mind to it you will hear me yell at headquarters."

He smiled grimly.

Chapter II: House of Mystery

THE REED house is on Beauregard Square. It is a small, exclusive community, the Beauregard neighborhood; a dozen or more solid citizens built their homes there in the early 70's, occupying large lots, the houses flush with the streets and with gardens behind. Six on one street, six on another, back to back with the gardens in the center, they occupied the whole block. And the gardens were not fenced off, but made a sort of small park unsuspected from the streets. Here and there bits of flowering shrubbery sketchily outlined a property, but the general impression was of lawn and trees, free of access to all the owners. Thus with the square in front and the gardens in the rear, the Reed house faced in two directions on the early spring green.

In the gardens the old tar walks were still there, and a fountain which no longer played, but on whose stone coping I believe the young Beauregard Squarites made their first climbing ventures.

The gardens were always alive with birds, and later on from my windows I learned the reason. It seems to have been a custom sanctified by years, that the crumbs from the twelve tables should be thrown into the dry basin of the fountain for the birds. It was a common sight to see stately butlers and chic little waitresses in black and white coming out after luncheon or dinner with silver trays of crumbs. Many a scrap of gossip, as well as scrap of food, has been passed along at the old stone fountain, I believe. I know that it was there that I heard of the "basement ghost" of Beauregard Square—a whisper at first, a panic later.

I arrived at eight o'clock and rang the doorbell twice. The door was opened at once by Mr. Reed, a tall, blond young man carefully dressed. He threw away his cigarette when he saw me and shook hands. The hall was brightly lighted and most cheerful; in fact the whole house was ablaze with light. Certainly nothing could be less mysterious than the house, or than the debonair young man who motioned me into the library.

"I told Mrs. Reed I would talk to you before you go upstairs," he said. "Will you sit down?"

I sat down. The library was even brighter than the hall, and now I saw that although he smiled as cheerfully as ever his face was almost colorless, and his eyes, which looked frankly enough into mine for a moment, went wandering off round the room. I had the impression somehow that Mr. Patton had had of the nurse at headquarters that morning—that he looked as if he expected a knife in his back. It seemed to me that he wanted to look over his shoulder and by sheer will power did not.

"You know the rule, Miss Adams," he said: "When there's an emergency get a trained nurse. I told you our emergency—no servants and two small children."

"This should be a good time to secure servants," I said briskly. "City houses are being deserted for country places, and a percentage of servants won't leave town."

He hesitated. "We've been doing very nicely, although of course it's hardly more than just living. Our meals are sent in from a hotel, and—well, we thought, since we are going away so soon, that perhaps we could manage."

The impulse was too strong for him at that moment. He wheeled and looked behind him, not a hasty glance, but a deliberate inspection that took in every part of that end of the room. It was so unexpected that it left me gasping.

The next moment he was himself again.

"When I say that there is no illness," he said, "I am hardly exact. There is no illness, but there has been an epidemic of children's diseases among the Beauregard Square children and we are keeping the youngsters indoors."

"Don't you think they could be safeguarded without being shut up in the house?"

He responded eagerly. "If I only thought—" he checked himself. "No," he said decidedly; "for a time at least I believe it is not wise."

I did not argue with him. There was nothing to be gained by antagonizing him. And as Mrs. Reed came in just then, the subject was dropped. She was hardly more than a girl, almost as blond as her husband, very pretty, and with the weariest eyes I have ever seen, unless perhaps the eyes of a man who has waited a long time for deathly tuberculosis.

I liked her at once. She did not attempt to smile. She rather clung to my hand when I held it out.

"I am glad St. Luke's still trusts us," she said. "I was afraid the other nurse— Frank, will you take Miss Adams's suitcase upstairs?"

She held out a key. He took it, but he turned at the door.

"I wish you wouldn't wear those things, Anne. You gave me your promise yesterday, you remember."

"I can't work round the children in anything else," she protested.

"Those things" were charming. She wore a rose silk negligee trimmed with soft bands of lace and blue satin flowers, a petticoat to match that garment, and a lace cap.

He hesitated in the doorway and looked at her—a curious glance, I thought, full of tenderness, reproof—apprehension perhaps.

"I'll take it off, dear," she replied to the glance. "I wanted Miss Adams to know that, even if we haven't a servant in the house, we are at least civilized. I—I haven't taken cold." This last was clearly an afterthought.

He went out then and left us together. She came over to me swiftly.

"What did the other nurse say?" she demanded.

"I do not know her at all. I have not seen her."

"Didn't she report at the hospital that we were—queer?"

I smiled. "That's hardly likely, is it?"

Unexpectedly she went to the door opening into the hall and closed it, coming back swiftly.

"Mr. Reed thinks it is not necessary, but—there are some things that will puzzle you. Perhaps I should have spoken to the other nurse. If—if anything strikes you as unusual, Miss Adams, just please don't see it! It is all right, everything is all right. But something has occurred—not very much, but disturbing—and we are all of us doing the very best we can."

She was quivering with nervousness.

I was not the police agent then, I'm afraid.

"Nurses are accustomed to disturbing things. Perhaps I can help."

"You can, by watching the children. That's the only thing that matters to me—the children. I don't want them left alone. If you have to leave them call me."

"Don't you think I will be able to watch them more intelligently if I know just what the danger is?"

I think she very nearly told me. She was so tired, evidently so anxious to shift her burden to fresh shoulders.

"Mr. Reed said," I prompted her, "that there was an epidemic of children's diseases. But from what you say—"

But I was not to learn, after all, for her husband opened the hall door.

"Yes, children's diseases," she said vaguely. "So many children are down. Shall we go up, Frank?"

The extraordinary bareness of the house had been dawning on me for some time. It was well lighted and well furnished. But the floors were innocent of rugs, the handsome furniture was without arrangement and, in the library at least, stood huddled in the center of the room. The hall and stairs were also uncarpeted, but there were marks where carpets had recently lain and had been jerked up.

The progress up the staircase was not calculated to soothe my nerves. The thought of my little revolver, locked in my suitcase, was poor comfort. For with every four steps or so Mr. Reed, who led the way, turned automatically and peered into the hallway below; he was listening, too, his head bent slightly forward. And each time that he turned, his wife behind me turned also. Cold terror suddenly got me by the spine, and yet the hall was bright with light.

(Note: Surely fear is a contagion. Could one isolate the germ of it and find an antitoxin? Or is it merely a form of nervous activity run amuck, like a runaway locomotive, colliding with other nervous activities and causing catastrophe? Take this up with Mr. Patton. But would he know? He, I am almost sure, has never been really afraid.)

I had a vision of my oxlike predecessor making this head-over-shoulder journey up the staircase, and in spite of my nervousness I smiled. But at that moment Mrs. Reed behind me put a hand on my arm, and I screamed. I remember yet the way she dropped back against the wall and turned white.

Mr. Reed whirled on me instantly. "What did you see?" he demanded.

"Nothing at all." I was horribly ashamed. "Your wife touched my arm unexpectedly. I dare say I am nervous."

"It's all right, Anne," he reassured her. And to me, almost irritably: "I thought you nurses had no nerves."

"Under ordinary circumstances I have none."

It was all ridiculous. We were still on the staircase.

"Just what do you mean by that?"

"If you will stop looking down into that hall I'll be calm enough. You make me jumpy."

He muttered something about being sorry and went on quickly. But at the top he went through an inward struggle, evidently succumbed, and took a final furtive survey of the hallway below. I was so wrought up that had a door slammed anywhere just then I think I should have dropped where I stood.

The absolute silence of the house added to the strangeness of the situation. Beauregard Square is not close to a trolley line, and quiet is the neighborhood tradition. The first rubber-tired vehicles in the city drew up before Beauregard Square houses. Beauregard Square children speak in low voices and never bang their spoons on their plates. Beauregard Square servants wear felt-soled shoes. And such outside noises as venture to intrude themselves must filter through double brick walls and doors built when lumber was selling by the thousand acres instead of the square foot.

Through this silence our feet echoed along the bare floor of the upper hall, as well lighted as belowstairs and as dismantled, to the door of the day nursery. The door was locked—double locked, in fact. For the key had been turned in the old-fashioned lock, and in addition an ordinary bolt had been newly fastened on the outside of the door. On the outside! Was that to keep me in? It was certainly not to keep anyone or anything out. The feeblest touch moved the bolt.

We were all three outside the door. We seemed to keep our compactness by common consent. No one of us left the group willingly; or, leaving it, we slid back again quickly. That was my impression, at least. But the bolt rather alarmed me.

"This is your room," Mrs. Reed said. "It is generally the day nursery, but we have put a bed and some other things in it. I hope you will be comfortable."

I touched the bolt with my finger and smiled into Mr. Reed's eyes.

"I hope I am not to be fastened in!" I said.

He looked back squarely enough, but somehow I knew he lied.

"Certainly not," he replied, and opened the door.

If there had been mystery outside, and bareness, the nursery was charming—a corner room with many windows, hung with the simplest of nursery papers and full of glass-doored closets filled with orderly rows of toys. In one corner a small single bed had been added without spoiling the room. The window sills were full of flowering plants. There was a bowl of goldfish on a stand, and a tiny dwarf parrot in a cage was covered against the night air by a bright afghan. A white-tiled bathroom connected with this room and also with the night nursery beyond.

Mr. Reed did not come in. I had an uneasy feeling, however, that he was just beyond the door. The children were not asleep. Mrs. Reed left me to let me put on my uniform. When she came back her face was troubled.

"They are not sleeping well," she complained. "I suppose it comes from having no exercise. They are always excited."

"I'll take their temperatures," I said. "Sometimes a tepid bath and a cup of hot milk will make them sleep."

The two little boys were wide awake. They sat up to look at me and both spoke at once.

"Can you tell fairy tales out of your head?"

"Did you see Chang?"

They were small, sleek-headed, fair-skinned youngsters, adorably clean and rumpled.

"Chang is their dog, a Pekinese," explained the mother. "He has been lost for several days."

"But he isn't lost, Mother. I can hear him crying every now and then. You'll look again, Mother, won't you?"

"We heard him through the furnace pipe," shrilled the smaller of the two. "You said you would look."

"I did look, darlings. He isn't there. And you promised not to cry about him, Freddie."

Freddie, thus put on his honor, protested he was not crying for the dog. "I want to go out and take a walk, that's why I'm crying," he wailed. "And I want Mademoiselle, and my buttons are all off. And my ear aches when I lie on it."

The room was close. I threw up the windows, and turned to find Mrs. Reed at my elbows. She was glancing out apprehensively.

"I suppose the air is necessary," she said, "and these windows are all right. But—I have a reason for asking it—please do not open the others."

She went very soon, and I listened as she went out. I had promised to lock the door behind her, and I did so. The bolt outside was not shot.

After I had quieted the children with my mildest fairy story I made a quiet inventory of my new quarters. The rough diagram of the second floor is the one I gave Mr. Patton later. That night, of course, I investigated only the two nurseries. But, so strangely had the fear that hung over the house infected me, I confess that I made my little tour of bathroom and clothes-closet with my revolver in my hand!

I found nothing, of course. The disorder of the house had not extended itself here. The bathroom was spotless with white tile, the large clothes-closet which opened off the passage between the two rooms was full of neatly folded clothing for the children. The closet was to play its part later, a darkish little room faintly lighted by a ground-glass transom opening into the center hall, but dependent mostly on electric light.

Outside the windows Mrs. Reed had asked me not to open was a porte-cochère roof almost level with the sills. Then was it an outside intruder she feared? And in that case, why the bolts on the outside of the two nursery doors? For the night nursery, I found, must have one also. I turned the key, but the door would not open.

I decided not to try to sleep that night, but to keep on watch. So powerfully had the mother's anxiety about her children and their mysterious danger impressed me that I made frequent excursions into the back room. Up to midnight there was nothing whatever to alarm me. I darkened both rooms and sat, waiting for I know not what; for some sound to show that the house stirred, perhaps. At a few minutes after twelve faint noises penetrated to my room from the hall, Mr. Reed's nervous voice and a piece of furniture scraping over the floor. Then silence again for half an hour or so.

Then—I was quite certain that the bolt on my door had been shot. I did not hear it, I think. Perhaps I felt it. Perhaps I only feared it. I unlocked the door; it was fastened outside.

There is a hideous feeling of helplessness about being locked in. I pretended to myself at first that I was only interested and curious. But I was frightened; I know that now. I sat there in the dark and wondered what I would do if the house took fire, or if some hideous tragedy enacted itself outside that locked door and I were helpless.

By two o'clock I had worked myself into a panic. The house was no longer silent. Someone was moving about downstairs, and not stealthily. The sounds came up through the heavy joists and flooring of the old house.

I determined to make at least a struggle to free myself. There was no way to get at the bolts, of course. The porte-cochere roof remained and the transom in the clothes-closet. True, I might have raised an alarm and been freed at once, but naturally I rejected this method. The roof of the porte-cochere proved impracticable. The tin bent and cracked under my first step. The transom then.

I carried a chair into the closet and found the transom easy to lower. But it threatened to creak. I put liquid soap on the hinges—it was all I had, and it worked very well—and lowered the transom inch by inch. Even then I could not see over it. I had worked so far without a sound, but in climbing to a shelf my foot slipped and I thought I heard a sharp movement outside. It was five minutes before I stirred. I hung there, every muscle cramped, listening and waiting. Then I lifted myself by sheer force of muscle and looked out. The upper landing of the staircase, brilliantly lighted, was to my right. Across the head of the stairs had been pushed a cotbed, made up for the night, but it was unoccupied.

Mrs. Reed, in a long, dark ulster, was standing beside it, staring with fixed and glassy eyes at something in the lower hall.

Chapter III: Deadly Fear

SOME TIME after four o'clock my door was unlocked from without; the bolt slipped as noiselessly as it had been shot. I got a little sleep until seven, when the boys trotted into my room in their bathrobes and slippers and perched on my bed.

"It's a nice day," observed Harry, the elder. "Is that bump your feet?"

I wriggled my toes and assured him he had surmised correctly.

"You're pretty long, aren't you? Do you think we can play in the fountain today?"

"We'll make a try for it, son. It will do us all good to get out into the sunshine."

"We always took Chang for a walk every day, Mademoiselle and Chang and Freddie and I."

Freddie had found my cap on the dressing-table and had put it on his yellow head. But now, on hearing the beloved name of his pet, he burst into loud grief-stricken howls.

"Want Mam'selle," he cried. "Want Chang too. Poor Freddie!"

The children were adorable. I bathed and dressed them and, mindful of my predecessor's story of crackers and milk, prepared for an excursion kitchenward. The nights might be full of mystery, murder might romp from room to room, but I intended to see that the youngsters breakfasted. But before I was ready to go down breakfast arrived.

Perhaps the other nurse had told the Reeds a few plain truths before she left; perhaps, and this I think was the case, the cloud had lifted just a little. Whatever it may have been, two rather flushed and blistered young people tapped at the door that morning and were admitted, Mr. Reed first, with a tray, Mrs. Reed following with a coffeepot and cream.

The little nursery table was small for five, but we made room somehow. What if the eggs were underdone and the toast dry? The children munched blissfully. What if Mr. Reed's face was still drawn and haggard and his wife a limp little huddle on the floor? She sat with her head against his knee and her eyes on the little boys, and drank her pale coffee slowly. She was very tired, poor thing. She dropped asleep sitting there, and he sat for a long time, not liking to disturb her.

It made me feel homesick for the home I didn't have. I've had the same feeling before, of being a rank outsider, a sort of defrauded feeling. I've had it when I've seen the look in a man's eyes when his wife comes to after an operation. And I've had it, for that matter, when I've put a new baby in its mother's arms for the first time. I had it for sure that morning, while she slept there and he stroked her pretty hair.

I put in my plea for the children then.

"It's bright and sunny," I argued. "And if you are nervous I'll keep them away from other children. But if you want to keep them well you must give them exercise."

It was the argument about keeping them well that influenced him, I think. He sat silent for a long time. His wife was still asleep, her lips parted.

"Very well," he said finally, "from two to three, Miss Adams. But not in the garden back of the house. Take them on the street."

I agreed to that. "I shall want a short walk every evening myself," I added. "That is a rule of mine. I am a more useful person and a more agreeable one if I have it."

I think he would have demurred if he dared. But one does not easily deny so sane a request. He yielded grudgingly.

That first day was calm and quiet enough. Had it not been for the strange condition of the house and the necessity for keeping the children locked in I would have smiled at my terror of the night. Luncheon was sent in; so was dinner. The children and I lunched and supped alone. As far as I could see, Mrs. Reed made no attempt at housework; but the cot at the head of the stairs disappeared in the early morning and the dog did not howl again.

I took the boys out for an hour in the early afternoon. Two incidents occurred, both of them significant. I bought myself a screw driver—that was one. The other was our meeting with a slender young woman in black who knew the boys and stopped them. She proved to be one of the dismissed servants—the waitress, she said.

"Why, Freddie!" she cried. "And Harry too! Aren't you going to speak to Nora?"

After a moment or two she turned to me, and I felt she wanted to say something, but hardly dared.

"How is Mrs. Reed?" she asked. "Not sick, I hope?" She glanced at my St. Luke's cloak and bonnet.

"No, she is quite well."

"And Mr. Reed?"

"Quite well also."

"Is Mademoiselle still there?"

"No, there is no one there but the family. There are no maids in the house."

She stared at me curiously. "Mademoiselle has gone? Are you cer— Excuse me, miss. But I thought she would never go. The children were like her own."

"She is not there, Nora."

She stood for a moment debating, I thought. Then she burst out, "Mr. Reed made a mistake, miss. You can't take a houseful of first-class servants and dismiss them the way he did, without half an hour to get out bag and baggage, without making talk. And there's talk enough all through the neighborhood."

"What sort of talk?"

"Different people say different things. They say Mademoiselle is still there, locked in her room on the third floor. There's a light there sometimes, but nobody sees her. And other folks say Mr. Reed is crazy. And there is worse being said than that."

But she refused to tell me any more—evidently concluded she

had said too much and got away as quickly as she could, looking rather worried.

I was a trifle over my hour getting back, but nothing was said. To leave the clean and tidy street for the disordered house was not pleasant. But once in the children's suite, with the goldfish in the aquarium darting like tongues of flame in the sunlight, with the tulips and hyacinths of the window-boxes glowing and the orderly toys on their white shelves, I felt comforted. After all, disorder and dust did not imply crime.

But one thing I did that afternoon—did it with firmness and no attempt at secrecy, and after asking permission of no one. I took the new screw driver and unfastened the bolt from the outside of my door.

I was prepared, if necessary, to make a stand on that issue. But although it was noticed, I knew, no mention was made to me.

Mrs. Reed pleaded a headache that evening, and I believe her husband ate alone in the dismantled dining-room. For every room on the lower floor, I had discovered, was in the same curious disorder.

At seven Mr. Reed relieved me to go out. The children were in bed. He did not go into the day nursery, but placed a straight chair outside the door of the back room and sat there, bent over, elbows on knees, chin cupped in his palm, staring at the staircase. He roused enough to ask me to bring an evening paper when I returned.

When I am on a department case I always take my off-duty in the evening by arrangement and walk round the block. Some time in my walk I am sure to see Mr. Patton himself if the case is big enough, or one of his agents if he cannot come. If I have nothing to communicate it resolves itself into a bow and nothing more.

I was nervous on this particular jaunt. For one thing my St. Luke's cloak and bonnet marked me at once, made me conspicuous; for another, I was afraid Mr. Patton would think the Reed house no place for a woman and order me home.

It was a quarter to eight and quite dark before he fell into step beside me.

"Well," I replied rather shakily; "I'm still alive, as you see."

"Then it is pretty bad?"

"It's exceedingly queer," I admitted, and told my story. I had meant to conceal the bolt on the outside of my door, and one or two other things, but I blurted them all out right then and there, and felt immeasurably better at once.

He listened intently.

"It's fear of the deadliest sort," I finished.

"Fear of the police?"

"I—I think not. It is fear of something in the house. They are always listening and watching at the top of the front stairs. They have lifted all the carpets, so that every footstep echoes through the whole house. Mrs. Reed goes down to the first door, but never alone. Today I found that the back staircase is locked off at top and bottom. There are doors."

I gave him my rough diagram of the house. It was too dark to see it.

"It is only tentative," I explained. "So much of the house is locked up, and every movement of mine is under surveillance. Without baths there are about twelve large rooms, counting the third floor. I've not been able to get there, but I thought that tonight I'd try to look about."

"You had no sleep last night?"

"Three hours—from four to seven this morning."

We had crossed into the public square and were walking slowly under the trees. Now he stopped and faced me.

"I don't like the look of it, Miss Adams," he said. "Ordinary panic goes and hides. But here's a fear that knows what it's afraid of and takes methodical steps for protection. I didn't want you to take the case, you know that; but now I'm not going to insult you by asking you to give it up. But I'm going to see that you are protected. There will be someone across the street every night as long as you are in the house."

"Have you any theory?" I asked him. He is not strong for theories generally. He is very practical. "That is, do you think the other nurse was right and there is some sort of crime being concealed?"

"Well, think about it," he prompted me. "If a murder has been committed, what are they afraid of? The police? Then why a trained nurse and all this caution about the children? A ghost? Would they lift the carpets so they could hear the specter tramping about the house?"

"If there is no crime, but something—a lunatic perhaps?" I asked.

"Possibly. But then why this secrecy and keeping out the police? It is, of course, possible that your respected employers have both gone off mentally, and the whole thing is a nightmare delusion. On my word it sounds like it. But it's too much for credulity to believe they've both gone crazy with the same form of delusion."

"Perhaps I'm the lunatic," I said despairingly. "When you reduce it like that to an absurdity I wonder if I didn't imagine it all, the lights burning everywhere and the carpets up, and Mrs. Reed staring down the staircase, and I locked in a room and hanging on by my nails to peer out through a closet transom."

"Perhaps. But how about the deadly sane young woman who preceded you? She had no imagination. Now about Reed and his wife—how do they strike you? They get along all right and that sort of thing, I suppose?"

"They are nice people," I said emphatically. "He's a gentleman and they're devoted. He just looks like a big boy who's got into an awful mess and doesn't know how to get out. And she's backing him up. She's a dear."

"Humph!" said Mr. Patton. "Don't suppress any evidence because she's a dear and he's a handsome big boy, Miss Adams!"

"I didn't say he was handsome," I snapped.

"Did you ever see a ghost or think you saw one?" he inquired suddenly.

"No, but one of my aunts has. Hers always carry their heads. She asked one a question once and the head nodded."

"Then you believe in things of that sort?"

"Not a particle—but I'm afraid of them."

He smiled, and shortly after that I went back to the house. I think he was sorry about the ghost question, for he explained that he had been trying me out, and that I looked well in my cloak and bonnet. "I'm afraid of your chin generally," he said; "but the white lawn ties have a softening effect. In view of the ties I have almost the courage—"

"Yes?"

"I think not, after all," he decided. "The chin is there, ties or no ties. Good night, and—for heaven's sake don't run any unnecessary risks."

The change from his facetious tone to earnestness was so unexpected that I was still standing there on the pavement when he plunged into the darkness of the square and disappeared.

Chapter IV: Terror Above

AT TEN minutes after eight I was back in the house. Mr. Reed admitted me, going through the tedious process of unlocking outer and inner vestibule doors and fastening them again behind me. He inquired politely if I had had a pleasant walk, and without waiting for my reply fell to reading the evening paper. He seemed to have forgotten me absolutely. First he scanned the headlines; then he turned feverishly to something farther on and ran his fingers down along a column. His lips were twitching, but evidently he did not find what he expected—or feared—for he threw the paper away and did not glance at it again. I watched him from the angle of the stairs.

Even for that short interval Mrs. Reed had taken his place at the children's door. She wore a black dress, long sleeved and high at the throat, instead of the silk negligee of the previous evening, and she held a book. But she was not reading. She smiled rather wistfully when she saw me.

"How fresh you always look!" she said. "And so self-reliant. I wish I had your courage."

"I am perfectly well. I dare say that explains a lot. Kiddies asleep?"

"Freddie isn't. He has been crying for Chang. I hate night, Miss Adams. I'm like Freddie. All my troubles come up about this time. I'm horribly depressed." Her blue eyes filled with tears.

"I haven't been sleeping well," she confessed.

I should think not!

Without taking off my things I went down to Mr. Reed in the lower hall.

"I'm going to insist on something," I said. "Mrs. Reed is highly nervous. She says she has not been sleeping. I think if I gave her an opiate and she gets an entire night's sleep it may save her a breakdown."

I looked straight in his eyes, and for once he did not evade me.

"I'm afraid I've been very selfish," he said. "Of course she must have sleep. I'll give you a powder, unless you have something you prefer to use."

I remembered then that he was a chemist, and said I would gladly use whatever he gave me.

"There is another thing I wanted to speak about, Mr. Reed," I said. "The children are mourning their dog. Don't you think he may have been accidentally shut up somewhere in the house in one of the upper floors?"

"Why do you say that?" he demanded sharply.

"They say they have heard him howling."

He hesitated for barely a moment. Then: "Possibly," he said. "But they will not hear him again. The little chap has been sick, and he— died today. Of course the boys are not to know."

No one watched the staircase that night. I gave Mrs. Reed the opiate and saw her comfortably into bed. When I went back fifteen minutes later she was resting, but not asleep. Opiates sometimes make people garrulous for a little while—sheer comfort, perhaps, and relaxed tension. I've had stockbrokers and bankers in the hospital give me tips, after a hypodermic of morphia, that would have made me wealthy had I not been limited to my training allowance of twelve dollars a month.

"I was just wondering," she said as I tucked her up, "where a woman owes the most allegiance—to her husband or to her children?"

"Why not split it up," I said cheerfully, "and try doing what seems best for both?"

"But that's only a compromise!" she complained, and was asleep almost immediately. I lowered the light and closed the door, and shortly after I heard Mr. Reed locking it from the outside.

With the bolt off my door and Mrs. Reed asleep my plan for the night was easily carried out. I went to bed for a couple of hours and slept calmly. I awakened once with the feeling that someone was looking at me from the passage into the night nursery, but there was no one there. However, so strong had been the feeling that I got up and went into the back room. The children were asleep, and all doors opening into the hall were locked. But the window on to the porte-cochere roof was open and the curtain blowing. There was no one on the roof.

It was not twelve o'clock and I still had an hour. I went back to bed.

At one I prepared to make a thorough search of the house. Looking from one of my windows I thought I saw the shadowy figure of a man across the street, and I was comforted. Help was always close, I felt. And yet, as I stood inside my door in my rubber-soled shoes, with my ulster over my uniform and a revolver and my skeleton keys in my pockets, my heart was going very fast. The stupid story of the ghost came back and made me shudder, and the next instant I was remembering Mrs. Reed the night before, staring down into the lower hall with fixed glassy eyes.

My plan was to begin at the top of the house and work down. The thing was the more hazardous, of course, because Mr. Reed was most certainly somewhere about. I had no excuse for being on the third floor. Down below I could say I wanted tea, or hot water—anything. But I did not expect to find Mr. Reed up above. The terror, whatever it was, seemed to lie below.

Access to the third floor was not easy. The main staircase did not go up. To get there I was obliged to unlock the door at the rear of the hall with my own keys. I was working in bright light, trying my keys one after another, and watching over my shoulder as I did so. When the door finally gave it was a relief to slip into the darkness beyond, ghosts or no ghosts.

I am always a silent worker. Caution about closing doors and squeaking hinges is second nature to me. One learns to be cautious when one's only chance of sleep is not to rouse a peevish patient and have to give a body-massage, as like as not, or listen to domestic troubles—"I said" and "he said"—until one is almost crazy.

So I made no noise. I closed the door behind me and stood blinking in the darkness. I listened. There was no sound above or below. Now houses at night have no terror for me. Every nurse is obliged to do more or less going about in the dark. But I was not easy. Suppose Mr. Reed should call me? True, I had locked my door and had the key in my pocket. But a dozen emergencies flew through my mind as I felt for the stair rail.

There was a curious odor through all the back staircase, a pungent, aromatic scent that, with all my familiarity with drugs, was strange to me. As I slowly climbed the stairs it grew more powerful. The air was heavy with it, as though no windows had been opened in that part of the house. There was no door at the top of this staircase, as there was on the second floor. It opened into an upper hall, and across from the head of the stairs was a door leading into a room. This door was closed. On this staircase, as on all the others, the carpet had been newly lifted. My electric flash showed the white boards and painted borders, the carpet tacks, many of them still in place. One, lying loose, penetrated my rubber sole and went into my foot.

I sat down in the dark and took off the shoe. As I did so my flash, on the step beside me, rolled over and down with a crash. I caught it on the next step, but the noise had been like a pistol shot.

Almost immediately a voice spoke above me sharply. At first I thought it was out in the upper hall. Then I realized that the closed door was between it and me.

"Ees that you, Meester Reed?"

Mademoiselle!

"Meester Reed!"—plaintively. "Eet comes up again, Meester Reed! I die! Tomorrow I die!"

She listened. On no reply coming she began to groan rhythmically, to a curious accompaniment of creaking. When I had gathered up my nerves again I realized that she must be sitting in a rocking-chair. The groans were really little plaintive grunts.

By the time I had got my shoe on she was up again, and I could hear her pacing the room, the heavy step of a woman well fleshed and not young. Now and then she stopped inside the door and listened; once she shook the knob and mumbled querulously to herself.

I recovered the flash, and with infinite caution worked my way to the top of the stairs. Mademoiselle was locked in, doubly bolted in. Two strong bolts, above and below, supplemented the door lock.

Her ears must have been very quick, or else she felt my softly padding feet on the boards outside, for suddenly she flung herself against the door and begged for a priest, begged piteously, in jumbled French and English. She wanted food; she was dying of hunger. She wanted a priest.

And all the while I stood outside the door and wondered what I should do. Should I release the woman? Should I go down to the lower floor and get the detective across the street to come in and force the door? Was this the terror that held the house in thrall—this babbling old Frenchwoman calling for food and a priest in one breath?

Surely not. This was a part of the mystery, not all. The real terror lay below. It was not Mademoiselle, locked in her room on the upper floor, that the Reeds waited for at the top of the stairs. But why was Mademoiselle locked in her room? Why were the children locked in? What was this thing that had turned a home into a jail, a barracks, that had sent away the servants, imprisoned and probably killed the dog, sapped the joy of life from two young people? What was it that Mademoiselle cried "comes up again"?

I looked toward the staircase. Was it coming up the staircase?

I am not afraid of the thing I can see, but it seemed to me, all at once, that if anything was going to come up the staircase I might as well get down first. A staircase is no place to meet anything, especially if one doesn't know what it is.

I listened again. Mademoiselle was quiet. I flashed my light down the narrow stairs. They were quite empty. I shut off the flash and went down. I tried to go slowly, to retreat with dignity, and by the time I had reached the landing below I was heartily ashamed of myself. Was this shivering girl the young woman Mr. Patton called his right hand?

I dare say I should have stopped there, for that night at least. My nerves were frayed. But I forced myself on. The mystery lay below. Well, then, I was going down. It could not be so terrible. At least it was nothing supernatural. There must be a natural explanation. And then that silly story about the headless things must pop into my head and start me down trembling.

The lower rear staircase was black dark, like the upper, but just at the foot a light came in through a barred window. I could see it plainly and the shadows of the iron grating on the bare floor. I stood there listening. There was not a sound.

It was not easy to tell exactly what followed. I stood there with my hand on the rail. I'd been very silent; my rubber shoes attended to that. And one moment the staircase was clear, with a patch of light at the bottom. The next, something was there, halfway down—a head, it seemed to me, with a pointed hood like a monk's cowl. There was no body. It seemed to lie at my feet. But it was living. It moved. I could tell the moment when the eyes lifted and saw my feet, the slow back-tilting of the head as they followed up my body. All the air was squeezed out of my lungs; a heavy hand seemed to press on my chest. I remember raising a shaking hand and flinging my flashlight at the head. The flash clattered on the stair tread, harmless. Then the head was gone and something living slid over my foot.

I stumbled back to my room and locked the door. It was two hours before I had strength enough to get my aromatic ammonia bottle.

Chapter V: A Ghost Walks

It seemed to me that I had hardly dropped asleep before the children were in the room, clamoring.

"The goldfish are dead!" Harry said, standing soberly by the bed. "They are all dead with their stummicks turned up."

I sat up. My head ached violently.

"They can't be dead, old chap." I was feeling about for my kimono, but I remembered that when I had found my way back to the nursery after my fright on the back stairs I had lain down in my uniform. I crawled out, hardly able to stand. "We gave them fresh water yesterday, and—"

I had got to the aquarium. Harry was right. The little darting flames of pink and gold were still. They floated about, rolling gently as Freddie prodded them with a forefinger, dull eyed, pale bellies upturned. In his cage above the little parrot watched out of a crooked eye.

I ran to the medicine closet in the bathroom. Freddie had a weakness for administering medicine. I had only just rescued the parrot from the result of his curiosity and a headache tablet the day before.

"What did you give them?" I demanded.

"Bread," said Freddie stoutly.

"Only bread?"

"Dirty bread," Harry put in. "I told him it was dirty."

"Where did you get it?"

"On the roof of the porte-cochere!"

Shade of Montessori! The rascals had been out on that sloping tin roof. It turned me rather sick to think of it.

Accused, they admitted it frankly.

"I unlocked the window," Harry said, "and Freddie got the bread. It was out in the gutter. He slipped once."

"Almost went over and made a squash on the pavement," added Freddie. "We gave the little fishes the bread for breakfast, and now they're gone to God."

The bread had contained poison, of course. Even the two little snails that crawled over the sand in the aquarium were motionless. I sniffed the water. It had a slightly foreign odor. I did not recognize it.

Panic seized me then. I wanted to get away and take the children with me. The situation was too hideous. But it was still early. I could only wait until the family roused. In the meantime, however, I made a nerve-racking excursion out onto the tin roof and down to the gutter. There was no more of the bread there. The porte-cochere was at the side of the house. As I stood balancing myself perilously on the edge, summoning my courage to climb back to the window above, I suddenly remembered the guard Mr. Patton had promised and glanced toward the square.

The guard was still there. More than that, he was running across the street toward me. It was Mr. Patton himself. He brought up between the two houses with absolute fury in his face.

"Go back!" he waved. "What are you doing out there, anyhow? That roof's as slippery as the devil!"

I turned meekly and crawled back with as much dignity as I could. I did not say anything. There was nothing I could bawl from the roof. I could only close and lock the window and hope that the people in the next house still slept. Mr. Patton must have gone shortly after, for I did not see him again.

I wondered if he had relieved the night watch, or if he could possibly have been on guard himself all that chilly April night.

Mr. Reed did not breakfast with us. I made a point of being cheerful before the children, and their mother was rested and brighter than

I had seen her. But more than once I found her staring at me in a puzzled way. She asked me if I had slept.

"I wakened only once," she said. "I thought I heard a crash of some sort. Did you hear it?"

"What sort of a crash?" I evaded.

The children had forgotten the goldfish for a time. Now they remembered and clamored their news to her.

"Dead?" she said, and looked at me.

"Poisoned," I explained. "I shall nail the windows over the porte-cochere shut, Mrs. Reed. The boys got out there early this morning and picked up something—bread, I believe. They fed it to the fish and—they are dead."

All the light went out of her face. She looked tired and harassed as she got up.

"I wanted to nail the window," she said vaguely, "but Mr. Reed—Suppose they had eaten that bread, Miss Adams, instead of giving it to the fish!"

The same thought had chilled me with horror. We gazed at each other over the unconscious heads of the children and my heart ached for her. I made a sudden resolution.

"When I first came," I said to her, "I told you I wanted to help. That's what I'm here for. But how am I to help either you or the children when I do not know what danger it is that threatens? It isn't fair to you, or to them, or even to me."

She was much shaken by the poison incident. I thought she wavered.

"Are you afraid the children will be stolen?"

"Oh, no."

"Or hurt in any way?" I was thinking of the bread on the roof.

"No."

"But you are afraid of something?"

Harry looked up suddenly. "Mother's never afraid," he said stoutly.

I sent them both in to see if the fish were still dead.

"There is something in the house downstairs that you are afraid of?" I persisted.

She took a step forward and caught my arm. "I had no idea it would be like this, Miss Adams. I'm dying of fear!"

I had a quick vision of the swathed head on the back staircase, and some of my night's terror came back to me. I believe we stared at each other with dilated pupils for a moment. Then I asked:

"Is it a real thing?—surely you can tell me this. Are you afraid of a reality, or—is it something supernatural?" I was ashamed of the question. It sounded so absurd in the broad light of that April morning.

"It is a real danger," she replied. Then I think she decided that she had gone as far as she dared, and I went through the ceremony of letting her out and of locking the door behind her.

The day was warm. I threw up some of the windows and the boys and I played ball, using a rolled handkerchief. My part, being to sit on the floor with a newspaper folded into a bat and to bang at the handkerchief as it flew past me, became automatic after a time.

As I look back I see a pair of disordered young rascals in Russian blouses and bare round knees doing a great deal of yelling and some very crooked throwing; a nurse sitting tailor fashion on the floor, alternately ducking to save her cap and making vigorous but ineffectual passes at the ball with her newspaper bat. And I see sunshine in the room and the dwarf parrot eating sugar out of his claw. And below, the fish in the aquarium floating belly-up with dull eyes.

Mr. Reed brought up our luncheon tray. He looked tired and depressed, and avoided my eyes. I watched him while I spread the bread and butter for the children. He nailed shut the windows that opened on to the porte-cochere roof and when he thought I was not looking he examined the registers in the wall to see if the gratings were closed. The boys put the dead fish in a box and made him promise a decent interment in the garden. They called on me for an epitaph, and I scrawled on top of the box:

These fish are dead

Because a boy called Fred
Went out on a porch roof when he should
Have been in bed.

I was much pleased with it. It seemed to me that an epitaph, which can do no good to the departed, should at least convey a moral. But to my horror Freddie broke into loud wails and would not be comforted.

It was three o'clock, therefore, before they were both settled for their afternoon naps and I was free. I had determined to do one thing, and to do it in daylight—to examine the back staircase inch by inch. I knew I would be courting discovery, but the thing had to be done, and no power on earth would have made me essay such an investigation after dark.

It was all well enough for me to say to myself that there was a natural explanation; but this had been a human head, of a certainty; that something living and not spectral had slid over my foot in the darkness. I would not have gone back there again at night for youth, love, or money. But I did not investigate the staircase that day, after all.

I made a curious discovery after the boys had settled down in their small white beds. A venturesome fly had sailed in through an open window, and I was immediately in pursuit of him with my paper bat. Driven from the cornice to the chandelier, harried here, swatted there, finally he took refuge inside the furnace register.

Perhaps it is my training—I used to know how many million germs a fly packed about with it, and the generous benevolence with which it distributed them; I've forgotten—but the sight of a single fly maddens me. I said that to Mr. Patton once, and he asked what the sight of a married one would do. So I sat down by the register and waited. It was then that I made the curious discovery that the furnace belowstairs was burning, and burning hard. A fierce heat assailed me as I opened the grating. I drove the fly out of cover, but I had no time for him. The furnace going full on a warm spring day! It was strange.

Perhaps I was stupid. Perhaps the whole thing should have been clear to me. But it was not. I sat there bewildered and tried to figure it out. I went over it point by point:

The carpets up all over the house, lights going full all night and doors locked.

The cot at the top of the stairs and Mrs. Reed staring down.

The bolt outside my door to lock me in.

The death of Chang.

Mademoiselle locked in her room upstairs and begging for a priest.

The poison on the porch roof.

The head without a body on the staircase and the thing that slid over my foot.

The furnace going, and the thing I recognized as I sat there beside the register—the unmistakable odor of burning cloth.

Should I have known? I wonder. It looks so clear to me now.

I did not investigate the staircase for the simple reason that my skeleton key, which unfastened the lock of the door at the rear of the second-floor hall, did not open the door. I did not understand at once and stood stupidly working with the lock. The door was bolted on the other side. I wandered as aimlessly as I could down the main staircase and tried the corresponding door on the lower floor. It, too, was locked. Here was an impasse for sure. As far as I could discover the only other entrance to the back staircase was through the window with the iron grating.

As I turned to go back I saw my electric flash, badly broken, lying on a table in the hall. I did not claim it.

The lower floor seemed entirely deserted. The drawing-room and library were in their usual disorder, undusted and bare of floor. The air everywhere was close and heavy; there was not a window open. I sauntered through the various rooms, picked up a book in the library as an excuse and tried the door of the room behind. It was locked. I thought at first that something moved behind it, but if anything lived there it did not stir again. And yet I had a vivid impression that just on the other side of the door ears as keen as mine were listening. It was broad day, but I backed away from the door and out into the wide hall. My nerves were still raw, no doubt, from the night before.

I was to meet Mr. Patton at half after seven that night, and when Mrs. Reed relieved me at seven I had half an hour to myself. I spent it in Beauregard Gardens, with the dry fountain in the center. The place itself was charming, the trees still black but lightly fringed with new green, early spring flowers in the borders, neat paths and, bordering it all, the solid, dignified backs of the Beauregard houses. I sat down on the coping of the fountain and surveyed the Reed house. Those windows above were Mademoiselle's. The shades were drawn, but no light came through or round them. The prisoner—for prisoner she was by every rule of bolt and lock—must be sitting in the dark. Was she still begging for her priest? Had she had any food? Was she still listening inside her door for whatever it was that was "coming up"?

In all the other houses windows were open; curtains waved gently in the spring air; the cheerful signs of the dinner hour were evident nearby—moving servants, a gleam of stately shirt bosom as a butler mixed a salad, a warm radiance of candlelight from dining-room tables and the reflected glow of flowers. Only the Reed house stood gloomy, unlighted, almost sinister.

Beauregard Place dined early. It was one of the traditions, I believe. It liked to get to the theater or the opera early, and it believed in allowing the servants a little time in the evenings. So, although it was only something after seven, the evening rite of the table crumbs began to be observed. Came a colored butler, bowed to me with a word of apology, and dumped the contents of a silver tray into the basin; came a pretty mulatto, flung her crumbs gracefully and smiled with a flash of teeth at the butler.

Then for five minutes I was alone.

It was Nora, the girl we had met on the street, who came next. She saw me and came round to me with a little air of triumph.

"Well, I'm back in the square again, after all, miss," she said. "And a better place than the Reeds'. I don't have the doilies to do."

"I'm very glad you are settled again, Nora."

She lowered her voice. "I'm just trying it out," she observed. "The girl that left said I wouldn't stay. She was scared off. There have been some queer doings—not that I believe in ghosts or anything like that. But my mother in the old country had the second-sight, and if there's anything going on I'll be right sure to see it."

It took encouragement to get her story, and it was secondhand at that, of course. But it appeared that a state of panic had seized the Beauregard servants. The alarm was all belowstairs and had been started by a cook who, coming in late and going to the basement to prepare herself a cup of tea, had found her kitchen door locked and a light going beyond. Suspecting another maid of violating the tea canister she had gone soft-footed to the outside of the house and had distinctly seen a gray figure crouching in a corner of the room. She had called the butler, and they had made an examination of the entire basement without result. Nothing was missing from the house.

"And that figure has been seen again and again, miss," Nora finished. "McKenna's butler Joseph saw it in this very spot, walking without a sound and the street light beyond there shining straight through it. Over in the Smythe house the laundress, coming in late and going down to the basement to soak her clothes for the morning, met the thing on the basement staircase and fainted dead away."

I had listened intently. "What do they think it is?" I asked.

She shrugged her shoulders and picked up her tray.

"I'm not trying to say and I guess nobody is. But if there's been a murder it's pretty well known that the ghost walks about until the burial service is read and it's properly buried."

She glanced at the Reed house.

"For instance," she demanded, "where is Mademoiselle?"

"She is alive," I said rather sharply. "And even if what you say were true, what in the world would make her wander about the basements?

It seems so silly, Nora, a ghost haunting damp cellars and laundries with stationary tubs and all that."

"Well," she contended, "it seems silly for them to sit on cold tombstones—and yet that's where they generally sit, isn't it?"

Mr. Patton listened gravely to my story that night.

"I don't like it," he said when I had finished. "Of course the head on the staircase is nonsense. Your nerves were ragged and our eyes play tricks on all of us. But as for the Frenchwoman—"

"If you accept her you must accept the head," I snapped. "It was there—it was a head without a body and it looked up at me."

We were walking through a quiet street, and he bent over and caught my wrist.

"Pulse racing," he commented. "I'm going to take you away, that's certain. I can't afford to lose my best assistant. You're too close, Miss Adams; you've lost your perspective."

"I've lost my temper!" I retorted. "I shall not leave until I know what this thing is, unless you choose to ring the doorbell and tell them I'm a spy."

He gave in when he saw that I was firm, but not without a final protest. "I'm directly responsible for you to your friends," he said. "There's probably a young man somewhere who will come gunning for me if anything happens to you. And I don't care to be gunned for. I get enough of that in my regular line."

"There is no young man," I said shortly.

"Have you been able to see the cellars?"

"No, everything is locked off."

"Do you think the rear staircase goes all the way down?"

"I haven't the slightest idea."

"You are in the house. Have you any suggestions as to the best method of getting into the house? Is Reed on guard all night?"

"I think he is."

"It may interest you to know," he said finally, "that I sent a reliable to break in there last night quietly, and that he—couldn't do it. He got a leg through a cellar window, and came near not getting it out again. Reed was just inside in the dark." He laughed a little, but I guessed that the thing galled him.

"I do not believe that he would have found anything if he had succeeded in getting in. There has been no crime, Mr. Patton, I am sure of that. But there is a menace of some sort in the house."

"Then why does Mrs. Reed stay and keep the children if there is danger?"

"I believe she is afraid to leave him. There are times when I think that he is desperate."

"Does he ever leave the house?"

"I think not, unless—"

"Yes?"

"Unless he is the basement ghost of the other houses."

He stopped in his slow walk and considered it.

"It's possible. In that case I could have him waylaid tonight in the gardens and left there, tied. It would be a holdup, you understand. The police have no excuse for coming in yet. Or, if we found him breaking into one of the other houses we could get him there. He'd be released, of course, but it would give us time. I want to clean the thing up. I'm not easy while you are in that house."

We agreed that I was to wait inside one of my windows that night, and that on a given signal I should go down and open the front door. The whole thing, of course, was contingent on Mr. Reed leaving the house some time that night. It was only a chance.

"The house is barred like a fortress," Mr. Patton said as he left me. "The window with the grating is hopeless. We tried it last night."

Chapter VI: Terror Below

I FIND that my notes of that last night in the house on Beauregard Square are rather confused, some written at the time, some just before. For instance, on the edge of a newspaper clipping I find this:

Evidently this is the item. R—— went pale on reading it. Did not allow wife to see paper.

The clipping is an account of the sudden death of an elderly gentleman named Smythe, one of the Beauregard families.

The next clipping is less hasty and is on a yellow symptom record. It has been much folded—I believed I tucked it in my apron belt:

If the rear staircase is bolted everywhere from the inside, how did the person who locked it, either Mr. or Mrs. Reed, get back into the body of the house again? Or did Mademoiselle do it? In that case she is no longer a prisoner and the bolts outside her room are not fastened.

At eleven o'clock tonight Harry wakened with earache. I went to the kitchen to heat some mullein oil and laudanum. Mrs. Reed was with the boy and Mr. Reed was not in sight. I slipped into the library and used my skeleton keys on the locked door to the rear room. It was empty even of furniture, but there is a huge box there, with a lid that fastens down with steel hooks. The lid is full of small airholes. I had no time to examine further.

It is one o'clock. Harry is asleep and his mother is dozing across the foot of his bed. I have found the way to get to the rear staircase. There are outside steps from the basement to the garden. The staircase goes down all the way to the cellar evidently. Then the lower door in the cellar must be only locked, not bolted from the inside. I shall try to get in the cellar.

The next is a scrawl:

Cannot get to the outside basement steps. Mr. Reed is wandering round lower floor. I reported Harry's condition and came up again. I must get to the back staircase.

I wonder if I have been able to convey, even faintly, the situation in that highly respectable old house that night: The fear that hung over it, a fear so great that even I, an outsider and stout of nerve, felt it and grew cold; the unnatural brilliancy of light that bespoke dread of the dark; the hushed voices, the locked doors and staring, peering eyes; the babbling Frenchwoman on an upper floor, the dead fish, the dead dog. And, always in my mind, that vision of dread on the back staircase and the thing that slid over my foot.

At two o'clock I saw Mr. Patton, or whoever was on guard in the park across the street, walk quickly toward the house and disappear round the corner toward the gardens in the rear. There had been no signal, but I felt sure that Mr. Reed had left the house. His wife was still asleep across Harry's bed. As I went out I locked the door behind me, and I took also the key to the night nursery. I thought that something disagreeable, to say the least, was inevitable, and why let her in for it?

The lower hall was lighted as usual and empty. I listened, but there were no restless footsteps. I did not like the lower hall. Only a thin wooden door stood between me and the rear staircase, and anyone who thinks about the matter will realize that a door is no barrier to a head that can move about without a body. I am afraid I looked over my shoulder while I unlocked the front door, and I know I breathed better when I was out in the air.

I wore my dark ulster over my uniform and I had my revolver and keys. My flash, of course, was useless. I missed it horribly. But to get to the staircase was an obsession by that time, in spite of my fear of it, to find what it guarded, to solve its mystery. I worked round the house, keeping close to the wall, until I reached the garden. The night was the city night, never absolutely dark. As I hesitated at the top of the basement steps it seemed to me that figures were moving about among the trees.

The basement door was unlocked and open. I was not prepared for that, and it made me, if anything, more uneasy. I had a box of matches with me, and I wanted light as a starving man wants food. But I dared not light them. I could only keep a tight grip on my courage and go on. A small passage first, with whitewashed stone walls, cold and scaly under my hand; then a large room, and still darkness. Worse than darkness, something crawling and scratching round the floor.

I struck my match, then, and it seemed to me that something white flashed into a corner and disappeared. My hands were shaking, but I managed to light a gas jet and to see that I was in the laundry. The staircase came down here, narrower than above, and closed off with a door.

The door was closed and there was a heavy bolt on it but no lock.

And now, with the staircase accessible and a gaslight to keep up my courage, I grew brave, almost reckless. I would tell Mr. Patton all about this cellar, which his best men had not been able to enter. I would make a sketch for him—coal-bins, laundry tubs, everything. Foolish, of course, but hold the gas jet responsible—the reckless bravery of light after hideous darkness.

So I went on, forward. The glow from the laundry followed me. I struck matches, found potatoes and cases of mineral water, bruised my knees on a discarded bicycle, stumbled over a box of soap. Twice out of the corner of my eye and never there when I looked I caught the white flash that had frightened me before. Then at last I brought up before a door and stopped. It was a curiously barricaded door, nailed against disturbance by a plank fastened across, and, as if to make intrusion without discovery impossible, pasted round every crack and over the keyhole with strips of strong yellow paper. It was an ominous door. I wanted to run away from it, and I wanted also desperately to stand and look at it and imagine what might lie beyond. Here again was the strange, spicy odor that I had noticed in the back staircase.

I think it is indicative of my state of mind that I backed away from the door. I did not turn and run. Nothing in the world would have made me turn my back to it.

Somehow or other I got back into the laundry and jerked myself together. It was ten minutes after two. I had been just ten minutes in the basement!

The staircase daunted me in my shaken condition. I made excuses for delaying my venture, looked for another box of matches, listened at the end of the passage, finally slid the bolts and opened the door. The silence was impressive. In the laundry there were small, familiar sounds—the dripping of water from a faucet, the muffled measure of a gas meter, the ticking of a clock on the shelf. To leave it all, to climb into that silence—

Lying on the lower step was a curious instrument. It was a sort of tongs made of steel, about two feet long, and fastened together like a pair of scissors, the joint about five inches from the flattened ends. I carried it to the light and examined it. One end was smeared with blood and short, brownish hairs. It made me shudder, but— from that time on I think I knew. Not the whole story, of course, but somewhere in the back of my head, as I climbed in that hideous quiet, the explanation was developing itself. I did not think it out. It worked itself out as, step after step, match after match, I climbed the staircase.

Up to the first floor there was nothing. The landing was bare of carpet. I was on the first floor now. On each side, doors, carefully bolted, led into the house. I opened the one into the hall and listened. I had been gone from the children fifteen minutes and they were on my mind. But everything was quiet.

The sight of the lights and the familiar hall gave me courage. After all, if I was right, what could the head on the staircase have been but an optical delusion? And I was right. The evidence—the tongs—was in my hand. I closed and bolted the door and felt my way back to the stairs. I lighted no matches this time. I had only a few, and on this landing there was a little light from the grated window, although the staircase above was in black shadow.

I had one foot on the lowest stair, when suddenly overhead came the thudding of hands on a closed door. It broke the silence like an explosion. It sent chills up and down my spine. I could not move for a moment. It was the Frenchwoman!

I believe I thought of fire. The idea had obsessed me in that house of locked doors. I remember a strangling weight of fright on my chest and of trying to breathe. Then I started up the staircase, running as fast as I could lift my weighted feet, I remember that, and getting up perhaps a third of the way. Then there came a plunging forward into space, my hands out, a shriek frozen on my lips, and—quiet.

I do not think I fainted. I know I was conscious of my arm doubled under me, a pain and darkness. I could hear myself moaning, but almost as if it were someone else. There were other sounds, but they did not concern me much. I was not even curious about my location. I seemed to be a very small consciousness surrounded by a great deal of pain.

Several centuries later a light came and leaned over me from somewhere above. Then the light said, "Here she is!"

"Alive?" I knew that voice, but I could not think whose it was.

"I'm not—Yes, she's moaning."

They got me out somewhere and I believe I still clung to the tongs. I had fallen on them and had a cut on my chin. I could stand, I found, although I swayed. There was plenty of light now in the back hallway, and a man I had never seen was investigating the staircase.

"Four steps off," he said. "Risers and treads gone and the supports sawed away. It's a trap of some sort."

Mr. Patton was examining my broken arm and paid no attention. The man let himself down into the pit under the staircase. When he straightened, only his head rose above the steps. Although I was white with pain to the very lips I laughed hysterically.

"The head!" I cried. Mr. Patton swore under his breath.

They half led, half carried me into the library. Mr. Reed was there, with a detective on guard over him. He was sitting in his old position, bent forward, chin in palms. In the blaze of light he was a pitiable figure, smeared with dust, disheveled from what had evidently been a struggle. Mr. Patton put me in a chair and dispatched one of the two men for the nearest doctor.

"This young lady," he said curtly to Mr. Reed, "fell into that damnable trap you made in the rear staircase."

"I locked off the staircase—but I am sorry she is hurt. My—my wife will be shocked. Only I wish you'd tell me what all this is about. You can't arrest me for going into a friend's house."

"If I send for some member of the Smythe family will they acquit you?"

"Certainly they will," he said. "I—I've been raised with the Smythes. You can send for anyone you like." But his tone lacked conviction.

Mr. Patton made me as comfortable as possible, and then, sending the remaining detective out into the hall, he turned to his prisoner.

"Now, Mr. Reed," he said. "I want you to be sensible. For some days a figure has been seen in the basements of the various Beauregard houses. Your friends, the Smythes, reported it. Tonight we are on watch, and we see you breaking into the basement of the Smythe house. We already know some curious things about you, such as dismissing all the servants on half an hour's notice and the disappearance of the French governess."

"Mademoiselle! Why, she—" He checked himself.

"When we bring you here tonight, and you ask to be allowed to go upstairs and prepare your wife, she is locked in. The nurse is missing. We find her at last, also locked away and badly hurt, lying in a staircase trap, where someone, probably yourself, has removed the steps. I do not want to arrest you, but, now I've started, I'm going to get to the bottom of all this."

Mr. Reed was ghastly, but he straightened in his chair.

"The Smythes reported this thing, did they?" he asked. "Well, tell me one thing. What killed the old gentleman—old Smythe?"

"I don't know."

"Well, go a little further." His cunning was boyish, pitiful. "How did he die? Or don't you know that either?"

Up to this point I had been rather a detached part of the scene, but now my eyes fell on the tongs beside me.

"Mr. Reed," I said, "isn't this thing too big for you to handle by yourself?"

"What thing?"

"You know what I mean. You've protected yourself well enough, but even if the—the thing you know of did not kill old Mr. Smythe you cannot tell what will happen next."

"I've got almost all of them," he muttered sullenly. "Another night or two and I'd have had the lot."

"But even then the mischief may go on. It means a crusade; it means rousing the city. Isn't it the square thing now to spread the alarm?"

Mr. Patton could stand the suspense no longer.

"Perhaps, Miss Adams," he said, "you will be good enough to let me know what you are talking about."

Mr. Reed looked up at him with heavy eyes.

"Rats," he said. "They got away, twenty of them, loaded with bubonic plague."

I went to the hospital the next morning. Mr. Patton thought it best. There was no one in my little flat to look after me, and although the pain in my arm subsided after the fracture was set I was still shaken.

He came the next afternoon to see me. I was propped up in bed, with my hair braided down in two pigtails and great hollows under my eyes.

"I'm comfortable enough," I said, in response to his inquiry; "but I'm feeling all of my years. This is my birthday. I am thirty today."

"I wonder," he said reflectively, "if I ever reach the mature age of one hundred, if I will carry in my head as many odds and ends of information as you have at thirty!"

"I?"

"You. How in the world did you know, for instance, about those tongs?"

"It was quite simple. I'd seen something like them in the laboratory here. Of course I didn't know what animals he'd used, but the grayish brown hair looked like rats. The laboratory must be the cellar room. I knew it had been fumigated—it was sealed with paper, even over the keyhole."

So, sitting there beside me, Mr. Patton told me the story as he had got it from Mr. Reed—a tale of the offer in an English scientific journal of a large reward from some plague-ridden country of the East for an anti-plague serum. Mr. Reed had been working along bacteriological lines in his basement laboratory, mostly with guinea pigs and tuberculosis. He was in debt; the offer loomed large.

"He seems to think he was on the right track," Mr. Patton said. "He had twenty of the creatures in deep zinc cans with perforated lids. He says the disease is spread by fleas that infest the rats. So he had muslin as well over the lids. One can had infected rats, six of them. Then one day the Frenchwoman tried to give the dog a bath in a laundry tub and the dog bolted. The laboratory door was open in some way and he ran between the cans, upsetting them. Every rat was out in an instant. The Frenchwoman was frantic. She shut the door and tried to drive the things back. One bit her on the foot. The dog was not bitten, but there was the question of fleas.

"Well, the rats got away, and Mademoiselle retired to her room to die of plague. She was a loyal old soul; she wouldn't let them call a doctor. It would mean exposure, and after all what could the doctors do? Reed used his serum and she's alive.

"Reed was frantic. His wife would not leave. There was the Frenchwoman to look after, and I think she was afraid he would do something desperate. They did the best they could, under the circumstances, for the children. They burned most of the carpets for fear of fleas, and put poison everywhere. Of course he had traps too.

"He had brass tags on the necks of the rats, and he got back a few—the uninfected ones. The other ones were probably dead. But he couldn't stop at that. He had to be sure that the trouble had not spread. And to add to their horror the sewer along the street was being relaid, and they had an influx of rats into the house. They found them everywhere in the lower floor. They even climbed the stairs. He says that the night you came he caught a big fellow on the front staircase. There was always the danger that the fleas that carry the trouble had deserted the dead creatures for new fields. They took up all the rest of the carpets and burned them. To add to the general misery the dog Chang developed unmistakable symptoms and had to be killed."

"But the broken staircase?" I asked. "And what was it that Mademoiselle said was coming up?"

"The steps were up for two reasons: The rats could not climb up, and beneath the steps Reed says he caught in a trap two of the tagged ones. As for Mademoiselle the thing that was coming up was her temperature—pure fright. The head you saw was poor Reed himself, wrapped in gauze against trouble and baiting his traps. He caught a lot in the neighbors' cellars and some in the garden."

"But why," I demanded, "why didn't he make it all known?"

Mr. Patton laughed while he shrugged his shoulders.

"A man hardly cares to announce that he has menaced the health of a city."

"But that night when I fell—was it only last night?—someone was pounding above. I thought there was a fire."

"The Frenchwoman had seen us waylay Reed from her window. She was crazy."

"And the trouble is over now?"

"Not at all," he replied cheerfully. "The trouble may be only beginning. We're keeping Reed's name out, but the Board of Health has issued a general warning. Personally I think his six pets died without passing anything along."

"But there was a big box with a lid—"

"Ferrets," he assured me. "Nice white ferrets with pink eyes and a taste for rats." He held out a thumb, carefully bandaged. "Reed had a couple under his coat when we took him in the garden. Probably one ran over your foot that night when you surprised him on the back staircase."

I went pale. "But if they are infected!" I cried; "and you are bitten—"

"The first thing a nurse should learn," he bent forward smiling, "is not to alarm her patient."

"But you don't understand the danger," I said despairingly. "Oh, if only men had a little bit of sense!"

"I must do something desperate then? Have the thumb cut off, perhaps?"

I did not answer. I lay back on my pillows with my eyes shut. I had given him the plague, had seen him die and be buried, before he spoke again.

"The chin," he said, "is not so firm as I had thought. The outlines are savage, but the dimple— You poor little thing; are you really frightened?"

"I don't like you," I said furiously. "But I'd hate to see anyone with—with that trouble."

"Then I'll confess. I was trying to take your mind off your troubles. The bite is there, but harmless. Those were new ferrets; had never been out."

I did not speak to him again. I was seething with indignation. He stood for a time looking down at me; then, unexpectedly, he bent over and touched his lips to my bandaged arm.

"Poor arm!" he said. "Poor, brave little arm!" Then he tiptoed out of the room. His very back was sheepish.

THE MYSTERY IN ROOM 913
Cornell Woolrich
Detective: Striker

ARGUABLY THE greatest suspense writer of the twentieth century, Cornell (George Hopley) Woolrich (1903-1968) was born in New York City, grew up in South America and New York, and was educated at Columbia University, to which he left his literary estate.

A sad and lonely man who desperately dedicated books to his typewriter and to his hotel room, Woolrich was almost certainly a closeted homosexual (his marriage was terminated almost immediately) and an alcoholic, so anti-social and reclusive that he refused to leave his hotel room when his leg became infected, ultimately resulting in its amputation.

Perhaps not surprisingly, then, the majority of his work has an overwhelming darkness, and few of his characters, whether good or evil, have much hope for happiness—or even justice. No twentieth-century author equaled Woolrich's ability to create suspense, and Hollywood producers recognized it early on; few writers have had as many films based on their work as Woolrich.

The major films began with *Convicted* (1938), based on the short story "Angel Face," starring Rita Hayworth, and continued with *Street of Chance* (1942), based on *The Black Curtain*, with Burgess Meredith and Claire Trevor; *The Leopard Man* (1943), inspired by *Black Alibi*, with Dennis O'Keefe and Jean Brooke; *Phantom Lady* (1944), a film noir classic based on the novel of the same title, with Ella Raines and Alan Curtis; *Mark of the Whistler* (1944), based on "Chance," with Richard Dix and Janis Carter; *Deadline at Dawn* (1946), a much-changed film than the novel of the same title, with Susan Hayward; the Hitchcock classic *Rear Window* (1954), based on "It Had to Be Murder," with Grace Kelly and James Stewart; the Francois Truffaut-directed *The Bride Wore Black* (1968), with Jeanne Moreau; and at least fifteen others.

"The Mystery in Room 913" was originally published in the June 4, 1938, issue of *Detective Fiction Weekly*; it was first collected in *Somebody on the Phone* (Philadelphia, J.B. Lippincott, 1950).

The Mystery in Room 913
By Cornell Woolrich

THEY THOUGHT it was the Depression the first time it happened. The guy had checked in one night in the black March of '33, in the middle of the memorable bank holiday. He was well-dressed and respectable looking. He had baggage with him, plenty of it, so he wasn't asked to pay in advance. Everyone was short of ready cash that week. Besides, he'd asked for the weekly rate.

He signed the register *James Hopper, Schenectady*, and Dennison, eyeing the red vacancy-tags in the pigeonholes, pulled out the one in 913 at random and gave him that. Not the vacancy tag, the room. The guest went up, okayed the room, and George the bell hop was sent up with his bags. George came down and reported a dime without resentment; it was '33, after all.

Striker had sized him up, of course. That was part of his duties, and the house detective found nothing either for him or against him. Striker had been with the St. Anselm two years at that time. He'd had his salary cut in '31, and then again in '32, but so had everyone else on the staff. He didn't look much like a house dick, which was why he was good for the job. He was a tall, lean, casual-moving guy, without that annoying habit most hotel dicks have of staring people out of countenance. He used finesse about it; got the same results, but with sort of a blank, idle expression as though he were thinking of something else. He also lacked the usual paunch, in spite of his sedentary life, and never wore a hard hat. He had a little radio in his top-floor cubbyhole and a stack of vintage "fantastics," pulp magazines dealing with super-science and the supernatural, and that seemed to be all he asked of life.

The newcomer who had signed as Hopper came down again in about half an hour and asked Dennison if there were any good movies nearby. The clerk recommended one and the guest went to it. This was about eight p. m. He came back at eleven, picked up his key, and went up to his room. Dennison and Striker both heard him whistling lightly under his breath as he stepped into the elevator. Nothing on his mind but a good night's rest, apparently.

Striker turned in himself at twelve. He was subject to call twenty-four hours a day. There was no one to relieve him. The St. Anselm was on the downgrade, and had stopped having an assistant house dick about a year before.

He was still awake, reading in bed, about an hour later when the desk man rang him. "Better get down here quick, Strike! Nine-thirteen's just fallen out!" The clerk's voice was taut, frightened.

Striker threw on coat and pants over his pajamas and got down as fast as the creaky old-fashioned elevator would let him. He went out to the street, around to the side under the thirteen-line.

Hopper was lying there dead, the torn leg of his pajamas rippling in the bitter March night wind. There wasn't anyone else around at that hour except the night porter, the policeman he'd called, and who had called his precinct house in turn, and a taxi driver or two. Maxon, the midnight-to-morning clerk (Dennison went off at 11:30), had to remain at his post for obvious reasons. They were just standing there waiting for the morgue ambulance; there wasn't anything they could do.

Bob, the night porter, was saying: "I thought it was a pillow someone drop out the window. I come up the basement way, see a thick white thing lying there, flappin' in th' wind. I go over, fix to kick it with my foot—" He broke off. "Golly, man!"

One of the drivers said, "I seen him comin' down." No one disputed the point, but he insisted, "No kidding, I seen him coming down! I was just cruisin' past, one block over, and I look this way, and I see—whisht, *ungh*—like a pancake!"

The other cab driver, who hadn't seen him coming down, said: "I seen you head down this way, so I thought you spotted a fare, and I chased after you."

They got into a wrangle above the distorted form. "Yeah, you're always chiselin' in on my hails. Follyn' me around. Can't ye get none o' your own?"

Striker crossed the street, teeth chattering, and turned and looked up the face of the building. Half the French window of 913 was open, and the 100m was lit up. All the rest of the line was dark, from the top floor down.

He crossed back to where the little group stood shivering and stamping their feet miserably. "He sure picked a night for it!" winced the cop. The cab driver opened his mouth a couple of seconds ahead of saying something, which was his speed, and the cop turned on him irritably. "Yeah, we know! You seen him coming down. Go home, will ya!"

Striker went in, rode up, and used his passkey on 913. The light was on, as he had ascertained from the street. He stood there in the doorway and looked around. Each of the 13's, in the St. Anselm, was a small room with private bath. There was an opening on each of the four sides of these rooms: the tall, narrow, old-fashioned room-door leading in from the hall; in the wall to the left of that, the door to the bath, of identical proportions; in the wall to the right of the hall door, a door giving into the clothes closet, again of similar measurements. These three panels were in the style of the nineties, not your squat modern aperture. Directly opposite the room door was a pair of French windows looking out onto the street. Each of them matched the door measurements. Dark blue roller-shades covered the glass on the inside.

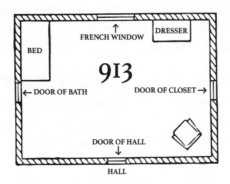

But Striker wasn't thinking about all that particularly, just then. He was interested only in what the condition of the room could tell him: whether it had been suicide or an accident. The only thing disturbed in the room was the bed, but that was not violently disturbed as by a struggle, simply normally disarranged as by someone sleeping. Striker, for some reason or other, tested the sheets with the back of his hand for a minute. They were still warm from recent occupancy. Hopper's trousers were neatly folded across the seat of a chair. His shirt and underclothes were draped over the back of it. His shoes stood under it, toe to toe and heel to heel. He was evidently a very neat person.

He had unpacked. He must have intended to occupy the room for the full week he had bargained for. In the closet, when Striker opened it, were his hat, overcoat, jacket, and vest, the latter three on separate hangers. The dresser drawers held his shirts and other linen. On top of the dresser was a white-gold wristwatch, a handful of change, and two folded squares of paper. One was a glossy handbill from the show the guest had evidently attended only two hours ago. *Saturday through Tuesday—the laugh riot, funniest, most tuneful picture of the year, "Hips Hips Hooray!" Also "Popeye the Sailor."* Nothing in that to depress anyone.

The other was a note on hotel stationery—*Hotel Management: Sorry to do this here, but I had to do it some-where.*

It was unsigned. So it was suicide after all. One of the two window halves, the one to the right, stood inward to the room. The one he had gone through.

"You the house man?" a voice asked from the doorway.

Striker turned and a precinct detective came in. You could tell he was that. He couldn't have looked at a dandelion without congenital suspicion or asked the time of day without making it a leading question. "Find anything?"

Striker handed over the note without comment.

Perry, the manager, had come up with him, in trousers and bathrobe. He was a stout, jovial-looking man ordinarily, but right now he was only stout. "He hadn't paid yet, either," he said ruefully to the empty room. He twisted the cord of his robe around one way, then he undid it and twisted it around the other way. He was very unhappy. He picked the wristwatch up gingerly by the end of its strap and dangled it close to his ear, as if to ascertain whether or not it had a good movement.

The precinct dick went to the window and looked down, opened the bath door and looked in, the closet door and looked in. He gave the impression of doing this just to give the customers their money's worth; in other words, as far as he was concerned, the note had clinched the case.

"It's the old suey, all right," he said and, bending over at the dresser, read aloud what he was jotting down. "James Hopper, Skun-Skunnect—"

Striker objected peevishly. "Why did he go to bed first, then get up and go do it? They don't usually do that. He took the room for a week, too."

The precinct man raised his voice, to show he was a police detective talking to a mere hotel dick, someone who in his estimation wasn't a detective at all. "I don't care if he took it for six months! He left this note and hit the sidewalk, didn't he? Whaddaya trying to do, make it into something it ain't?"

The manager said, "Ssh! if you don't mind," and eased the door to, to keep other guests from overhearing. He sided with the precinct man, the wish being father to the thought. If there's one thing that a hotel man likes less than a suicide, it's a murder. "I don't think there's any doubt of it."

The police dick stooped to reasoning with Striker. "You were the first one up here. Was there anything wrong with the door? Was it forced open or anything?"

Striker had to admit it had been properly shut; the late occupant's key lay on the dresser where it belonged at that very moment.

The police dick spread his hands, as if to say: "There you are, what more do you want?"

He took a last look around, decided the room had nothing more to tell him. Nor could Striker argue with him on this point. The room had nothing more to tell anyone. The dick gathered up Hopper's watch, change, and identification papers, to turn them over to the police property-clerk, until they were claimed by his nearest of kin. His baggage was left in there temporarily; the room was darkened and locked up once more.

Riding down to the lobby, the dick rubbed it in a little. "Here's how those things go," he said patronizingly. "No one got in there or went near him, so it wasn't murder. He left a note, so it wasn't an accident. The word they got for this is suicide. Now, y'got it?"

Striker held his palm up and fluttered it slightly. "Teacher, can I leave the room?" he murmured poignantly.

The stout manager, Perry, had a distrait, slightly anticipatory expression on his moon face now; in his mind it was the next day, he had already sold the room to someone else, and had the two dollars in the till. Heaven, to him, was a houseful of full rooms.

The body had already been removed from the street outside. Somewhere, across a coffee counter, a cab driver was saying: "I seen him coming down."

The city dick took his departure from the hotel, with the magnanimous assurance: "It's the depresh. They're poppin' off like popcorn all over the country this week. *I* ain't been able to cash my pay check since Monday."

Perry returned to his own quarters, with the typical managerial admonition, to Maxon and Striker, "Soft pedal, now, you two. Don't let this get around the house." He yawned with a sound like air brakes, going up in the elevator. You could still hear it echoing down the shaft after his feet had gone up out of sight.

"Just the same," Striker said finally, unasked, to the night clerk, "I don't care what that know-it-all says, Hopper didn't have suicide on his mind when he checked in here at 7:30. He saw a show that was full of laughs, and even came home whistling one of the tunes from it. We both heard him. He unpacked all his shirts and things into the bureau drawers. He intended staying. He went to bed first; I felt the covers, they were warm. Then he popped up all of a sudden and took this standing broadjump."

"Maybe he had a bad dream," Maxon suggested facetiously. His was a hard boiled racket. He yawned, muscularly magnetized by his boss's recent gape, and opened a big ledger. "Some of 'em put on a fake front until the last minute—whistle, go to a show, too proud to take the world into their confidence, and then—bang—they've crumpled. How do you or I know what was on his mind?"

And on that note it ended. As Maxon said, there was no accounting for human nature. Striker caught the sleepiness from the other two, widened his jaws terrifyingly, brought them together again with a click. And yet somehow, to him, this suicide hadn't run true to form.

He went back up to his own room again with a vague feeling of dissatisfaction, that wasn't strong enough to do anything about, and yet that he couldn't altogether throw off. Like the feeling you get when you're working out a crossword puzzle and one of the words fills up the space satisfactorily, but doesn't seem to have the required meaning called for in the solution.

The St. Anselm went back to sleep again, the small part of it that had been awake. The case was closed.

People came and went from 913 and the incident faded into the limbo of half-forgotten things. Then in the early Fall of '34 the room came to specific attention again.

A young fellow in his early twenties, a college type, arrived in a roadster with just enough baggage for overnight. No reservation or anything. He signed on as Allan Hastings, Princeton, New Jersey. He didn't have to ask the desk if there were any shows. He knew his own way around. They were kind of full-up that weekend. The only red vacancy-tag in any of the pigeonholes was 913. Dennison gave him that—had no choice.

The guest admitted he'd been turned away from two hotels already. They all had the S. R. O. sign out. "It's the Big Game, I guess," he said.

"What Big Game?" Striker was incautious enough to ask.

"Where've you been all your life?" he grinned. But not offensively.

Some football game or other, the house dick supposed. Personally a crackling good super-science story still had the edge on twenty-two huskies squabbling over a pig's inflated hide, as far as he was concerned.

Hastings came back from the game still sober. Or if he'd had a drink it didn't show. "We lost," he said casually at the desk on his way up, but it didn't seem to depress him any. His phone, the operator reported later, rang six times in the next quarter of an hour, all feminine voices. He was apparently getting booked up solid for the rest of the weekend.

Two girls and a fellow, in evening clothes, called for him about nine. Striker saw them sitting waiting for him in the lobby, chirping and laughing their heads off. He came down in about five minutes, all rigged up for the merry-merry, even down to a white carnation in his lapel.

Striker watched them go, half wistfully. "That's the life," he said to the man behind the desk.

"May as well enjoy it while you can," said Dennison philosophically. "Here today and gone tomorrow."

Hastings hadn't come back yet by the time Striker went up and turned in. Not that Striker was thinking about him particularly, but he just hadn't seen him. He read a swell story about mermaids kidnaping a deep-sea diver, and dropped off to sleep.

The call came through to his room at about four thirty in the morning. It took him a minute or two to come out of the deep sleep he'd been in.

"Hurry it up, will you, Strike?" Maxon was whining impatiently. "The young guy in 913 has taken a flier out his window."

Striker hung up, thinking blurredly, "Where've I heard that before—913?" Then he remembered—last year, from the very same room.

He filled the hollow of his hand with cold water from the washstand, dashed it into his eyes, shrugged into some clothing, and ran down the fire stairs at one side of the elevator shaft. That was quicker than waiting for the venerable mechanism to crawl up for him, then limp down again.

Maxon, who was a reformed drunk, gave him a look eloquent of disgust as Striker chased by the desk. "I'm getting off the wagon again if this keeps up—then I'll have some fun out of all these bum jolts."

There was more of a crowd this time. The weather was milder and there were more night-owls in the vicinity to collect around him and gape morbidly. The kid had fallen farther out into the street than Hopper—he didn't weigh as much, maybe. He was lying there face down in the shape of a Greek cross. He hadn't undressed yet, either. Only his shoes and dinner jacket had been taken off. One strap of his black suspenders had torn off, due to the bodily contortion of the descent or from the impact itself. The white of his shirt was pretty badly changed by now, except the sleeves. He'd had a good-looking face; that was all gone too. They were turning him over as Striker came up.

The same cop was there. He was saying to a man who had been on his way home to read the after-midnight edition of the coming morning's newspaper: "Lemme have your paper, Mac, will you?"

The man demurred, "I ain't read it myself yet. I just now bought it."

The cop said, "You can buy another. We can't leave him lying like this."

The thing that had been Hastings was in pretty bad shape. The cop spread the paper, separating the sheets, and made a long paper-covered mound. The stain even came through that a little, more like gasoline than anything else. Came through a headline that said something about the King of Jugoslavia being assassinated at Marseilles.

Striker thought, with a touch of mysticism, "Half a world away from each other this afternoon; now they're both together—somewhere—maybe."

The same precinct-dick showed up in answer to the routine notification that had been phoned in. His greeting to Striker was as to the dirt under his feet. "You still on the face of the earth?"

"Should I have asked your permission?" answered the hotel man drily.

Eddie Courlander—that, it seemed, was the police dick's tag—squatted down, looked under the pall of newspapers, shifted around, looked under from the other side.

"Peek-a-boo!" somebody in the small crowd said irreverently.

Courlander looked up threateningly. "Who said that? Gawan, get outa here, wise guys! If it happened to one of youse, you wouldn't feel so funny."

Somebody's night-bound coupé tried to get through, honked imperiously for clearance, not knowing what the obstruction was. The cop went up to it, said: "Get back! Take the next street over. There's a guy fell out of a window here."

The coupé drew over to the curb instead, and its occupants got out and joined the onlookers. One was a girl carrying a night club favor, a long stick topped with paper streamers. She squealed, "*Ooou, ooou-ooou,*" in a way you couldn't tell if she was delighted or horrified.

Courlander straightened, nodded toward Striker. "What room'd he have? C'mon in."

He didn't remember that it was the same one. Striker could tell that by the startled way he said, "Oh, yeah, that's right too!" when he mentioned the coincidence to him.

Perry and the night porter were waiting outside the room door. "I wouldn't go in until you got here," the manager whispered virtuously to the cop. "I know you people don't like anything touched." Striker, however, had a hunch there was a little superstitious fear at the back of this as well, like a kid shying away from a dark room.

"You're thinking of murder cases," remarked Courlander contemptuously. "Open 'er up."

The light was on again, like the previous time. But there was a great difference in the condition of the room. Young Hastings obviously hadn't had Hopper's personal neatness. Or else he'd been slightly lit up when he came in. The daytime clothes he'd discarded after coming back from the game were still strewn around, some on chairs, some on the floor. The St. Anselm didn't employ maids to straighten the rooms after five in the evening. His patent-leathers lay yards apart as though they had been kicked off into the air and left lying where they had come down. His bat-wing tie was a black snake across the carpet. There was a depression and creases on the counterpane on top of the bed, but it hadn't been turned down. He had therefore lain down on the bed, but not in it.

On the dresser top stood a glittering little pouch, obviously a woman's evening bag. Also his carnation, in a glass of water. Under that was the note. Possibly one of the shortest suicide notes on record. Three words. *What's the use?*

Courlander read it, nodded, showed it to them. "Well," he said, "that tells the story."

He shrugged.

In the silence that followed the remark, the phone rang sharply, unexpectedly. They all jolted a little, even Courlander. Although there was no body in the room and never had been, it was a dead man's room. There was something macabre to the peal, like a desecration. The police dick halted Striker and the manager with a gesture.

"May be somebody for him," he said, and went over and took it. He said, "Hello?" in a wary, noncommittal voice. Then he changed to his own voice, said: "Oh. Have you told her yet? Well, send her up here. I'd like to talk to her."

He hung up, explained: "Girl he was out with tonight is down at the desk, came back to get her bag. He must have been carrying it for her. It has her latchkey in it and she couldn't get into her own home."

Perry turned almost unconsciously and looked into the dresser mirror to see if he needed a shave. Then he fastidiously narrowed the neck opening of his dressing gown and smoothed the hair around the back of his head, which was the only place he had any.

The dick shoved Hastings's discarded clothes out of sight on the closet floor. This was definitely not a murder case, so there was no reason to shock the person he was about to question, by the presence of the clothes.

There was a short tense wait while she was coming up on the slow-motion elevator. Coming up to see someone that wasn't there at all. Striker said rebukingly, "This is giving it to her awful sudden, if she was at all fond of the guy."

Courlander unwittingly gave an insight into his own character when he said callously, "These girls nowadays can take it better than we can—don't worry."

The elevator panel ticked open, and then she came into the square of light thrown across the hall by the open doorway. She was a very pretty girl of about twenty-one or -two, tall and slim, with dark red hair, in a long white satin evening gown. Her eyes were wide with startled inquiry, at the sight of the three of them, but not frightened yet. Striker had seen her once before, when she was waiting for Hastings in the lobby earlier that evening. The other man of the original quartette had come up with her, no doubt for propriety's sake, and was standing behind her. They had evidently seen the second girl home before coming back here. And the side street where he had fallen was around the corner from the main entrance to the hotel.

She crossed the threshold, asked anxiously, "Is Allan—Is Mr. Hastings ill or something? The desk man said there's been a little trouble up here."

Courlander said gently, "Yes, there has." But he couldn't make anything sound gentle. The closest he could get to it was a sort of passive truculence.

She looked around. She was starting to get frightened now. She said, "What's happened to him? Where is he?" Then she saw the right half of the window standing open. Striker, who was closest to it, raised his arm and pushed it slowly closed. Then he just looked at her.

She understood, and whimpered across her shoulder, "Oh, Marty!" and the man behind her put an arm around her shoulder to support her.

They sat down. She didn't cry much—just sat with her head bent looking over at the floor. Her escort stood behind her chair, hands on her shoulders, bucking her up.

Courlander gave her a minute or two to pull herself together, then he started questioning. He asked them who they were. She gave her name. The man with her was her brother; he was Hastings's classmate at Princeton.

He asked if Hastings had had much to drink.

"He had a few drinks," she admitted, "but he wasn't drunk. Mart and I had the same number he did, and we're not drunk." They obviously weren't.

"Do you know of any reason, either one of you, why he should have done this?"

The thing had swamped them with its inexplicability, it was easy to see that. They just shook their heads dazedly.

"Financial trouble?"

The girl's brother just laughed—mirthlessly. "He had a banking business to inherit, some day—if he'd lived."

"Ill health? Did he study too hard, maybe?"

He laughed again, dismally. "He was captain of the hockey team, he was on the baseball team, he was the bright hope of the swimming team. Why should he worry about studying? Star athletes are never allowed to flunk."

"Love affair?" the tactless flatfoot blundered on.

The brother flinched at that. This time it was the girl who answered. She raised her head in wounded pride, thrust out her left hand.

"He asked me to marry him tonight. He gave me this ring. That was the reason for the party. Am I so hard to take?"

The police dick got red. She stood up without waiting to ask whether she could go or not. "Take me home, Mart," she said in a muffled voice. "I've got some back crying to catch up on."

Striker called the brother back again for a minute, while she went on alone toward the elevator; shoved the note before him. "Was that his handwriting?"

He pored over it. "I can't tell, just on the strength of those three words. I've never seen enough of it to know it very well. The only thing I'd know for sure would be his signature—he had a cockeyed way of ending it with a little pretzel twist—and that isn't on there." Over his shoulder, as he turned to go once more, he added: "That was a favorite catchword of his, though. 'What's the use?' I've often heard him use it. I guess it's him all right."

"We can check it by the register," Striker suggested after they'd gone.

The dick gave him a scathing look. "Is it your idea somebody else wrote his suicide note for him? That's what I'd call service!"

"Is it your idea he committed suicide the same night he got engaged to a production number like you just saw?"

"Is it your idea he didn't?"

"Ye-es," said Striker with heavy emphasis, "but I can't back it up."

"You bet you can't!"

The register showed a variation between the two specimens of handwriting, but not more than could be ascribed to the tension and nervous excitement of a man about to end his life. There wasn't enough to the note for a good handwriting expert to have got his teeth into with any degree of certainty.

"How long had he been in when it happened?" Striker asked Maxon.

"Not more than half an hour. Bob took him up a little before four."

"How'd he act? Down in the mouth, blue?"

"Blue nothing, he was tappin' out steps there on the mosaic, waitin' for the car to take him up."

Bob, the night man-of-all-work, put in his two cents' worth without being asked: "On the way up he said to me, 'Think this thing'll last till we get up there? I'd hate to have it drop me now. I got engaged tonight.'"

Striker flashed the police dick a triumphant look. The latter just stood by with the air of one indulging a precocious child. "Now ya through, little boy?" he demanded. "Why don't you quit trying to make a noise like a homicide dick and stick to your own little racket?

"It's a suicide, see?" continued the police dick pugnaciously, as though by raising his voice he was deciding the argument. "I've cased the room, and I don't care if he stood on his head or did somersaults before he rode up." He waved a little black pocket-notebook under

Striker's nose. "Here's my report, and if it don't suit you, why don't you take it up with the Mayor?"

Striker said in a humble, placating voice: "Mind if I ask you something personal?"

"What?" said the precinct man sourly.

"Are you a married man?"

"Sure I'm married. What's that to—?"

"Think hard. The night you became engaged, the night you first proposed to your wife, did you feel like taking your own life afterward?"

The police dick went "Arrrr!" disgustedly, flung around on his heel, and stalked out, giving the revolving door an exasperated twirl that kept it going long after he was gone.

"They get sore, when you've got 'em pinned down," Striker remarked wryly.

Perry remonstrated impatiently, "Why are you always trying to make it out worse than it is? Isn't it bad enough without looking for trouble?"

"If there's something phony about his death, isn't it worse if it goes undetected than if it's brought to light?"

Perry said, pointedly thumbing the still-turning door, "*That* was the police we just had with us."

"We were practically alone," muttered his disgruntled operative.

And so they couldn't blame it on the depression this time. That was starting to clear up now. And besides, Allan Hastings had come from well-to-do people. They couldn't blame it on love either. Perry half-heartedly tried to suggest he hadn't loved the girl he was engaged to, had had somebody else under his skin maybe, so he'd taken this way to get out of it.

"That's a woman's reason, not a man's," Striker said disgustedly. "Men don't kill themselves for love; they go out and get tanked, and hop a train for some place else, instead!" The others both nodded, probing deep within their personal memories. So that wouldn't wash either.

In the end there wasn't anything they could blame it on but the room itself. "That room's jinxed," Maxon drawled slurringly. "That's two in a row we've had in there. I think it's the thirteen on it. You oughta change the number to 912½ or 914½ or something, boss."

That was how the legend first got started.

Perry immediately jumped on him full-weight. "Now listen, I won't have any of that nonsense! There's nothing wrong with that room! First thing you know the whole hotel'll have a bad name, and then where are we? It's just a coincidence, I tell you, just a coincidence!"

Dennison sold the room the very second day after to a middle-aged couple on a visit to the city to see the sights. Striker and Maxon sort of held their breaths, without admitting it to each other. Striker even got up out of bed once or twice that first night and took a prowl past the door of 913, stopping to listen carefully. All he could hear was a sonorous baritone snore and a silvery soprano one, in peaceful counterpoint.

The hayseed couple left three days later, perfectly unharmed and vowing they'd never enjoyed themselves as much in their lives.

"Looks like the spirits are lying low," commented the desk man, shoving the red vacancy-tag back into the pigeonhole.

"No," said Striker, "looks like it only happens to singles. When there's two in the room nothing ever happens."

"You never heard of anyone committing suicide in the presence of a second party, did you?" the clerk pointed out not unreasonably. "That's one thing they gotta have privacy for."

Maybe it had been, as Perry insisted, just a gruesome coincidence. "But if it happens a third time," Striker vowed to himself, "I'm going to get to the bottom of it if I gotta pull the whole place down brick by brick!"

The Legend, meanwhile, had blazed up high and furious with the employees; even the slowest-moving among them had a way of hurrying past Room 913 with sidelong glances and fetish mutterings when any duty called them to that particular hallway after dark. Perry raised hell about it, but he was up against the supernatural now; he and his threats of discharge didn't stack up at all against that. The penalty of repeating the rumor to a guest was instant dismissal if detected by the management. *If.*

Then just when the legend was languishing from lack of any further substantiation to feed upon, and was about to die down altogether, the room came through a third time!

The calendar read Friday, July 12th, 1935, and the thermometers all read ninety-plus. He came in mopping his face like everyone else, but with a sort of professional good humor about him that no one else could muster just then. That was one thing that tipped Striker off he was a salesman. Another was the two bulky sample cases he was hauling with him until the bellboy took them over. A third was his ability to crack a joke when most people felt like eggs in a frying pan waiting to be turned over.

"Just rent me a bath without a room," he told Dennison. "I'll sleep in the tub all night with the cold water running over me."

"I can give you a nice inside room on the fourth." There were enough vacancies at the moment to offer a choice, these being the dog days.

The newcomer held up his hand, palm outward. "No thanks, not this kind of weather. I'm willing to pay the difference."

"Well, I've got an outside on the sixth, and a couple on the ninth."

"The higher the better. More chance to get a little circulation into the air."

There were two on the ninth, 13 and 19. Dennison's hand paused before 13, strayed on past it to 19, hesitated, came back again. After all, the room had to be sold. This was business, not a kid's goblin story. Even Striker could see that. And it was ten months now since— There'd been singles in the room since then, too. And they'd lived to check out again.

He gave him 913. But after the man had gone up, he couldn't refrain from remarking to Striker: "Keep your fingers crossed. That's the one with the jinx on it." As though Striker didn't know that! "I'm going to do a little more than that," he promised himself privately.

He swung the register around toward him so he could read it. *Amos J. Dillberry, City,* was inscribed on it. Meaning this was the salesman's headquarters when he was not on the road, probably. Striker shifted it back again.

He saw the salesman in the hotel dining-room at mealtime that evening. He came in freshly showered and laundered, and had a wise-crack for his waiter. That was the salesman in him. The heat certainly hadn't affected his appetite any, the way he stoked.

"If anything happens," thought Striker with gloomy foreboding, "that dick Courlander should show up later and try to tell me this guy was depressed or affected by the heat! He should just try!"

In the early part of the evening the salesman hung around the lob-by a while, trying to drum up conversation with this and that swelter-ing fellow-guest. Striker was in there too, watching him covertly. For once he was not a hotel dick sizing somebody up hostilely, he was a hotel dick sizing somebody up protectively. Not finding anyone partic-ularly receptive, Dillberry went out into the street about ten, in quest of a soul-mate.

Striker stood up as soon as he'd gone, and took the opportunity of going up to 913 and inspecting it thoroughly. He went over every square inch of it; got down on his hands and knees and explored all along the baseboards of the walls; examined the electric outlets; held matches to such slight fissures as there were between the tiles in the bathroom; rolled back one half of the carpet at a time and inspected the floorboards thoroughly; even got up on a chair and fiddled with the ceiling light fixture, to see if there was anything tricky about it. He couldn't find a thing wrong. He tested the windows exhaustively, working them back and forth until the hinges threatened to come off. There wasn't anything defective or balky about them, and on a scorch-ing night like this the inmate was bound to leave them wide open and let it go at that, not fiddle around with them in any way during the middle of the night. There wasn't enough breeze, even this high up, to swing a cobweb.

He locked the room behind him, went downstairs again with a helpless dissatisfied feeling of having done everything that was humanly possible—and yet not having done anything at all, really. What was there he could do?

Dillberry reappeared a few minutes before twelve, with a package cradled in his arm that was unmistakably for refreshment purposes up in his room, and a conspiratorial expression on his face that told Striker's experienced eyes what was coming next. The salesman obviously wasn't the solitary drinker type.

Striker saw her drift in about ten minutes later, with the air of a lady on her way to do a little constructive drinking. He couldn't place her on the guest list, and she skipped the desk entirely—so he bracketed her with Dillberry. He did exactly nothing about it—turned his head away as though he hadn't noticed her.

Maxon, who had just come on in time to get a load of this, looked at Striker in surprise. "Aren't you going to do anything about that?" he murmured. "She's not one of our regulars."

"I know what I'm doing," Striker assured him softly. "She don't know it, but she's subbing for night watchman up there. As long as he's not alone, nothing can happen to him."

"Oh, is that the angle? Using her for a chest protector, eh? But that just postpones the showdown—don't solve it. If you keep using a spare to ward it off, how you gonna know what it is?"

"That," Striker had to admit, "is just the rub. But I hate like the devil to find out at the expense of still another life."

But the precaution was frustrated before he had time to see whether it would work or not. The car came down almost immediately afterward, and the blonde was still on it, looking extremely annoyed and quenching her unsatisfied thirst by chewing gum with a sound like castanets. Beside her stood Manager Perry, pious determination transforming his face.

"Good night," he said, politely ushering her off the car.

"Y'couldda at least let me have one quick one, neat, you big over-stuffed blimp!" quoth the departing lady indignantly. "After I helped him pick out the brand!"

Perry came over to the desk and rebuked his house-man: "Where are your eyes, Striker? How did you let that come about? I happened to spot her out in the hall waiting to be let in. You want to be on your toes, man."

"Sorry, chief," said Striker.

"So it looks like he takes his own chances," murmured Maxon, when the manager had gone up again.

"Then I'm elected, personally," sighed Striker. "Maybe it's just as well. Even if something had happened with her up there, she didn't look like she had brains enough to be able to tell what it was afterward."

In the car, on the way to his own room, he said, "Stop at nine a minute—and wait for me." This was about a quarter to one.

He listened outside 13. He heard a page rustle, knew the salesman wasn't asleep, so he knocked softly. Dillberry opened the door.

"Excuse me for disturbing you. I'm the hotel detective."

"I've been quarantined once tonight already," said the salesman, but his characteristic good humor got the better of him even now. "You can come in and look if you want to, but I know when I'm licked."

"No, it isn't about that." Striker wondered how to put it. In loyalty to his employer he couldn't very well frighten the man out of the place. "I just wanted to warn you to please be careful of those windows. The guard rail outside them's pretty low, and—"

"No danger," the salesman chuckled. "I'm not subject to dizzy spells and I don't walk in my sleep."

Striker didn't smile back. "Just bear in mind what I said, though, will you?"

Dillberry was still chortling good-naturedly. If he *did* lose his balance during the night and go out, thought Striker impatiently, it would be like him still to keep on sniggering all the way down.

"What are you worried they'll do—creep up on me and bite me?" kidded the salesman.

"Maybe that's a little closer to the truth than you realize," Striker said to himself mordantly. Looking at the black, night-filled aperture across the lighted room from them, he visualized it for the first time as a hungry, predatory maw, with an evil active intelligence of its own, swallowing the living beings that lingered too long within its reach, sucking them through to destruction, like a diabolic vacuum-cleaner. It looked like an upright, open black coffin there, against the cream-painted walls; all it needed was a silver handle at each end. Or like a symbolic Egyptian doorway to the land of the dead, with its severe proportions and pitch-black core and the hot, lazy air coming through it from the nether-world.

He was beginning to hate it with a personal hate, because it baffled him, it had him licked, had him helpless, and it struck without warning—an unfair adversary.

Dillberry giggled, "You got a look on your face like you tasted poison! I got a bottle here hasn't been opened yet. How about rinsing it out?"

"No, thanks," said Striker, turning away. "And it's none of my business, I know, but just look out for those windows if you've got a little something under your belt later."

"No fear," the salesman called after him. "It's no fun drinking alone. Too hot for that, anyway."

Striker went on up to his own room and turned in. The night air had a heavy, stagnant expectancy to it, as if it were just waiting for something to happen. Probably the heat, and yet he could hardly breathe, the air was so leaden with menace and sinister tension.

He couldn't put his mind to the "fantastic" magazine he'd taken to bed with him—he flung it across the room finally. "You'd think I knew, ahead of time!" he told himself scoffingly. And yet deny it as he might, he did have a feeling that tonight was going to be one of those times. Heat jangling his nerves, probably. He put out his light—even the weak bulb gave too much warmth for comfort—and lay there in the dark, chain-smoking cigarettes until his tongue prickled.

An hour ticked off, like drops of molten lead. He heard the hour of three strike faintly somewhere in the distance, finally. He lay there, tossing and turning, his mind going around and around the problem. What *could* it have been but two suicides, by coincidence both from the one room? There had been no violence, no signs of anyone having got in from the outside.

He couldn't get the infernal room off his mind; it was driving him nutty. He sat up abruptly, decided to go down there and take soundings. Anything was better than lying there. He put on shirt and pants, groped his way to the door without bothering with the light—it was too hot for lights—opened the door and started down the hall. He left the door cracked open behind him, to save himself the trouble of having to work a key on it when he got back.

He'd already rounded the turn of the hall and was at the fire door giving onto the emergency stairs, when he heard a faint trill somewhere behind him. The ding-a-ling of a telephone bell. Could that be his? If it was— He tensed at the implication. It kept on sounding; it must be his, or it would have been answered by now.

He turned and ran back, shoved the door wide open. It was. It burst into full-bodied volume, almost seemed to explode in his face. He found the instrument in the dark, rasped, "Hello?"

"Strike?" There was fear in Maxon's voice now. "It's—it's happened again."

Striker drew in his breath, and that was cold too, in all the heat of the stuffy room. "Nine-thirteen?" he said hoarsely.

"Nine-thirteen!"

He hung up without another word. His feet beat a pulsing tattoo racing down the hall. This time he went straight to the room, not down to the street. He'd seen too often what "they" looked like, down below, after they'd grounded. This time he wanted to see what that hell box, that four-walled coffin, that murder crate of a room looked like. Right after. Not five minutes or even two, but right after—as fast as it was humanly possible to get there. But maybe five minutes had passed, already; must have, by the time it was discovered, and he was summoned, and he got back and answered his phone. Why hadn't he stirred his stumps a few minutes sooner? He'd have been just in time, not only to prevent, but to see what it was—if there was anything to see.

He got down to the ninth, heat or no heat, in thirty seconds flat, and over to the side of the building the room was on. The door was yawning wide open, and the room light was out. "Caught you, have I?" flashed grimly through his mind. He rounded the jamb like a shot, poked the light switch on, stood crouched, ready to fling himself—

Nothing. No living thing, no disturbance.

No note either, this time. He didn't miss any bets. He looked into the closet, the bath, even got down and peered under the bed. He peered cautiously down from the lethal window embrasure, careful where he put his hands, careful where he put his weight.

He couldn't see the street, because the window was too high up, but he could hear voices down there plainly in the still, warm air.

He went back to the hall and stood there listening. But it was too late to expect to hear anything, and he knew it. The way he'd come galloping down like a war-horse would have drowned out any sounds of surreptitious departure there might have been. And somehow, he couldn't help feeling there hadn't been any, anyway. The evil was implicit in this room itself—didn't come from outside, open door to the contrary.

He left the room just the way he'd found it, went below finally. Maxon straightened up from concealing something under the desk, drew the back of his hand recklessly across his mouth. "Bring on your heebie-jeebies," he said defiantly. "See if I care—now!"

Striker didn't blame him too much at that. He felt pretty shaken himself.

Perry came down one car-trip behind him. "I never heard of anything like it!" He was seething. "What kind of a merry-go-round is this anyway?"

Eddie Courlander had been sent over for the third time. Happened to be the only one on hand, maybe. The whole thing was just a monotonous repetition of the first two times, but too grisly—to Striker, anyway—to be amusing.

"This is getting to be a commutation trip for me," the police dick announced with macabre humor, stalking in. "The desk lieutenant only has to say, 'Suicide at a hotel,' and I say right away, 'The St. Anselm,' before he can tell me."

"Only it isn't," said Striker coldly. "There was no note."

"Are you going to start that again?" growled the city dick.

"It's the same room again, in case you're interested. Third time in a little over two years. Now, don't you think that's rubbing it in a little heavy?"

Courlander didn't answer, as though he *was* inclined to think that, but—if it meant siding with Striker—hated to have to admit it.

Even Perry's professional bias for suicide—if the alternative had to be murder, the *bête-noir* of hotel men—wavered in the face of this triple assault. "It does look kind of spooky," he faltered, polishing the center of his bald head. "All the rooms below, on that line, have those same floor-length windows, and it's never taken place in any of the others."

"Well, we're going to do it up brown this time and get to the bottom of it!" Courlander promised.

They got off at the ninth. "Found the door open like this, too," Striker pointed out. "I stopped off here on my way down."

Courlander just glanced at him, but still wouldn't commit himself. He went into the room, stopped dead-center and stood there looking around, the other two just behind him. Then he went over to the bed, fumbled a little with the covers. Suddenly he spaded his hand under an edge of the pillow, drew it back again.

"I thought you said there was no note?" he said over his shoulder to Striker.

"You not only thought. I did say that."

"You still do, huh?" He shoved a piece of stationery at him. "What does this look like—a collar button?"

It was as laconic as the first two. *I'm going to hell, where it's cool!* Unsigned.

"That wasn't in here when I looked the place over the first time," Striker insisted with slow emphasis. "That was planted in here between then and now!"

Courlander flung his head disgustedly. "It's white, isn't it? The bedclothes are white too, ain't they? Why don't you admit you missed it?"

"Because I know I didn't! I had my face inches away from that bed, bending down looking under it."

"Aw, you came in half-asleep and couldn't even see straight, probably!"

"I've been awake all night, wider awake than you are right now!"

"And as for your open door—" Courlander jeered. He bent down, ran his thumbnail under the panel close in to the jamb, jerked something out. He stood up exhibiting a wedge made of a folded-over paper match-cover. "He did that himself, to try to get a little circulation into the air in here."

Striker contented himself with murmuring, "Funny no one else's door was left open." But to himself he thought, ruefully, "It's trying its best to look natural all along the line, like the other times; which only proves it isn't."

The city dick answered, "Not funny at all. A woman alone in a room wouldn't leave her door open for obvious reasons; and a couple in a room wouldn't, because the wife would be nervous or modest about it. But why shouldn't a guy rooming by himself do it, once his light was out, and if he didn't have anything of value in here with him? That's why his was the only door open like that. The heat drove him wacky; and when he couldn't get any relief no matter what he did—"

"The heat did nothing of the kind. I spoke to him at twelve and he was cheerful as a robin."

"Yeah, but a guy's resistance gets worn down, it frays, and then suddenly it snaps." Courlander chuckled scornfully. "It's as plain as day before your eyes."

"Well," drawled Striker, "if this is your idea of getting to the bottom of a thing, baby, you're easily pleased! I'll admit it's a little more work to keep digging, than just to write down 'suicide' in your report and let it go at that," he added stingingly.

"I don't want any of your insinuations!" Courlander said hotly. "Trying to call me lazy, huh? All right," he said with the air of doing a big favor, "I'll play ball with you. We'll make the rounds giving off noises like a detective, if that's your idea."

"You'll empty my house for me," Perry whined.

"Your man here seems to think I'm laying down on the job." Courlander stalked out, hitched his head at them to follow.

"You've never played the numbers, have you?" Striker suggested stolidly. "No number ever comes up three times in a row. That's what they call the law of averages. Three suicides from one room doesn't conform to the law of averages. And when a thing don't conform to that law, it's phony."

"You forgot your lantern slides, perfessor," sneered the police dick. He went next door and knuckled 915, first gently, then resoundingly.

The door opened and a man stuck a sleep-puffed face out at them. He said, "Whad-dye want? It takes me half the night to work up a little sleep and then I gotta have it busted on me!" He wasn't just faking being asleep—it was the real article; anyone could see that. The light hurt his eyes; he kept blinking.

"Sorry, pal," Courlander overrode him with a businesslike air, "but we gotta ask a few questions. Can we come in and look around?"

"No, ya can't! My wife's in bed!"

"Have her put something over her, then, 'cause we're comin'!"

"I'm leaving the first thing in the morning!" the man threatened angrily. "You can't come into my room like this, without a search warrant!" He thrust himself belligerently into the door opening.

"Just what have you got to hide, Mr. Morris?" suggested Striker mildly.

The remark had an almost magical effect on him. He blinked, digested the implication a moment, then abruptly swept the door wide open, stepped out of the way.

A woman was sitting up in bed struggling into a wrapper.

Courlander studied the wall a minute. "Did you hear any noise of any kind from the next room before you fell asleep?"

The man shook his head, said: "No."

"About how long ago did you fall asleep?"

"About an hour ago," said the man sulkily.

Courlander turned to the manager. "Go back in there a minute, will you, and knock on the wall with your fist from that side. Hit it good."

The four of them listened in silence; not a sound came through. Perry returned, blowing his breath on his stinging knuckles.

"That's all," Courlander said to the occupants. "Sorry to bother you." He and Striker went out again. Perry lingered a moment to try to smoothe their ruffled plumage.

They went down to the other side of the death chamber and tried 911. "This witch," said Perry, joining them, "has got ears like a dictaphone. If there was anything to hear, she heard it all right! I don't care whether you disturb her or not. I've been trying to get rid of her for years."

She was hatchet-faced, beady-eyed, and had a cap with a drawstring tied closely about her head. She seemed rather gratified at finding herself an object of attention, even in the middle of the night, as though she couldn't get anyone to listen to her most of the time.

"Asleep?" she said almost boastfully. "I should say not! I haven't closed my eyes all night." And then, overriding Courlander's attempt at getting in a question, she went on: "Mr. Perry, I know it's late, but as long as you're here, I want to show you something!" She drew back into the center of the room, crooked her finger at him ominously. "You just come here!"

The three men advanced alertly and jockeyed into positions from which they could see.

She swooped down, flung back a corner of the rug, and straightened up again, pointing dramatically. A thin film of dust marked the triangle of flooring that had just been bared. "What do you think of that?" she said accusingly. "Those maids of yours, instead of sweeping the dust *out* of the room, sweep it under the rug."

The manager threw his hands up over his head, turned, and went out. "The building could be burning," he fumed, "and if we both landed in the same firemen's net, she'd still roll over and complain to me about the service!"

Striker lingered behind just long enough to ask her: "You say you've been awake all night. Did you hear anything from the room next door, 913, during the past half-hour or so?"

"Why, no. Not a sound. Is there something wrong in there?" The avid way she asked it was proof enough of her good faith. He got out before she could start questioning him.

Courlander grinned, "I can find a better explanation even than the heat for him jumping, now," he remarked facetiously. "He musta seen *that* next door to him and got scared to death."

"That would be beautifully simple, wouldn't it?" Striker said cuttingly. "Let's give it one more spin," he suggested. "No one on either side of the room heard anything. Let's try the room directly underneath—813. The closet and bath arrangement makes for soundproof side-partitions, but the ceilings are pretty thin here."

Courlander gave the manager an amused look, as if to say, "Humor him!"

Perry, however, rolled his eyes in dismay. "Good heavens, are you trying to turn my house upside-down, Striker? Those are the Youngs, our star guests, and you know it!"

"D'you want to wait until it happens a fourth time?" Striker warned him. "It'll bring on a panic if it does."

They went down to the hallway below, stopped before 813. "These people are very wealthy," whispered the manager apprehensively. "They could afford much better quarters. I've considered myself lucky that they've stayed with us. Please be tactful. I don't want to lose them." He tapped apologetically, with just two finger-nails.

Courlander sniffed and said, "What's that I smell?"

"Incense," breathed the manager. "*Sh!* Don't you talk out of turn now."

There was a rustling sound behind the door, then it opened and a young Chinese in a silk robe stood looking out at them. Striker knew him, through staff gossip and his own observation, to be not only thoroughly Americanized in both speech and manner but an American by birth as well. He was Chinese only by descent. He was a lawyer and made huge sums looking after the interests of the Chinese businessmen down on Pell and Mott Streets—a considerable part of which he lost again betting on the wrong horses, a pursuit he was no luckier at than his average fellow citizen. He was married to a radio singer. He wore horn-rimmed glasses.

"Hi!" he said briskly. "The Vigilantes! What's up, Perry?"

"I'm so sorry to annoy you like this," the manager began to whine.

"Skip it," said Young pleasantly. "Who could sleep on a night like this? We've been taking turns fanning each other in here. Come on in."

Even Striker had never been in the room before; the Youngs were quality folk, not to be intruded upon by a mere hotel-detective. A doll-like creature was curled up on a sofa languidly fanning herself, and a scowling Pekinese nestled in her lap. The woman wore green silk pajamas. Striker took note of a tank containing tropical fish, also a lacquered Buddha on a table with a stick of sandalwood burning before it.

Striker and Courlander let Perry put the question, since being tactful was more in his line. "Have you people been disturbed by any sounds coming from over you?"

"Not a blessed thing," Mrs. Young averred. "Have we, babe? Only that false-alarm mutter of thunder that didn't live up to its promise. But that came from outside, of course."

"Thunder?" said Striker, puzzled. "What thunder? How long ago?"

"Oh, it wasn't a sharp clap," Young explained affably. "'Way off in the distance, low and rolling. You could hardly hear it at all. There was a flicker of sheet-lightning at the same time—that's how we knew what it was."

"But wait a minute," Striker said discontentedly. "I was lying awake in my room, and I didn't hear any thunder, at any time tonight."

"There he goes again," Courlander slurred out of the corner of his mouth to Perry.

"But your room's located in a different part of the building," Perry interposed diplomatically. "It looks out on a shaft, and that might have muffled the sound."

"Thunder is thunder. You can hear it down in a cellar, when there is any to hear," Striker insisted.

The Chinese couple good-naturedly refused to take offense. "Well, it was very low, just a faint rolling. We probably wouldn't have noticed it ourselves, only at the same time there was this far-off gleam of lightning, and it seemed to stir up a temporary breeze out there, like when a storm's due to break. I must admit we didn't feel any current of air here inside the room, but we both saw a newspaper or rag of some kind go sailing down past the window just then."

"No. that wasn't a—" Striker stopped short, drew in his breath, as he understood what it was they must have seen.

Perry was frantically signaling him to shut up and get outside.

Striker hung back long enough to ask one more question. "Did your dog bark or anything, about the time this—'promise of a storm' came up?"

"No, Shan's very well behaved," Mrs. Young said fondly.

"He whined, though," her husband remembered. "We thought it was the heat."

Striker narrowed his eyes speculatively. "Was it right at that same time?"

"Just about."

Perry and Courlander were both hitching their heads at him to come out, before he spilled the beans. When he had joined them finally, the city dick flared up: "What'd you mean by asking that last one? You trying to dig up spooks, maybe?—hinting that their dog could sense something? All it was is, the dog knew more than they did. It knew that wasn't a newspaper flicked down past their window. That's why it whined!"

Striker growled stubbornly, "There hasn't been any thunder or any lightning at any time tonight—I know what I'm saying! I was lying awake in my room, as awake as they were!"

Courlander eyed the manager maliciously. "Just like there wasn't any farewell note, until I dug it out from under the pillow."

Striker said challengingly, "You find me *one other person*, in this building or outside of it, that saw and heard that 'thunder and lightning' the same as they did, and we'll call it quits!"

"Fair enough. I'll take you up on that!" Courlander snapped. "It ought to be easy enough to prove to you that that wasn't a private preview run off in heaven for the special benefit of the Chinese couple."

"And when people pay two hundred a month, they don't lie," said Perry quaintly.

"We'll take that projecting wing that sticks out at right-angles," said the dick. "It ought to have been twice as clear and loud out there as down on the eighth. Or am I stacking the cards?"

"You're not exactly dealing from a warm deck," Striker said. "If it was heard below, it could be heard out in the wing, and still have something to do with what went on in 913. Why not pick somebody who was out on the streets at the time and ask him? There's your real test."

"Take it or leave it. I'm not running around on the street this hour of the night, asking people 'Did you hear a growl of thunder thirty minutes ago?' I'd land in Bellevue in no time!"

"This is the bachelor wing," Perry explained as they rounded the turn of the hall. "All men. Even so, they're entitled to a night's rest as well as anyone else. Must you disturb *everyone* in the house?"

"Not my idea," Courlander rubbed it in. "That note is still enough for me. I'm giving this guy all the rope he needs, that's all."

They stopped outside 909. "Peter the Hermit," said Perry disgustedly. "Aw, don't take him. He won't be any help. He's nutty. He'll start telling you all about his gold mines up in Canada."

But Courlander had already knocked. "He's not too nutty to know thunder and lightning when he hears it, is he?"

Bedsprings creaked, there was a slither of bare feet, and the door opened.

He was about sixty, with a mane of snow-white hair that fell down to his shoulders, and a long white beard. He had mild blue eyes, with something trusting and childlike about them. You only had to look at them to understand how easy it must have been for the confidence men, or whoever it was, to have swindled him into buying those worthless shafts sunk into the ground up in the backwoods of Ontario.

Striker knew the story well; everyone in the hotel did. But others laughed, while Striker sort of understood—put two and two together. The man wasn't crazy, he was just disappointed in life. The long hair and the beard, Striker suspected, were not due to eccentricity but probably to stubbornness; he'd taken a vow never to cut his hair or shave until those mines paid off. And the fact that he hugged his room day and night, never left it except just once a month to buy a stock of canned goods, was understandable too. He'd been "stung" once, so now he was leery of strangers, avoided people for fear of being "stung" again. And then ridicule probably had something to do with it too. The way that fool Courlander was all but laughing in his face right now, trying to cover it with his hand before his mouth, was characteristic.

The guest was down on the register as Atkinson, but no one ever called him anything but Peter the Hermit. At irregular intervals he left the hotel, to go "prospecting" up to his mine-pits, see if there were any signs of ore. Then he'd come back again disappointed, but without having given up hope, to retire again for another six or eight months. He kept the same room while he was away, paying for it just as though he were in it.

"Can we come in, Pops?" the city dick asked, when he'd managed to straighten his face sufficiently.

"Not if you're going to try to sell me any more gold mines."

"Naw, we just want a weather report. You been asleep or awake?"

"I been awake all night, practickly."

"Good. Now tell me just one thing. Did you hear any thunder at all, see anything like heat-lightning flicker outside your window, little while back?"

"Heat-lightning don't go with thunder. You never have the two together," rebuked the patriarch.

"All right, all right," said Courlander wearily. "Any kind of lightning, plain or fancy, and any kind of thunder?"

"Sure did. Just once, though. Tiny speck of thunder and tiny mite of lightning, no more'n a flash in the pan. Stars were all out and around too. Darnedest thing I ever saw!"

Courlander gave the hotel dick a look that should have withered him. But Striker jumped in without waiting. "About this flicker of lightning. Which direction did it seem to come from? Are you sure it came from above and not"—he pointed meaningly downward—"from *below* your window?"

This time it was the Hermit who gave him the withering look. "Did you ever hear of lightning coming from below, son? Next thing you'll be trying to tell me rain falls up from the ground!" He went over to the open window, beckoned. "I'll show you right about where it panned out. I was standing here looking out at the time, just happened to catch it." He pointed in a northeasterly direction. "There. See that tall building up over thattaway? It come from over behind there—miles away, o' course—but from that part of the sky."

Courlander, having won his point, cut the interview short. "Much obliged, Pops. That's all."

They withdrew just as the hermit was getting into his stride. He rested a finger alongside his nose, trying to hold their attention, said confidentially: "I'm going to be a rich man one of these days, you wait'n see. Those mines o' mine are going to turn into a bonanza." But they closed the door on him.

Riding down in the car, Courlander snarled at Striker: "Now, eat your words. You said if we found one other person heard and saw that thunder and sheet-lightning—"

"I know what I said," Striker answered dejectedly. "Funny—private thunder and lightning that some hear and others don't."

Courlander swelled with satisfaction. He took out his notebook, flourished it. "Well, here goes, ready or not! You can work yourself up into a lather about it by yourself from now on. I'm not wasting any more of the city's time—or my own—on anything as self-evident as this!"

"Self-evidence, like beauty," Striker reminded him, "is in the eye of the beholder. It's there for some, and not for others."

Courlander stopped by the desk, roughing out his report. Striker, meanwhile, was comparing the note with Dillberry's signature in the book. "Why, this scrawl isn't anything like his John Hancock in the ledger!" he exclaimed.

"You expect a guy gone out of his mind with the heat to sit down and write a nice copybook hand?" scoffed the police dick. "It was in his room, wasn't it?"

This brought up their former bone of contention. "Not the first time I looked."

"I only have your word for that."

"Are you calling me a liar?" flared Striker.

"No, but I think what's biting you is, you got a suppressed desire to be a detective."

"I think," said Striker with deadly irony, "you have too."

"Why, you—!"

Perry hurriedly got between them. "For heaven's sake," he pleaded wearily, "isn't it hot enough and messy enough, without having a fist fight over it?"

Courlander turned and stamped out into the suffocating before-dawn murk. Perry leaned over the desk, holding his head in both hands. "That room's a jinx," he groaned, "a hoodoo."

"There's nothing the matter with the room—there can't possibly be," Striker pointed out. "That would be against nature and all natural laws. That room is just plaster and bricks and wooden boards, and they can't hurt anyone—in themselves. Whatever's behind this is some human agency, and I'm going to get to the bottom of it if I gotta sleep in there myself!" He waited a minute, let the idea sink in, take hold of him, then he straightened, snapped his fingers decisively. "That's the next step on the program! I'll be the guinea pig, the white mouse! That's the only way we can ever hope to clear it up."

Perry gave him a bleak look, as though such foolhardiness would have been totally foreign to his own nature, and he couldn't understand anyone being willing to take such an eerie risk.

"Because I've got a hunch," Striker went on grimly. "It's not over yet. It's going to happen again and yet again, if we don't hurry up and find out what it is."

Now that the official investigation was closed, and there was no outsider present to spread rumors that could give his hotel a bad name, Perry seemed willing enough to agree with Striker that it wasn't normal and natural. Or else the advanced hour of the night was working suggestively on his nerves. "B-but haven't you any idea at all, just as a starting point," he quavered, "as to what it could be—if it is anything? Isn't it better to have some kind of a theory? At least know what to look for, not just shut yourself up in there blindfolded?"

"I could have several, but I can't believe in them myself. It could be extra-mural hypnosis—that means through the walls, you know. Or it could be fumes that lower the vitality, depress, and bring on suicide mania—such as small quantities of monoxide will do. But this is summertime and there's certainly no heat in the pipes. No, there's only one way to get an idea, and that's to try it out on myself. I'm going to sleep in that room myself tomorrow night, to get the *feel* of it. Have I your okay?"

Perry just wiped his brow, in anticipatory horror. "Go ahead if you've got the nerve," he said limply. "You wouldn't catch me doing it!"

Striker smiled glumly. "I'm curious—that way."

Striker made arrangements as inconspicuously as possible the next day, since there was no telling at which point anonymity ended and hostile observation set in, whether up in the room itself or down at the registration desk, or somewhere midway between the two. He tried to cover all the externals by which occupancy of the room could be detected without at the same time revealing his identity. Dennison, the day clerk, was left out of it entirely. Outside of Perry himself, he took only Maxon into his confidence. No one else, not even the cleaning help. He waited until the night clerk came on duty at 11:30 before he made the final arrangements, so that there was no possibility of foreknowledge.

"When you're sure no one's looking—and not until then," he coached the night clerk, "I want you to take the red vacancy-tag out of the pigeonhole. And sign a phony entry in the register—John Brown, anything at all. We can erase it in the morning. That's in case the leak is down here at this end. I know the book is kept turned facing you, but there *is* a slight possibility someone could read it upside-down while stopping by here for their key. One other important thing: I may come up against something that's too much for me, whether it's physical or narcotic or magnetic. Keep your eye on that telephone switchboard in case I need help in a hurry. If 913 flashes, don't wait to answer. I mayn't be able to give a message. Just get up there in a hurry."

"That's gonna do you a lot of good," Maxon objected fearfully. "By the time anyone could get up there to the ninth on that squirrel-cage, it would be all over! Why don't you plant Bob or someone out of sight around the turn of the hall?"

"I can't. The hall may be watched. If it's anything external, and not just atmospheric or telepathic, it comes through the hall. It's got to. That's the only way it can get in. This has got to look *right*, wide open, unsuspecting, or whatever it is won't strike. No, the switchboard'll be my only means of communication. I'm packing a Little Friend with me, anyway, so I won't be exactly helpless up there. Now remember, 'Mr. John Brown' checked in here unseen by the human eye sometime during the evening. Whatever it is, it can't be watching the desk *all* the time, twenty-four hours a day. And for pete's sake, don't take any nips tonight. Lock the bottle up in the safe. My life is in your hands. Don't drop it!"

"Good luck and here's hoping," said Maxon sepulchrally, as though he never expected to see Striker alive again.

Striker drifted back into the lounge and lolled conspicuously in his usual vantage-point until twelve struck and Bob began to put the primary lights out. Then he strolled into the hotel drug store and drank two cups of scalding black coffee. Not that he was particularly afraid of not being able to keep awake, tonight of all nights, but there was nothing like making sure. There might be some soporific or sedative substance to overcome, though how it could be administered he failed to see.

He came into the lobby again and went around to the elevator bank, without so much as a wink to Maxon. He gave a carefully studied yawn, tapped his fingers over his mouth. A moment later there was a whiff of some exotic scent behind him and the Youngs had come in, presumably from Mrs. Young's broadcasting station. She was wearing an embroidered silk shawl and holding the Peke in her arm.

Young said, "Hi, fella." She bowed slightly. The car door opened.

Young said, "Oh, just a minute—my key," and stepped over to the desk.

Striker's eyes followed him relentlessly. The register was turned facing Maxon's way. The Chinese lawyer glanced down at it, curved his head around slightly as if to read it right side up, then took his key, came back again. They rode up together. The Peke started to whine. Mrs. Young fondled it, crooned: "*Sh*, Shan, be a good boy." She explained to Striker, "It always makes him uneasy to ride up in an elevator."

The couple got off at the eighth. She bowed again. Young said, "G'night." Striker, of course, had no idea of getting off at any but his usual floor, the top, even though he was alone in the car. He said in a low voice to Bob: "Does that dog whine other times when you ride it up?"

"No, sir," the elevator man answered. "It nevah seem' to mind until tonight. Mus' be getting ritzy."

Striker just filed that detail away: it was such a tiny little thing.

He let himself into his little hole-in-the-wall room. He pulled down the shade, even though there was just a blank wall across the shaft from his window. There was a roof-ledge farther up. He took his gun out of his valise and packed it in his back pocket. That was all he was taking with him; no fantastics tonight. The fantasy was in real life, not on the printed page.

He took off his coat and necktie and hung them over the back of a chair. He took the pillow off his bed and forced it down under the bedclothes so that it made a longish mound. He'd brought a newspaper up with him. He opened this to double-page width and leaned it up against the head of the bed, as though someone were sitting up behind it reading it. It sagged a little, so he took a pin and fastened it to the woodwork. He turned on the shaded reading-lamp at his bed-side, turned out the room light, so that there was just a diffused glow. Then he edged up to the window sidewise and raised the shade again, but not all the way, just enough to give a view of the lower part of the bed if anyone were looking down from above—from the cornice, for instance. He always had his reading lamp going the first hour or two after he retired other nights. Tonight it was going to burn all night. This was the only feature of the arrangement Perry would have disap-proved of, electricity bills being what they were.

That took care of things up here. He edged his door open, made sure the hallway was deserted, and sidled out in vest, trousers, and carrying the .38. He'd done everything humanly possible to make the thing foolproof, but it occurred to him, as he made his way noiselessly to the emergency staircase, that there was one thing all these precau-tions would be sterile against, if it was involved in any way, and that was mind-reading. The thought itself was enough to send a shudder up his spine, make him want to give up before he'd even gone any further, so he resolutely put it from him. Personally he'd never been much of a believer in that sort of thing, so it wasn't hard for him to discount it. But disbelief in a thing is not always a guarantee that it does not exist or exert influence, and he would have been the first to admit that.

The safety stairs were cement and not carpeted like the hallways, but even so he managed to move down them with a minimum of sound once his senses had done all they could to assure him the whole shaft was empty of life from its top to its bottom.

He eased the hinged fire-door on the ninth open a fraction of an inch, and reconnoitered the hall in both directions; forward through the slit before him, rearward through the seam between the hinges. This was the most important part of the undertaking. Everything de-pended on this step. It was vital to get into that room unseen. Even if he did not know what he was up against, there was no sense letting what he was up against know who he was.

He stood there for a long time like that, without moving, almost without breathing, narrowly studying each and every one of the in-scrutably closed doors up and down the hall. Finally he broke for it.

He had his passkey ready before he left the shelter of the fire-door. He stabbed it into the lock of 913, turned it, and opened the door with no more than two deft, quick, almost soundless movements. He had to work fast, to get in out of the open. He got behind the door once he was through, got the key out, closed the door—and left the room dark. The whole maneuver, he felt reasonably sure, could not have been accomplished more subtly by anything except a ghost or wraith.

He took a long deep breath behind the closed door and relaxed—a little. Leaving the room dark around him didn't make for very much peace of mind—there was always the thought that *It* might already be in here with him—but he was determined not to show his face even to the blank walls.

He was now, therefore, Mr. John Brown, Room 913, for the rest of the night, unsuspectingly waiting to be—whatever it was had hap-pened to Hopper, Hastings, Dillberry. He had a slight edge on them because he had a gun in his pocket, but try to shoot a noxious vapor (for instance) with a .38 bullet!

First he made sure of the telephone, his one lifeline to the outside world. He carefully explored the wire in the dark, inch by inch from the base of the instrument down to the box against the wall, to make sure the wire wasn't cut or rendered useless in any way. Then he opened the closet door and examined the inside of that, by sense of touch alone. Nothing in there but a row of empty hangers. Then he cased the bath, still without the aid of light; tried the water faucets, the drains, even the medicine chest. Next he devoted his attention to the bed it-self, explored the mattress and the springs, even got down and swept an arm back and forth under it, like an old maid about to retire for the night. The other furniture also got a health examination. He tested the rug with his foot for unevennesses. Finally there remained the win-dow, that mouthway to doom. He didn't go close to it. He stayed well back within the gloom of the room, even though there was nothing, not even a rooftop or water tank, opposite, from which the interior of this room could be seen; the buildings all around were much lower. It couldn't tell him anything; it seemed to be just a window embrasure. If it was more than that, it was one up on him.

Finally he took out his gun, slipped the safety off, laid it down beside the phone on the nightstand. Then he lay back on the bed, shoes and all, crossed his ankles, folded his hands under his head, and lay staring up at the pool of blackness over him that was the ceiling. He couldn't hear a thing, after that, except the whisper of his breathing, and he had to listen close to get even that.

The minutes pulled themselves out into a quarter hour, a half, a whole one, like sticky taffy. All sorts of horrid possibilities occurred to him, lying there in the dark, and made his skin crawl. He remembered the Conan Doyle story, "The Speckled Band," in which a deadly snake had been lowered through a transom night after night in an effort to get it to bite the sleeper. That wouldn't fit this case. He'd come upon the scene too quickly each time. You couldn't juggle a deadly snake—had to take your time handling it. None of his three predecessors had been heard to scream, nor had their broken bodies shown anything but the impact of the fall itself. None of the discoloration or rigidity of snake venom. He'd looked at the bodies at the morgue.

But it was not as much consolation as it should have been, in the dark. He wished he'd been a little braver—one of these absolutely fearless guys. It didn't occur to him that he was being quite brave enough already for one guy, coming up here like this. He'd stretched himself out in here without any certainty he'd ever get up again alive.

He practiced reaching for the phone and for his gun, until he knew just where they both were by heart. They were close enough. He didn't even have to unlimber his elbow. He lit a cigarette, but shielded the match carefully, with his whole body turned toward the wall, so it wouldn't light up his face too much. John Brown could smoke in bed just as well as House Dick Striker.

He kept his eyes on the window more than anything else, almost as if he expected it to sprout a pair of long octopus arms that would reach out, grab him, and toss him through to destruction.

He asked himself fearfully: "Am I holding it off by lying here awake like this waiting for it? Can it *tell* whether I'm awake or asleep? Is it on to me, whatever it is?" He couldn't help wincing at the implication of the supernatural this argued. A guy could go batty thinking things like that. Still, it couldn't be denied that the condition of the bed, each time before this, proved that the victims had been asleep and not awake just before it happened.

He thought, "I can pretend I'm asleep, at least, even if I don't actually go to sleep." Nothing must be overlooked in this battle of wits, no matter how inane, how childish it seemed at first sight.

He crushed his cigarette out, gave a stage yawn, meant to be heard if it couldn't be seen, threshed around a little like a man settling himself down for the night, counted ten, and then started to stage-manage his breathing, pumping it slower and heavier, like a real sleeper's. But under it all he was as alive as a third rail and his heart was ticking away under his ribs like a taximeter.

It was harder to lie waiting for it this way than it had been the other, just normally awake. The strain was almost unbearable. He wanted to leap up, swing out wildly around him in the dark, and yell: "Come on, you! Come on and get it over with!"

Suddenly he tensed more than he was already, if that was possible, and missed a breath. Missed two—forgot all about timing them. Something—what was it?—something was in the air; his nose was warning him, twitching, crinkling, almost like a retriever's. Sweet, foreign, subtle, something that didn't belong. He took a deep sniff, held it, while he tried to test the thing, analyze it, differentiate it, like a chemist without apparatus.

Then he got it. If he hadn't been so worked up in the first place, he would have got it even sooner. Sandalwood. Sandalwood incense. That meant the Chinese couple, the Youngs, the apartment below. They'd been burning it last night when he was in there, a stick of it in front of that joss of theirs. But how could it get up here? And how could it be harmful, if they were right in the same room with it and it didn't do anything to them?

How did he know they were in the same room with it? A fantastic picture flashed before his mind of the two of them down there right now, wearing gauze masks or filters over their faces, like operating surgeons. Aw, that was ridiculous! They'd been in the room a full five minutes with the stuff—he and Perry and Courlander—without masks, and nothing had happened to them.

But he wasn't forgetting how Young's head had swung around a little to scan the reversed register when they came in tonight—nor how their dog had whined, like it had whined when Dillberry's body fell past their window, when—Bob had said—it never whined at other times.

He sat up, pulled off his shoes, and started to move noiselessly around, sniffing like a bloodhound, trying to find out just how and where that odor was getting into the room. It must be at some particular point more than another. It wasn't just *soaking* up through the floor. Maybe it was nothing, then again maybe it was something. It didn't seem to be doing anything to him so far. He could breathe all right, he could think all right. But there was always the possibility that it was simply a sort of smoke-screen or carrier, used to conceal or transport some other gas that was to follow. The sugar-coating for the poison!

He sniffed at the radiator, at the bathroom drains, at the closet door, and in each of the four corners of the room. It was faint, almost unnoticeable in all those places. Then he stopped before the open window. It was much stronger here; it was coming in here!

He edged warily forward, leaned out a little above the low guardrail, but careful not to shift his balance out of normal, for this very posture of curiosity might be the crux of the whole thing, the incense a decoy to get them to lean out the window. Sure, it was coming out of their open window, traveling up the face of the building, and—some of it—drifting in through his. That was fairly natural, on a warm, still night like this, without much circulation to the air.

Nothing happened. The window didn't suddenly fold up and throw him or tilt him forward, the guard rail didn't suddenly collapse before him and pull him after it by sheer optical illusion (for he wasn't touching it in any way). He waited a little longer, tested it a little longer. No other result. It was, then, incense and nothing more.

He went back into the room again, stretched out on the bed once more, conscious for the first time of cold moisture on his brow, which he now wiped off. The aroma became less noticeable presently, as though the stick had burned down. Then finally it was gone. And he was just the way he'd been before.

"So it wasn't that," he dismissed it, and reasoned, "It's because they're Chinese that I was so ready to suspect them. They always seem sinister to the Occidental mind."

There was nothing else after that, just darkness and waiting. Then presently there was a gray line around the window enclosure, and next he could see his hands when he held them out before his face, and then the night bloomed into day and the death watch was over.

He didn't come down to the lobby for another hour, until the sun was up and there was not the slimmest possibility of anything happening any more—this time. He came out of the elevator looking haggard, and yet almost disappointed at the same time.

Maxon eyed him as though he'd never expected to see him again. "Anything?" he asked, unnecessarily.

"Nothing," Striker answered.

Maxon turned without another word, went back to the safe, brought a bottle out to him.

"Yeah, I could use some of that," was all the dick said.

"So I guess this shows," Maxon suggested hopefully, "that there's nothing to it after all. I mean about the room being—"

Striker took his time about answering. "It shows," he said finally, "that whoever it is, is smarter than we gave 'em credit for. Knew enough not to tip their mitts. Nothing happened because someone knew I was in there, knew who I was, and knew *why* I was in there. And *that* shows it's somebody in this hotel who's at the bottom of it."

"You mean you're not through yet?"

"Through yet? I haven't even begun!"

"Well, what're you going to do next?"

"I'm going to catch up on a night's sleep, first off," Striker let him know. "And after that, I'm going to do a little clerical work. Then when that's through, I'm going to keep my own counsel. No offense, but"— he tapped himself on the forehead—"only this little fellow in here is going to be in on it, not you nor the manager nor anyone else."

He started his "clerical work" that very evening. Took the old ledgers for March 1933 and September 1934 out of the safe, and copied out the full roster of guests from the current one (July 1935). Then he took the two bulky volumes and the list of present guests up to his room with him and went to work.

First he cancelled out all the names on the current list that didn't appear on either of the former two rosters. That left him with exactly three guests who were residing in the building now and who also had been in it at the time of one of the first two "suicides." The three were Mr. and Mrs. Young, Atkinson (Peter the Hermit), and Miss Flobelle Heilbron (the cantankerous vixen in 911). Then he cancelled those of the above that didn't appear on *both* of the former lists. There was only one name left uncancelled now. There was only one guest who had been in occupancy during *each and every one* of the three times that a "suicide" had taken place in 913. Atkinson and Miss Heilbron had been living in the hotel in March 1933. The Youngs and Miss Heilbron had been living in the building in September, 1934. Atkinson (who must have been away the time before on one of his nomadic "prospecting trips"), the Youngs, and Miss Heilbron were all here now. The one name that recurred triply was Miss Flobelle Heilbron.

So much for his "clerical work." Now came a little research work.

She didn't hug her room quite as continuously and tenaciously as Peter the Hermit, but she never strayed very far from it nor stayed away very long at a time—was constantly popping in and out a dozen times a day to feed a cat she kept.

He had a word with Perry the following morning, and soon after lunch the manager, who received complimentary passes to a number of movie theaters in the vicinity, in return for giving them advertising space about his premises, presented her with a matinee pass for that afternoon. She was delighted at this unaccustomed mark of attention, and fell for it like a ton of bricks.

Striker saw her start out at two, and that gave him two full hours. He made a bee-line up there and pass-keyed himself in. The cat was out in the middle of the room nibbling at a plate of liver which she'd thoughtfully left behind for it. He started going over the place. He didn't need two hours. He hit it within ten minutes after he'd come into the room, in one of her bureau-drawers, all swathed up in intimate wearing-apparel, as though she didn't want anyone to know she had it.

It was well-worn, as though it had been used plenty—kept by her at nights and studied for years. It was entitled *Mesmerism, Self-Taught; How to Impose Your Will on Others.*

But something even more of a giveaway happened while he was standing there holding it in his hand. The cat raised its head from the saucer of liver, looked up at the book, evidently recognized it, and whisked under the bed, ears flat.

"So she's been practicing on you, has she?" Striker murmured. "And you don't like it. Well, I don't either. I wonder who else she's been trying it on?"

He opened the book and thumbed through it. One chapter heading, appropriately enough, was *Experiments at a Distance*. He narrowed his eyes, read a few words. "In cases where the subject is out of sight, behind a door or on the other side of a wall, it is better to begin with simple commands, easily transferable. 1—Open the door. 2—Turn around, etc."

Well, "jump out of the window" was a simple enough command. Beautifully simple—and final. Was it possible that old crackpot was capable of—? She was domineering enough to be good at it, heaven knows. Perry'd wanted her out of the building years ago, but she was still in it today. Striker had never believed in such balderdash, but suppose—through some fluke or other—it had worked out with ghastly effect in just this one case?

He summoned the chambermaid and questioned her. She was a lumpy, work-worn old woman, and had as little use for the guest in question as anyone else, so she wasn't inclined to be reticent. "Boss me?" she answered, "Man, she sure do!"

"I don't mean boss you out loud. Did she ever try to get you to do her bidding without, uh, talking?"

She eyed him shrewdly, nodded. "Sure nuff. All the time. How you fine out about it?" She cackled uproariously. "She dippy, Mr. Striker, suh. I *mean!* She stand still like this, look at me *hard*, like this." She placed one hand flat across her forehead as if she had a headache. "So nothing happen', I just mine my business. Then she say: 'Whuffo you don't do what I just tole you?' I say, 'You ain't tole me nothing yet.' She say, 'Ain't you got my message? My sum-conscious done tole you, "Clean up good underneath that chair."'

"I say, 'Yo sum-conscious better talk a little louder, den, cause I ain't heard a thing—and I got good ears!'"

He looked at her thoughtfully. "Did you ever *feel* anything when she tried that stunt? Feel like doing the things she wanted?"

"Yeah man!" she vigorously asserted. "But not what she wanted! I feel like busting dis yere mop-handle on her haid, dass what I feel!"

He went ahead investigating after he'd dismissed her, but nothing else turned up. He was far from satisfied with what he'd got on Miss Heilbron, incriminating as the book was. It didn't *prove* anything. It wasn't strong enough evidence to base an accusation on.

He cased the Youngs' apartment that same evening, while they were at the wife's broadcasting studio. This, over Perry's almost apoplectic protests. And there, as if to confuse the issue still further, he turned up something that was at least as suspicious in its way as the mesmerism handbook. It was a terrifying grotesque mask of a demon, presumably a prop from the Chinese theater down on Doyer Street. It was hanging at the back of the clothes closet, along with an embroidered Chinese ceremonial robe. It was limned in some kind of luminous or phosphorescent paint that made it visible in the gloom in all its bestiality and horror. He nearly jumped out of his shoes himself at first sight of it. And that only went to show what conceivable effect it could have seeming to swim through the darkness in the middle of the night, for instance, toward the bed of a sleeper in the room above. That the victim would jump out of the window in frenzy would be distinctly possible.

Against this could be stacked the absolute lack of motive, the conclusive proof (two out of three times) that no one had been in the room with the victim, and the equally conclusive proof that the Youngs hadn't been in the building at all the first time, mask or no mask. In itself, of course, the object had as much right to be in their apartment as the mesmerism book had in Miss Heilbron's room. The wife was in theatrical business, liable to be interested in stage curios of that kind.

Boiled down, it amounted to this: that the Youngs were still very much in the running.

It was a good deal harder to gain access to Peter the Hermit's room without tipping his hand, since the eccentric lived up to his nickname to the fullest. However, he finally managed to work it two days later, with the help of Peter, the hotel exterminator, and a paperful of red ants. He emptied the contents of the latter outside the doorsill, then Perry and the exterminator forced their way in on the pretext of combating the invasion. It took all of Perry's cajolery and persuasiveness to draw the Hermit out of his habitat for even half an hour, but a professed eagerness to hear all about his "gold mines" finally turned the trick, and the old man was led around the turn of the hall. Striker jumped in as soon as the coast was clear and got busy.

It was certainly fuller of unaccountable things than either of the other two had been, but on the other hand there was nothing as glaringly suspicious as the mask or the hypnotism book. Pyramids of hoarded canned-goods stacked in the closet, and quantities of tools and utensils used in mining operations; sieves, pans, shorthandled picks, a hooded miner's lamp with a reflector, three fishing rods and an assortment of hooks ranging from the smallest to big triple-toothed monsters, plenty of tackle, hip boots, a shotgun, a pair of scales (for assaying the gold that he had never found), little sacks of worthless ore, a mallet for breaking up the ore specimens, and the pair of heavy knapsacks that he took with him each time he set out on his heartbreaking expeditions. It all seemed legitimate enough. Striker wasn't enough of a mining expert to know for sure. But he was enough of a detective to know there wasn't anything there that could in itself cause the death of anyone two rooms over and at right angles to this.

He had, of necessity, to be rather hasty about it, for the old man could be heard regaling Perry with the story of his mines just out of sight around the turn of the hall the whole time Striker was in there. He cleared out just as the exterminator finally got through killing the last of the "planted" ants.

To sum up: Flobelle Heilbron still had the edge on the other two as chief suspect, both because of the mesmerism handbook and because of her occupancy record. The Chinese couple came next, because of the possibilities inherent in that mask, as well as the penetrative powers of their incense and the whining of their dog. Peter the Hermit ran the others a poor third. Had it not been for his personal eccentricity and the location of his room, Striker would have eliminated him altogether.

On the other hand, he had turned up no real proof yet, and the motive remained as unfathomable as ever. In short, he was really no further than before he'd started. He had tried to solve it circumstantially, by deduction, and that hadn't worked. He had tried to solve it first hand, by personal observation, and that hadn't worked. Only one possible way remained, to try to solve it at *second hand*, through the eyes of the next potential victim, who would at the same time be a material witness—if he survived. To do this it was necessary to anticipate it, *time* it, try to see if it had some sort of spacing or rhythm to it or was just hit-or-miss, in order to know more or less when to expect it to recur. The only way to do this was to take the three dates he had and average them.

Striker took the early part of that evening off. He didn't ask permission for it, just walked out without saying anything to anyone about it. He was determined not to take anyone into his confidence this time.

He hadn't been off the premises a night since he'd first been hired by the hotel, and this wasn't a night off. This was strictly business. He had seventy-five dollars with him that he'd taken out of his hard-earned savings at the bank that afternoon. He didn't go where the lights were bright. He went down to the Bowery.

He strolled around a while looking into various barrooms and "smoke houses" from the outside. Finally he saw something in one that seemed to suit his purpose, went in and ordered two beers.

"Two?" said the barman in surprise. "You mean one after the other?"

"I mean two right together at one time," Striker told him.

He carried them over to the table at the rear, at which he noticed a man slumped with his head in his arms. He wasn't asleep or in a drunken stupor. Striker had already seen him push a despairing hand through his hair once.

He sat down opposite the motionless figure, clinked the glasses together to attract the man's attention. The derelict slowly raised his head.

"This is for you," Striker said, pushing one toward him.

The man just nodded dazedly, as though incapable of thanks any more. Gratitude had rusted on him from lack of use.

"What're your prospects?" Striker asked him bluntly.

"None. Nowhere to go. Not a cent to my name. I've only got one friend left, and I was figgerin' on looking him up 'long about midnight. If I don't tonight, maybe I will tomorrow night. I surely will one of these nights, soon. His name is the East River."

"I've got a proposition for you. Want to hear it?"

"You're the boss."

"How would you like to have a good suit, a clean shirt on your back for a change? How would you like to sleep in a comfortable bed tonight? In a three-dollar room, all to yourself, in a good hotel uptown?"

"Mister," said the man in a choked voice, "if I could do that once again, just once again, I wouldn't care if it was my last night on earth! What's the catch?"

"What you just said. It's liable to be." He talked for a while, told the man what there was to know, the little that he himself knew. "It's not certain, you understand. Maybe nothing'll happen at all. The odds are about fifty-fifty. If nothing does happen, you keep the clothes, the dough, and I'll even dig up a porter's job for you. You'll be that much ahead. Now I've given it to you straight from the shoulder. I'm not concealing anything from you, you know what to expect."

The man wet his lips reflectively. "Fifty-fifty—that's not so bad. Those are good enough odds. I used to be a gambler when I was young. And it can't hurt more than the river filling up your lungs. I'm weary of dragging out my days. What've I got to lose? Mister, you're on." He held out an unclean hand hesitantly. "I don't suppose you'd want to—"

Striker shook it as he stood up. "I never refuse to shake hands with a brave man. Come on, we've got a lot to do. We've got to find a barbershop, a men's clothing store if there are any still open, a luggage shop, and a restaurant."

An hour and a half later a taxi stopped on the corner diagonally opposite the St. Anselm, with Striker and a spruce, well-dressed individual seated in it side by side. On the floor at their feet were two shiny, brand-new valises, containing their linings and nothing else.

"Now there it is over there, on the other side," Striker said. "I'm going to get out here, and you go over in the cab and get out by yourself at the entrance. Count out what's left of the money I gave you."

His companion did so laboriously. "Forty-nine dollars and fifty cents."

"Don't spend another penny of it, get me? I've already paid the cab-fare and tip. See that you carry your own bags in, so they don't notice how light they are. Remember, what's left is all yours if—"

"Yeah, I know," said the other man unabashedly. "If I'm alive in the morning."

"Got your instructions straight?"

"I want an outside room. I want a ninth floor outside room. No other floor will do. I want a ninth floor outside room with a bath."

"That'll get you the right one by elimination. I happen to know it's vacant. You won't have to pay in advance. The two bags and the out-fit'll take care of that. Tell him to sign Harry Kramer for you—that what you said your name was? Now this is your last chance to back out. You can still welsh on me if you want—I won't do anything to you."

"No," the man said doggedly. "This way I've got a chance at a job tomorrow. The other way I'll be back on the beach. I'm glad somebody finally found some use for me."

Striker averted his head, grasped the other's scrawny shoulder en-couragingly. "Good luck, brother—and God forgive me for doing this, if I don't see you again." He swung out of the cab, opened a newspaper in front of his face, and narrowly watched over the top of it until the thin but well-dressed figure had alighted and carried the two bags up the steps and into a doorway from which he might never emerge alive.

He sauntered up to the desk a few minutes later himself, from the other direction, the coffee shop entrance. Maxon was still blotting the ink on the signature.

Striker read, *Harry Kramer, New York City*—913.

He went up to his room at his usual time, but only to get out his gun. Then he came down to the lobby again. Maxon was the only one in sight. Striker stepped in behind the desk, made his way back to the telephone switchboard, which was screened from sight by the tiers of mailboxes. He sat down before the switchboard and shot his cuffs, like a wireless operator on a ship at sea waiting for an SOS. The St. Anselm didn't employ a night operator. The desk clerk attended to the calls himself after twelve.

"What's the idea?" Maxon wanted to know.

Striker wasn't confiding in anyone this time. "Can't sleep," he said noncommittally. "Why should you object if I give you a hand down here?"

Kramer was to knock the receiver off the hook at the first sign of danger, or even anything that he didn't understand or like the looks of. There was no other way to work it than this, roundabout as it was. Striker was convinced that if he lurked about the ninth floor corridor within sight or earshot of the room, he would simply be banishing the danger, postponing it. He didn't want that. He wanted to know what it was. If he waited in his own room he would be even more cut off. The danger signal would have to be relayed up to him from down here. The last three times had shown him how ineffective that was.

A desultory call or two came through the first hour he was at the board, mostly requests for morning calls. He meticulously jotted them down for the day operator. Nothing from 913.

About two o'clock Maxon finally started to catch on. "You going to work it all night?"

"Yeh," said Striker shortly. "Don't talk to me. Don't let on I'm behind here at all."

At two thirty-five there were footsteps in the lobby, a peculiar sobbing sound like an automobile tire deflating, and a whiff of sandalwood traveled back to Striker after the car had gone up. He called Maxon guardedly back to him.

"The Youngs?"

"Yeah, they just came in."

"Was that their dog whining?"

"Yeah. I guess it hadda see another dog about a man."

Maybe a dead man, thought Striker morosely. He raised the plug toward the socket of 913. He ought to call Kramer, make sure he stayed awake. That would be as big a giveaway as pussyfooting around the hall up there, though. He let the plug drop back again.

About three o'clock more footsteps sounded. Heavy ones stamping in from the street. A man's voice sounded hoarsely. "Hey, desk! One of your people just tumbled out, around on the side of the building!"

The switchboard stool went over with a crack, something blurred streaked across the lobby, and the elevator darted crazily upward. Striker nearly snapped the control lever out of its socket, the way he bore down on it. The car had never traveled so fast before, but he swore horribly all the way up. Too late again!

The door was closed. He needled his passkey at the lock, shouldered the door in. The light was on, the room was empty. The window was wide open, the guy was gone. The fifty-fifty odds had paid off— the wrong way.

Striker's face was twisted balefully. He got out his gun. But there was only empty space around him.

He was standing there like that, bitter, defeated, granite-eyed, the gun uselessly in his hand, when Perry and Courlander came. It would be Courlander again, too!

"Is he dead?" Striker asked grimly.

"That street ain't quilted," was the dick's dry answer. He eyed the gun scornfully. "What're you doing? Holding the fort against the Indians, sonny boy?"

"I suggest instead of standing there throwing bouquets," Striker said, "you phone your precinct house and have a dragnet thrown around this building." He reached for the phone. Courlander's arm quickly shot out and barred him. "Not so fast. What would I be doing that for?"

"Because this is murder!"

"Where've I heard that before?" He went over for the inevitable note. "What's this?" He read it aloud. "'Can't take it any more.'"

"So you're still going to trip over those things!"

"And you're still going to try to hurdle it?"

"It's a fake like all the others were. I knew that all along. I couldn't prove it until now. This time I can! Finally."

"Yeah? How!"

"Because the guy couldn't write! Couldn't even write his own name! He even had to have the clerk sign the register for him downstairs. And if that isn't proof enough there's been somebody else in this room, have a look at that." He pointed to the money Kramer had left neatly piled on the dresser top. "Count that! Four-fifty. Four singles and a four-bit piece. He had forty-nine dollars and fifty cents on him when he came into this room, and he didn't leave the room. He's down there in his underwear now. Here's all his outer clothing up here. What became of that forty-five bucks?"

Courlander looked at him. "How do you know so much about it? How do you know he couldn't write, and just what dough he had?"

"Because I planted him up here myself!" Striker ground out exasperatedly. "It was a set-up! I picked him up, outfitted him, staked him, and brought him in here. He ran away to sea at twelve, never even learned his alphabet. I tested him and found out he was telling the truth. He couldn't write a word, not even his own name! Now do you understand? Are you gonna stand here all night or are you going to do something about it?"

Courlander snatched up the phone, called his precinct house. "Courlander. Send over a detail, quick! St. Anselm. That suicide reported from here has the earmarks of a murder."

"Earmarks!" scoffed Striker. "It's murder from head to foot, with a capital *M!*" He took the phone in turn. "Pardon me if I try to lock the stable door after the nag's been stolen. . . . H'lo, Maxon? Anyone left the building since this broke, anyone at all? Sure of that? Well, see that no one does. Call in that cop that's looking after the body. Lock up the secondary exit through the coffee shop. No one's to leave, no one at all, understand?" He threw the phone back at Courlander. "Confirm that for me, will you? Cops don't take orders from me. We've got them! They're still in the building some place! There's no way to get down from the roof. It's seven stories higher than any of the others around it."

But Courlander wasn't taking to cooperation very easily. "All this is based on your say-so that the guy couldn't write and had a certain amount of money on him when he came up here. So far so good. But something a little more definite than that better turn up. Did you mark the bills you gave him?"

"No, I didn't," Striker had to admit. "I wasn't figuring on robbery being the motive. I still don't think it's the primary one, I think it's only incidental. I don't think there is any consistent motive. I think we're up against a maniac."

"If they weren't marked, how do you expect us to trace them? Everyone in this place must have a good deal more than just forty-five dollars to their name! If you did plant somebody, why didn't you back him up, why didn't you look after him right? How did you expect to be able to help him if you stayed all the way downstairs, nine floors below?"

"I couldn't very well hang around outside the room. That would've been tipping my hand. I warned him, put him on his guard. He was to knock the phone over. That's all he had to do. Whatever it was, was too quick even for that."

Two members of the Homicide Squad appeared. "What's all the fuss and feathers? Where're the earmarks you spoke of, Courlander? The body's slated for an autopsy, but the examiner already says it don't look like anything but just the fall killed him."

"The house dick here," Courlander said, "insists the guy couldn't write and is short forty-five bucks. He planted him up here because he has an idea those other three cases—the ones I covered, you know—were murder."

They started to question Striker rigorously as though he himself were the culprit. "What gave you the idea it would happen tonight?"

"I didn't know it would happen tonight. I took a stab at it, that's all. I figured it was about due somewhere around now."

"Was the door open or locked when you got up here?"

"Locked."

"Where was the key?"

"Where it is now—over there on the dresser."

"Was the room disturbed in any way?"

"No, it was just like it is now."

They took a deep breath in unison, a breath that meant they were being very patient with an outsider. "Then what makes you think somebody beside himself was in here at the time?"

"Because that note is in here, and he couldn't write! Because there's forty-five dollars—"

"One thing at a time. Can you prove he couldn't write?"

"He proved it to *me!*"

"Yes, but can you prove it to *us?*"

Striker caught a tuft of his own hair in his fist, dragged at it, let it go again. "No, because he's gone now."

The other one leaned forward, dangerously casual. "You say you warned him what to expect, and yet he was willing to go ahead and chance it, just for the sake of a meal, a suit of clothes, a bed. How do you explain that?"

"He was at the end of his rope. He was about ready to quit anyway." Striker saw what was coming.

"Oh, he was? How do you know?"

"Because he told me so. He said he was—thinking of the river."

"*Before* you explained your proposition or after?"

"Before," Striker had to admit.

They blew out their breaths scornfully, eyed one another as though this man's stupidity was unbelievable. "He brings a guy up from the beach," one said to the other, "that's already told him *beforehand* he's got doing the Dutch on his mind, and then when the guy goes ahead and does it, he tries to make out he's been murdered."

Striker knocked his chair over, stood up in exasperation. "But can't you get it through your concrete domes? What was driving him to it? The simplest reason in the world! *Lack of shelter, lack of food, lack of comfort.* Suddenly he's given all that at one time. Is it reasonable to suppose he'll cut his own enjoyment of it short, put an end to it halfway through the night? Tomorrow night, yes, after he's out of here, back where he was again, after the let-down has set in. But not tonight."

"Very pretty, but it don't mean a thing. The swell surroundings only brought it on quicker. He wanted to die in comfort, in style, while he was about it. That's been known to happen too, don't forget. About his not being able to write, sorry, but"—they flirted the sheet of notepaper before his eyes—"this evidence shows he *was* able to write. He must have put one over on you. You probably tipped your mitt in giving him your writing test. He caught on you were looking for someone who couldn't write, so he played 'possum. About the money—well, it musta gone out the window with him even if he *was* just in his underwear, and somebody down there snitched it before the cop came along. No evidence. The investigation's closed as far as we're concerned." They sauntered out into the hall.

"Damn it," Striker yelled after them, "you can't walk out of here! You're turning your backs on a murder!"

"We *are* walking out," came back from the hallway. "Put that in your pipe and smoke it!" The elevator door clicked mockingly shut.

Courlander said almost pityingly, "It looks like tonight wasn't your lucky night."

"It isn't yours either!" Striker bellowed. He swung his fist in a barrelhouse right, connected with the city dick's lower jaw, and sent him volplaning back on his shoulders against the carpet.

Perry's moon-face and bald head were white as an ostrich egg with long-nursed resentment. "Get out of here! You're fired! Bring bums into my house so they can commit suicide on the premises, will you? You're through!"

"Fired?" Striker gave him a smouldering look that made Perry draw hastily back out of range. "I'm quitting, is what you mean! I wouldn't even finish the night out in a murder nest like this!" He stalked past the manager, clenched hands in pockets, and went up to his room to pack his belongings.

His chief problem was to avoid recognition by any of the staff, when he returned there nearly a year later. To achieve this after all the years he'd worked in the hotel, he checked in swiftly and inconspicuously. The mustache he had been growing for the past eight months and which now had attained full maturity, effectively changed the lower part of his face. The horn-rimmed glasses, with plain inserts instead of ground lenses, did as much for the upper part, provided his hat brim was tipped down far enough. If he stood around, of course, and let them stare, eventual recognition was a certainty, but he didn't. He'd put on a little added weight from the long months of idleness in the furnished room. He hadn't worked in the interval. He could no doubt have got another berth, but he considered that he was still on a job—even though he was no longer drawing pay for it—and he meant to see it through.

A lesser problem was to get the room itself. If he couldn't get it at once, he fully intended taking another for a day or two until he could, but this of course would add greatly to the risk of recognition. As far as he could tell, however, it was available right now. He'd walked through the side street bordering the hotel three nights in a row, after dark, and each time that particular window had been unlighted. The red tag would quickly tell him whether he was right or not.

Other than that, his choice of this one particular night for putting the long-premeditated move into effect was wholly arbitrary. The interval since the last time it had happened roughly approximated the previous intervals, and that was all he had to go by. One night, along about now, was as good as another.

He paid his bill at the rooming house and set out on foot, carrying just one bag with him. His radio and the rest of his belongings he left behind in the landlady's charge, to be called for later. It was about nine o'clock now. He wanted to get in before Maxon's shift. He'd been more intimate with Maxon than the other clerks, had practically no chance of getting past Maxon unidentified.

He stopped in at a hardware store on his way and bought two articles: a long section of stout hempen rope and a small sharp "fruit" or "kitchen" knife with a wooden handle. He inserted both objects in the bag with his clothing, right there in the shop, then set out once more. He bent his hat brim a little lower over his eyes as he neared the familiar hotel entrance, that was all. He went up the steps and inside unhesitatingly. One of the boys whom he knew by sight ducked for his bag without giving any sign of recognition. That was a good omen. He moved swiftly to the desk without looking around or giving anyone a chance to study him at leisure. There was a totally new man on now in Dennison's place, someone who didn't know him at all. That was the second good omen. And red was peering from the pigeon-hole of 913.

His eye quickly traced a vertical axis through it. Not another one in a straight up-and-down line with it. It was easy to work it if you were familiar with the building layout, and who should be more familiar than he?

He said, "I want a single on the side street, where the traffic isn't so heavy." He got it the first shot out of the box!

He paid for it, signed *A. C. Sherman, New York,* and quickly stepped into the waiting car, with his head slightly lowered but not enough so to be conspicuously furtive.

A minute later the gauntlet had been successfully run. He gave the boy a dime, closed the door, and had gained his objective undetected. Nothing had been changed in it. It was the same as when he'd slept in it that first time, nearly two years ago now. It was hard to realize, looking around at it, that it had seen four men go to their deaths. He couldn't help wondering, "Will I be the fifth?" That didn't frighten him any. It just made him toughen up inside and promise, "Not without a lotta trouble, buddy, not without a lotta trouble!"

He unpacked his few belongings and put them away as casually as though he were what he seemed to be, an unsuspecting newcomer who had just checked into a hotel. The coiled rope he hid under the mattress of the bed for the time being; the fruit knife and his gun under the pillows.

He killed the next two hours, until the deadline was due; undressed, took a bath, then hung around in his pajamas reading a paper he'd brought up with him.

At twelve he made his final preparations. He put the room light out first of all. Then in the dark he removed the whole bedding, mattress and all, transferred it to the floor, laying bare the framework and bolted-down coils of the bed. He looped the rope around the bed's midsection from side to side, weaving it inextricably in and out of the coils. Then he knotted a free length to a degree that defied undoing, splicing the end for a counter-knot.

He coiled it three times around his own middle, again knotting it to a point of Houdini-like bafflement. In between there was a slack of a good eight or ten feet. More than enough, considering the ease with which the bed could be pulled about on its little rubber-tired casters, to give him a radius of action equal to the inside limits of the room. Should pursuit through the doorway become necessary, that was what the knife was for. He laid it on the nightstand, alongside his gun.

Then he replaced the bedding, concealing the rope fastened beneath it. He carefully kicked the loose length, escaping at one side, out of sight under the bed. He climbed in, covered up.

The spiny roughness and constriction of his improvised safety-belt bothered him a good deal at first, but he soon found that by lying still and not changing position too often, he could accustom himself to it, even forget about it.

An hour passed, growing more and more blurred as it neared its end. He didn't try to stay awake, in fact encouraged sleep, feeling that the rope would automatically give him more than a fighting chance, and that to remain awake and watchful might in some imponderable way ward off the very thing he was trying to come to grips with.

At the very last he was dimly conscious, through already somnolent faculties, of a vague sweetness in the air, lulling him even further. Sandalwood incense. "So they're still here," he thought indistinctly. But the thought wasn't sufficient to rouse him to alertness; he wouldn't let it. His eyelids started to close of their own weight. He let them stay down.

Only once, after that, did his senses come to the surface. The scratchy roughness of the rope as he turned in his sleep. "Rope," he thought dimly, and placing what it was, dropped off into oblivion again.

The second awakening came hard. He fought against it stubbornly, but it slowly won out, dragging him against his will. It was two-fold. Not dangerous or threatening, but mentally painful, like anything that pulls you out of deep sleep. Excruciatingly painful. He wanted to be let alone. Every nerve cried out for continued sleep, and these two spear-heads-noise and glare—continued prodding at him, tormenting him.

Then suddenly they'd won out. *Thump!*—one last cruelly-jolting impact of sound, and he'd opened his eyes. The glare now attacked him in turn; it was like needles boring into the pupils of his defense-less, blurred eyes. He tried to shield them from it with one protective hand, and it still found them out. He struggled dazedly upright in the bed. The noise had subsided, was gone, after that last successful bang. But the light—it beat into his brain.

It came pulsing from beyond the foot of the bed, so that meant it was coming through the open bathroom door. The bed was along the side wall, and the bathroom door should be just beyond its foot. He must have forgotten to put the light out in there. What a brilliance! He could see the light through the partly open door, swinging there on its loose, exposed electric-cord. That is to say, he could see the pulsing gleam and dazzle of it, but he couldn't get it into focus; it was like a sunburst. It was torture, it was burning his sleepy eyeballs out. Have to get up and snap it out. How'd that ever happen anyway? Maybe the switch was defective, current was escaping through it even after it had been turned off, and he was sure he had turned it off.

He struggled out of bed and groped toward it. The room around him was just a blur, his senses swimming with the combination of pitch-blackness and almost solar brilliance they were being subjected to. But it was the bathroom door that was beyond the foot of the bed, that was one thing he was sure of, even in his sleep-fogged condition.

He reached the threshold, groped upward for the switch that was located above the bulb itself. To look upward at it was like staring a blast-furnace in the face without dark glasses. It had seemed to be dangling there just past the half-open door, so accessible. And now it seemed to elude him, swing back a little out of reach. Or maybe it was just that his fumbling fingers had knocked the loose cord into that strange, evasive motion.

He went after it, like a moth after a flame. Took a step across the threshold, still straining upward after it, eyes as useless as though he were standing directly in a lighthouse beam.

Suddenly the door sill seemed to rear. Instead of being just a flat strip of wood, partitioning the floor of one room from the other, it struck him sharply, stunningly, way up the legs, just under the knee-caps. He tripped, overbalanced, plunged forward. The rest was hallucination, catastrophe, destruction.

The light vanished as though it had wings. The fall didn't break; no tiled flooring came up to stop it. The room had suddenly melted into disembodied night. No walls, no floor, nothing at all. Cool air of out-of-doors was rushing upward into the vacuum where the bathroom apparently had been. His whole body was turning completely over, and then over again, and he was going down, down, down. He only had time for one despairing thought as he fell at a sickening speed: "I'm *outside* the building!"

Then there was a wrench that seemed to tear his insides out and snap his head off his neck. The hurtling fall jarred short, and there was a sickening, swaying motion on an even keel. He was turning slowly like something on a spit, clawing helplessly at the nothingness around him. In the cylindrical blackness that kept wheeling about him he could make out the gray of the building wall, recurring now on this side, now on that, as he swiveled. He tried to get a grip on the wall with his fingertips, to steady himself, gain a fulcrum! Its sandpapery roughness held no indentation to which he could attach himself even by one wildly searching thumb.

He was hanging there between floors at the end of the rope which had saved his life. There was no other way but to try to climb back along its length, until he could regain that treacherous guard-rail up there over his head. It could be done, it had to be. Fortunately the rope's grip around his waist was automatic. He was being held without having to exert himself, could use all his strength to lift himself hand over hand. That shouldn't be impossible. It was his only chance, at any rate.

The tall oblong of window overhead through which he had just been catapulted bloomed yellow. The room lights had been put on. Someone was in there. Someone had arrived to help him. He arched his back, straining to look up into that terrifying vista of night sky overhead—but that now held the warm friendly yellow patch that meant his salvation.

"Grab that rope up there!" he bellowed hoarsely. "Pull me in! I'm hanging out here! Hurry! There isn't much time!"

Hands showed over the guard-rail. He could see them plainly, tinted yellow by the light behind them. Busy hands, helping hands, answering his plea, pulling him back to the safety of solid ground.

No, wait! Something flashed in them, flashed again. Sawing back and forth, slicing, biting into the rope that held him, just past the guardrail. He could feel the vibration around his middle, carried down to him like the hum along a wire. Death-dealing hands, completing what had been started, sending him to his doom. With his own knife, that he'd left up there beside the bed!

The rope began to fritter. A little severed outer strand came twining loosely down the main column of it toward him like a snake. Those hands, back and forth, like a demon fiddler drawing his bow across a single tautened violin-string in hurried, frenzied funeral-march that spelled Striker's doom!

"Help!" he shouted in a choked voice, and the empty night sky around seemed to give it mockingly back to him.

A face appeared above the hands and knife, a grinning derisive face peering down into the gloom. Vast mane of snow-white hair and long white beard. It was Peter the Hermit.

So now he knew at last—too late. Too late.

The face vanished again, but the hands, the knife, were busier than ever. There was a microscopic dip, a *give*, as another strand parted, forerunner of the hurtling, whistling drop to come, the hurtling drop that meant the painful, bone-crushing end of him.

He burst into a flurry of helpless, agonized motion, flailing out with arms and legs—at what, toward what? Like a tortured fly caught on a pin, from which he could never hope to escape.

Glass shattered somewhere around him; one foot seemed to puncture the solid stone wall, go all the way through it. A red-hot wire stroked across his instep and he jerked convulsively.

There was a second preliminary dip, and a wolf-howl of joy from above. He was conscious of more yellow light, this time from below, not above. A horrified voice that was trying not to lose its self-control sounded just beneath him somewhere. "Grab this! Don't lose your head now! Grab hold of this and don't let go whatever happens!"

Wood, the wood of a chair back, nudged into him, held out into the open by its legs. He caught at it spasmodically with both hands, riveted them to it in a grip like rigor mortis. At the same time somebody seemed to be trying to pull his shoe off his foot, that one foot that had gone in through the wall and seemed to be cut off from the rest of him.

There was a nauseating plunging sensation that stopped as soon as it began. His back went over until he felt like he was breaking in two, then the chair back held, steadied, reversed, started slowly to draw him with it. The severed rope came hissing down on top of him. From above there was a shrill cackle, from closer at hand a woman's scream of pity and terror. Yellow closed around him, swallowed him completely, took him in to itself.

He was stretched out on the floor, a good solid floor—and it was over. He was still holding the chair in that vise-like grip. Young, the Chinese lawyer, was still hanging onto it by the legs, face a pasty gray. Bob, the night porter, was still holding onto his one ankle, and blood was coming through the sock. Mrs. Young, in a sort of chain arrangement, was hugging the porter around the waist. There was broken glass around him on the floor, and a big pool of water with tropical fish floundering in it from the overturned tank. A dog was whining heartbreakingly somewhere in the room. Other than that, there was complete silence.

None of them could talk for a minute or two. Mrs. Young sat squarely down on the floor, hid her face in her hands, and had brief but high-powered hysterics. Striker rolled over and planted his lips devoutly to the dusty carpet, before he even took a stab at getting to his shaky and undependable feet.

"What the hell happened *to you?*" heaved the lawyer finally, mopping his forehead. "Flying around out there like a bat! You scared the daylights out of me."

"Come on up to the floor above and get all the details," Striker invited. He guided himself shakily out of the room, stiff-arming himself against the door frame as he went. His legs still felt like rubber, threatening to betray him.

The door of 913 stood open. In the hallway outside it he motioned them cautiously back. "I left my gun in there, and he's got a knife with him too, so take it easy." But he strode into the lighted opening as though a couple of little items like that weren't stopping him after what he'd just been through and nearly didn't survive.

Then he stopped dead. There wasn't anyone at all in the room—any more.

The bed, with the severed section of rope still wound securely around it, was upturned against the window opening, effectively blocking it. The entire bedding, mattress and all, had slid off it, down into the street below. It was easy to see what had happened. The weight of his body, dangling out there, had drawn it first out into line with the opening (and it moved so easily on those rubber-tired casters!), then tipped it over on its side. The mattress and all the encumbering clothes had spilled off it and gone out of their own weight, entangling, blinding, and carrying with them, like a linen avalanche, whatever and whoever stood in their way. It was a fitting finish for an ingenious, heartless murderer.

The criminal caught neatly in his own trap.

"He was too anxious to cut that rope and watch me fall at the same time," Striker said grimly. "He leaned too far out. A feather pillow was enough to push him over the sill!"

He sauntered over to the dresser, picked up a sheet of paper, smiled a little—not gaily. "My 'suicide note'!" He looked at Young. "Funny sensation, reading your own farewell note. I bet not many experience it! Let's see what I'm supposed to have said to myself. 'I'm at the end of my rope. 'Queer, how he hit the nail on the head that time! He made them short, always. So there wouldn't be enough to them to give the handwriting away. He never signed them, either.

Because he didn't know their names. He didn't even know what they looked like."

Courlander's voice sounded outside, talking it over with someone as he came toward the room. ". . . mattress and all! But instead of him landing on it, which might have saved his life, *it* landed on *him*. Didn't do him a bit of good! He's gone forever."

Striker, leaning against the dresser, wasn't recognized at first.

"Say, wait a minute, where have I seen *you* before?" the city dick growled finally, after he'd given a preliminary look around the disordered room.

"What a detective you turned out to be!" grunted the shaken Striker rudely.

"Oh, it's you, is it? Do you haunt the place? What do you know about this?"

"A damn sight more than you!" was the uncomplimentary retort. "Sit down and learn some of it—or are you still afraid to face the real facts?"

Courlander sank back into a chair mechanically, mouth agape, staring at Striker.

"I'm not going to *tell* you about it," Striker went on. "I'm going to demonstrate. That's always the quickest way with kindergarten-age intelligences!" He caught at the overturned bed, righted it, rolled it almost effortlessly back into its original position against the side wall, *foot facing directly toward the bathroom door.*

"Notice that slight vibration, that humming the rubber-tired casters make across the floorboards? That's the 'distant thunder' the Youngs heard that night. I'll show you the lightning in just a minute. I'm going over there to his room now. Before I go, just let me point out one thing: the sleeper goes to bed in an unfamiliar room, and his last recollection is of the bathroom door being down there at the foot, the windows over here on this side. He wakes up dazedly in the middle of the night, starts to get out of bed, and comes up against the wall first

of all. So then he gets out at the opposite side; but this has only succeeded in disorienting him, balling him up still further. All he's still
sure of, now, is that the bathroom door is somewhere down there *at
the foot of the bed!* Now just watch closely and you'll see the rest of it in
pantomime. I'm going to show you just how it was done."

He went out and they sat tensely, without a word, all eyes on the
open window.

Suddenly they all jolted nervously, in unison. A jumbo, triple-
toothed fishhook had come into the room, through the window, on
the end of three interlocked rods—a single line running through them
from hook to reel. It came in diagonally, from the projecting wing.
It inclined of its own extreme length, in a gentle arc that swept the
triple-threat hook down to floor level. Almost immediately, as the unseen "fisherman" started to withdraw it, it snagged the lower right-
hand foot of the bed. It would have been hard for it not to, with its
three barbs pointing out in as many directions at once. The bed started
to move slowly around after it, on those cushioned casters. There was
not enough vibration or rapidity to the maneuver to disturb a heavy
sleeper. The open window was now at the foot of the bed, where the
bathroom had been before the change.

The tension of the line was relaxed. The rod jockeyed a little until
the hook had been dislodged from the bed's "ankle." The liberated rod
was swiftly but carefully withdrawn, as unobtrusively as it had appeared a moment before.

There was a short wait, horrible to endure. Then a new object appeared before the window opening—flashing refracting light, so that
it was hard to identify for a minute even though the room lights were
on in this case and the subjects were fully awake. It was a lighted miner's lamp with an unusually high-powered reflector behind it. In addition to this, a black object of some kind, an old sweater or miner's shirt,
was hooded around it so that it was almost invisible from the street or
the windows on the floor below—all its rays beat inward to the room.
It was suspended from the same trio of interlocked rods.

It swayed there motionless for a minute, a devil's beacon, an invitation to destruction. Then it nudged inward, knocked repeatedly against the edge of the window frame, as though to deliberately awaken whoever was within. Then the light coyly retreated a little farther out into the open, but very imperceptibly, as if trying to snare something into pursuit. Then the light suddenly whisked up and was gone, drawn up through space.

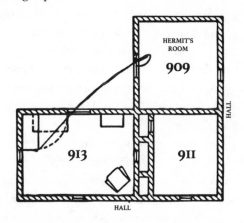

With unbelievable swiftness, far quicker than anybody could have come up from the street, the closed door flew back at the touch of Striker's passkey, he darted in, tossed the "suicide note" he was holding onto the dresser, then swiveled the bed back into its original position in the room, scooped up imaginary money.

He stepped out of character and spread his hands conclusively. "See? Horribly simple and—simply horrible."

The tension broke. Mrs. Young buried her face against her husband's chest.

"He was an expert fisherman. Must have done a lot of it up around those mines of his," Striker added. "Probably never failed to hook that bed first cast off the reel. This passkey, that let him in here at will, must have been mislaid years ago and he got hold of it in some way. He brooded and brooded over the way he'd been swindled; this was his way of getting even with the world, squaring things. Or maybe he actually thought these various people in here were spies who came to learn the location of his mines. I don't know, I'm no psychiatrist. The money was just secondary, the icing to his cake. It helped him pay for his room here, staked him to the supplies he took along on his 'prospecting' trips.

"A few things threw me off for a long time. He was away at the time young Hastings fell out. The only possible explanation is that that, alone of the four, was a genuine suicide. By a freak coincidence it occurred in the very room the Hermit had been using for his murders. And this in spite of the fact that Hastings had less reason than any of the others; he had just become engaged. I know it's hard to swallow, but we'll have to. I owe you an apology on that one suicide, Courlander."

"And I owe you an apology on the other three, and to show you I'm no bad loser, I'm willing to make it in front of the whole Homicide Squad of New York."

Young asked curiously, "Have you any idea of just where those mines of his that caused all the trouble are located? Ontario, isn't it? Because down at the station tonight a Press Radio news flash came through that oil had been discovered in some abandoned gold-mine pits up there, a gusher worth all kinds of money, and they're running around like mad trying to find out in whom the title to them is vested. I bet it's the same ones!"

Striker nodded sadly. "I wouldn't be surprised. That would be just like one of life's bum little jokes on us."

DISCUSSION QUESTIONS

- Which of the detectives was your favorite? Why?

- Reading this anthology, did you learn anything about the Golden Age detective story genre that you didn't already know? If so, what?

- How did the cultural history of the era play into these stories? Did anything help date them for you?

- Were you able to solve any of the mysteries before the main character? If so, which ones?

- Did any stories surprise you in terms of subject, character, or setting? If so, which ones?

- Did any stories remind you of work from authors today? If so, which ones?

- What characteristics do you think made these authors so popular in their day? Do you think readers today still want the same things from their reading material?

AMERICAN MYSTERY CLASSICS

from

AMERICAN MYSTERY CLASSICS

from